After Life

Dean Crawford

Copyright © 2013 Fictum Ltd

All rights reserved.

ISBN-10: 151484379X
ISBN-13: 978-1514843796

Also by Dean Crawford:

The Warner & Lopez Series

The Ethan Warner Series

The Atlantia Series

And many more novels at…

www.deancrawfordbooks.com

"While I thought that I was learning how to live, I have been learning how to die."

Leonardo da Vinci

They say that you see a bright tunnel of light, just before the end.

They say that there is nothing to be afraid of, that when it comes it fills your world and changes everything. That all of the emotions that you once felt just slip away like an old skin. Scoured of all life's labours, what remains is nothing more than light, like starlight, bright and yet as ephemeral and distant as the edge of the universe.

That's what dying was like.

But now, of course, death is no longer the end.

The soft, warm and welcoming tunnel of light still emerges from the darkness of oblivion, swelling around you in a warm and comforting blanket, but then it vanishes in a blur of sharp colours, geometric whorls and spirals that bury deep into your core. Some people even say that at the last moment, just before the tunnel of light faded away they saw people waiting for them, people that they felt certain they knew. Then, all of a sudden you feel as though you're flying faster than light itself. Memories long forgotten race through the field of your awareness: these days, your life flashes in front of your eyes after you die.

Sentience comes slowly. It's as though the brain has to recalibrate itself to view the world through different eyes. There are new sensations. I wouldn't call them physical feelings as such, just an awareness of objects and their proximity hovering like ghosts in a new and unusual world. Not that they matter all that much, of course, because if I wanted to I could walk right through them.

First thing I did was look at my hands. I'd spent the last twenty six years of my life with crippling arthritis that had reduced my fingers to bony digits covered with thin, almost translucent skin. I was a decrepit bag of bones that you could barely call alive at all. Now my hands looked perfect, which was exactly how they should have looked. I didn't pay this much money for anything less than perfection. Sure, it was weird to be able to see right through them to the projection platform beneath my feet but hell, with me feeling no pain for the first time in nearly three decades I could deal with that.

I guess I wish that it had happened sooner. My death, I mean. Hard not to when I could have saved myself two decades of daily pain and humiliation and just ended it all. Look at me now, compared to how I was then. I was ninety four years old, hadn't been able to get out of my bed on my own for over a decade, could barely see past the end of my own bloated nose and spent much of my time dribbling my dinners down my chest. Now I look and feel like a teenager again, full of spirit and verve. I'm a Holosap, and man am I glad that my life ended because that's when it really got going.

Trust me, this is worth it. It's the best thing you'll ever do with your afterlife.

Marvin Rockefeller III

For and on behalf of *Re–Volution Ltd*

1

Whitehall, London

United Kingdom

There was no time to waste.

He ran through the darkened and rain soaked streets, street lights illuminating his path in pools of sparkling light that danced erratically like distant lightning storms as the city's power supply surged and fluttered. Patches of mist drifted in cold banks to obscure the lights of the financial district way off to the east that flickered like a distant galaxy of dying stars. His footfalls echoed down the winding streets in percussion to the hymn of terror coming from the wider city as a million souls cried out in fear.

He could see them flocking across the Thames to the south, thousands of flaming torches streaming across the remaining bridges above the cold water, a last bastion of civilisation besieged by a cruel darkness beyond. Elsewhere in the black and bitter water, refugees from the darkness tried to swim to safety, their torches extinguished as the current and icy waters drew them to their deaths. Further to the south the sky glowed a fiery red as the country beyond was consumed by an inferno wrought by the hellish devices of man. But he barely cast a glance at the turmoil of flame as he ran, his tired old lungs throbbing painfully in his chest.

There was a far greater threat than The Falling bearing down upon the city.

He reached the end of Whitehall and staggered to the ornate gated doorway of an imposing Georgian building guarded by two uniformed soldiers. He stumbled to a halt before them, his chest heaving as he rested his hands on his knees.

One of the soldiers stepped forward, his gloved hands gripping his rifle cautiously. A tall black man bearing the insignia of an Army lieutenant, he moved to the old man's side.

'Professor Anderson? Are you all right sir?'

Anderson lifted his head, his face sheened with sweat. 'I will be, Lieutenant Connelly, just as soon as you open those doors.'

'Is it happening, sir?'

The old man nodded, managed to stand upright again. 'It's happening.'

Connelly turned to his colleague, Private Watkins, and nodded. The soldier whirled and removed a glove to swipe his hand across a sensor screen set into the wall. The gates clicked and Watkins pushed through them. Lieutenant Connelly took the old man's arm and guided him through the doors as outside the shouts and shrieks rose in volume from the Thames nearby. The gates and then the doors thumped closed behind them with a boom that echoed through the building as Watkins locked them once again.

'Where to?' Lieutenant Connelly asked.

Anderson waved the two soldiers to follow him through the building. There were no lights on, but the windows glowed with the flickering light of countless torches burning nearby as survivors flooded into the city. Every now and again, in the distance, Anderson heard a deep boom rumble out in the night as another bridge was blasted into pieces by the Royal Engineers.

'How long do we have?' he asked Lieutenant Connelly, 'until the city is sealed off?'

Connelly shrugged as he followed Anderson down an ornate staircase that led toward the building's expansive basement.

'Maybe an hour,' he replied. 'Once the main access routes are secured they'll start sealing up the sewers, the tube stations, places like that. Why?'

Anderson did not reply as he reached the basement level, their way now illuminated by strips of glowing blue fluorescent tubing. A series of transparent doors made from bullet proof plastic stood between them and a further, larger steel door. One by one, Anderson accessed the different sections. Each was pressurised to a different degree, offering three levels of protection against atmospheric contaminants from entering whatever lay beyond.

Lieutenant Connelly hesitated as Anderson reached the steel door. 'Private Watkins and my own security clearance is not sufficient for us to be down here, professor. Perhaps we should return to our sentry posts and let you perform your duties alone.'

Anderson hefted the door's seal and replied over his shoulder as he did so. 'The city is under siege and extreme circumstances require extreme responses,' he said. 'Consider yourselves cleared by me. If I do not do now what I have to, there will be more to worry about than The Falling.'

As if in reply, from the building above came the faint clatter of machine gun fire from nearby Westminster.

'They're securing the bridge,' Connelly said in a leaden tone, 'cutting the survivors off.'

'Then we must hurry,' Anderson insisted.

He spun the steel wheel and a hiss of pressurised air escaped from whatever was concealed within. Connelly and Watkins hefted their weapons onto their shoulders and helped him push the door open. A glow from the room reached out to bathe the three men in a ray of ultra–violet light that seemed somehow alien.

Within lay a remarkable sight that, even after years spent labouring within the very same room, never failed to take Anderson's breath away.

A series of eighteen supercomputers, linked in parallel, lined one wall of the large basement, which was intersected vertically by thick concrete stanchions that supported the vast weight of the building above. The computers' glossy black faces blinked with tiny coloured lights as they hummed in digital harmony. Anderson moved through the forest of stanchions to a central area in the basement that had been cleared to make space for a large, angular platform of matt black plastic and rubber walkways that rose a couple of feet off the basement floor. Thick cables snaked their way from the platform up the walls as though a gigantic, angular black spider were nesting in the centre of the basement, while to their right stood a computer terminal where several monitors flashed information and streams of binary code.

In the centre of the platform, standing alone with hands clasped calmly before him stood a figure staring down at Anderson and the two soldiers.

'Good evening, professor.'

The voice was monotone and tainted with a faint warble, as though it were being heard from underwater through a stream of bubbles.

'Good evening, Adam,' Anderson replied.

Lieutenant Connelly and Private Watkins remained rooted to the spot and stared up at the projection. 'What the hell is that?'

Adam stood six feet tall, his body lightly muscular and athletic, his shoulders broad and his scalp hairless. In fact, there appeared to be no hair on his body at all. His hands were covering his crotch, but it quickly became obvious as he turned to watch Anderson that he possessed no genitalia. His face was smooth, perfectly symmetrical, his movements as fluid as warm running oil. But what was most remarkable about Adam was that he glowed with a soft, electric–blue light touched with a faint aurora of green and that the back of the basement was clearly visible through him. Adam's body was translucent.

Anderson barely looked up at the soldiers as he replied, his fingers racing across a keyboard at the terminal that was merely a clear plastic sheet onto which the shape of keys were being projected by beams of light.

'Adam,' he replied, 'is a Holonomic Entity.'

Lieutenant Connelly cautiously approached the platform, his eyes fixed upon those of Adam. Adam returned the gaze with equal curiosity. His eyes glowed with a strange light, a distant star of awareness gleaming within them.

'Is it, *alive*?' Watkins asked.

Anderson nodded as he typed furiously. 'Adam is fully self-aware, which is what is going to make this so very difficult for me to do.'

'What is happening, professor?' Adam asked as he turned to watch Anderson, a frown appearing on his impossibly symmetrical features.

Anderson tapped a few glowing keys and then hit a final one, hard. He stood up from the terminal and turned to Adam.

'I am sorry,' he said, his face torn with something that looked to be genuine grief. 'I have made a terrible mistake. I am erasing you from the system, Adam.'

The holographic man stared back at Anderson for several moments before replying.

'Where will I go?' he asked.

There was something uncomfortably child–like about the question, unrestrained curiosity thinly veiling a fear of the unknown.

Anderson hesitated for a moment. 'Somewhere nice,' he replied, 'somewhere better.'

'Wait a moment,' Lieutenant Connelly snapped. 'I'm guessing you can't just turn all of this stuff off without orders.'

Anderson shook his head. 'Believe me, this experiment must be destroyed while it still can be.'

'I'm not going to stand here and let you shut this down without confirming it with my superior officer.'

'Your superior officer,' Anderson explained, 'will know nothing about this.'

'Then explain it to me, right now.'

'There's no time!'

Lieutenant Connelly pulled his rifle into his shoulder and aimed it at Anderson. 'Make time,' he growled.

Anderson glanced at the entrance to the basement as though he were being watched and spoke quickly.

'This is the cure for The Falling,' he said.

'A cure?' Watkins gasped. 'There's a cure?'

'There is no cure,' Connelly insisted.

'Precisely,' Anderson agreed. 'There is no biological cure for The Falling, which means the only way to evade infection is to become invulnerable to the disease. Adam here represents my attempt to create a human being that is not physical in its presence, but digital. I applied an electrical charge to a human brain and then scanned it down to a level so tiny that I could see the interactions between individual neurons. I then digitised the scan and uploaded it into a computer program which mimics neuronal processes. Adam is the result.'

The soldier glanced sideways at Adam. 'He's alive because you scanned a dead person's brain?'

Anderson clenched his fists by his side. 'Kind of. We must hurry.'

'Hurry where? And what were you doing on that computer?'

'Saving humanity,' Anderson shot back, 'and covering its arse at the same time.' Anderson looked up at Adam. 'I truly am sorry, my friend.'

Adam's frown mutated into concern. 'I don't understand.'

'How the hell can he do that?' Watkins asked. 'See? Hear?'

'Twisted light,' Anderson snapped, 'microphones and vocal resonance amplifiers. We don't have time for this!'

Lieutenant Connelly looked around him at the laboratory, and then his eyes settled on a small holograph sitting on a table beside Anderson's computer terminal, an image of a young girl of maybe six or seven years old smiling happily. Beneath it in glowing script was a poem of some kind.

Yes, thou shalt know, spite of thy past Distress,
And all those Ills which thou so long hast mourn'd
Heav'n has no Rage, like Love to Hatred turn'd,
Nor Hell a Fury, like a Woman scorn'd.

William Congreve, *The Mourning Bride*, 1697

Lieutenant Connelly lowered his rifle. 'You lost your daughter to The Falling,' he recalled. 'You're going to end this, after all that you lost, all that you sacrificed?'

Anderson hesitated, looking at the image of his daughter, but it was Adam's voice that replied.

'Don't do this, professor,' he pleaded. 'I don't want to die.'

Lieutenant Connelly looked up at the humanoid form looking down at them and heard Professor Anderson's reply as though it came from another world.

'You never lived, Adam. You're not like us.' Anderson hesitated. 'You're not like me. You're the birth, Adam, but the end must come with Eve.'

Anderson sensed the two soldiers look up once again at Adam, and wasn't sure whether he imagined or heard the gasp of realisation from them both.

'You scanned your own brain,' Lieutenant Connelly whispered. 'Adam is *you*.'

As Anderson watched, Adam's glowing form began to sparkle and shimmer as though it were breaking down before their very eyes.

'He's me,' Anderson whispered in reply, 'but he's not *me*.'

And then he whispered words that barely reached Lieutenant Connelly's ears.

'Heav'n has no rage, like love to hatred turned…'

The holonomic entity's voice became pleading. 'Father, don't do this.'

Anderson whispered again and was about to reply to Adam when the glass doors to the basement exploded in a shower of sparkling crystals that crashed through the basement in a lethal cloud of shrapnel. Anderson spun away from the horrendous blast, saw Private Watkins and Lieutenant Connelly scythed down by the debris as their weapons flew from their grasp. Anderson felt the shockwave hit him and hurl him backwards against the computer terminal with a thud that echoed through his skull and blurred his vision.

Heavily armed troops in black fatigues and face masks poured into the basement, spreading out as the huge computers sparked and shuddered as their damaged circuits fried and melted. Anderson turned his head, his ears still ringing, and saw Adam watching him with a strange, confused expression painted on his features. Gradually, as Anderson watched, Adam's face began to melt away in a drifting vortex of light particles as though a gentle breeze were gusting through the basement and blowing him away one atom at a time.

A galaxy of tiny, bright lights, like falling stars spilled away from his body and his face, and as he tumbled into a collapsing cloud of binary code Anderson heard Adam's voice cry out in an increasingly distorted wail of pain, his face stricken with fear.

'Why, father?'

Adam's countenance vanished as his body tumbled into a seething torrent of light that ran like water across the projection platform and vanished from sight as his cry echoed and faded into digital oblivion. Anderson leaned back against the terminal, exhausted, and was still staring at the platform when the troops surrounded him, their rifles all pointed at his head.

They parted as a young man strode between them, brushing dust off of his expensive suit as though mildly irritated to be down in the basement at all. He stopped in front of Anderson and looked down at the injured man.

'The Board is very disappointed in you, Cecil,' he said. 'They will not look kindly upon what you have done here tonight.'

'They're too dangerous,' Anderson gasped. 'They're not like us.'

'Which is precisely why they should become us,' the man replied. 'Or we them, depending on how you look at it.'

Anderson shook his head. 'It's too late. Adam is gone.'

'Yes,' the man replied, 'but I am still here, and like many others I have no desire to die from The Falling. Tell me, where have you sent the data? We know it went out of here only moments ago and we will find it eventually.'

'I don't know where it went,' Anderson gasped. 'That's kind of the point, isn't it?'

The man grinned. 'You're a clever man, professor, but unfortunately you underestimate my persistence. I take it that you have scanned your own brain and that you think that if I kill you, you will automatically upload into the computers somewhere?'

Anderson's smile slipped.

'Indeed,' the man said. From his pocket he retrieved a long black cylinder, an inch thick, with two chrome probes projecting from one end. He pointed the probes toward Anderson. 'I can assure you that we will replicate your technology, professor. How long that will take depends on what you decide to do now.'

Anderson glanced at the now darkened projection platform where Adam had once stood and let out a bitter chuckle. 'Go to hell.'

'You first,' the man replied.

The man gestured to Anderson with an angry flick of his hand. The troops grabbed the old man and pinned him down. Without hesitation, the man knelt down and rammed the probes up into Anderson's nostrils with a grunt of effort.

Anderson screamed in agony as the two probes crunched through his sinuses and pierced his frontal lobes. The man squeezed a button on the device and pain seared through Anderson's skull like liquid fire. Anderson smelled the burning of his own flesh and heard the sound of the laser cutter clicking noisily as it scythed through flesh and bone. His body thrashed and writhed as the device sliced upward toward his brain and his screams mutated into strained choking. The man pressed the button again and the pain vanished as Anderson slumped, his eyes throbbing in agonising pulses as blood poured from his nose to drench his shirt. He gasped as the man leaned in.

'One last time, Cecil.'

Anderson, his body exhausted and his mind weary of life, managed to twist his lips into an awkward, bitter smile.

'Nor hell a fury, like a woman scorned..,' he gasped.

The man frowned in confusion and then with a scowl he jammed the device further up into Anderson's skull and activated it once more. The old man felt the computer chip implanted in his frontal lobes melt as the cutter reached it within the agonised confines of his brain.

And then, mercifully, there was blackness.

* * *

Twenty five years later...

2

Dario LeMarke had never faced death before, but now he was doing it on two fronts at the same time.

Turbulent grey clouds tumbled above the crumbling remains of the city as though hoping to escape the silent, haunted streets, occasional stabs of bright sunlight beaming down and glinting off the few windows that remained intact south of the Thames. Dario laboured as fast as he could along the cracked, weed infested tarmac of York Road, dodging between the scorched and rusting hulks of abandoned taxis slumped on deflated tyres. Behind him the giant London Eye lay crippled, creepers and vines trailing in the wind from its useless support wires, the upper half of the wheel missing and the observation cars scattered where they had fallen decades before.

Dario's old lungs ached and his breath wheezed in his throat as he looked over his shoulder at the giant Ferris wheel looming above the dense foliage clogging the road and the beasts creeping through it.

There were two of them, lumbering after him on mangy legs with their tongues hanging loose from yellow–fanged jaws. Drool spilled like suet from their mouths, draped across stems of dense grass like gossamer webs in their wake. Dogs, large dogs, the only kind left after The Falling. Smaller, selectively bred species had died out decades ago, unable to survive in the wild when mankind had vanished in a panicked stampede into the few remaining enclaves of safety.

Dario knew that he could not enter the city: not because he was not welcome, and not because he could not reach safety before the dogs caught up with him. No. He could not enter the city because he was a *carrier*.

Dario clutched in one hand a plastic cylinder which he had sealed in a transparent bag. The cylinder contained a hunk of fresh meat, the cylinder itself perforated to allow the scent to drift on the air. An enticing target for the few mammals that remained alive in what had once been England's capital city. Dario glimpsed Westminster through gaps in the buildings to his right as he ran toward Westminster Bridge, Big Ben's tower looming over the glittering surface of the Thames.

Just a little bit further.

Dario looked at the hand in which he held the cylinder, saw the painful blisters and the small chunks of desiccated flesh tumbling away on the wind as he ran. He stifled a whimper and reminded himself of his blessings. He had enjoyed a good life, or as good as one could expect after the catastrophe. He was sixty three years old and left behind him a family with a good chance of survival, especially if he could get this sample back to the guard station erected across Westminster Bridge. There was no other way across the river – the authorities had destroyed all other bridges over the Thames decades ago and boats were fired upon without hesitation, the river surging around the aged wrecks of countless refugee vessels.

Dario had made it as far as the collapsed hulk of the old IMAX cinema, like a beached whale with its ribcage jutting up into the grey sky. He had leaned on a wall encrusted with filth and vines as he tried to catch his breath, when he had first seen the dogs behind him. Lean, skeletal, yellow eyed, more like wolves than dogs now.

The dogs had loped under what had once been the railway line, padding quietly after him. No hurry – they knew a wounded prey when they saw it. Dario's legs had trembled beneath him from more than fatigue: the tendons, muscles and nerves were all being eaten away by the fungus that infected him as it had infected billions before him. The horror of it was that the fungus had been present for millennia, living right alongside every human being on Earth, just waiting for the chance to get *inside* somebody, to grow, to mutate, to proliferate and become what it had become. Pandemic.

Dario had pushed himself off the wall and began walking as fast as he could toward Westminster Bridge and its guard house. The dogs lumbered after him still, closer now, somehow sensing that their chance to eat was slipping away. They would know the boundaries of their territory well. They would not let him escape.

Facing death from within and behind, Dario pushed on and hoped against hope that the men in the guardhouse would soon see him and come to his aid, for he knew that this would be his last mission and he hoped fervently that it would not be in vain.

Dario was a scientist, one of many brave souls who periodically ventured out into the wilderness in search of a cure for The Falling. Although not a biologist, Dario's qualifications were in demand and he could not avoid his sense of duty to others of greater need. Trapped south of the river since becoming infected during a routine mission, Dario had devoted his last remaining days to high risk excursions to seek species immune to The Falling. Many did not return from such missions, prey to the handful of animals that had somehow survived the pandemic that had struck so many vertebrate species. It was those animals whom Dario had been targeting, waiting with his bait, waiting for them to sink their teeth into the cylinder and the meat and pass on their DNA for him to study. The cure, he felt certain, lay within one of those rare and resilient beasts.

Dario raised the cylinder above his head and cried out, a torn out canine tooth from one of the dogs rattling alongside the meat inside the cylinder as he turned onto Westminster Bridge.

'Here!'

The guard house remained silent. Dario began to run again, his legs unsteady as though he were drunk as his brain struggled to send the correct messages to them. The surface of the bridge was rugged and broken, filled with grass and mosses that clung to the railings like green snakes and seemed to reach out to trip his weary legs. Behind him the city loomed in a curious mixture of dirty grey concrete and green foliage as though nature were eating the buildings alive, more forest now than city. Closer, the dogs began to run.

'Here!' Dario screamed, his voice choking off with the effort.

He got to within sixty yards of the tower, heard the pads of the heavy dogs behind him slapping down on the surface of the bridge, when his legs finally gave way and he crashed down painfully onto his knees. The cylinder bounced away into the grass nearby. Dario tried to reach out for it, but he heard the animals behind him and rolled onto his back.

The first dog landed on him heavily and powerful jaws clamped around Dario's neck and squeezed with unimaginable force as yellow fangs sank deep into his neck. Dario's scream was choked off as the second animal's fangs bit into his groin in an attempt to paralyse him. Dario writhed in agony as his throat collapsed and his vision began to pulse with light as his brain was starved of oxygen, his head twisted to the left by the dog's powerful bite. Dario glimpsed the Parliament buildings one last time, and then mercifully his consciousness slipped away.

*

'There, south side, fifty yards!'

The police cruiser accelerated through the barrier as it rose up, the gate guards hauling it out of the way just in time. Four men sat inside, all wearing respirators and armoured clothing and all carrying assault weapons.

The heavily armoured cruiser raced to the far side of the bridge, where the carefully tended tarmac ended and the waist high grasses and weeds swayed in the breeze drifting down river, the natural divide marked by a ten foot high steel and razor wire fence.

'There he is,' pointed the driver.

The car screeched to a halt and the four men tumbled out as they ran to a steel framed door in the fence. They drove keys into padlocks, yanked the doors opened and two men raced through the grasses as the other two guarded the fence.

The lead trooper, an officer, saw the dogs look up, their gruesome fangs stained red and dripping with infected meat.

Both men fired an instant later, the gunshots kicking up chunks of tarmac around the dogs. The animals bared their fangs but a second burst sent them fleeing off the bridge, back to the ruined cityscape.

The officer shouldered his rifle and knelt down alongside the old man's body. Dario was barely conscious now, his throat ripped to shreds by the dogs. The officer reached down and turned Dario's head to get his attention. The old man's skin was flaking from his body, his hands a mess of necrotised flesh and sagging tendons.

'Professor, can you hear me?'

The old man coughed, his voice rattling through damaged vocal chords. 'The sample, it's here.'

'Is it viable?' he asked.

Before Dario could answer, the officer's companion called out. 'Got it.' The officer looked over his shoulder to see his colleague holding a cylinder in a bag, an ugly chunk of meat slopped within alongside a yellowing fang. 'What do you want me to do with it?'

'You heard what they said,' the officer snapped. 'Give it to me.'

The trooper handed the officer the cylinder. He walked to the railings and opened first the bag, then the cylinder. Moments later, the chunk of meat and the tooth were spinning away down into the Thames, followed by the cylinder and the bag.

A desperate voice croaked from behind him. 'No.'

The officer returned to Dario's side. 'Sorry old man,' he said as he looked down at Dario's body. The officer reached down to his utility belt and retrieved a long, slim and needle sharp blade. With a grunt of effort he drove the blade through Dario's chest and his heart. Blood spilled around the wound as the old man thrashed and his fractured heart bled out into his chest cavity. Dario LeMarke finally died, the officer's hands on his shoulders to restrain him in his last agonised moments.

'Okay, let's get him back.'

Together, they hauled Dario's corpse back to the razor wire fence and lay it down alongside their cruiser as their colleagues closed the fence back up again.

The officer opened the cruiser's trunk and hauled out a glossy black box the size of a house brick that he set down alongside Dario's remains. His colleague quickly uncoiled two cables attached to the box, each with electrodes at the end which he without hesitation shoved up Dario's nostrils with a heave of effort, the skin bulging as the nodes moved toward Dario's frontal lobes.

'Contact,' he said as the box nearby flashed a series of lights, 'charge detected.'

'Light him up,' said the officer, 'quickly.'

The officer flipped several switches on the box and a whirr of circuitry told him what he needed to know.

'Neurological networks are sound, we've got a current. He's got Futurance, last updated two months ago.'

'Good. Shut him down,' the officer ordered.

The trooper obeyed and pulled the device from Dario's face and looked at the officer.

'I'll take care of the corpse. Get out of here.'

The trooper obeyed, and moments later the cruiser was accelerating away from the scene. It passed an ambulance making its way onto the bridge from the north, where the immaculate city skyline was briefly bathed in a wash of sunlight.

The officer slipped his blade back into its sheath then pulled a small can of yellow paint and sprayed a big, bright X across the old man's chest, careful to make sure the paint concealed the chest wound as much as possible. The officer turned and watched as the ambulance got through the last checkpoint and made its way slowly up onto the bridge. Nobody liked dealing with infected corpses and nobody would want to risk infection during an autopsy on Dario's crumbling remains, so they wouldn't find the knife wound to his heart.

Dario's body would be incinerated within an hour or two.

And he would remember nothing of how he had died.

* * *

3

'Tell me how you feel.'

Arianna Volkov sat in a comfortable chair that had once belonged to her father, made of old leather that had aged but still retained the unique odour that had made her feel so comfortable as a child riding around in Alexei Volkov's big old Bentley. That was, of course, when there were still cars being used on the streets of London.

The antique chair was at odds with the sparse room. The colours were warm, and the blinds let in enough of the early sunlight bleeding through the city smog to fill the room with a fiery glow, but there was little furniture. A chromium Crucifix adorned the wall opposite the window, the silvery surface reflecting the sunrise as though it were aflame.

'I'm not sure,' came a reply.

The man was standing before Arianna, his hands in his pockets and a confused look upon his features, as though he were contemplating a difficult equation or mathematical model. In Arianna's experience they were some of the most difficult to fit in, the scientists and the mathematicians. Arianna did not much like them and their cold, dispassionate view of the universe. Maybe that was why they struggled to cope, even though they were the people who had first wielded the new power of life over death. Reaping the whirlwind, they had sought the impossible but knew not what to do with it.

'You know that you are the same person as you were before,' Arianna soothed, watching the man's emotions flicker like conflicting radio waves across his features. 'The same person.'

The man looked up at her. 'I know.'

'So tell me how you feel.'

The man looked down at his feet. 'Trapped,' he said finally. 'I can't move beyond this spot.'

'Only while your identity is confirmed,' Arianna reminded him, 'that's just the law. You'll be free to move at will along light paths and in the colony soon enough, professor.'

The man nodded as though he had forgotten. One hand reached up to rub his temples, and then he stopped as he realised that the act no longer held the purpose it once had. Arianna watched as he lowered the arm, his hand briefly passing straight through a glass vase standing nearby on a table.

Professor Dario LeMarke was a mathematician of enormous renown and one of the first people to outline the real potential for Holonomic

Brain Theory, a name that made Arianna shudder with its complex scientific undertones. LeMarke had devoted his entire career to that theory and doing so had made him an extremely wealthy man all of his life, right up to him being infected with The Falling. He had died just two days ago of a heart attack, aged sixty three, while returning from an expedition outside the city in search of a cure for disease. The police report confirmed an attack by wild dogs.

'But I'm still trapped,' LeMarke insisted. 'There's nowhere else to go for me now but here.'

LeMarke tapped his own head. Unable yet to judge distance correctly, and with his holonomic brain not yet having fully adjusted to its new configuration, LeMarke's finger entered his skull as cleanly as a hot knife through butter. The brief overlap caused a flutter of distorted pixilation, as though LeMarke were a reflection in a pool of water where a pebble had been dropped. Arianna knew that the lack of coordination was both a psychological and physiological feature considered similar to those caused by amputation, whereby a replacement prosthetic limb took time to be accepted by the owner's brain. For a short while, the owner would be unable to accurately manipulate their foreign limb.

'Your mind is still the same,' Arianna replied. 'Only your circumstances have changed.'

LeMarke nodded vaguely. He understood, she knew, but understanding and accepting were two vastly different states when undergoing such a dramatic transformation. In her career, Arianna had successfully integrated over four hundred struggling *holosaps* into their new lives, helping them cope with the mental anguish of being effectively both alive and dead at the same time.

LeMarke's image flickered, a tiny glitch in the transmission. Arianna glanced out of the windows across the city. The Thames wound its way between tower blocks like a snake of molten metal, the sun blazing to the east behind towering cumulonimbus soaring like angel's wings into the heavens. A flicker of distant lightning danced low across the skyline. The spring storms were starting again, right on time. She could see dark grey veils of rain falling over the forests that entombed the south.

'How did I die?' LeMarke asked.

Arianna did not look at the data–roll by her side, a sheet of glossy electro–paper that detailed LeMarke's final moments. She liked her clients to see that she had read their cases in detail.

'You were working outside of the city,' she said. 'A pair of wild dogs got the better of you. You died before the gate guards on Westminster Bridge could reach you.'

'Will I *feel* again, Reverend?' LeMarke asked her.

She smiled. The questions were always the same and always followed the same format. It didn't matter if the newly uploaded *holosap* was a mathematician or just a lucky lottery winner, the human desire for contact and comfort was undiminished. The scientists might rely upon evidence to move forward in life but in matters spiritual they still, like all human beings, deferred to other authorities.

'Your brain will rewire itself, just as it would when you were physically alive,' she replied. 'The holonomic networks act like neural networks, able to reconnect after trauma. You know this, Professor.'

LeMarke gave a meek smile, glanced at her. 'Sometimes you've just got to hear it.'

'I know,' Arianna said. 'Your sense of taste, touch, even smell will eventually return, although they will differ from how you remember them. How that happens is your expertise Professor, not mine, but happen it will. Coordination will improve, cognition will become less erratic and further memories should form naturally within just a few days. Right now, the best thing that you can do is simply try to relax and wait for it all to come to you.'

'Just like that, eh?'

'Just like that,' Arianna confirmed. 'Don't try to force it, just let your body do its thing.'

LeMarke chuckled as he looked at her. 'My body?'

'Is exactly as it was before,' Arianna said, 'as is your brain. You may be a product of quantum light but you're still a human being. Don't let anybody tell you any different, especially yourself.'

It was sound advice that fell like honey from her lips, but it tasted sour. Arianna believed not in immortality but in a higher power, and somehow it seemed to her that uploading upon death to become a *holosap* was somehow dodging a bullet that was inevitably going to find you in the end. She didn't understand how *holosaps* could see, hear, touch or think, although she recalled from memory that the living human brain actually worked much like a hologram. When holographic brains first emerged they had automatically created neuronal links to the senses that mimicked normal brains; eyes, ears, hands and so on. But, trapped in a computer, they had been unable to express their senses in the normal way. Everybody knew the first words uttered by the very first holosap, *Adam*, when his computer generated brain had completed its neuronal links and achieved self-awareness for the first time.

'Where am I?'

Adam, the creation of celebrated neurobiologist Cecil Anderson, had been born and deactivated many times by his sensitive creator. Modern human rights groups liked to remind *holosap* objectors that the longer Adam had been trapped inside a computer the more agitated and upset *"he"* became. Human beings, they pointed out, were nothing without language and movement. It was only when Anderson created a human hologram and projected the digital brain's primary sensorium into three–dimensional space using a phenomenon known as "hard light" that Adam finally was able to express himself as a human being and his fearful, angry persona vanished.

Unfortunately, even Anderson had not been able to predict the rapidity with which the holonomic brain melded to its holographic body. Sight, hearing and even a quasi–sense of touch were generated by the holonomic networks until the *holosap* looked, felt and acted just like its deceased human counterpart. A new species had appeared, had *evolved* some said, and there had been no turning back.

God created Man in His own image, had once been the legend. Then, in the secular age, that *Man had created God in his own image*. Now, in this latest chapter in the crucible of human endeavour, *Homo sapiens* had created *Holo Sapiens* in his own image, and rendered God irrelevant.

Arianna realised not for the first time that despite her distaste she also viewed LeMarke, like all *holosaps*, as just another human being. About a third of her clients were living humans suffering from all manner of bereavements, illnesses, injuries and such like. As a bereavement counsellor and priest, her job was simply to ease their transition from a state of injury or grieving to one of contentment, or as close as she could get them to it. Ultimately it was down to the individual to finish the job. Arianna merely provided support and consolation, and she suspected that her presence as an ordained priest, one of the last now in a firmly secular world, gave them some sense of comfort when the divine was viewed with suspicion at the best of times and outright disdain the rest.

She did not *like* holosaps, however. Who did, really? The whole thing was an abomination of what it meant to actually be alive. Sure there weren't many of them, just a few thousand, but that was only because so few people could afford the astronomical sums required to properly insure their minds for future use. *Futurance*, the lawyers called it, somewhat cynically. Those who could upload were invariably powerful and influential, and nobody doubted their influence on the living members of government.

'This is going to take some getting used to,' LeMarke said finally.

'Just like us all, human and *holosap* alike,' Arianna replied.

LeMarke looked at her for a moment as though considering his words. His eyes dropped to her white collar, stark above her black shirt and trousers, and then drifted across to the chrome Crucifix on her office wall. 'Do you, still, *believe*? I mean really believe, despite all of this?'

'With all of my heart.'

'Do you have an upload waiting?'

Arianna kept her voice even. 'Yes, it was gifted me but I don't intend to use it.'

'Use it,' LeMarke said, 'because people like you are needed wherever you may be.'

Arianna smiled as LeMarke turned for the office door and then checked himself.

'You're getting there,' she observed. 'By the time we've had another couple of visits there'll be no stopping you.'

Arianna stood up and saw LeMarke move to shake her hand. This time he caught himself a little quicker, grinned ruefully and reached out to a spot of thin air at his side. LeMarke's image blinked out and vanished. Only the projection plate remained, set into the carpeted floor. A gentle, digitised voice echoed through the office.

'Connection disengaged.'

'In every sense,' Arianna murmured to herself.

A blinking light signalled another communication, but this time from the living. Arianna smiled as she tapped the screen. Another holographic projection appeared, but this time it was relayed directly via a camera in another building in the city, the holographic imagery clearer and sharper than LeMarke's ephemeral form.

'Papa!'

Alexei Volkov was a tall, broad shouldered man with a round, content face born of decades of experiencing both the best and the worst the world had to offer.

'*Rebyohnuk*,' Alexei replied with a broad grin in lightly accented Russian, '*my child*. Have you finished your morning's work yet?'

'Got another client before lunch, Gregory Detling,' Arianna said. 'What's up?'

'I need to see you, if you can spare the time?' Alexei said. 'After Gregory's appointment, of course.'

There was no urgency on his face, no timbre of alarm in his voice, but somehow Arianna sensed something behind his words. 'Is everything okay?' she asked.

'Everything's fine,' Alexei assured her. 'Can you make it to The Ivory for lunch, say two hours' time?'

'Wouldn't miss it, papa,' she smiled.

'*Ti takaya chudesnaya*,' Alexei winked.

'Oh, I'm wonderful now, am I?' she giggled. 'And you are too kind. See you later.'

Arianna disconnected the transmission and grabbed her jacket, slipped it over her shoulders and walked from her office. The tiny church, once known as St Matthews, sounded hollow as she walked between the pews. Long gone were the days when the faithful rejoiced in these halls, or any other for that matter. The need for faith, for a belief in the afterlife, had long since been swept aside in the wake of mankind's digital immortality.

On the ancient brickwork of the church was a faded piece of crude graffiti that somehow she had never quite been able to remove.

"You haven't lived until you've lived again."

She had never figured out whether the graffiti had been made by a believer, a cynic or a comic.

The street outside was quiet. Scattered sunlight glinted off countless windows, the brightly illuminated tower blocks contrasting sharply with the deep grey clouds looming across the horizon and trailing skirts of falling rain beyond the river. Arianna walked toward the embankment, veering off through Whitehall and then away from the river again until she approached the towering edifice of the Re–Volution building.

Her appointment was with a *holosap* by the name of Gregory Detling, a former property magnate who was making waves across the city. He had uploaded six years previously after a heart attack had ended his ninety four year tenure as a human being on Earth. He had been survived by his beloved wife, Svetlana Rokovitch, a Moscovian who had fled the Motherland long before The Falling and settled in London to work as a model. Fifty nine years younger than her husband, their relationship had endured even his death when she had, to the amazement of the media, declined her share of his considerable fortune and placed it in trust for him. The laws governing *holosap* control of privately owned corporations had long been debated by parliament, amid claims by human rights groups that *holosaps* should be able to continue their work after death.

Two years after Gregory Detling's upload, Svetlana had died in a train wreck. Her cranial injuries were such that she was unable to upload, leaving her husband bereft. Now, he had initiated a legal challenge at the High Court asserting his right to *die again*, and requested Arianna as his spiritual advisor. Her father Alexei was openly backing Detling's legal challenge. An ardent supporter of the right–to–die–again campaign, he funded victims who wished to recant their uploads, something that Re–Volution forbade on the grounds of lost revenue.

Arianna strode into the expansive lobby of the building, checking her reflection in a mirror. Long, light brown hair in a neat pony tail, two–piece black power suit with its stark white collar. Modest heels. She didn't look too bad, she guessed, and a damned sight better than she would have done without the salary she pulled down from the Hope Reunion Church and her freelance psychology work for Re–Volution.

Across one wall was emblazoned an emblem tagged with the Re–Volution logo: a human figure holding a stylised glowing torch aloft before them.

See the light.

The echoing of conversations competed with countless footfalls as members of staff hurried from one meeting to the next. Between them, on pathways of thick glass that crossed the lobby floor in a giant X, several *holosaps* strolled and conversed. Streams of light flickered and glowed beneath their feet as they walked. A pair saw her and nodded in greeting as they passed by, their shoulders occasionally passing through each other as they strolled.

Arianna smiled politely but kept her head down. She had almost reached the security checkpoint when she remembered that she had left her security card back at the church. She cursed, turned and hurried for the exit, glass doors shielded with mirrors that made the lobby seem darker and the *holosaps* brighter than they should be. She pushed through the doors and sucked in a lungful of fresh air.

The pavement was peppered with big spots of damp as the first heavy raindrops splattered down from the turbulent sky above. She could smell the odour of rain, of the dirt ingrained into the pavement wafting up as it was drenched as she opened an umbrella and stepped out into the road.

Pedestrians hurried to avoid the rainstorm, sheltering their heads from the giant droplets as a crack of thunder split the heavens above and reverberated through Arianna's chest. She checked both ways for the hiss of gas–powered taxis but saw none as she hurried across the street. The rain began to fall from behind her, driven by the storm front's winds, and as she stepped up onto the pavement she turned her umbrella and lowered it across the back of her head to protect her as another crack of thunder smashed across the sky.

The shockwave hit her first. It felt as though a car had driven into her at speed. The air spilled from her lungs as her vision blurred, and she thought that she felt hundreds of raindrops hit her umbrella until she saw chunks of glass and masonry blast by in a cloud of debris.

Heat scorched her legs and hands as she was lifted off the pavement and hurled over a low wall onto a damp lawn. Arianna hit the muddy ground, and as the blast thundered over her she glimpsed the lower floors of the Re–Volution building vanish in a boiling cloud of smoke and flame as a galaxy of glass stars rained down across her.

* * *

4

Alexei Volkov was not a man who delighted in his fortune. Not any more, anyway.

His embankment house overlooked the surging waters of the Thames River, the churning green water swollen from the rain seething down from heavily laden skies and running in rivulets down the glass before him. Some of the other gated homes nearby glowed from lights turned on against the growing gloom despite the hour, the owners risking the crippling electricity bills for the sake of a little heat and light.

Alexei's home was filled with windows of triple-glazed glass that allowed prodigious quantities of natural light to flood into its interior. He had been raised by poor parents on the Kamchatka Peninsular, about as far from the rest of humanity as it was possible to get. Both of his younger brothers had died before their tenth birthdays of illnesses brought on by poverty and a lack of medical care. Alexei alone had survived, and had realised that his only chance of living a full life was to get the hell out of Siberia and join the rest of civilisation.

It was a great irony that having escaped from the icy grip of Kamchatka, Alexei had then made his fortune in water. The dramatic alteration of the planet's climate over his lifetime had seen the Mediterranean and Africa paralysed by drought to the extent that their entire populations had either perished or sought refuge further north in Europe. Sensing an opportunity, Alexei had invested in defunct container ships that had once carried oil and had them refitted to carry fresh water. Thus had his company, H2O2U, been born. Forty years later, it was one of the few major corporations still standing independent of either government or the *holosaps*.

Water was the one thing that his adoptive motherland had plenty of. As the locals often said, they were *pissed on* daily either by the *holosaps* or the sky. The shifting climate had resulted in disruption of both the jet stream and the ocean circulation around the United Kingdom. Contrary to long–held popular beliefs, global warming had not resulted in a balmy English climate but in fact had heralded falling average temperatures, bitter winters and damp, stormy summers.

At least now, Alexei mused, the English had some real weather to worry about.

A deep boom shook him from his thoughts as it reverberated through the building and he glanced out of a broad window across the city. A flare of lightning snaked white fire across the clouds above, briefly illuminating the gloomy skyline in a halo of light and casting into sharp relief a billowing black plume of oily smoke rising from within the city.

His first thought was for his adopted daughter, Arianna. She worked close to where he assumed the blast had detonated. Revolutionaries, those opposed to the *holosaps* on religious grounds, frequently attacked the company's distinctive headquarters, claiming God's will as the motivation for their atrocities. His second thought was for his deceased wife, Natalya, whose passing had forged within his heart a dense pall of sadness that time would not heal. A victim of The Falling, she had died long before uploading as a *holosap* was possible.

Alexei squinted his ageing eyes to focus on the plume, and saw a reflection dance in front of the windows. Alarm fired through his synapses and he whirled in time to see a masked man plunge something deep into Alexei's belly. Pain bolted through Alexei's stomach and danced through his tendons as electrical currents seethed through his body.

Alexei gagged as his legs collapsed beneath him, the sound of a Taser device clicking in his ears as he squirmed in agony on the polished floor. Through his pain and his blurred vision he saw more men flood into his living room, all of them wearing face masks, black combat suits and carrying weapons. Rough hands bound his wrists and his ankles and he was dragged through the room and down a corridor to his bedroom.

Alexei felt himself being lifted onto his bed and pinned down as the rough hands loosed the restraints on his limbs only to refasten them to the ornate iron bedstead. Thick tape was affixed across his mouth, making his breathing difficult as he tried to suck in air.

The men stood back. Six of them in all. The eyes of strangers watched him without emotion through plastic eye shields as a seventh man walked in and closed the bedroom door behind him. He was shorter than the rest, thin and wiry, his features hidden behind a black balaclava. He reached up to a small panel on the wall and swept one gloved finger across it. The digital display lit up and in an instant the windows turned opaque, blocking out the view from beyond. The man then turned on the bedroom lights and walked slowly toward Alexei's bed.

The man dragged a chair from a desk nearby and set it alongside the bed. He sat down, his squinting eyes never shifting from Alexei's.

'This will not hurt for very long,' the man said in a soft voice.

Alexei began trying to shout for help through his gag, but his cries were weak and his breathing laboured as he tried to get more air into his lungs.

'There is no sense in struggling,' the man said. 'This will all be over shortly.'

The man reached into a pocket and produced two strips of what looked like chewing gum, each a different colour and packaged in slim polythene bags. He examined the bags with interest as he spoke.

'Remarkable, the inventiveness of mankind,' the man said conversationally. 'Inert plastic when sealed within these small bags, but a lethal source of ignition when bound together.' He looked at Alexei. 'I doubt that anybody would be surprised that now, in the twilight of your life, you have chosen to end this existence and move on to greater things?'

Alexei glared at the man, radiated fury, but his anger was hopelessly futile.

'I can assure you, Alexei,' he said, 'that despite what you may think, this if for the best. It is for a better future, for all of us. It is time we shook off these puny, vulnerable shells and become what we should have long ago been: Gods, in all but name.'

The man reached out a hand behind him. One of the armed soldiers produced a long, thin plastic case not much longer than Alexei's finger. The man opened the case and produced a syringe filled with an amber fluid.

Alexei's eyes widened and he tried to scream again through his gag. The man took his time, not reacting to Alexei's muffled protests as he leaned forward and wrenched one of Alexei's sleeves up to reveal a thick vein. Moments later, the needle slipped in and the man slowly injected the fluid into Alexei's arm.

'Alcohol,' the man said as he slipped the needle out, 'just in case the coroner bothers with an autopsy, and a mild paralysis agent called *Pancuronium bromide*.'

Alexei felt the alcohol hit his system almost immediately, felt as though he had been drinking all day even though he hadn't touched a drop in twenty years. Nausea poisoned his guts and sent hot flushes through his body as his limbs fell still.

The man stood up from the bed and opened the two packs of plastic. Alexei felt tears stream from his eyes as he looked up imploringly at the man, unable now even to move his head.

'Don't worry,' his attacker said softly as he wound the two pieces of plastic together and tossed them underneath the bed. 'You'll thank me for this, before long.'

The six armed men turned and left the room. Their leader waited in silence for several long seconds, looking down at Alexei's body before he then removed the restraints from his wrists and ankles. He turned off the bedroom lights and the privacy fogging on the windows and moved to look out over the city. Although he could not hear sirens he could see them flashing through London's murky streets as emergency vehicles and law enforcement rushed to the nearby explosion.

He checked his watch and nodded in satisfaction as tendrils of smoke coiled from beneath the bed and crept like snakes across the bed sheets.

Alexei tried to scream through his gag but he could barely breath as the sheets burst into flame.

The man turned and strode from the bedroom, disappeared down the stairs and left Alexei alone and immobilised on the bed. The smell of smoke, the heat of flames and a strange chemical taint hit his senses. And then white pain touched his body.

He squeezed his eyes tight shut as his late father's words drifted through his mind.

'What is interminable now will be but a short memory, for all things good and bad eventually come to an end.'

Alexei felt tears of raw fear spill down his cheeks as the mattress beneath him burst into flames that spat thick smoke billowing up toward the ceiling. The heat and the pain roared upward and he screamed and tried to move as it seared his body like a furnace, but not a single muscle would respond. Through his agony he felt his skin slough from his body and glimpsed his flesh bubbling on his chest as his shirt ignited.

The flames and the smoke consumed him in a crucible of pain worse than anything he could have imagined as he literally burned alive in a funeral pyre.

His last thought was of the peaceful wilds of the Kamchatka Peninsular he had left behind so long ago, and his kindly old parents waving him goodbye for the last time.

* * *

5

'Can you see my hand?'

Flashing lights flared in Arianna's field of vision, pulsing like nightclub strobes through the gloom. A star–shaped blur hovered before them and she blinked as she tried to focus. A palm and fingers swam into her vision in front of a concerned paramedic.

'Yes,' she replied.

Nausea bolted through her stomach and she coughed as she sat on the damp pavement. The paramedic sat down beside her and rested a comforting arm and a thermal blanket across her shoulders.

'Easy now,' he reassured her. 'You'll be fine in a few minutes.'

Arianna's head ached and there was a painful ringing in her ears as she looked about her.

The street was full of fire trucks and ambulances. It had been a long time since she had seen so many motor vehicles all in one place: most ordinary citizens could not afford luxury items such as vehicles, the fuel to power them mainly reserved for emergency services and what was left of the military. A galaxy of emergency lights flashed through a fine drizzle of rain, some of it natural and some of it drifting from the fire hoses spraying into a writhing inferno of flame still consuming the lower floors of the Re–Volution building.

'What happened?' Arianna managed to ask as she spotted gurneys being manhandled through the foyer's shattered windows.

'Terrorist attack I think,' the medic replied with a shake of his head. 'Some of those religious warriors were seen fleeing the scene. They were trying to hit the company's quantum storage units. You were lucky â€" your umbrella and that wall shielded you from the worst of the blast and debris.'

Arianna nodded absent–mindedly, her brain not yet fully engaged with the world around her. One of the greatest of the seismic cultural changes wrought by the arrival of the *holosaps* was the collapse of organised religion. Most had degenerated over the generations since into a scattered coalition of cults and inevitably there were those who were still willing to use violence to undertake *God's work*. Most targeted Re–Volution in one way or another, under a banner of outrage at the abomination of the dead now walking amongst the living. Arianna had seen plenty of marches attended by people bearing banners that complained of the preference for "Death before Life", espoused "Pro–Life" laws or simply threatened death to anybody who did not subscribe to their own archaic point of view.

'Water,' she rasped.

The medic turned and poured chilled water into a plastic cup for her. She sipped it gratefully as she watched police cordoning off the street nearby, hundreds of onlookers watching. Some of the more shabbily dressed were clapping and hooting.

'You work here?' the medic asked her as he gestured at the building and looked at her clerical collar.

Arianna glanced him over before she replied. Young, dark haired but pale skinned, likely poor much like herself. Nobody went abroad anymore for holidays in the sun, the risk of infection being too great and there being no aircraft available to fly them there.

'Not really,' she replied, 'I'm a bereavement counsellor.'

'Must be weird,' he said conversationally as he watched the nearby crowds, 'counselling the already dead about the afterlife that we now control.'

'It's not an easy thing to do,' she replied, 'make the switch overnight from living being to hologram.'

'They should try living in the real world for a while,' the medic replied. 'Poor things, years of living in luxury and then they get immortality tagged on while we all suffer down here until we just die.' He closed a box containing basic medical supplies. 'Personally I wish somebody would blow this whole damned building off the map for good.'

Arianna looked at him for a moment before she replied.

'They'd build another. It's equality you should seek, not revenge.'

'Tell that to my deceased parents.'

'Or mine?' she challenged lightly.

The medic looked at her for a moment. 'Are you on their side or ours?'

'I'm on the side of life,' she replied and gestured to the medical symbol on his shoulder insignia, 'just like you should be.'

The medic got up from the pavement. 'You're all done here, have a nice day.'

Arianna took the hint and got up, her legs a little unsteady beneath her as she looked at small abrasions on her palms. The road was littered with a sparkling sheet of shattered glass and chunks of masonry where the blast had torn a jagged twenty metre hole in the building's entrance. Smoke still writhed and coiled out of broken windows further up where the fire had spread to the second floor offices, but the fire hoses were playing water across them and killing the flames.

'Arianna?'

A man hurried toward her, his grey suit stained with water and grime, his face twisted with concern. Larry Wilkes was an executive at Re–Volution and one of the few people that she could actually stand to be in the same room with. Twice her age and with a belly that sagged over his trousers, he had a buoyant attitude that more than made up for his haggard appearance.

'You okay?' he asked her.

'I'll live..,' Arianna replied, using one of the company's iconic catch phrases with a bitter tone attached.

Larry managed a grin beneath his stubble. '… another day. Is the word getting out about what happened?'

'Antisaps,' she replied, sheltering from the rain against a wall in a side street opposite the Re–Volution building, 'some kind of terrorist hit. Are you all right?'

'Second floor,' Larry said. 'Felt like the building was coming down there for a bit, but we all got out okay. The lobby's a mess.'

'Casualties?' Arianna asked furtively.

'Several fatalities,' Larry informed her. 'Revo's security personnel are rushing a few of them down to the theatres right now before they fade out.'

Arianna nodded. There was usually a time window of about eight minutes after death that the human brain could be successfully wired for upload. Random electrical impulses, wayward neurons and cortex activity still occurred in the human body for a few minutes after clinical death, creating a brief period of opportunity before the brain began to decompose and the essential neural networks were lost forever. Long standing Re–Volution employees were able to forgo their pensions in exchange for a free upload to the "light colony", a digital world entirely contained within Re–Volution's data storage systems that was rumoured to be a place better than heaven, devoid of all ills. Few declined, mainly because few could afford either the upload or the alternative, the company's new Futurance scheme, which for an exorbitant fee allowed a full brain back–up to be updated every six months. *Die another day*, was the catchphrase attached to that particular service.

'But it's not the human casualties that bother me,' Larry added.

It took Arianna a few moments to realise what he meant. 'Oh, no. They got through?'

'The blast was a distraction,' Larry said. 'Two of the terrorists made it to the basement in the confusion and managed to hit the servers with a suicide belt.'

Arianna felt her shoulders sag. 'How many?'

'One hundred eighteen confirmed *holosap* casualties, maybe another forty to add if the techs can't retrieve the data.'

Arianna slumped against the wall.

The servers was a generalised name for some of the world's most remarkable computers. Quantum–storage systems had once been the preserve of the military and government, but now Re–Volution owned six of them, which were linked to each other via a vast supporting "cloud" system of ordinary processors. The quantum computers held the digitized lives of thousands of *holosaps*, preserving them for all eternity. Unless, of course, somebody destroyed the servers.

'The press will have a field day with this,' Larry went on. 'As soon as they realise the scale of the hit it will be all over the glossies: the biggest mass murder of *holo*–history.'

Arianna nodded but she was not interested in the headlines that would flash up on electronic broadsheets in pockets all across the city. She felt weighed down by the knowledge that dozens, if not hundreds of grieving relatives would flock to her offices to receive support for their loss. Again. As if it were not enough that their relatives had died of old age or disease or accidents, now they would have lost them all over again along with their money. Re–Volution's contract clauses ensured that it shared no liability for what the company termed *"acts of Nature or third–party attacks on company property"*.

Arianna sighed and pulled her raincoat closer about her. The damp air had matted her hair across her faced and she felt exhausted. Larry looked like he was about to say something when he was interrupted by the sound of footsteps through nearby puddles on the debris strewn street.

Two police detectives strode up to them, badge–shields hanging round their necks and heavy looking pistols poking from shoulder holsters beneath their jackets.

'Miss Volkov?' the older of the two asked.

Arianna nodded. The older detective was probably not much more than thirty five but his features carried the lines of a man who had seen more than his fair share of murder and mayhem. Thick brown hair framed grey eyes, and the hard line of his lips above a tense jaw spoke of a daily battle for justice in a city that few believed would endure for much longer. He squinted as a flare of sunlight streamed briefly through the turbulent clouds above as the thunderstorm moved on.

The younger man, also dark haired but shorter and stockier, spoke quietly.

'Detectives Myles Bourne and Han Reeves. Miss Volkov, can we ask you to come with us? There's been a murder.'

Arianna stared at Bourne. 'You boys sure have to work hard for those badges these days.'

Han Reeves's jaw fractured into a brittle grin.

'A hundred or more *holosaps* and several humans have died right here,' Larry said, intervening, 'and Arianna here has already had a hell of a day. Maybe this could wait until tomorrow?'

Han's grin slipped away.

'Maybe you could get lost,' the detective replied to Larry, 'before I arrest you for obstructing police business?'

Larry stood his ground. 'She's been through enough already.'

Han seemed to be deciding whether or not he could take Larry seriously. Arianna felt a rush of compassion toward her friend for his noble stance, but she had a voice of her own and the impression that Han Reeves would put Larry horizontal without breaking a sweat.

'Detective Reeves,' she said, pushing past Larry. 'I'll come with you. Can I clean up first at my place? I've narrowly avoided being blown up and its playing havoc with my hair.'

The glint of steel in Han's eyes faded away. 'Fine.'

'Can I ask why I have to be there?' Arianna asked. 'What does the murder have to do with me?'

'The victim is a man named Alexei Volkov,' Han replied. 'Your father.'

Arianna felt her breath catch in her throat. The world seemed to tilt slightly beneath her feet.

'Alexei is dead?' she gasped. 'When? How?'

Han glanced suspiciously at Larry. 'We'll talk in the car.'

The detectives turned away and marched toward a police cruiser parked further down the street. Larry grabbed Arianna's arm and squeezed, his features taut with concern.

'My God, Arianna, I'm so sorry.'

Arianna could not find her voice to reply. She felt as though she were occupying somebody else's body, witnessing events that were not real.

'Don't trust them,' Larry insisted. 'The police are as corrupt as the criminals these days. God only knows what's going on.'

Arianna managed a feeble nod and headed off in pursuit of the detectives. Han Reeves waited for her at the rear door of the cruiser and held it open for her as she climbed aboard. The interior smelled of plastic and of hot electronics. Two display screens dominated the centre of the dashboard, and a holographic map hovered in front of the passenger seat and displayed their location north west of the Thames.

Han Reeves climbed in as Myles started the engine and they pulled out of the street. Arianna felt the unfamiliar throb of the large engine under the hood as the car surged away.

'Alexei Volkov was your adoptive father,' Han said.

'He was,' Arianna replied, her voice robbed of emotion. 'What happened?'

'Suicide,' Han replied. 'Right now he's not much more than ash and a bad smell.'

Arianna felt a twist of nausea in the back of her throat. 'Thanks for the concern.'

Han did not look at her. 'I have a job to do. Somebody else can send flowers.'

'You're sure it was a suicide?'

'Very,' Han confirmed. 'Forensics teams are on site but we wanted you to come in and view the scene.'

'Me?'

'You,' Myles said as he drove the cruiser, its lights flashing and reflecting off the damp tarmac, 'because you're one of the few people who actually knew the guy.'

'He was a recluse, right?' Han added.

'He was,' Arianna replied. 'He took very few visitors, and even I only travelled to his house once every fortnight or so.'

'Why?' Han pressed. 'What was his issue?'

'I can't say,' Arianna replied, 'but I can say with some certainty that he was not suicidal the last time I spoke with him.'

'Which was when?' Myles asked.

'Barely an hour ago.'

'And he gave no indications of being depressed?' Han asked. 'Did he reveal anything to you that might have suggested concerns for the future, for family or friends?'

'Nothing,' Arianna insisted. 'He had no other family, or many friends for that matter. In fact he was quite upbeat and had arranged for us to meet for lunch today at The Ivory.'

'The restaurant?' Han asked. Arianna nodded without speaking. 'Hell of a place,' Han observed. 'Amazing that somebody with all that wealth would choose to take their own life, especially when they've got an upload waiting for them anyway. Why rush?'

'My father had absolutely no intention of uploading when his time came,' Arianna pointed out. 'He was as opposed to being a *holosap* as I am.'

Han glanced at her collar. 'So we understand.'

'What's that supposed to mean, detective?'

'Alexei Volkov was one of the earliest financial supporters of what became Re–Volution,' Han explained. 'He backed out just after The Falling overcame the population, never explained why.'

'Because it was an unholy mess,' Arianna replied. 'Alexei knew the difference between science and idiocy.'

'Idiocy?' Han echoed her. 'I guess being beamed up into immortality is only idiocy if you don't like it. Odd, though, how Alexei commits suicide right after a bomb hits the *Revo* building, don't you think?'

Arianna stared at Detective Reeves. 'You seriously think he did it,' she said flatly.

'Or you did,' Han replied, 'because you were the last person to see him alive.'

* * *

6

The mansion was located on the Embankment, with a small mooring behind security gates blocking access from the Thames. No boats were allowed due to the smuggling that plagued the city, a black market trade in items from the dangerous wilderness beyond the river sought by the rich and obtained by criminals willing to risk infection travelling into the forests. Arianna got out into the chill air, surrounded once again by flashing hazard lights that reflected off the mansion of glass as though it were a gigantic kaleidoscope, rainbow hues contrasting with the grey sky.

Han and Myles led her past the police cordons and into the mansion.

White tiled floors and minimalistic polished steel furniture dominated Alexei's refuge. Canvasses of impressionist works hung in flashes of colour on the otherwise sparse walls as Han led her up a spiral staircase to the second floor.

The harsh taint of smoke and chemicals stung her throat as they reached a corridor that led into the north wing and the master bedroom. The fittings near the door were charred and crumbling, everything cast in shades of black. Arianna slowed as a forensics team in white overalls and masks moved past them, and a uniformed officer guarding the entrance to the bedroom waved them through.

Arianna saw the smouldering bed almost immediately, dominating the far end of the room. A charred square of brittle metal springs draped in loops of white foam that had been hosed in from outside. A cold wind gusted through the room where the fire crews had deliberately fired projectiles through the toughened windows to gain access for their hoses.

Draped across the skeletal metallic bed was the body of Alexei Volkov. Arianna choked back a sob of grief and loathing as the smell of burned flesh coated the back of her throat with something slimy.

'Breathe slow,' Han advised her. 'Your brain will adjust soon enough and scrub the smell from your mind.'

'And the memory?' she coughed.

'That's there forever I'm afraid.'

Arianna edged forward and saw that Alexei's corpse was charred beyond recognition, a blackened hulk of scorched tissue scoured of any recognisable features.

'Are you sure it's Alexei?' Arianna asked, tears blurring her eyes.

'Forensics have taken blood samples from his core,' Myles answered for Han. 'They'll probably check his teeth too to confirm the identity.'

'There was no sign of forced entry,' Han added, 'and no security alerts from the home's systems. It looks like Alexei died here alone.'

'Did he upload in time?'

'Re–Volution's people got here at the same time as the emergency services,' Myles reported. 'His implant signalled them as soon as Alexei's heart stopped beating. They got him wired up once the fire was out but we don't yet know if the transfer was completed. It took the fire crews several minutes to control the blaze and gain access to the body.'

Arianna closed her eyes in regret. 'The heat might have damaged his brain. If they couldn't upload him, we won't know what happened.'

'Which is why you're here,' Han explained. 'Did Alexei present any indication that he was going to commit suicide despite what he said to you about meeting for lunch?'

'None,' Arianna replied firmly. 'He was an extremely wealthy man but he came from a very poor background. He used to tell me about his childhood in Siberia. He was the eldest and only survivor of three children. He knew how lucky he was to have this life, and spent most of his time donating to and supporting charities across the globe before The Falling. It's part of the reason why he supported early work into holonomic entities – he knew the pain of losing siblings, and wanted to prevent others from having to go through the same loss.'

Han nodded and scanned the grim scene with a practiced eye.

'The problem I've got is that this blaze was started deliberately by *somebody*,' he said. 'It burned with incredible ferocity and speed, which means an accelerant was used. But we have no evidence of anybody entering or exiting the building.'

'What about the security cameras?' Arianna asked. 'Wouldn't they have seen something?'

'First place we looked,' Myles said. 'Nobody on them. Alexei was alone.'

'Then why the suspicion?' Arianna asked Han. 'My opinion is just that, an opinion. Maybe there were things that Alexei did not want to share with me, fears or emotions or regrets that he buried deep inside that eventually caught up with him?'

'Maybe,' Han agreed, 'or maybe those thoughts were planted inside him by a psychologist.'

Han looked down at her for a moment. Arianna coughed out a bitter laugh.

'Seriously? You're saying I'm a suspect?'

'Right now everybody with a connection to Alexei Volkov is a suspect.'

'That's more than ridiculous,' Arianna gasped. 'I was nearly blown into a million pieces less than an hour ago! I hadn't been in this house for several days! How on Earth can you suspect me of murdering him?'

Myles stepped forward and produced a data–roll. He slid the glossy electronic screen onto a charred bedside table and pointed at the documents glowing inside it.

'Is it true that six months ago, on your thirtieth birthday, Alexei Volkov gifted to you the promise of an upload?'

Arianna struggled to speak. 'Yes, it is.'

Arianna had been stunned when her reclusive philanthropist father revealed that he had reserved her a place as a *holosap*. The cost of a place was equivalent to about thirty years' of her salary, far beyond her means. For most people an upload was merely the stuff of dreams, like a win on those old fashioned lotteries that used to operate in better days. Alexei had said that although he understood her opposition to uploading, she was the only heir to his fortune and as was her nature would probably seek to help others before helping herself. He had insisted: no upload, no inheritance, and written it into his will.

Arianna had never wanted Alexei's money, an inheritance that most people would gladly have killed for. She had occasionally fantasised about handing out his billions to the poor and the needy living in the rat–runs of the East End, but somehow the thought of doing so had always seemed like a betrayal of Alexei's hardships, the jewel of his determination cast away to others less able.

Alexei had begged her to agree, if only to protect his fortune from the government who would no doubt attempt to claim it in his absence and her refusal. Accept, he had said, and at least you will be able to control its distribution.

Arianna had been implanted with her revised chip two weeks later.

Every single person in the city possessed a chip, implanted between the frontal lobes of the brain when the recipient was aged four years, as a requirement by law. The procedure was simple and painless, the chip slightly smaller and shorter than a matchstick and inserted under local anaesthetic. Standard chips performed two main functions: firstly, they monitored a person's location in the city. Second, they monitored their body's vitals and kept a watch for the first tell–tale signs of The Falling, signalling an infection inside the city and triggering an immediate quarantine signal to law enforcement.

Advanced chips performed a third function via bio–neural networking. Two biological growths extended gradually from the top of the chip into the frontal lobes of the brain, providing a natural link between the human brain and the chip. The link recorded every facet of the person's daily life through the signals processed within their mind, a sort of mobile Big Brother, which was then stored by Re–Volution. Should the person die, and be fortunate enough to possess an upload, the data was then uploaded into a *holosap*. The brain, scanned in tremendous detail during the initial download, was then rebuilt and the memories on the chip inserted as part of the program.

Immortality, forged in binary code and stored forever.

'And is it true,' Myles went on, 'that the upload would be automatically verified to you only upon Alexei's death?'

'Yes,' Arianna said, and sighed. 'Alexei disliked holosaps as much as I do, so he held back on activating the upload, something which I did not question at all.'

Han gestured to the billionaire's corpse lying on the remains of the bed. 'Maybe something changed for you?'

Arianna felt a surge of liquid anger flush hot down her spine.

'Don't you think that if I was going to kill him I'd have just shot him in the head?'

'That would be an obvious murder,' Han pointed out. 'This is much more ambiguous. The use of the accelerant could have been by Alexei himself, but we just can't be sure. That means it is a suspected homicide.'

Arianna gaped at him as she struggled to understand why she would even be under suspicion on such lame evidence.

'Alexei was old,' she uttered. 'He would have died eventually, probably of natural causes. If it was the upload I was after all I had to do was wait. And how could I have got in here and burned him when I was sitting on my arse with bleeding ears several miles away across the damned city?'

Han raised an eyebrow in interest at her tirade. 'Which you escaped from just in the nick of time, and I didn't tell you Alexei's time of death, Miss Volkov.'

Arianna laughed again. 'Call yourselves detectives? The bed is still dripping with retardant foam, the room stinks and you guys are both clean shaven which suggests you're fresh to the case.'

Han and Myles exchanged a glance. 'There are other detective teams,' Han replied. 'Foam hangs around for days, as does smoke, and I shave every morning.'

'Then we both have a shaky theory,' Arianna shot back.

Han grinned. 'Except that we both know you're capable of murder, Miss Volkov.'

Arianna stared at the detective for a long moment. She felt her lips quivering and hot tears beading on her eyes.

'How could you know that?' she managed to ask. 'That's personal information. You have no right to…'

'We attained warrants almost immediately,' Myles cut her off. 'In the case of any mortality or fatal accident, we have the right to suspend personal confidentiality orders if there is sufficient suspicion of foul play. The swift and uncharacteristic nature of Alexei Volkov's apparent suicide was considered by the Attorney General sufficient to warrant data retrieval on any persons either related or closely affiliated with the victim.'

Han Reeves spoke softly.

'It's my bet that we will find evidence of an accelerant, perhaps somewhere in the remains of the bed, that could have been placed there to ignite beneath the victim. More to the point, The Falling will breach the city eventually, and anybody without an active upload will likely be abandoned, just like people were when London was quarantined.'

Arianna staggered sideways slightly and put her hand down on a scorched table top that still felt warm to the touch. Detective Han Reeves' voice reached her as though from the opposite side of the universe.

'We know about your husband's death,' he said, 'and that you escaped conviction on the thinnest of alibis. Miss Volkov, I'm sorry to say that you are the only person who had access to this room, a motive to kill Alexei Volkov and a likely will to do so.'

*** * ***

7

Bayou La Tour, Louisiana

Gulf of Mexico

'Air lock activated, please check your HazMat suits and air cylinders.'

Marcus D'Souza tried to ignore the cloying heat and glanced down at two pressure gauges attached to a utility belt on his suit and saw them both reading acceptable levels. As he did so, a smaller man with a balding head and dressed in a quaint tweed suit and patterned bow–tie head walked slowly around him, checking that his Hazmat suit was sealed.

'You ever think about switching that tweed for something else?'

Dr Reed shook his head as he examined Marcus's boot bindings. 'No. I loved it.'

Marcus didn't miss the doctor's past tense reply.

Dr Reed stood up, and in the heat his projected image flickered slightly. Reed had died some years earlier from *The Falling*. Or, to be more accurate, the British expert in infectious disease had decided to take his own life in Gabon after becoming infected during a research mission. *The Falling's* flesh eating nature tended to attack brains as well as everything else, preventing upload for those deeply infected, and Reed had decided to take no chances. As a valuable field research scientist, his upload had been sanctioned and paid for by the British government.

'All seals are secure,' Reed said as he stood up. 'You're good to go, as you Yanks say.'

'Okay Kerry, let's do it.'

The voice of Dr Kerry Hussein, Marcus's companion in the remote field station, echoed through his protective headgear.

'Doors opening in five seconds. Take care out there.'

Moments later, the airlock hissed as air pressure from within drove a breeze out into the muggy heat of Louisiana's burning skies. Marcus walked swiftly out into the bayou and turned, giving a camera above the airlock a quick thumbs–up. The airlock doors hissed shut again and he was alone but for Dr Reed's *holosap* and thick clouds of insects buzzing lazily on the hot air.

Marcus turned and looked out across the bayou.

Through rolling banks of bugs flowing like rivers through the air he could see the distant and crumbling city of New Orleans, a monument of city blocks and roads shimmering in the heat, and closer by the virtually unrecognisable town of Lafitte. Even from a mile away he could see that the buildings were caked in filth and thick vegetation, windows broken and the roofs of smaller buildings either sagging inward or already collapsed beneath the weight of foliage.

The forests and the swamps had reclaimed the cities far faster than anybody could have imagined, mostly down to the fact that there were no longer any herbivorous mammals left to consume them. Likewise, the insects thrived with no birds to pluck them from the air or rodents to hunt them on the ground.

'Let's go,' Dr Reed said, his voice sounding small in the wilderness. 'You've only got an hour's worth of air.'

Marcus heard his own breathing rasp as he sucked in blessedly cool air from his compressed tanks, that air already filtered and cleaned in the laboratory. His suit had the capacity to filter air directly from the environment around him, but neither he nor any other researcher working in one of the many remote stations around the world fancied taking that chance, not with a pandemic as virulent as The Falling.

'This way,' he said.

Dr Reed followed Marcus, who had a small digital display projected onto the clear visor of his head gear. The display was of a grid system laid out over the terrain before him, each grid representing an area of land that had already been searched, sometimes with small chunks of text denoting discoveries of interest.

Marcus headed through the grid toward its edge, where an old road ran through the bayou toward the looming city nearby.

'Any sign of life?' Marcus asked.

Kerry Hussein's voice came back to him from the compound.

'Nothing yet but keep your eyes open, the heat's affecting the sensors.'

Marcus nodded to himself inside the headgear, and glanced to his right to see Dr Reed pacing alongside him.

'You'd better take the lead,' Marcus said, 'in case anything nasty jumps out at us. Head for Lafitte.'

Dr Reed obeyed without question, despite his greater experience as a scientist. The simple fact was that since becoming a *holosap* Reed was automatically required to obey Marcus, a living human. Although Marcus enjoyed being the senior scientist, he knew that the reasons for the altered pecking order after death were more to do with practicality than discrimination: as a *holosap* Dr Reed could not physically manipulate anything in the world around him. However, it also meant that he could not be infected by The Falling, or harmed by any other of the many *nasties*, as Kerry named them, living in the bayou.

Dr Reed took point a few feet ahead of Marcus and headed down the cracked, weed infested asphalt road toward the abandoned city ahead. His *holosap* was being beamed directly from the research station, his visual and audio provided by Marcus's equipment along with algorithms that created an "off–set", allowing him a sort of quasi–freedom of movement as long as he stayed within visual range of Marcus.

He led the way for several minutes before pausing beside a pool of brackish water. Marcus stopped beside him and scooped a half–quart of green water into a transparent cylinder and sealed the lid.

'It's everywhere.'

The seething heat would have been bad enough even without the Level 4 Hazmat suit as Marcus swilled the water in the cylinder.

'At what density?' asked Dr Reed.

The searing equatorial sun caused his holographic image to appear washed out and there was a slight flicker caused by the extreme range of the projection.

'Stand by,' Marcus said.

He turned the cylinder over on itself a few times and then depressed a small button set into the lid. A squirt of blue liquid was injected into the green water and Marcus shook the cylinder for a few seconds before holding it in the shade of his body.

Dr Reed watched as within the now pale yellow fluid floated a billion tiny black flecks.

'Overwhelming,' Marcus replied finally. 'Concentrations are likely now high enough that even mild exposure to infected water would kill any human being within a matter of hours.'

Marcus, Kerry and Dr Reed had arrived in Louisiana four months previously, despatched from what was left of New York City to search for any species that may have survived or developed a resistance to The Falling. The tragedy of mankind's greatest pandemic was that it had originated somewhere in the American deep south, specifically in the Bayou in Louisiana, according to genetic analysis of victims of the disease.

Marcus was standing in what was believed to be Ground Zero.

No warm or cold blooded vertebrates had yet been found that were not vulnerable to The Falling, which got its name from the extraordinary speed with which its victims were overcome. The fungal infection attacked flesh, and in doing so rapidly degraded things like nerves, tendons and muscles, common features of all mammals. One of the first things that happened as an infection took hold was loss of local motor control, depending on where the infection was introduced to the body.

The reality of the pandemic was far more horrific than any Hollywood movie. The infection spread easily through bodily fluids, sweat, saliva and even hair follicles. By the time the first symptoms were showing in victims around the Gulf of Mexico, tens of thousands of people had been infected. Flights out of New Orleans transmitted the disease across the continental United States and around the globe before it had even been properly identified and studied. Attempts at global quarantine were hopeless – the disease was already present in millions within days of its discovery in Louisiana.

Symptoms appeared typically within eight to twelve hours of infection. Rashes and blisters on the skin quickly festered and bled, helping to spread the disease to carers and family members alike. The fungus did not really *eat* flesh, but merely hastened its decay by feeding on tissue and veins, cutting off the flow of blood to muscles and organs and causing them to rot.

Within twenty four hours infected victims might be completely immobilised, or have flesh falling in chunks from their face, chest or abdomen, depending on where the infection struck first. At times in some cities it seemed as though leprosy had returned from the Middle Ages to haunt the present, infected people begging and crying for surcease from their agony. Some victim's vocal chords and tongues became infected first, causing starvation and dehydration as their ruined throats no longer allowed food to pass through or they died from asphyxiation as their throats collapsed into their lungs.

Marcus had been trying to stem the tide of victims in New York City until the pull–out was enforced. Doctors were replaced by the National Guard as strict curfew and quarantines were put in place, but by then everybody knew it was too late. The streets were full of people bleeding from every orifice, some with limbs hanging by threads or already bloody stumps of meat. The zombie apocalypse realised, but with the added reality of true suffering as otherwise sentient human beings rotted into pieces while still alive.

The worst of it though, for Marcus, was not the human tragedy but the global tragedy. All vertebrates were affected alike: dogs, cats, mice, birds, cattle, everything. Birds dropped out of the sky as wings were severed in flight. Cattle lay dead and bloated in fields across the Midwest. Rodents sprawled on asphalt, rigid with death and teeth bared. They were fed upon by others, who then contracted the infection.

Six months. That was how long it took for over six billion human beings to die, along with at least eighty per cent of all vertebrate species. Only the bugs, some species of fish and other marine species remained. The collapse of the entire food chain had sparked the biggest mass extinction since the Cretaceous Period some sixty–five million years before, and Marcus was now standing perilously exposed at the very spot where the devastating pandemic had begun.

'We're here,' Dr Reed said, pausing on the edge of a river bank.

Marcus slowed, noticed the gently swaying reed banks brushing into Reed's legs, vanishing only to reappear again moments later.

'The river's the border, can't cross beyond it,' Marcus said.

'I can,' Reed smiled.

The *holosap* stepped out and strode across the green surface of the river. He even still had his hands in his pockets, like it was nothing.

Marcus shivered. Like most all folk, he'd never really got used to the idea of people being dead and alive at the same time. Seeing shit like this didn't much help his unease. He knew it was all something to do with quantum computers, bent light and who the hell knew what else, but his field was classical biology and that's where he intended his expertise to stay. Besides, he couldn't afford an upload even if he'd wanted one. Dr Reed's Nobel laureate and expertise were his key to immortality. By contrast, Marcus was a novice.

Dr Reed was almost across the river when Marcus saw the threat.

'Reed, move, now!'

It was an instinctive act born of human nature, to alert a fellow human being to danger. Marcus had barely got the words out of his mouth when Dr Reed turned casually to observe the shape speeding silkily through the water toward him. Moments later the snake jerked as its head lifted out of the murky green water and slashed fangs across Dr Reed's leg.

The snake flashed through the *holosap* and splashed back into the water to disappear into its murky depths.

'Nerodia rhombifer,' Dr Reed observed with interest. 'Very poisonous and one of the few surviving vertebrate species.'

Marcus got his heartbeat back under control.

'Diamondback water snake,' he replied. 'They shouldn't have lasted this long out here without anything to eat.'

'Agreed,' Dr Reed said, looking about from the opposite river bank. 'But we've only seen a few of them along this stretch of water, and snakes can go for extremely long periods without food.'

'Not for twenty–five years they can't,' Marcus argued. 'They don't eat insects and this water's far too brackish for fish. There's something else out here, a survivor.'

It was nature's way that just as some species evolved to become efficient killers, so others would evolve in response a defence mechanism against those predators. If a mutation appeared quickly enough that defended well enough against the new attack, the defending species would survive and propagate its defence throughout the population through breeding. If it did not, it became extinct.

'Nutria,' Dr Reed said. 'It was present in sufficient numbers to have perhaps evolved immunity to the disease.' He looked up at Marcus. 'Like us, it needed to adapt to survive.'

Nutria was an Argentinian species of rodent that looked somewhat like a cross between a rat and a beaver. Up to fifteen or so pounds in weight, they devoured up to a quarter of their bodyweight each day by eating the vegetation that bound soil together. The erosion it had caused before The Falling has resulted in vast programs to eradicate and even eat the species. Now, Marcus would have given up almost anything to locate a single one of them, because their habitat and diet meant that of all species on the planet they were the most likely to have developed an immunity to The Falling.

'We'll set traps, all along here,' he said, indicating the river banks. 'We've never seen mink, otter or any other species that could have thrived when the eagles and 'gators went, so it's probably nutria.'

'There!'

Dr Reed pointed across the river and Marcus saw another snake appear as it lunged toward him. He leaped backward as the snake's brilliant white fangs flashed in the sunlight as droplets of water sparkled like diamond chips in the sunlight.

Marcus staggered over the rough ground as the snake struck into the reeds at the water's edge, and something burst from within them. Marcus saw the big rodent lurch away from the snake's fangs with a high–pitched squeal of terror. It's thick wet fur was covered in strips of reed and grass from where it had been concealed in the undergrowth.

'Grab it!'

Dr Reed's voice was almost a screech as Marcus regained his balance and hurled himself down on the fat nutria. The rodent squealed again as Marcus landed on it and wrapped his arms around it.

'It's too wet!' he yelled. 'I can't keep hold of it!'

The surface of his HazMat suit was drenched from the nutria, which scrambled desperately to escape his grip. Marcus tightened his hold on the nutria but it squirmed free of his arms.

Marcus, on his knees, let himself fall flat on top of the creature to pin it in place.

'I've got it!'

Marcus heard the sound before he saw the snake. The hiss was the only warning he got before the bright fangs flashed across his face and smacked against his face mask before falling away toward the nutria's head poking from beneath his chest. Dr Reed yelled at him.

'Marcus, pit viper!'

Marcus grabbed the snake's head with one gloved hand and yanked it away from the nutria. The viper recoiled and changed position as it tried to wrap itself around Marcus's arm.

'Throw it clear!'

Dr Reed's cry came too late. Marcus panicked.

He hurled the snake but as soon as he released his grip the viper, still coiled around his forearm, struck again and white pain ripped through his arm as the snake's fangs sliced straight through his Hazmat Suit and into his flesh.

Marcus screamed in pain and released the nutria as he grabbed at the snake just behind its head and pulled it away from his arm. The snake coiled around his right arm, but this time Marcus turned the snake head–down toward the ground and rammed it into the soil. He heard a soft cracking sound, and the snake slumped like a rope onto the ground.

'Marcus!'

Dr Reed scrambled to his side and looked at his arm.

Marcus could see the two pin–prick holes in his HazMat suit, and the blood spilling from the two puncture wounds somewhere within as the pain spread up his arm.

'The nutria,' Marcus gasped.

'It's over there,' Dr Reed pointed. 'Come on, we need to get you back to the compound right now!'

Marcus staggered to his feet and Dr Reed guided him to where the nutria was laying in the thick grass, its chest heaving as it struggled to escape, one leg dragging uselessly behind it where Marcus's weight must have broken it.

'We've got only a few minutes before you're dead,' Dr Reed urged. 'Hurry.'

Marcus winced in pain as he picked the nutria up in his uninjured arm and then staggered toward the distant compound, Dr Reed by his side.

* * *

8

Marcus felt this heart start to thump inside his chest, more from than just fear now. He sensed, somehow, the lethal neurotoxins flooding into his nervous system from the snakebite, threatening to shut down his lungs, liver and kidneys before paralysing his heart in a final and massive cardiac arrest.

He blinked sweat from his eyes and willed his legs to push him onward.

Beyond where they struggled through the listless palm trees and swamps lay the Gulf of Mexico, the Caribbean and the Atlantic Ocean, and beyond the rest of the world, immense expanses of wilderness and all of it filled to the brim with a fungus that had been responsible for wiping out some ninety per cent of all mammalian life on the planet. Including his own wife and three children.

Not a virus. Not a bacteria. A fungus.

Nobody was quite sure how it had made the leap into mammals, and the likely explanation after years of study was that the outbreak had occurred in many places, many times before truly taking hold.

Marcus remembered the old zombie movies, of people walking about with flesh hanging off their bodies, desperate for human blood and biting anything that moved. The reality had been far more horrifying in its simplicity than anybody could ever have imagined. He looked down at the galaxy of black specks floating now in what looked like yellow pus in the cylinder in his hand, the nutria making small noises as it dangled in the crook of his arm. Already a cloud of insects were humming around the cylinder.

'Apophysomyces,' he whispered, and shivered in the heat as his body started to react to the snake venom coursing through his veins.

The fungus was commonplace around the world and probably had been for millions of years, for it made its home in common soil, wood and water. Usually entirely harmless to humans, it only made its real danger known when introduced *inside* the human body, perhaps through a scratch or wound. There, it became an infection known as Zygomycosis, causing thrombosis but also tissue necrosis. In short, the usually benign fungus began consuming flesh, essentially causing the victim to decay from within as the infection shut off blood flow to infected areas of the body. The more the infection spread the faster the body decayed, and it was one of the fastest spreading fungal infections known to man.

Prognosis from infection to death was usually less than forty–eight hours, all of it spent in the agony of necrosis and then organ failure as the body turned to a bloodied mush from the inside out.

'Keep moving,' Reed said, his voice touched with concern. 'We don't know if your air filters are as effective in this heat.'

Marcus nodded, his breathing rasping in his ears along with Kerry's voice coming from the research station.

'Marcus, you've got elevated levels across the board. Are you okay?'

'Snake bite,' Marcus gasped in reply.

'Shit!' He heard the panic sear Kerry's voice. *'Species?'*

'Cottonmouth,' Marcus replied, 'pit viper.'

Same family as Copperhead and rattlers. Severe hemotoxic venom. Death within a few hours if untreated. They'd all been briefed before departing for the Bayou, in search of the source of The Falling, and preparations had been made.

'I'll get the antivenin ready,' Kerry replied, 'hurry.'

Marcus nodded, almost to himself, as he stumbled through the foliage and tried to focus on putting one foot in front of the other.

It was the so–called *sentinel* species, amphibians, that showed the first signs of the impending apocalypse a quarter of a century ago, when Marcus was just a child. Delicate, sensitive to climate and temperature, they began dying in ever increasing numbers in tropical regions around the globe from rapid and advanced necrosis. Scientists examined them, unable to pinpoint the exact cause of the infections.

Cases of *The Falling*, as it became known, began to rise as climate change altered ocean salinity and temperature and caused an increase in micro–species such as algae, bacteria and fungi. The same altered climate conditions had caused an increase in the frequency and ferocity of tropical storms that annually battered the east coasts of South and North America, Mexico and the Caribbean, the warming waters fuelling the storms that swept through annually. DNA analysis by World Health Organisation scientists confirmed that several strains of *Apophysomyces* were responsible, revealing that the fungus was well established in all areas of the globe and had simply been unleashed by increasing storm events due to climate change. Hurricanes, tornadoes, cyclones and all manner of violent natural events helped to churn up the soil, broke down trees and flooded landscapes, spreading the fungus from its natural environment into new terrain where evolution took its natural course. Strains of the fungus emerged that could survive the upheavals, reducing its proximity to humans and animals, increasing its virulence and survival rates.

The devastation caused by these storms also produced an increase in injuries associated with soil laden debris, which in turn led to the increase in infections in both human and other mammalian species across the gulf. Bodies pierced by wooden splinters, lesions stained by damp soil, mixed blood and other bodily fluids in the chaotic aftermath of major tropical storms provided a lush breeding ground for fungal growths. At some point, somewhere near the Florida panhandle, the fungus had made the leap from fungal parasite to airborne contagion, probably through mutation and infection in a victim's lungs via ingestion. Able to pass on as easily as a common cold, the effects after The Falling became an airborne pathogen were horrendous.

Beginning in the paranasal sinuses, the infection spread with extreme rapidity throughout the body, often killing its host within twenty four hours as necrosis collapsed the airways and throat. Its rapid mortality in immuno–suppressed individuals transferred to an equally voracious mortality in healthy humans and animals. Even as the first World Health Organisation warnings were hitting the headlines as infections broke out all over the gulf and the southern United States, air travel meant that the outbreak moved faster than any containment strategy world governments could implement. Poor sanitation and health centres in economically depressed countries led to the first pandemics as the infection spread unchecked.

Cuba, Havana and Mexico were the first to be quarantined, along with Belize and Puerto Rico. Florida followed, then Georgia. Within days the east coast of the USA was a no–go zone. Outbreaks in West Africa, Spain, Portugal and the Mediterranean followed, the disease spreading with what seemed like impossible speed across the world's equatorial regions.

It has been, as the American president had once said to his beleaguered nation, *"only a matter of time before humankind's arrogant abuse of his environment provoked the wrath of nature. Now, shall we reap the whirlwind."*

Seven billion souls lost. Less than a billion left alive now, in cities–under–siege scattered across the globe. The fungus had made the leap to other species of mammal in less than a year. Ninety per cent of species had succumbed: horses, cats, dogs, rodents. Avian species, once infected, had been the most prolific carriers, but the skies were now empty in all but the northern most countries, hence the profusion of airborne insects: they had flourished in the absence of rodents and birds.

'Hurry,' Reed said, his flickering *holosap* image becoming more defined as they got closer to the compound. 'You only have a few minutes remaining on your filter.'

Marcus quickened his pace, but even in his increasingly desperate state he was careful to avoid touching any foliage around him for fear of further compromising his Hazmat suit.

'Nearly there,' he breathed, his voice heavy with the exertion in the crushing heat.

The northern hemisphere was where the pandemic's dramatic advance was finally slowed. Colder seas, bitter winters and permafrost defied *Apophysomyces* and created a natural barrier. Boston, New York, London, Reykjavik, Moscow, Tokyo and Vancouver had all been spared – for a while. All had likewise been forced to become fortress cities as millions tried to flock in from the south, desperate to escape the disease that then flourished in the slums they created outside city walls around the globe. Images of thousands of men, women and children screaming for help as their bodies decayed, their flesh literally falling from their bodies, haunted Marcus's dreams as they had done for years now.

Only Marcus's credentials as a biologist had saved him. His family had died in a refugee camp somewhere in Pennsylvania that was finally overrun by the disease two years after it had first emerged.

'Reed, one–seven–nine–five–Hotel, request entry to decon' unit, over?'

Reed was calling ahead for Marcus, letting him conserve his filter by not talking, although by now the sheer heat was enough for Marcus to be sucking in air in wheezing breaths as he struggled to the edge of the compound.

'Roger, Reed nine–five–Hotel, I have you visual. D'Souza, six–eight–seven–three–Bravo, confirm filter green?'

'Confirmed, Bravo,' Marcus gasped his reply. 'Suit breached, filter at two minutes remaining.'

'Roger, enter now.'

The compound was a large dome of rigid, pearlescent plastic that shone in the harsh sunlight as though somebody had dropped a gigantic upturned dish in the middle of the bayou.

An exterior door to the compound opened with a hydraulic hiss, leading to a tunnel of plastic and more safety doors. Marcus heard the whisper of air moving out of the tunnel: the dome maintained an air pressure higher than that of the outside environment, ensuring that if it was breached, air could only flow *out of* and not *into* the dome, thus preventing contamination by any airborne pathogen.

'Bravo and Hotel inside the entry port,' Reed said, and promptly vanished.

Hotel and Bravo were the dispassionate but universal radio call–signs for *Holosap* and *Biological*, a quick and simple way to distinguish between the living and the after–living, as Marcus's mother used to call them. The memory made him smile as his suit was doused in chemicals able to kill *Apophysomyces* dead on contact, the liquids spraying from multiple hoses set into the tunnel walls. Outside of the soil or a living host, like many infectious diseases *Apophysomyces* was easily destroyed by suitable chemicals. The nutria tucked under his arm squirmed violently as it was drenched but he managed to hold onto it.

Marcus completed his decontamination routine before dragging himself out of his suit and entering the compound itself, the door shutting behind him swiftly and trapping the animal inside.

The living space within was reasonably large and designed for permanent, self–sufficient habitation. Solar powered, it contained gardens for growing food, livestock pens, living quarters and a water–filtration unit all arranged around the laboratory at its heart. Everything was designed to sustain two people for a long duration stay.

Kerry hurried down through the compound toward him.

'Marcus!'

Marcus, his body throbbing with pain and his vision blurring, collapsed against a wall and slid to his knees, his breathing choked in his throat and his heart racing.

Kerry, her long dark hair flying in a tight pony–tail behind her, dropped to her knees in full flight and slid across the polished tiles of the compound to his side, shoving a syringe between her teeth as she collided with him and yanked his shirt sleeve up his arm.

Marcus saw the bite marks on his arm, saw the inflamed and swollen flesh either side of the puncture wounds as Kerry pulled the syringe from between her teeth and eased the needle beneath his skin right above the wound. Marcus winced as the needle went in and the bitterly cold antivenin flooded into his arm.

Kerry emptied the syringe into him, slid the needle out and pressed one finger over the puncture wound. She reached up and with one hand gently pushed Marcus's damp hair from out of his eyes.

'Hang in there,' she said. 'It'll take a while for this stuff to work its magic.'

Marcus nodded as he saw Dr Reed appear ghost–like nearby, his projection flickering as he watched.

'You'll live,' the biologist said prophetically. 'Couple of hours and you should start to clear up, then we can get back to work.'

Kerry glanced over her shoulder at him. 'You're all heart, you know that?'

'He's alive,' Reed pointed out, 'which is more than can be said for me. How are your samples coming along?'

Kerry stood up from Marcus's side, careful to cap the syringe. 'Multiple tests but nothing's coming up.'

'We've got some more samples for you,' Marcus said weakly and gestured behind him to the airlock. 'Water and a nutria.'

'You got a live one?' Kerry asked in amazement.

Without waiting for a reply, she dashed to the decon' unit door and peered inside to see the mammal sniffing its way around the confines of its new prison.

'It looks healthy, apart from that leg!'

'It's doing better than me,' Marcus whimpered. 'Took a bite for that damned thing.'

Kerry appeared not to hear him. 'Is the water from the same site?'

'Yes,' Dr Reed replied, 'within fifty to seventy metres.'

Kerry whirled from the door and began marching toward her laboratory. 'I'll get right on it.'

She breezed past Marcus, who glanced up at her. 'Any chance of some help here?'

'You'll live, so grow some balls okay?' she called over her shoulder as she vanished into a nearby corridor. 'But do shout if you think you're dying again.'

Marcus sighed and looked across at Dr Reed.

'Humans,' the *holosap* muttered with a shake of his head and a wry smile.

Marcus watched the *holosap* flicker out and vanish, probably to reappear somewhere else in the compound. He shivered, partly from the poison wracking his body and partly from the odd sensation of living in a compound that was, in some respects, haunted.

He didn't like to dwell on it much, but now, slumped against the wall after nearly dying from a fatal snakebite, he wondered whether he too could live on after his body had succumbed to whatever fate awaited it.

There were one hundred trillion neural connections in the human brain, and those synaptic connections could be recorded, copied and resurrected much like a computer hard drive. Decades ago, scientists had taken heated diamond knives and divided human brains into slices one forty–thousandth the width of a human hair. They had then sliced them down to a thousandth of even that slenderest width, so small that the connections between individual neurons became visible.

Mankind's ability to store data had grown so rapidly that long before the end of the first decade of the twenty first century, man was recording more data in two days than his entire history up to that point. Digital life loggers, as they had been known, had been recording their lives via cameras and thus creating recordings more accurate than could be created by the fallible human memory. Even by the early 21st Century, Functional Magnetic Resonance Imaging scans coupled with blood–flow monitors had enabled scientists to "read minds" by matching brain blood flow to images watched by test subjects on a monitor. Even when denied a link to what the subjects were seeing, the programs devised showed a pixellated image of the subject's view, a window into their minds. The truly digital brain, made possible by advances in quantum storage, had been just around the corner.

So, unfortunately, had The Falling.

Scientists had tried regenerating victim's bodies, growing new organs via healthy cadavers to combat the disease; livers, lungs, hearts generated via donor stem–cells. Brains were mostly water like many organs and could be recreated, but not with the essential essence of the original owner: the memories, the personality, the soul. But only through the digitizing and copying of a human brain at immense resolutions could their essence at the time of death be captured, and their souls saved for perpetuity.

Death, as they said back in the day at MIT, was just a mitochondrial chain–reaction, and even that could be stopped with sulphide, cyanide and carbon–monoxide, effectively arresting death in mid flow.

Marcus shivered as he wondered what his own cells were going through.

The generation of a *holosap* merely required the mapping of the owner's brain, much of which was made possible by earlier work in numerous fields. Microscopic probes lit up synapses in living neurons in real–time by attaching fluorescent markers onto synaptic proteins, allowing scientists to see how neurons changed with new data; "hard light", which used the properties of photons to manipulate their momentum to mimic molecules with mass and thus encode light data into a cohesive holographic image of the deceased human; modulators to produce the image in full colour with a thirty hertz refresh rate in three dimensional space; and quantum storage units to hold the data accumulated by a lifetime's experiences in place.

There was only one thing that Marcus felt the folks at Re–Volution hadn't got quite right.

Kerry reappeared with a blanket and knelt down beside him, covering his shoulders as she tugged at his arm.

'Come on,' she said, 'it's off to bed with you. I don't want you dying in the hall.'

'You're all heart,' Marcus mumbled in reply.

Marcus felt that there was a stark difference between Kerry and Dr Reed, between a human being and their *holosap* digital cousins. Kerry had come back to check on him.

Dr Reed's *holosap* had not.

9

London

Arianna felt numb as she sat in a holding cell at the police station.

A paper cup of water trembled in her grasp as she stared down at it, strangely fascinated by the ripples within. *You're in denial. Your brain is seeking ways to avoid thinking about what has happened.* Focus. Think.

She didn't want to think, didn't want to consider what had happened. There was no sense to it, no reason that she could think of to explain why she was now sitting here in a tiny cell after being arrested at the site of her adoptive father's gruesome death. Just a few hours before, everything had been absolutely fine.

Arianna could not even look at a picture of her son, Connor. Her belongings had been confiscated upon her arrival at the station. Often, in times of crisis she had looked longingly at her son's image and asked herself what she would have done for him were he here, drawing strength and moral integrity from his memory. Though she could not admit it to herself, often she found more strength in her son that in god Himself.

'Oh God, Connor.'

Five years old. Blond and with cute green eyes that had matched his father's, the only bit of that man she allowed into her conscience these days. Connor had been the light of her life and his absence ached through her heart with its every beat.

And now this.

Water spilled across her hands and she blinked. The paper cup was crushed in her clenched fist, liquid running in droplets across her shoes.

'*Volkov!*'

The sharp command jolted Arianna off the uncomfortably hard bench in the cell. She looked up at the digital speaker on the wall above the door. '*Stand facing away from the cell door. Place your hands behind your back and then stand within reach of the hatch!*'

Arianna obeyed the command as a small hatch opened in the cell door at waist height. Moments later rough hands cuffed her wrists and the cell door opened. She was led by a portly officer bearing the stripes of a sergeant to an interview room further down the corridor. Inside awaited Detectives Han Reeves and Myles Bourne.

Arianna was guided into a seat behind a table in the room and her cuffs were removed before the sergeant left the room.

'Tuesday, five forty–eight pm,' Reeves intoned for the benefit of the recorder set into the wall alongside the table. 'Detectives Bourne and Reeves, interview of suspect Arianna Volkov for murder and acts of terrorism against ...'

'*What?!*' Arianna gaped at Reeves, who didn't miss a beat as he continued.

'... the corporate headquarters of Re–Volution Ltd in the city.'

'You're accusing me of terrorism now?' she uttered in disbelief. 'I nearly died in that explosion!'

'Indeed,' Han agreed, 'but conveniently you did not. The explosion occurred just at the right time to provide you with cover on the opposite side of the street. You entered the building, then immediately exited again and crossed the street. You walked to the very spot, the *only* spot, that close to the blast that allowed you to survive. Two other pedestrians fifty yards further away from the building died from shrapnel and debris wounds.'

Arianna struggled to speak.

'For God's sake, how the hell are you coming up with all of this? I forgot my security pass and turned to go back for it. I work for that company, detective!'

'My point exactly,' Han agreed, 'lots of very wealthy and very dead clients. Lots of people who would need counselling, for a generous fee no doubt.'

'That's thin,' Arianna uttered. 'People die all the time without needing me to blow them up.'

'As a stand–alone conviction we agree,' Myles said, 'that the charge might be considered thin. But when we combine your miraculous survival with what happened to Alexei Volkov, and your previous convictions...'

Arianna stared at the younger man for a long beat before she spoke carefully. 'Connor's father wrecked my life.'

'Tell me,' Han said. 'Explain to me what happened.'

Arianna's fingernails bit into her palms. She focused on her fists, forced them to relax.

'I got pregnant,' she said, almost whispering, as though the words would not hurt so much if she could barely hear them. 'When he, the father, found out he told me he wanted to terminate the baby.'

'And you disagreed,' Han said.

'There are only a few million people left alive on this Earth, detective,' Arianna shot back, 'the idea of ruining a life that hadn't even begun yet didn't appeal to me.'

'Maybe your partner felt becoming a father would ruin his life?' Myles suggested.

Arianna glared at Myles but said nothing.

'So then you took his life from him,' Han replied as he looked down at a charge sheet before him on the table. 'You hit him across the head three times with an iron bar, the last blow struck when he was already unconscious. He was in hospital for two months in a coma before he died. No upload.'

'He threatened my child,' Arianna snapped, 'told me that if I didn't terminate the pregnancy he'd do it for me.'

'So you said in court,' Myles replied. 'No witnesses though, and no testimony from your former partner's friends, colleagues or family suggesting any hint of violence toward you.'

'They wouldn't have,' Arianna said. 'They all saw me as the rich girl with the powerful father. They hated me.'

'How come you ended up with this guy then?' Han challenged her.

'I didn't,' Arianna said. 'It was a mistake. He was from the rat–runs, someone I'd known since growing up in the boarding houses. We'd kept in touch. He was into bootlegging, you know? Alcohol. We sampled some of his stock. Things got out of hand.'

'Your father must have been appalled.'

Arianna cringed. 'He understood well enough.'

'And your son?' Myles asked.

Arianna glared at the young detective. 'He died, aged five, from The Falling,' she spat, some of the old fury rising in her blood. 'He couldn't be uploaded because he was too young to have an implant fitted.' Arianna fought back tears. 'Re–Volution isn't interested in saving children, they don't possess enough personal wealth to make it *financially viable*.'

Han Reeves leaned forward on the table, his voice a little softer now. 'You see where we're coming from here, right Arianna? You're a woman who has been in court for murdering a man; you had both motive, means and access to Alexei Volkov at the time of his murder and you were both the last person to see Alexei alive and the last person to leave the Re–Volution building before the blast that killed dozens of its employees.'

'To what end?' Arianna uttered. 'I kill Alexei and then try to destroy the very place that can protect my future? What the hell sense does that make?'

'We're just trying to establish the facts, Miss Volkov, and...'

'You're trying to establish a case,' Arianna cut him off. 'You're not looking at facts, you're making up connections and hoping that they'll stick.'

Han smiled without warmth. 'A person will go a long way to protect their immortality.'

Arianna maintained a calm expression as she replied.

'Including not making things worse than they already were. I have no intention of using my upload.'

'So you say,' Myles agreed. 'But what people say and what they actually do often bear little resemblance to each other.'

Arianna almost laughed at the absurdity of it all. 'If I was going to kill Alexei, why would I go to the trouble of burning him to death? Do you think he just lay down and let it happen?'

'You tell us,' Han suggested.

Arianna banged a fist down on the table. 'So you guys can call it case-closed and go on your merry way? Like hell. I want my lawyer. And what's happened to Alexei Volkov? Has he been uploaded yet?'

'We're waiting on confirmation from Re–Volution,' Myles said. 'They've been informed of the situation.'

'Misinformed you mean,' Arianna said.

'How often do you attend your church, Arianna?' Han asked.

'What's that got to do with anything?'

'I think that you know.'

Arianna stared at the detective for a long beat. 'My church does not condone terrorism.'

'Does any?' Han asked rhetorically. 'But we both know that many attacks have been made against the Re–Volution building by religiously motivated groups of all kinds, including the Hope Reunion Church and....'

'I minister at my church because there's not much else to have faith in, detective,' Arianna replied, hearing the bitterness still in her own voice, 'least of all the law. Since the idea of an afterlife was erased by Re–Volution there aren't many places of worship left. It's not surprising the radicals use them to plan their attacks.'

Han Reeves smiled tightly but did not reply.

Arianna could not blame the detective's reasoning. Since the emergence of the first *holosap* the faiths of countless cultures around the world had begun to collapse like a deck of cards. She figured that it was probably fair to admit that this was not entirely the fault of Re–Volution: organised religion had been crumbling for centuries beforehand. But now the last nail in the figurative coffin had been hammered firmly in place by the realisation that death was no longer the final event in a life. That a new species of man had emerged for whom immortality was a realistic proposition, for whom sickness and frailty were a thing of the past, for whom the future was eternally bright. They even had a new, Latin name for them:

Homo immortalis.

The name sent a shudder down her spine, coined as it was by the newly uploaded billionaires and former politicians, their heavily greased palms now glowing in holographic glory as they fought for the right to continue expanding their bloated empires from beyond the grave. Laws had been passed in parliament to prevent them from ever holding power or chairing the corporations they had built during their lifetimes, but everybody knew that the law was a charade. Lobbying was part and parcel of politics, and with the growing *holosap* community consisting entirely of an elite able to afford the tremendous cost of being uploaded, there was no shortage of funding for their demands.

Soon, the Court of Human Rights was forging laws preventing the *holosap's* power source from ever being switched off. Then came the laws allowing *holosaps* oversight of the sprawling corporations they had left behind, and laws allowing them the right to walk amongst the living. It was inevitable that eventually they would achieve the status of a new species, Homo immortalis, and that they would then be able to sit in Parliament, vote once again, and begin the business of what Arianna believed would be a new class war.

Those left behind, those for whom faith in life after death and a God was the foundation of their existence suddenly found themselves staring gods in the face and knowing not what to do about it. Violence directed at the *holosaps* as an abomination only strengthened the case for Homo immortalis's ascent to power, the uprising playing directly into their hands as the most aggressive and dangerous of their opponents were arrested and jailed one after the other. Now, the *holosaps* had conquered in all but name and the two thousand year rule of the church was but a faint memory lingering in the minds of the faithful few who remained.

'Strange,' Han Reeves said, 'how many religiously motivated terrorist attacks there are, and how few people are still able to call them as such.'

'They use religion as an excuse.'

'They use it as a reason,' Han snapped back, 'and they always have. It is possible, Ms Volkov, that you are innocent of any crime. But right now, you are our number one suspect and every piece of evidence we have points to you as the guilty party.'

Arianna managed to keep her mouth shut. Right now she knew that the detective was trying to get her riled up and it was working. Say nothing until the lawyer gets here. Just hold them at bay until then.

A knock sounded at the door. It opened and a desk sergeant poked his head into the room.

'Alexei Volkov is here, detectives.'

* * *

10

The *holosap* projection platform was located in what Arianna assumed doubled as both an observation room and a place where suspects could be lined up for identification by their beleaguered victims. A one–way mirror looked out into a room where a height chart was crudely tacked to the wall.

Standing over the platform was Alexei Volkov.

Arianna stared at him from behind the mirror in the observation room as she stood between Han Reeves and Myles Bourne, her wrists back in the steel cuffs as two police detectives from the team entered the room opposite. Alexei watched them as they walked in and spoke to him.

'Our apologies, sir,' intoned one of the policemen, 'for having you brought here so soon after your unfortunate experience.'

Alexei nodded, his features blanched of colour and his expression trapped somewhere between outrage and bemusement. Arianna caught glimpses of him trying to adjust to his new and unfamiliar body and surroundings as he fielded the detective's questions.

'Sir, you are aware that you are now deceased, correct?'

Alexei nodded vacantly as he stared over the police officer's heads at the mirror opposite, no doubt fascinated by his own reflection. Arianna saw him reach up and touch his face, but of course he felt nothing, not yet. His fingers blended in with his cheek and he yanked them away quickly.

'Can you speak, sir, for the benefit of the recorders?'

'Yes,' Alexei replied, and then seemed surprised by the sound of his own voice and looked down at the projection platform beneath him. 'Yes, I am aware that I have died.'

Arianna knew that the voice was not generated by Alexei's *holosap* but by speakers built into the projection platform. Speech was made by the *holosap* within the quantum storage unit where their digital selves truly resided, down in the Re–Volution building's basement servers. Digital distortion ensured that the timbre of the voice matched that of the deceased's natural body and the fact that all of their projection data was emitted at the speed of light meant that there was no detectable lapse between physical movement and the emitted speech.

'Good,' replied the detective. 'Can you tell me what happened to you?'

'I was at home,' Alexei said. 'I went for a lie down. It's my age you see. I find that I need a nap in the afternoons. Am I really dead?'

Han Reeves glanced down at Arianna, who spoke on reflex as she watched Alexei.

'His brain hasn't yet connected all of its neural pathways in their new form. It'll take a little while but he'll soon feel his body again, sense his surroundings.'

'You mean he can't feel anything?' Myles asked.

'He can see and hear,' Arianna replied. 'The essential, deepest parts of the brain reconnect first upon upload because they're so primal. Other functions come later, like emotional connections, fine coordination and motor skills.'

'But he can't touch anything, right?' Han murmured.

'Not really,' Arianna confirmed. 'But within a few days the brain fills in the gaps, just like it does in a dream. Although he'll never touch anything again in a real sense, if he touches his face tomorrow his brain will let him *think* that he can feel it.'

Myles Bourne shook his head in apparent disgust as Alexei went on.

'... I don't remember much. I thought that there was somebody in my home, and then I was attacked from behind.'

'Did you see any faces?' asked one of the detectives. 'Any identifying marks?'

'Nothing,' Alexei replied. 'They dragged me into the bedroom and tied me down, then injected me with a paralysing agent. Then one of them ignited some kind of device beneath the bed. I could smell the burning, like chemicals of some kind. They ran, and I...' Alexei frowned, and then his eyes filled with horror. 'I burned, alive,' he whispered.

'His memory is returning in full,' Arianna realised.

The other detective leaned forward. 'Who was the last person to see you alive, Alexei?'

Alexei's brow furrowed as he thought.

'Arianna, my daughter,' he said finally. 'We spoke briefly via holo–link.'

'Can you confirm whether Miss Volkov had access to your home after the meeting?'

Alexei glared down at the detective. 'No, why?' Then his eyes flared wide. 'Do you have Arianna in custody?'

'Sir,' the detective said, 'right now we are pursuing all possible avenues of investigation and...'

'My attackers were all men,' Alexei growled. 'Not one of them was less than six feet tall!'

'That may be so,' the detective agreed, 'but they gained access to your home without forcing entry. Somebody had to let them in.'

'And you think that person was Arianna?' Alexei uttered. 'Let me tell you, young man, that even if in some bizarre alternate universe Arianna had decided to have me murdered she would not have been able to do so in my own home.'

'Why not, sir?'

'Because Arianna does not have a pass code to my security system.'

'Your own daughter does not have the code to your home?'

'Arianna is somewhat independent, detective. She prefers to live her own life and left home young for college and university. We always arranged to meet in advance.'

'Could she have obtained a code?' the detective questioned. 'Perhaps by observation?'

'It is doubtful,' Alexei said. 'I changed the code regularly, and only ever reset it *after* people had left the building.'

The detective squinted thoughtfully. 'You take many precautions, sir. Is it normal for you to be so…'

'Paranoid?' Alexei finished the sentence for the officer.

'For want of a better word.'

'I am a billionaire,' Alexei said without pride, as though his wealth were a burden, 'and there are many people who would wish to see me dead just for my success. Our world is suffering, most people are poor and desperate. To see people like myself live in luxury, safe in the knowledge that when we die we will in fact live again, is reason enough for desperate people to do desperate things, don't you think?'

'Have you been threatened before?' the detective asked.

'Every day of my life,' Alexei said, 'every single day. But if you're about to ask me whether I knew my attacker, or whether I could identify them in a line–up here, then I am sorry detective. As much as I would like to do so, I saw no faces and heard no voices. The only thing that I can say with absolute certainty is that Miss Volkov cannot have been directly responsible for my death as none of my attackers were female. In fact, as soon as this interview is complete I would like to meet her once again at her office or home. I am overwhelmed by the sense that I am made of a feeble column of air and if I move too quickly I will blow away with the wind.'

Han Reeves looked down at Arianna, who spoke softly.

'A common psychological reaction to being uploaded,' she explained. 'The *holosap* cannot understand how they can be alive and yet have no physical substance. Some become terrified of moving or speaking in case they fall apart. The doctors usually call it *vertigo* – like the fear of falling.'

Reeves nodded but didn't reply.

Alexei Volkov abruptly vanished as the connection was terminated and the detectives left the room and joined Reeves and Arianna in the observation room.

'I'm guessing that's sufficient evidence to get you off my damned back?' she inquired of Reeves.

'Not nearly,' Han shot back as he removed her cuffs. 'But right now without evidence we cannot hold you for more than twenty–four hours. If the terrorist attack produces a second lead I'll be advised to cut you loose.'

'You must be devastated.'

'I'm a patient man,' Han replied as he looked at her. 'I don't give in easily.'

'Good,' Arianna said, 'then get out of here and start looking for whoever blew that building up and murdered my father, because it sure as hell wasn't me! I suggest you let me go right now before I call my lawyer and start proceedings against you and this department for harassment and slander.'

Han Reeves held her gaze for several moments and then the lop–sided grin reappeared.

'As you wish,' he replied as he stepped back and gestured to the door with a grand sweep of his arm.

Arianna kept her chin held high as she walked from the room and turned left for the exit. Moments later, Han's voice called after her.

'Ma'am?'

Arianna rolled her eyes as she looked over her shoulder. 'Yes?'

Han leaned against the door frame with his hands in his pockets, smiled and gestured with a nod of his head toward the opposite end of the corridor. 'The exit's that way.'

Arianna managed a snort of irritation as she whirled on the spot and marched past him, ignoring the smug grin plastered across his face.

* * *

11

The city could seem such an alien place sometimes, filled with countless souls all on their crowded journeys and yet entirely alone.

Arianna watched through a window of the elevated train as it rattled between the jumbled masses of glossy black towers that reflected a galaxy of city lights shimmering through mists drifting like ghosts through the night. Crouched between the soaring blocks were ancient buildings preserved by historians and charities determined that their crumbling remains stand defiant against the equally beleaguered edifices of modern man. Their meagre, blocky hulks lay in deep shadow with no lights to warm their depths.

The E–train was empty but for a few late night commuters. The mist caused rivulets of rain to spill across the window, further blurring the cityscape.

Arianna looked away from the darkness outside and remained with her thoughts until the E–train eased into her stop and she disembarked. Cold, damp night air tainted by the smell of decay that filled the city, the distant hiss of vehicles and crowds drifting through the darkness.

Arianna hurried down off the platforms and onto streets slick with moisture. She walked alone, her heels clicking on the sidewalks as she fingered a personal defence device in her pocket and glanced over her shoulder every few seconds as the train hummed away overhead.

Nobody appeared from the shadows or watched her from windows. Nobody cared.

Arianna reached the church, opened the heavy side door and closed it behind her, triple–latching it before letting out a breath that felt as though it had been trapped in her lungs for an hour. *Jeez, what a day.* She walked through the church, illuminated only by a pair of softly glowing lamps near the altar, and through into her living quarters. She hit the lights, revelling in their warm glow as she headed for a shower.

She took her time, and was feeling almost human again when she noticed the transmission light blinking for attention from across the living room as she walked in while drying her hair with a towel. She strode across and hit a button on a small panel. A digitized voice purred back at her.

'*You have one transmission request: press one to accept, two to delete, three to…*'

Arianna cut the voice off with a jab of one finger into a keypad. A small *ping* let her know that her acceptance had been sent. Moments later the transmission platform in her apartment hummed and glowed into life. Alexei Volkov appeared before her, shimmering in the softly lit apartment as though he were somehow radioactive.

'What on earth happened to you today *rebyohnuk*?' he asked, his face wrought with concern. 'You look tired.'

'Everything, pretty much,' she replied, shaking the towel through her long brown hair. 'I was blown up, taken to the scene of your murder and then arrested all in one afternoon.'

'The Re–Volution building,' Alexei said. 'I heard about it almost as soon as I was uploaded. Apparently they had to use an off site storage facility to run my upload process. It took a little longer than usual. I'm lucky to be here: another few seconds and I wouldn't have made it.'

'Are you okay?' Arianna asked. 'No confusion, memory lapses, neurological issues, anything like that?'

'I'm *fine*,' Alexei insisted, opening his hands palm outward. 'They got all of me, I think. It's you I'm worried about.'

Arianna tossed her towel aside and brushed her hair back.

'You've just been brutally murdered,' she said, 'I survived and it's *me* you're worried about?'

Alexei smiled and shrugged. 'It's a new world and it feels strange, but that doesn't mean I forget who my family are.'

Arianna sighed. 'Thanks, Alexei, for coming here after everything that's happened to you. It's been a hell of a day.'

'For us both. See, *holosaps* and people can be friends after all. Who knew?'

It had been a long time since humanity had made the breakthrough, the first quantitative steps to altering the nature of what it meant to be *alive*. The earliest researchers, working on a new and radical theory of how the human brain operated, had intended to develop a method for repairing even the most horrendous brain injuries: their goal was to allow the paralysed to walk again, to allow the blind to see, the deaf to hear. The comatose to regain conscience.

Noble aims.

Arianna did not understand how they did it. Holonomic Brain Theory, as it had become known in its infancy, had bored her witless at school and like most science subjects seemed forever beyond the realm of her mental capacity, like a distant star simply too far away to ever see or examine. All that she had been able to retain was that for some reason, brains worked like a hologram, a three dimensional one at that, where the power of the neurons within was amplified massively by their ability to relay information in three dimensions. By contrast, ordinary computers worked via linear circuits that could not possibly hope to compete with the human brain, despite that brain being a lump of tissue requiring no more power than a light bulb.

This remarkable discovery had then been swiftly allied to two more extraordinary scientific breakthroughs made by people with brains the size of continents who no doubt viewed people like Arianna in the same way that she viewed single–celled organisms swimming in murky pools.

The first truly operable quantum computers made it beyond the secretive halls of the military and intelligence communities and into hospitals and public research companies. Essentially able to make calculations in multiple universes, whatever the hell that meant, a single one of the things could do more calculations in a second than every standard computer on the planet at that time. In other words, *super computers* took on a whole new meaning.

Somewhere, somebody far smarter than she had realised that combining the computers with modern brain–scanning techniques could, in theory, recreate parts of a brain in such detail that they could be modelled as three dimensional holograms that would integrate with an existing brain to replace damaged areas. Power for the holographic sections would come from the human body's own electrical output as the holographic brain sections did not need to be visible, the light only requiring weak output to perform its functions. In essence, a three dimensional holographic brain acted exactly like a three dimensional physical brain, a sort of ethereal replacement.

The success of the first small transplants opened the floodgates: laws were passed allowing the rapid spread of the technology into operating theatres across the country. Further laws allowed "brain bypass" operations in the event of major trauma from accidents or novel disease, the tactile nature of holographic light allowing the owner's newly created brains to seamlessly re–connect severed spinal cords. The still–working parts of the physical brain accepted the holographic replacements as though they were entirely natural, presumably because they operated in the exact same way. They carried information, like trillions of optical fibres. Paralysis victims learned to walk again. The blind, to see. The deaf, to hear.

It was, Arianna guessed, only a matter of time before somebody attempted the impossible and recreated a human being in entirely holographic form. Too curious to think about the dangers, too excited to consider the possible consequences. She herself had read of the early fears of pioneers in the field, that without natural selection there would be no way for the *holosaps* to evolve defences against flaws in the system. What if sickness could be digital as well as biological? What about identity theft? Could the human brain handle immortality without collapsing into psychosis or degeneration?

As ever the pioneers forged ahead regardless when The Falling emerged, a great sacrifice by the living on behalf of the partly dead.

'What did the police want with you?' Alexei asked.

Arianna blinked herself back into the present. 'They arrested me for your murder and for trying to blow up the Re–Volution building.'

'Pah! Damned fools, all of them.' He looked at her. 'You didn't, did you?'

Arianna stared at him. 'Seriously?'

'No. I know how you feel about *holosaps*.'

'I'm sorry you got uploaded,' Arianna said. 'I know it wasn't what you wanted.'

'It was the last thing I wanted,' Alexei sighed. 'But I was murdered, Re–Volution got the alert signal from my chip and rushed to the scene with the emergency services. They're not going to pass up the chance that I saw my killer and abandon any hope of a conviction. Sometimes it's helpful to be uploaded I suppose.'

'They wouldn't pass up the chance of your payment for upload either,' Arianna snorted as she finished drying her hair.

'At least I had the option,' Alexei shrugged.

Arianna glanced across the room before she could stop herself. A small holographic image of her son, Connor, hovered over the centre of her equally small dining table. Arianna felt tiny pricks of pain in the corners of her eyes. 'He still smiles, in my mind.'

'I'm sure he still smiles, wherever he is.'

Like most all folk, a place in the *holosap* colony was a dream that would remain forever beyond their reach. Most people could no longer afford even to be buried, their remains cast instead into mass crematorium furnaces and returned to the ashes and dust from whence they had come. That Connor had died a year before he could have had a chip fitted was a cruel blow that clashed with Arianna's deeply held beliefs. In a world where so few people had faith, how could God have forsaken her? How could Gods forsake any of His faithful? It would have been so easy to protect Connor. She could have gone to Alexei, tried to somehow save Connor's *essence* and perhaps even try to have him secretly uploaded, just in case. But she had not done so, because she believed.

Then again, no decent mother plans to lose their child.

In the end Connor had died peacefully in his sleep, Arianna wearing a hazardous materials suit and holding him in her arms while anaesthetics were pumped into Connor's body to ease his suffering. His heart gave out a few hours later.

'Are you all right my dear?'

Arianna realised that she was holding her hands clenched before her, her gaze passing straight through the holographic image of Connor and beyond into some interminable place wherein her grief resided, festering and sick.

'No,' she admitted.

Alexei watched her for a long moment before he spoke, and she could tell that he was choosing his words with care.

'My offer still stands, Arianna,' he said. 'I know that you are opposed to it but it is the least that I can do.'

Arianna sighed and turned to look at Alexei once more.

'I don't want to live for eternity,' she said finally. 'I know that you mean well papa, but I have to believe that he's out there somewhere waiting for me. I can't live a hundred lives wondering if my little boy needs me.'

Arianna realised that she sounded almost pleading.

'I know,' Alexei replied. 'I feel the same about my parents, and my brothers. I can see where Gregory Detling is coming from now.'

His gentle old smile calmed her now just as it had always done.

'Give the ticket to somebody who wants it,' she said finally, 'a child, somebody who won't survive without it.'

Alexei nodded, but concern creased his features as he watched her.

'Alexei, I'll be fine,' she insisted, snapping herself out of her torpor. 'It's what I want.'

'I know,' Alexei repeated. 'That's not what bothers me, Arianna.'

'What, then?'

'Just take extra care my dear, after all that's happened. Promise me.'

Arianna chuckled. 'I promise, okay? What's gotten into you? I'm a big girl now, I can take care of myself.'

'And I was a big man who could hold his own, too,' Alexei replied. 'What bothers me is that the people who attacked me knew enough to get into my house unopposed by the security systems. They must have studied me, my movements, my family.'

Arianna slowed as she looked at Alexei.

'You don't know that,' she said. 'It could have been an opportunistic attack.'

'I lied to the police,' Alexei said. 'I did hear their voices. They asked me questions, Arianna, like they were looking for something.'

'Looking for what?'

Alexei shook his head. 'I don't know. Please, just talk to the police. If my killers think that you might eventually identify them, they may try to ensure your silence.'

Arianna swallowed thickly. 'Do you really think they'd bother with me?'

'They were professionals, Arianna,' he said. 'And what's worse is the fact that I still have no idea why they killed me. You could be in great danger.'

* * *

12

Parliament, Westminster

'The time is now.'

The Prime Minister's voice carried solemnly across the gathered ministers crowding the chamber, spoken not with force but with a conviction that brooked no argument.

Tarquin St John stood upon a raised podium that overlooked the opposition, his gaze boring into every man's eyes. He was dressed in an expensive, dark suit that contrasted sharply with his shock of white hair. Shafts of intermittent sunlight shimmered down through the high chamber windows to glow like a halo around him.

'By what measure do we call ourselves human? Is it that we feel, or touch, or see or any one of our many senses? No? Then is it because we are self aware, sentient, conscious beings controlling our own destiny? Not that? Perhaps it is our empathy, or our spirit, or some ephemeral essence of which we are aware and yet unable to touch with our hands or our minds? I ask you, all of you, to tell me which of those many possible things separate us from our holographic brethren who even now stand among us as citizens of this once great, and still great, nation?'

The house remained silent, watching the Prime Minister with rapt expressions.

'Is it, then, my fellow human beings, that there is nothing that makes us different from the *holo sapiens* with whom we now share this world? But for our spite, our fear and our prejudice against those who are *different*?' St John's eyes swept the chamber as though encouraging any man to challenge him, and then gestured up to the highest tiers of the chamber. There, sitting on holographic seats, were ranks of perhaps thirty *holosaps*. 'Could you explain to our honourable friends here in the chamber why they are denied access to their companies, their fortunes and their futures?'

Murmurs drifted across the seated politicians and dignitaries like an errant ill wind as St John continued, his big, broad hands animated as he spoke as though he were silently scything down any opposition.

'Have we not been here before, so many times? Must I list the countless reasons mankind has subjugated, imprisoned, outcast and killed millions for nothing more than their appearance or disease, religion, race and colour. Is it right, in this day and age, that fully sentient, conscious and active human beings should be prevented from having their fair say in the matters of the world simply because they have undergone a transformation that was once considered the end of all things: death? There is no longer any such thing as death, only a new evolution of mankind's journey from primeval ape to sentient custodian of our world.

'Is what we have achieved so unusual? There are those few who scorn the *holosaps* as abominations, insults to the gods of times past. For millennia, in the face of the unknown we grovelled on our knees before gods in temples across the world, and what did it achieve compared to our ability to conquer that same unknown while standing on our feet?' He let the audience digest his words, let them wait for more. They waited. 'We have adapted, and we have overcome. One more step, one more leap, one more victory in a human story that has endured war, famine, disease, natural disasters and our own hellish destruction of the climate and environment and yet still prevailed. I motion this bill not because I believe that it is of benefit to our nation but because I believe that it is our future, that our ascent to immortality is not just another technological marvel but is now an essential component of our survival as a species upon our planet.'

St John's fist had been clenched before him as he spoke, and he gently let it unfold as he went on.

'It is said by our brightest researchers that no species of creature known to science has survived more than two million years before becoming extinct. Mankind has existed in much the same form for approximately that length of time. Our evolution has ceased as we have learned to manipulate our environment to suit our needs. Now, we are suffering the results of our greed and arrogance; fossil fuels are all but depleted, nations have fallen, grain is in short supply and our climate has changed beyond all recognition. Yet even all of these challenges could have been overcome were it not for The Falling, a crisis that even our best and brightest have failed to defeat. This, gentlemen, is where we should end. This moment should be the *final* chapter in our human story.'

St John swept the chamber once again with his icy gaze, and saw that every pair of eyes was upon him, that no man spoke, that all awaited his words.

'I truly believe that this is the *beginning*.'

Dozens of his party members bolted to their feet as a tsunami of rapturous applause thundered through the chamber and broke against the immovable might of Tarquin St John. He waited for their approval to die down before he spoke.

'It is rare that a citizen speaks to this chamber, but I would like to introduce you to Kieran Beck, the Chief Executive Officer of Re–Volution and the architect of our salvation.'

The ministers applauded loudly as Kieran Beck took the podium. Shorter than the Prime Minister by several inches, and with black hair swept across his forehead with such gelled precision as to appear painted–on, he smiled shyly at the men gathered before him.

'Gentlemen, I appreciate the chance to speak with you directly,' Beck said. 'I shall be brief. Humanity is facing extinction. In the absence of any cure for The Falling, and with resources almost completely exhausted, it would be as remiss of us all not to plan for the worst than it would be to hope for the best.'

Beck glanced at Tarquin St John briefly before continuing.

'The Prime Minister knows well how hard my staff and I have worked to provide a workable, long term solution to humanity's vulnerability to The Falling. It is not perfect, but then this is not a perfect world. If it were, The Falling would not have occurred. We cannot run any longer. We cannot hide any longer. Either we fall together as human beings or we stand together as holo sapiens: there can be no middle ground. My company offers you all an upload, regardless of your financial or personal status, in order to sustain the political power and structure of this country in the event that it is overrun by the disease which haunts us all.'

A gasp fluttered across the gathered ministers of all parties as Kieran Beck offered them a curt nod.

'Our survival is more important than revenue,' he said with a final flourish and a smile. 'Without good governance, the populace would be in chaos. I hope that my offer goes some way in helping you all to come to terms with the difficult decisions that will be made over the coming days.'

Kieran Beck stepped down off the podium, as the Prime Minister retook his position.

'I request, with all due respect,' St John urged, 'that the chamber pass the Bill of Rights that will finalise *holosap* independence in both civil and human rights, allowing them to once again become fully integrated members of society. I do this not for personal preference or gain, but because I believe that our ascent to a higher level of being was heralded by the appearance of the first *holosap*, and that we should embrace this new existence with open arms because to not do so is to consign the human race to extinction. They do not need to eat. They do not grow old. They do not start wars. They do not end lives. They do not deplete the world's resources and, most importantly of all, they do not suffer *disease*. The *holosaps* of this world are the greatest and most ecologically sound members of our society and dare I say it, the most *humane*!'

Another tumult of applause raced around the chamber as Tarquin St John raised his fist into the air once more and his voice thundered across the house.

'The age of *Homo sapiens* has ended! Let the age of *Homo immortalis* begin!'

The applause crashed through the house as St John took his seat once more among his fellow politicians. The Speaker of the House stood and addressed the audience in a voice that sounded thin after St John's grand oratory.

'We have fought long and hard for the recognition that our enlightened brothers deserve, the same human rights they and their forefathers fought hard to preserve during their tenures upon our planet. They deserve acceptance as a new species of human being, as *Homo immortalis*. Now, I ask of you on their behalf to pass the laws necessary to provide *holosaps* with a lasting dignity – independence of power and a say in the politics and the economies of today. Ladies and gentlemen of the house, I take it that there are no dissenters?'

St John swept the chamber with his gaze as though daring a man to speak out against him. His granite hewn features slipped a little when, from the gathered politicians, a single hand rose up.

'Minister Hart?'

A small man stood up, appearing uncomfortable under the gaze of several hundred pairs of eyes. A podgy hand dabbed at a sweaty forehead with a handkerchief, the densely gathered humanity creating a humid atmosphere within the chamber.

'Ladies and gentlemen,' Hart said in a voice so soft that it would not have been audible but for the amplifiers that were switched on suddenly to convey his words. 'I appreciate the vigour in the Prime Minister's speech, and I appreciate also how it has been used skilfully to manipulate the house into openly voting for the bill for *holosap* rights to pass. However I believe this to be a mistake.'

Another breeze of mutterings drifted through the air, this time cold and dismissive as though a hundred of Hart's peers were disapproving and rolling their eyes at him. The minister took a breath and continued.

'We already know well the suffering endured by mankind from The Falling,' he began. 'The figures speak for themselves. More than six billion people dead with no cure in sight. The sickness pervades all mammalian species, leading to famine and disease stalking entire regions hand in hand. Were it not for our innovative fishing techniques our own island would have fallen long ago too. We remain one of the last bastions of humankind, facing insurmountable odds. I put it to you that we have been in this position many times in the past and have prevailed. It seems to me that to grant control of parliament and industry entirely to the *holosaps* is to figuratively sign the death warrant for millions of citizen's lives, simply so the fortunate and wealthy few may enjoy an immortality free from the rigours of this disease. The action has little to do with compassion and much to do with selfishness and cowardice.'

Tarquin St John bolted out of his seat as a rush of exclamations flooded the chamber, hundreds of eyes swivelling to stare in disbelief at the diminutive Hart. St John pointed his arm and finger at Hart as though he were aiming a shotgun.

'You dare to insult me in the chamber sir?!' His voice was loud and deep enough to make it seem as though it were vibrating through the very walls. 'It is members of the *holosap* community who are out there in the world, right now, walking amongst the dead and the dying as they search for a cure for this disease! It is they who seek to protect humans, to protect *us*, and you call them cowards?!'

Hart cleared his throat.

'With all due respect Prime Minister, as you recently said yourself, *holosaps* cannot be infected with disease. There are also humans working alongside them, people who are facing genuine danger without the benefit of an upload to protect them, whom you seem not to have mentioned.'

St John trembled with indignation, his arm still pointed across the chamber at Hart.

'Do not dare to provoke outrage to defend your arguments, Hart. We have all spent years agonizing over how best to avoid this moment, ever since the first *holosap* was switched on. We know it's unjust, we know it's unfortunate and we all know that if there was any other way we would take it. But right now, here and now, we are fighting a rear guard action against a sickness that will consume us all if we do not act decisively!'

'I agree,' Minister Hart nodded. 'But running away and hiding does not find a cure for The Falling, and nor does handing the reins of power to *holosaps*. They have no need of political influence or the need to manage their corporations and empires: that was why laws were passed prohibiting them from doing so, to prevent a class war between the living and…, the *after*–living. They are effectively as immortal as their name suggests and have nothing to fear from disease or famine.' Minister Hart turned to address the chamber at large. 'What message do you think such an act will send to the nine million people living within our city walls? That we're handing power to several thousand people who are already dead? Do any of you really believe, given the tenacious history of our species, that those nine million people will simply give up their right to self-determination, to democracy, without a fight?'

The house remained silent and all eyes switched back to Tarquin St John. The big man faltered for a moment. It was Kieran Beck, seated behind him, who spoke.

'What do you propose instead, minister?'

Hart turned to the house speaker.

'That we do indeed put the matter to a vote, but not here. We put it to a referendum, to the people.'

'Pah!' St John snapped. 'They'll never back the proposal!'

Hart smiled. 'But isn't it the people that you purport to protect with your proposal?'

'It's not a matter of the proposal,' St John rallied. 'It's the people themselves. They're inclined to conspiracy theories and all manner of fantasies, projecting their politicians as uncaring of the human condition. History shows us that the people have never really trusted their leaders. They would reject the proposal on principle, not on any evidence that it is the best step for mankind to take at this juncture.'

Hart smiled.

'That, I'm afraid, is democracy. You do support democracy, don't you Prime Minister?'

St John's features screwed up in distaste.

'What kind of question is that?' he uttered. 'We're standing here debating this, aren't we?'

'Indeed we are,' Hart agreed. 'But what of the nine million citizens who have no means of uploading? The population is outgrowing our resources. We must expand and yet we cannot because beyond the city walls lies assured and painful death. The people have no place to go, and by creating this bill you're telling them that they're no longer the main concern for politics. You're telling them that they're already doomed and that you're putting *holosap* issues before theirs. Every word of your valiant speech, sir, is either incorrect or an outright lie.'

St John almost combusted on the spot as he turned to the Speaker of the House.

'This is not a house of insults and accusations!' he raged.

'Minister Hart has neither insulted nor accused,' the speaker said, 'at least in no terms more unreasonable than have you in your career, Prime Minister.'

St John fumed silently for a moment as Hart inclined his head to the speaker and went on.

'This bill is not about defending the rights of the *holosaps*, it is about taking away the rights of the human population from which they originated. It is no coincidence that the company which owns the rights to the technology, *Re–Volution*, also backs the honourable gentlemen's political campaigns. Nor is it a coincidence that in the event of The Falling breaching our city walls many of you, gentlemen, have in place the means to take your own lives and those of your families and be uploaded as *holosaps*.'

A rush of indignation staled the air, roars and waved fists flying like banners as Minister Hart stood his ground amid the tumult.

'You can shout all you want,' Hart spoke loudly enough for the amplifiers to carry his words above the protests, 'but the truth is the truth. Is there any man here who has not assured his family's safety in the event of humanity's final collapse? If the survival of mankind is your true motivation, then should it not be clear that all surviving humans are gifted the opportunity to upload and save themselves?' Hart looked around him and was rewarded with silence. 'Of course not, because that would mean Re–Volution missing out on immense revenue and becoming a charitable institution, something that it would not want when other *holosaps* are able to retake the reins of their huge fortunes. Greed is what is condemning our fellow citizens, and I see nothing humane in that.'

'Don't lecture us on issues of humanity, Hart,' he growled. 'Just because you don't want to upload should not mean that none of the rest of us should not have the opportunity.'

'Actually, I do have a ticket,' Hart replied, and then his face went cold. 'I'd just rather use it when I actually died and not as an excuse to abandon those who remain alive.'

'Nobody has done any such thing!' St John raged.

'No,' Hart agreed, 'not yet.' He looked around him at his fellow ministers. 'Gentlemen, if democracy dies here in this chamber today then so does humanity. The Prime Minister's proposal is, in my opinion, nothing more than the corporate desire of Re–Volution Limited and an act of eugenic genocide, the favouring of one species over another without consulting the people whom we claim to represent. It is their lives at risk, not ours: let them have the final say.'

Minister Hart retook his seat as St John made his final address to the chamber.

'Humanity is indeed at risk, and our survival now dependent on the technology we have created to take those able to afford it beyond the diseases and limitations of their biological brothers. Sooner or later, without it, our species will become extinct. Today is the day that you decide whether this is the end of mankind, or the beginning.'

St John sat down.

The chamber fell silent until the speaker finally made a decision.

'We call upon the honourable gentlemen to make their votes heard, in favour of a public referendum on the future of *holosap* involvement in politics and commerce.'

Minister Hart raised his hand. Across the chamber a small number of hands went up at the same time, like lone shoots blossoming across a silent and barren wasteland. The Prime Minister smiled as Hart's sigh of resignation was amplified across the chamber.

'Those against?' the speaker asked.

The air in the chamber trembled as several hundred hands lifted like a dense forest springing to life.

'Motion passed,' the speaker said without emotion. 'Ballots will be cast tomorrow for the final vote on *holosap* citizenship rights. This session is now closed.'

* * *

13

Bayou La Tour, Louisiana

The dreams came when he was asleep. Hot, heavy dreams fuelled by toxins poisoning his bloodstream, running like acid in his veins. His parents, screaming in fear for their infected children. His siblings, screaming in fear of the unknown. Himself, trying to console them but screaming inside his mind at a god he did not believe in for one chance, just one more chance, to save their lives. Nobody answered his prayers because nobody could. His mother died first, followed by their father and all three of his sisters, one by one in a horrific maelstrom of grief that consumed him every night but burned brighter and more painful now through the lens of venom and fever.

His family cried out for him one last time in the grinding pain and heavy darkness of his delirium.

'Marcus!'

Marcus jolted upright in his bed and sucked in a huge lungful of air, his chest streaming with sweat. He coughed, tears staining his eyes to mingle with the sweat speckling his skin.

Kerry hurried down through the compound toward what passed for the sick bay. 'Marcus! You've got to see this!'

Marcus blinked away the tears and looked down at his arm. It was still swollen around the bite but the skin no longer looked angry, and although he had a headache he felt somewhat better than he had a couple of hours ago. He lifted his head as Kerry burst in.

'Marcus, are you listening…?' Kerry broke off, her eyes fixed on his. 'You okay?'

Women. Marcus knew that they had a supernatural ability to detect emotion, especially in men, probably because most men tried so hard not to show them. Despite his skin being darkened by the fever and awash with sweat, Kerry could still detect a couple of tears like a shark could smell a bleeding fish from five miles away.

'I'm fine,' he replied. 'What's up?'

Kerry, with her infectious enthusiasm for all things microbial, gently guided him out of the bed and pulled him excitedly through the compound.

Marcus followed willingly, although Kerry had performed the same routine with him almost a dozen times in the long months that they had been living in the compound. The only difference had been whether she would lead him to the laboratory to relate another exciting biological discovery that had later failed replication, or to her quarters for an equally exciting investigation of a different kind.

Dr Reed appeared genie–like near the entrance to the laboratory and waved them forward. Reed's projector platforms were scattered throughout the chamber rather than forming continuous paths where he could "walk", like in the cities. Even in the tropics, the solar power cells generated energy sufficient to run the compound but not for the frivolous use of holographic entities.

Marcus did not miss the irony of the fact that it had taken a global extinction level event for humans to finally realise the importance of clean living and sustainability.

'What is it?' he asked.

'It's worth it,' Kerry insisted.

Marcus caught Reed's eye as he passed by into the laboratory, the *holosap's* expression one of concern but not alarm. Although to preserve their privacy there was no *holosap* projection unit in either Marcus or Kerry's living quarters, it didn't take a genius to work out that they slept together frequently. They were not romantically involved, but several months living in isolation with an attractive younger woman presented temptations to Marcus that no single man would likely be able to resist. Fortunately, Kerry had deigned to consider him a suitable partner.

Kerry led him into the laboratory, which was filled both with scientific equipment and a long row of fish tanks filled with countless colourful tropical species.

On one counter was a row of small cages, in each a species of local rodent, mostly mice and rats that had been collected before they too had become extinct. Several were dead, the cages that held their corpses double wrapped in plastic film to prevent contamination.

At the end, a single Nutria ran about in its cage. Kerry stopped and waved her hands at the cages. 'Ta–daaa!'

Marcus stared at the assembled rodents. 'Am I missing something?'

Kerry rolled her eyes. 'Derrr! The status cards?'

Marcus glanced at the cards attached to the end of the cage, filled with hand written data recording the age of the specimen, the test number, test type and the results. It only took him a second to digest the information on the card before him.

Infected, June 24th.
Test #: 4,267
Results: Immune response normal.

Marcus glanced at his watch. The date was the 25th June.

'I was out for a whole day?'

'It's developed immunity,' Kerry gabbled in delight, ignoring his last. 'The same test number killed the other specimens, but this little fella is still up and about with no evidence of necrosis in any of the plates I've run. He's clean!'

Marcus took a deep breath to clear his head of the last lingering phantoms of his nightmare and ordered his thoughts.

'Replication?' he demanded.

'Already underway,' Kerry confirmed and pointed to several mice in cages nearby. 'Subjects Alpha, Bravo and Charlie over there have been given the antigens I found in the Nutria and then infected. The clock's ticking on them too now.'

'The fish too,' Dr Reed added from one side. 'Kerry scanned for the same antigens in their tissue.'

Marcus turned to look at several fish tanks ranged behind him. 'Which one?'

'Pomacanthus imperator,' Kerry said and pointed at a tank full of fish with bright gold and dark blue stripes, 'the Emperor fish.'

Marcus's heart fluttered in his chest as he looked at the beautiful colours of the tropical fish as they flitted back and forth in its tank. Never had a name seemed to bear such importance as it now did.

It had long been known that salt water fish were immune to *The Falling*, a positive boon for humanity's survival, but nobody knew why. Only by analysing the DNA and trying to isolate the genes responsible for the immunity could mankind seek a cure to the disease that was decimating all life on Earth.

It had been discovered in tests that nearly eighty per cent of fish were resistant to the most common of antibiotics, tetracycline, which had become an issue as it exposed people to the risk of infections carried by those same fish. However, that same resistance combined with a saline environment may also have immunised fish against The Falling. What science had not been able to discover in time, before the catastrophic collapse of society, was just how that immunity worked.

'You've isolated the genes responsible?' Marcus gasped, looking at Kerry

'Done.'

'Download the information,' he ordered quickly. 'We need to get this back to London as soon as we can.'

'Already in progress,' Kerry said and then looked up at him. 'We've got it Marcus. We've found a cure for The Falling!'

* * *

14

London

Arianna awoke to utter silence.

She focused on her bedroom window, the sound of running water draining from the gutters and splattering through cracks and holes as a sullen sky wept upon the city. She hauled herself out of bed and strode across to the window, staring out through rivers of rain spilling down the glass at the distant hills to the south. Through the gloom she could see distant tower blocks coated in foliage beyond the city walls.

The whole world had never seemed so bleak.

She dressed and ate a breakfast that she didn't really want, Alexei Volkov's words revolving around in her mind. *"You could be in great danger"*. She supposed that she should take heed of the great man's words, but in all honesty she could think of no single reason as to why her life should be in danger. She was nobody: a number in the databases of the government, digits in a computer somewhere. She had nothing at all to fear.

Go to work.

Arianna stepped out of her church and onto the drenched pavement. She took a deep breath and told herself that paranoia was for fools. Nobody was out to get her because nobody was in the slightest bit interested in her, and that was true in any sense of the phrase. Her own bitterness made her laugh.

She put up her umbrella and strode out across a cracked road laced with weeds. Although the road was deserted at this early hour the sound of humanity surrounded her as she walked, every building densely populated, filled with whisperings and soft noises of people moving as though ashamed to reveal their presence. Much of London had degenerated into the same kind of squalor she had once read about during the Middle Ages, narrow and dangerous streets running with raw sewage and cheap alcohol, "gut–rot" as it had been known. Criminals ran underground networks, smuggling desirable and dangerous objects from out beyond the city walls. Gangs ruled many streets at night, young thugs out for anything they could get now that there simply were not enough police to patrol the streets. Arianna ministered to as many who would listen but had made no visible impact on the streets of her neighbourhood, the crime and neglect fuelled it seemed to her by the sheer futility of existence: the city was doomed, humanity was doomed, so what was the point in anything?

A woman appeared on the other side of the street, pushing a child in a pushchair concealed by a clear plastic cover. She wore a T–Shirt emblazoned with the legend: *There are only two certainties in life: death and…. Oh, crap*. Anti–*holosap* sentiment was rife in the city, another coal in the fire of resentment that seethed through the populace. They knew about the big referendum moving through parliament, the Bill of Rights that would see humans consigned to second class citizenry and the un–dead elevated to rule.

It was like a bizarre nightmare made real by man's dabbling in technology's dark arts, conjuring the unthinkable.

Arianna kept her head down and made no attempt at eye contact with the woman. She turned onto another street, heard the whisper of live current humming through the elevated train line above her head as she climbed the steps up onto the platform. The rain gusted a little as she saw the line snaking its way through the city blocks, swinging east toward Westminster. Shafts of sunlight broke through clouds out that way, glistening off the Thames in a bright flare that made her squint.

Several other people stood waiting for the train, most in business suits and sheltering beneath umbrellas. She found herself examining them, shielding her scrutiny beneath the rim of her umbrella. *Everything is normal. You are not a target despite what Alexei said. It's not like he's a government agent or something. He's a businessman and he's technically dead. Get over it.*

A glint of light on glass heralded the appearance of the train as it glided to a halt in a station barely half a mile away down the line, where it followed the embankment.

A man walked up onto the platform nearby. Middle aged but slim, dressed in casual clothes and a bulky jacket against the chill air. No umbrella, despite the rain. Even as she saw him, another pair of men appeared on the opposite end of the platform, both dressed in casual clothes and moving down the platform toward her.

Needles of concern tingled down her spine and sent a hot flush through Arianna's belly. *They're nothing to do with you*, she told herself. *You're being paranoid, reflecting the worst case scenario back onto yourself. Alexei was murdered. But there's absolutely nothing in the world that anybody could need from you. You have no money, no family and no future but for the implant stuck up your bloody nose.*

The implant.

Arianna sighed. It had taken a train of thought like this to reduce her to realising just how utterly insignificant she had become. The only thing of value she possessed was something that had never really belonged to her and she would gladly have removed. She truly did have nothing, and the realisation cut her deeply. *I'm on my own.*

Winter jacket guy had moved closer to her, but then the train was coming and people were naturally edging closer to the platform edge. The other two guys were also closer, still walking idly in her general direction. Arianna realised that she was at the far right of the platform, the two men already past the centre. Why would they walk all the way down here when the train was already moving alongside them?

'Miss Volkov?'

The voice snapped through her awareness like a bolt of electricity and she whipped her head around to see the man in the bulky jacket standing right alongside her.

'Yes?' she managed to say.

The man discreetly flashed a police badge at her. 'Officer Stewart. You're in great danger. Detective Han Reeves sent me.'

Arianna was about to ask Stewart what on earth he was talking about when the officer's eyes widened as he looked past her. Arianna turned to see the two men walking fast in her direction, their expressions hard and uncompromising.

'Come on, now!'

Stewart grabbed her arm and yanked her toward the platform exit as the two men broke into a run. Arianna glimpsed one of them reaching below his jacket to produce a heavy looking pistol before she was hauled out of sight through the exit.

Officer Stewart barged past a queue of people queuing for tickets and plunged down the exit steps with Arianna struggling to keep up.

'Who are they?' she yelled at Stewart.

'I wish we knew!' he shouted back. 'They've been watching you, that's all I know!'

Stewart reached the bottom of the stairs first and whirled, a pistol held double–handed as he aimed it at her. Arianna's heart almost stopped in her chest as Stewart shouted and leaped to one side.

'Down, now!'

A gunshot cracked over her head and Arianna dropped into a crouch as a deafening blast and a spurt of flame flared before her as Stewart fired up the staircase. She glimpsed the two men leap back out of sight at the top, heard screams of alarm from queuing passengers as they stampeded away from the noise.

Stewart grabbed Arianna and together they ran across the street, staying under the rail line as he led her down a trash strewn alley. The odour of puddles of stale water and decaying garbage assaulted Arianna's senses as they ran, their footfalls echoing through the alley.

'Where's Han?' she shouted.

'On his way!'

She burst out of the alley behind Stewart and looked over her shoulder to see their pursuers entering the alley at a run.

'This way,' Stewart snapped.

Arianna followed him down a side street between damp brick walls. She heard the sound of a car engine racing down the street ahead. Stewart turned in the alley and waved her past as he raised the pistol to point back at their pursuers. Arianna burst out of the alley and onto the street as a glossy black car screeched to a halt and a crescendo of gunshots shattered the air.

A door flew open before her and a suited man inside gestured frantically for her to get in. Arianna ducked and flinched as bullets zipped off the car's metal fenders and nicked masonry shrapnel off the walls.

'Get in!' the man bellowed.

Arianna dove into the back seat of the car. The man reached over her and yanked it shut, wafting cheap cologne in her face as he did so. Arianna felt the car lurch forwards as though the tinted windows she saw Officer Stewart hit in the shoulder by a bullet and collapse writhing onto the sidewalk.

'He's been hit!' she shouted.

The man beside her said nothing. The two men up front said nothing.

'An officer's down,' she repeated.

'He's not an officer,' said the man beside her.

The vehicle doors clicked as the locks closed.

'Who are you?' Arianna hissed at the man beside her. 'Let me out.'

'I can't do that Miss Volkov,' said the man. 'But I can assure you that you are safe and that you'll understand why in just a few minutes.'

'This is abduction.'

'This is a bloody rescue,' the man shot back at her. 'Perhaps you'd rather be back there and have a bullet in you right now?'

Arianna stared at him for a long moment. 'Who was chasing me?'

The car cruised swiftly through the streets, swerving to avoid the worst of the potholes and cracks as it headed for the glittering waters of the Thames.

'The police,' said the man next to her. 'They want you dead.'

* * *

15

Re–Volution Headquarters

Centre Point Tower

London

'When did this happen?'

Kieran Beck sat behind a broad mahogany desk, his back to windows that looked out over the rolling green waters of the Thames less than a mile away. So high was the tower that on a good day it was said you could see the south coast of England.

Before him on a projection platform inside his office stood a *holosap*, Dr Reed.

'Yesterday afternoon local time,' Reed replied. 'They're sleeping now.'

Kieran Beck leaned back in his chair, a slender gold pen held in one hand. The office surrounding them was vast, the entire top floor reserved for Beck as an office with an adjoining conference room. The three floors below were used by him as a living quarters, reducing his need for travel outside of the building.

'This changes everything,' Beck said finally. 'How sure are your researchers that their conclusions are valid and replicable?'

'There is some excitement here,' Reed said. 'So far, we have only a single live specimen that is able to resist the effects of *Apophysomyces*, but it is a very good start. Repeat experiments are underway and given the fast acting nature of the disease we're likely to have confirmation of the results within hours rather than days.'

Kieran looked at his pen thoughtfully. A cure for the disease, however unlikely, would bring about a true change in the policies he intended to be put in place by parliament. It was not impossible that millions of lives might be saved in cities across the globe, the last bastions of mankind suddenly freed from their rotting and sewage laden metropolis to once again venture out into the world. Other species, their DNA preserved in frozen stasis, might be reintroduced into the wild. Farms could once again work without being surrounded by electric fences, the farmers themselves no longer demanding danger money in order to provide what meagre supplies they could for the starving citizens of London, New York, Moscow and many other besieged cities.

'This is an historic moment,' Beck said as he looked up once more at Reed. 'The question is how do we prevent it from happening?'

Dr Reed stared back at Kieran but he said nothing. Beck smiled briefly, rueing the apparent humour of fate itself that now, at the moment of mankind's final elevation to greatness, a pair of anonymous scientists working half a world away had discovered genes that could erase the results of a lifetime's work in a single public announcement.

'What resources do we have in the gulf?' he asked.

Reed shrugged, his hands in his pockets, which was bizarre because there was no need. He didn't really have any hands, or pockets for that matter.

'None,' Reed replied. 'The outpost is close to what we believe was Ground Zero, and the infection rates there were so high that it was one of the first locations to be abandoned. Most of the population succumbed to the disease. American troops deployed the compound for us, but they haven't been back since and aren't likely to be in a hurry. They lost two out of three men to The Falling.'

'Good,' Beck replied. 'We'll let your researchers know that their work is greatly appreciated, that they'll probably win Nobel prizes or whatever the hell it is that these people expect, and that should keep them quiet. Once we've got the formula, elixir or whatever it's called…'

'Antidote,' Reed cut in helpfully, 'or vaccination.'

'… antidote, we'll replicate enough of it to fulfil our requirements and lock the rest of it away, understood?'

Reed seemed uncertain.

'They'll be looking for news reports,' he pointed out. 'They'll get suspicious if the news hasn't spread within a day or two.'

'A day or two is all we need,' Beck replied. 'Once parliament passes the *holosap's* bill of rights and access is granted to the political, economic and military sphere, it won't matter what your people say. Nobody that matters will be listening.'

'Sir, with all due respect I think that we should consider the possibility that other research stations around the world will eventually stumble across the same mutation. If either Kerry or Marcus were able to…'

'Fine,' Beck snapped as a light started flashing for attention on his desk's surface. 'I'll talk to a few people at Broadcasting House and ensure that all communications regarding this matter are blocked.'

'They're not idiots,' Reed smiled without warmth. 'One slip, one tiny inconsistency in any deception and they'll be likely to spot it. It's what they're trained to do.'

'What are you saying, Doctor Reed?'

'That any delay or hubris now could cause havoc later on,' he replied. 'To be sure, all witnesses should be silenced permanently.'

Beck watched the *holosap* for a long moment before he replied.

'I admire your candour, doctor, and I agree with your assessment. I have the ear of the defence minister. I'll ask him to talk to our counterparts in the US and assign a suitable team to the task. Now, if you'll excuse me?'

Dr Reed's image blinked out, and Beck pressed a button on a touch screen counter-sunk into the polished surface of his desk.

'What is it, Madeline?'

The voice of his secretary spoke through speakers concealed in the desk. *'Commissioner Raymond Forrester is here to see you, sir.'*

'He's here?' Beck repeated, somewhat alarmed. 'Not via transmission?'

'He's waiting for you.'

Reed sucked in a deep breath. 'Fine, send him in.'

The door opened and Police Commissioner Forrester strode in. A tall, black man in his early fifties, he exuded the same kind of confidence and charm that Kieran Beck prided himself on. The big difference was that Forrester was as straight as an arrow and one of the most respected men in the city. His approval ratings made Beck's look pitiful – not that he gave a shit. No sensible man was in this game for the kudos. This was survival of the fittest and the smartest.

'Kieran.'

'Raymond.'

A firm handshake and a winning smile reflected back at each of them, both men knowing that neither contained any warmth whatsoever.

'To what do I owe this honour?' Beck asked, perching on the edge of his desk because Forrester never sat down in this office.

'The hit on the Re–Volution buildings yesterday,' Forrester began. 'I want to know what you have learned about the event.'

Beck smiled. 'I wish we knew more, commissioner. Don't we all?'

'Don't piss me about,' Forrester said. 'Re–Volution have funded just about every political campaign the Prime Minister has been involved in and he's one of your biggest shareholders. Just because your status as an international company prevents law enforcement from searching the building doesn't mean that I won't figure out what's going on in here.'

'I don't doubt it,' Beck replied, 'although of course if that were entirely true you wouldn't be standing here. I take it that this has put enough of a rocket up your arse to honour me with a real visit instead of using the projectors?'

Kieran Beck gestured to the holographic projector, which was just as capable of beaming fully three dimensional images of living humans as *holosaps*.

Forrester's shoulders slumped slightly and he exhaled. Seeing the commissioner holding his cap beneath his arm made it seem like he was almost begging, like some modern day Oliver Twist, and the realisation pleased Beck immensely.

'Can we bury the political power hatchet just for a moment?' Forrester asked him. 'Several people have died as a result of the blast, not to mention over a hundred *holosaps*, and right now I have detectives trying to figure out who was behind it. There are lives at stake here Kieran, because whoever did this is likely to be bolstered by their success and will almost certainly try it again.'

'What do you want from me?'

'Answers,' Forrester urged. 'What does Re–Volution know about the attack?'

'That it was likely the work of religious objectors,' Beck replied without hesitation. 'They've been targeting *holosap* facilities here and across the world for years. You'd think that they'd have learned by now to let go of their so–called *faith* and accept that the world has moved on from gods and prayers.'

'And now the real information, please,' the commissioner replied with a tight grin. 'Fact is that we know that every major religious objector with the means and the will to have conducted these attacks has alibied out. They weren't behind this one, and that makes me wonder about some of the other attacks too.'

Beck stood up from his desk, his eyes levelled with Forrester's. 'Are you accusing me of something?'

'Are you hiding anything? I thought I was asking you what you *knew*, not what you've done.'

Beck held the commissioner's steady gaze for a few seconds and then turned away. He walked to the window and stared out across the city.

'I don't know what you're trying to achieve here, commissioner, but you're failing.'

Beck watched Forrester put his cap back on as he replied. 'I'm trying to think of noble reasons for why you would conceal evidence from the police investigators, and you're right, I'm failing.'

'Even if I could let you in, what would you be looking for?'

'I'd be looking for justice,' Forrester replied as he turned for the door. 'That's why I've failed to find it here.'

The office door opened and closed behind the commissioner, leaving Kieran Beck in contemplative silence. He looked out across the river for a few moments and then turned to his desk and opened a drawer.

He took out a sheet of electrofilm, the glossy translucent paper glowing into life at his touch and stiffening automatically, as he preferred. Beck swept a finger across the surface of the paper, shifting through files until he found the one he wanted.

An image of a woman appeared, in her thirties with long brown hair and clear green eyes that seemed both mysterious and sad. The name Volkov hovered beneath the image.

Kieran Beck stared at the image and then looked out through the windows at the distant forests to the south.

'It is almost time for us to finally meet, Arianna,' he whispered. 'It's been a long time coming.'

* * *

16

Arianna tried to contain her terror in her chest, where it chased back and forth as though trying to beat its way out.

She had been driven to a dock on the embankment several miles to the east of Westminster, and there forced to board a small boat which was mostly concealed beneath the waves like a tiny breaching submarine. Locked inside the hull, which was powered by the physical effort of four hooded men using chains, pulleys, gears and sheer physical effort, she was transported across the river and alighted at gunpoint into the abandoned wasteland of south London.

A second vehicle, battered and dirty, had awaited her. Once again, all of the occupants were hooded, their faces concealed.

The road surface was broken into a patchwork of shattered asphalt and dense grass, buildings lining the streets filled with gaping black holes where once windows had been. An emaciated fox scarred by patches of rotting flesh darted out from where it had been rummaging through trash spilling from an alley, nipping across the foliage filled street and vanishing into what had once been a convenience store, the signage faded and cracked. Across the wall of the building beside it was a faded slogan sprayed in paint across the brickwork.

Life's a bitch and then you… Oh crap.

'Where are you taking me?' she demanded again of her captors.

'Somewhere safe, believe it or not,' came the reply from the hooded driver, who guided the vehicle slowly through the ghostly remains of the city.

'Safe?' she uttered. 'This is the perfect location for a vector, a place where we could be infected!'

'We've taken precautions, just in case,' said his companion.

'Oh, thank God for that, otherwise I'd be worried.'

The hooded men said nothing more as the vehicle drove up a ramp into a loading bay at the rear of a large, dilapidated apartment building, the shutter doors that once protected the entrance rusted solid into their mounts. The sound of the car engine changed note as it echoed around the interior of the parking bays inside. Arianna saw rust, decay and damp brickwork everywhere and a dirty, stained elevator door nearby.

'Put this on,' said the man next to her as he handed her a translucent oxygen mask and a portable cylinder attached to it. 'Four minutes of air.'

'Four minutes?' she asked nervously.

'Head to the elevator. It will open.'

Arianna looked across at the elevator door nearby. It looked as though it had not moved for half a century.

'It's supposed to look old,' the driver informed her. 'I can assure you that it's perfectly serviceable though.'

Arianna figured that she had little choice. She slipped the mask over her head and opened the feeder valve on the cylinder. Cool air breezed into her nose and almost made her cough, but she could feel it bleeding out around the edges of the mask and knew that she could not become infected by any airborne pathogen as long as the air kept flowing.

'Go, now,' said her captor, 'and don't forget to switch the valve off once you're up there. You'll need the rest for the return journey.'

The car door unlocked automatically and Arianna climbed out. She shut the door and the vehicle reversed out of the building and drove away.

Arianna hurried across to the elevator, fearful of fox bites or dog attacks. The doors pinged and opened as she hurried inside. The building had power, although she could not imagine where from. She turned to look for which of the aged buttons to press, but before she could even decide the doors closed and the elevator climbed up to the top floor. When it opened again, Arianna stepped out into a perfectly furnished apartment. She twisted the cylinder valve to the off position and slipped the mask off her face as she stood and stared at the white leather sofa, tasteful kitchen and beautiful ornaments.

'What is this?' she whispered to herself.

'Your new home.' She whirled as a holographic projector hummed into life and Alexei Volkov smiled at her. 'You'll be safe here.'

'Alexei!' she gasped. 'What the hell is going on?'

Alexei raised his hands at her in defence.

'I'm sorry for the way in which I've handled this, Arianna,' he said quickly, 'but I had already tried to convince you that you were in danger and you would not listen.'

Arianna tried to think of a suitable response.

'They said that the police want me dead,' was all she managed to get out.

'Possibly,' Alexei nodded. 'There are bigger forces at work around us, Arianna. I believe that it was the police who murdered me, and that they were trying to pin the murder on you.'

'What the hell for?' Arianna asked. 'Why on earth would they have tried to murder you Alexei?'

'To silence me,' Alexei said and gestured to the kitchen. 'Please, fix yourself a drink and let me explain.'

'I'm not thirsty,' Arianna replied. 'Just tell me, everything.'

Alexei hesitated before speaking.

'Arianna, I have not been entirely honest with you over the time we have known each other. To put it simply, I was not sure whether I could trust you or not.'

Arianna almost laughed. 'Trust me? I'm your daughter.'

'No, Arianna,' Alexei smiled. 'You are my daughter to all intents and purposes, but we both know that you were adopted.'

Arianna smiled to hide the pain that sliced through her. It was rare for either of them to mention the fact that Arianna had been adopted at the age of seven years by Alexei, who himself was childless. Driven by a deep rooted need for financial success, by the time the businessman had even considered marriage or children The Falling had decimated the population and he was in his fifties.

'Why bring this up now?' she asked, not really able to look Alexei in the eye.

'Because you hate *holosaps*,' he said, 'you always have.'

'What does that have to do with me being here?'

'Because they're the ones behind all of this, and that means you're the least likely person I know to be working for them.'

Arianna felt briefly off–balance. 'I work for Re–Volution.'

'You're contracted to them,' Alexei corrected her. 'So are their cleaners, but they're not going to be informed of what's going on in board meetings any more than you are. Arianna, I believe that it is the intention of Re–Volution to eradicate what's left of humanity and preserve only *holosaps* for the future of our species.'

Arianna sat in silence for a moment as she digested what he was saying.

'What the hell good would that do?' she asked. 'They only exist because we do.'

'For now,' Alexei agreed. 'But plans are already in motion to change that, if you hadn't been watching the news.'

'The bill of rights,' she recalled dimly. 'Homo immortalis?'

'Holo sapiens was only ever a temporary name,' Alexei explained, 'coined more by popular culture than anything else. The new name implies the kind of permanence that I think we all fear. The proposed bill of rights for *holosaps* essentially means that they will be able to continue their lives as they would have done were they actually alive, in the traditional sense. They may return to their jobs, control their companies, influence politics in their favour and so on.'

Arianna shrugged.

'It doesn't mean anything,' she said. 'If they started to become a problem we could just pull the plug, right?'

'Wrong,' Alexei said, 'because doing so is now considered by law to be murder. That's the charge the people who caused the Re-Volution blast yesterday are facing: mass murder, genocide. Call it what you like, but switching off the *holosaps* is no longer an option. Their rights, *human* rights, will soon be enshrined in the same way as yours or mine.'

Arianna tried to understand the motivation behind the claim, but she simply could not fathom how a species, or whatever people called them, so dependent upon their creators could possibly seek to overthrow and even eradicate them.

'They'd be signing their own death warrants,' she said, 'so to speak.'

'Would they?' Alexei asked her. '*Holosaps* are sentient holograms, people as alive as they were before they died. Their only disadvantage is that they are non-physical, simply tricks of the light that with quantum physics become self-aware again. But that disadvantage is merely an inconvenience: think about it. We use touch screens, motion sensors, all manner of minimal contact devices. Given a year or two the *holosap* community could easily develop a means of controlling machinery, allowing them to build and control physical devices.'

'Perhaps,' Arianna conceded, 'but they're contained, unable to leave the walk lanes, projectors and the colony itself.'

'As a holder of Re-Volution's *Futurance*, their insurance program, I was able to read the bill of rights proposal a month ago,' Alexei said, 'long before it was revealed to the general public. Freedom of movement, without restriction in any normal field of operations and recreation enjoyed by normal human beings, is part of their charter.'

'You think that they could do that?' Arianna asked.

'Sure,' Alexei said. 'We're imaged by lasers, ultimately, which move at the speed of light. All we'd need is a sufficient number of relay stations in order to maintain the signal in any location on Earth and you're done.'

Arianna stood up and paced the living room as she thought.

'Why would the police be involved? And why would they try to kill you, or me for that matter?'

'Me, because I was always opposed to becoming a *holosap*,' Alexei replied for her. 'I guess that they figured if I decided to use my futurance that I might become a thorn in their side and oppose the bill from within.'

'But if that's true, then why didn't they just prevent you from uploading?' Arianna asked. 'If they wanted you out of the way, the last thing they should have done was let you become immortal.'

'I do not know,' Alexei said. 'I can only assume that they have their reasons. As for you, Arianna, there is something that you should know.'

Arianna sensed a blow coming, and waited silently for Alexei to continue.

'You will recall how I adopted you when you were seven years old, from the old boarding houses in Leadenhall?'

Arianna nodded. 'You saved my life, even before we'd first spoken.'

Alexei nodded, and his gentle smile seemed broader than ever. 'I was a billionaire, but nothing I have ever earned has given me such pleasure as saving you from that awful place. However, my selection was not entirely based on personal preference.'

Arianna felt something uncomfortable coil within her belly as Alexei went on.

'Twenty eight years ago, I was approached by a man who was involved in advanced research at a now defunct government facility. He was a genius who had decided to start his own company and develop something known as Holonomic Brain Theory.'

It did not take a genius to figure out who Alexei was referring to. 'Cecil Anderson.'

'The same,' Alexei confirmed. 'This was before The Falling had emerged. Cecil was seeking private funding and his work was remarkable to say the least. I backed his projects for several years, before Cecil died and the government took over his work.'

'He made the first digital brain, Adam, right?' Arianna asked. 'It went nuts a few times before he gave it a body to stand in, the first *holosap*.'

'He did,' Alexei confirmed. 'Cecil was driven initially by curiosity, then by greed, and finally by grief. His daughter died of The Falling and was buried down near Coulsden, back when they still bothered to bury the dead instead of burning them. The loss of my own family as a young boy drove me in much the same way to finance his work.'

'So, what's this got to do with your murder and the police?'

Alexei took a breath, an act entirely of habit rather than necessity, before he spoke. His voice trailed off in her mind as she digested what he was saying, as though his voice were from a dream.

'Cecil Anderson's daughter did not die,' he said finally. 'Cecil hid her away to protect her. He implanted her with a chip, fully ready for upload, then used his knowledge to erase any knowledge of his existence from her mind. She was placed in a boarding house in Leadenhall for several months before I was then to go in and find her, adopt her and protect her.'

Arianna sat in silence for what felt like an age, her eyes unfocused.

'He was my father?' she whispered.

'You are the daughter of Cecil Anderson,' Alexei confirmed. 'You were sent to the boarding houses a few days before Cecil was killed.'

Arianna blinked and looked up at Alexei. 'Cecil Anderson died of The Falling, didn't he?'

'He died at the hands of either government soldiers or private troops,' Alexei informed her. 'He would have been one of the first to upload if he could have. He believed in his work, but he also believed that *holosaps*, Adam in particular, were somehow dangerous. He was trying to shut his work down when the government intervened.'

'How do you know that?'

'Because I withdrew funding when it became clear that Adam, the first *holosap*, was unstable. He displayed psychotic tendencies, was angry, dangerous, impetuous and if he had been alive he would have been cruel. Cecil and I had a falling out of sorts. He believed that the work could be improved, whereas I felt it was a step too far. When I withdrew my funding, Cecil went elsewhere.'

'Re–Volution,' Arianna finished the sentence for him. 'They were already looking for a cure for The Falling.'

'And were failing dismally,' Alexei confirmed. 'Cecil's work was the perfect solution. Why find a cure when a hologram can't catch the disease? Can't catch any disease, for that matter. Re–Volution stepped in, but Cecil soon realised that I had been right, that he could not control his creations, that if they got loose they would see humanity as nothing but a threat to their own existence. He called me on the night that the city was quarantined, told me I was right and that he was going to shut it all down. I helped him hide you, Arianna, but after the quarantine I never saw him again.'

'And the first *holosaps* appeared a few years later,' Arianna recalled. 'Re–Volution saves the world.'

An image of Han Reeves appeared in Arianna's mind. Two police officers had tried to kill her. Could Detective Reeves have sent them, and if so, just how far did the conspiracy run in the force? Alexei answered her question with clairvoyant accuracy.

'You must remain out of sight for the moment,' he told her. 'You cannot trust the police or the government. For this to have happened requires collusion at the highest levels and until we can figure this out, you could be in danger.'

Arianna nodded, and looked about at the apartment.

'How come you were not staying here, if you feared for your own life?'

'If only I *had* feared for my life,' he said. 'I did not understand that I was in danger until it was too late.'

Arianna nodded. 'What do we do now?'

'You have a person on the inside now,' Alexei said. 'Me. We figure out who's behind this and we take them down.'

'How?'

'That's simple,' Alexei said with a grim smile, 'we cut t…..'

The holosap transmission flickered, Alexei's voice warbling with interference. Arianna saw him speaking but nothing but static and high-pitched squeals reached her ears.

'Alexei, I can't hear you!'

Alexei kept talking, but his image shuddered and then blinked out.

Moments later, as she stared at the projection platform, the locks on the apartment door clicked loudly, trapping her inside.

* * *

17

'What the hell happened?'

Detective Han Reeves stood alongside Myles Bourne in front of their superior officer, a former Guards man called Harrison Lee. Short, with cropped white hair and a stiff moustache that looked like a thin mouse perched on his top lip, Lee was not a man to be trifled with and somewhat reminded Han of a Confederate general or something.

'You let her go, and now she's disappeared?'

Han did the talking by instinct, diverting the flak from his partner.

'We didn't let anybody go, sir,' he explained. 'We couldn't get anything out of her here at the station and when Alexei Volkov turned up with her alibi we couldn't justify holding her for the full ninety six hours as a suspect. It was my idea to let her go and have a couple of guys put on observation.'

Lee ground his teeth in his jaw, making the mouse on his lip twitch as though awoken from a slumber.

'It would appear your men were not as bloody observant as they should have been, detective, because now we have both a murder to solve and a missing person. Who the hell took her?'

'We don't know,' Han replied. 'My men were ordered to keep their distance. The idea was to see what Arianna Volkov did after we released her, whether she would contact any criminal elements or people otherwise implicated in the Re–Volution blast case and Alexei Volkov's murder.'

'And did she?'

'Yes, sir,' Han said. 'Our men were observing her on the west–bound platform at Station Seventeen when they saw her being approached by an individual who then attempted to guide her away from my men. They pursued, and were fired upon from within the station. They lost Arianna after a getaway vehicle intercepted her, but we caught the shooter on the platform.'

'Where is he now?'

'Intensive care,' Myles replied. 'He was hit twice in the upper chest and shoulder and suffered a collapsed lung. Surgeons say he'll pull through but he's not answering any questions right now. My guess is he's just a hired hand and won't be able to provide us with any useful information.'

Lee nodded thoughtfully.

'Where was she taken?'

'No idea sir,' Han said. 'We managed to track the vehicle to the water but we lost it after that. The camera coverage is patchy at best.'

'Why would they take her over there?'

'As you know there's a strong criminal element sheltering from law enforcement south of the water sir,' Han pointed out. 'If Arianna is indeed involved in the crimes we're investigating and fears that she's been exposed, it's the perfect place to hide out.'

Lee peered at Han with interest.

'You're convinced that she's behind all of this, even though Alexei Volkov himself said that she could not have killed him?'

'She didn't have to pull the trigger to be involved, sir. Maybe she clocked the tail we put on her and decided to call in some help. So far she looks guilty of something, I'm just not sure what.'

It was a weak line and Han knew it. Just as likely, Arianna was grabbed and dragged into a vehicle before being spirited away across the Thames. Maybe people were already interrogating her.

'She could have run after the blast or after the murder,' Lee mused out loud, 'if she were indeed guilty of either. Yesterday, she was almost blown up and saw her adoptive father's charred remains lying in his bed. It seems unlikely that she would endure questions and accusations here, then just go home upon release and get a good night's sleep before heading to work as usual the following morning if she were guilty, don't you think?'

Han raised his chin, looking over Lee's head.

'It would stretch credibility a touch,' he conceded, 'although it could also be a remarkably astute bluff.'

'Bull crap,' Lee uttered. 'We work on the assumption that she has been abducted by persons unknown, for reasons unknown, and that she is in considerable danger if not dead already. Get on it, the both of you, and let me know as soon as you learn anything. Have you got her colleague in here yet?'

'Larry Wilkes,' Han Reeves said. 'He's waiting in my office right now.'

'Fine,' Forrester replied, 'pressure him but don't get carried away, understand? He could be as much of an innocent bystander in all of this as the Volkovs.'

Han spun on his heel and strolled out of the office with Myles right behind him. They walked down a corridor to the interview rooms and strode into one. Larry Wilkes sat behind a bare desk, a Styrofoam cup in his hand and a worried expression on his features. Han rested his hands on the table before Wilkes and glowered down at him as Myles closed the door.

'So, Larry,' he began, 'how about coming clean?'

'About what?'

'Re–Volution have not released any interior footage of the blast,' Han explained. 'They're hiding something, aren't they?'

'I wouldn't know.'

'You worked at Re–Volution on the second floor, right above the blast,' Myles Bourne snapped. 'You told Arianna that you came straight down afterward and saw the damage. Did you see anything else?'

Wilkes shook his head, his jowls trembling with the motion. 'No, I don't know. There was so much confusion, blood and bodies. I don't know what you want me to say?'

Han leaned in closer to Wilkes. 'Arianna Volkov, she's your friend, right?'

'Yes, she's…' Wilkes hesitated. 'She's a friend.'

Han smiled grimly. 'Got a fancy for the priest, have we Wilkes?'

'What do you want from me?'

'Arianna's whereabouts,' Myles said.

'What?'

'Arianna was abducted this morning from a train platform near her home,' Han said, 'and last seen near the Thames. It's believed she's been taken south of the river.'

Wilkes's face collapsed. 'Oh no, my God, she could die.'

'Very likely,' Han agreed, 'so right now we need to know what Re–Volution isn't telling us.'

Larry Wilkes clasped his hands together, his jowls trembling.

'I don't know,' he replied, 'for sure.'

'Don't know what for sure?' Han demanded.

Wilkes dragged a hand down his face. 'I didn't see anything.'

'We both know that's not true,' Han insisted. 'You were there and…'

'That's not what I mean!' Wilkes snapped. 'I mean I didn't see anything. No attackers, no terrorists, nothing. Just victims.' He sighed. 'Nobody saw anybody associated with anti–saps or other groups who have threatened us in the past. The only person who was in the lobby right before the blast was…'

'Arianna,' Han said as he glanced at his partner. 'She says she wasn't responsible for the blast.'

'She wouldn't do something like that,' Wilkes insisted. 'She doesn't like holosaps, granted, but then who does? But she's just not the sort to kill, even holosaps and especially not human beings caught in the blast. I don't know why she was there, but she couldn't have taken anything into the building and then walked out.'

Han leaned closer to Wilkes. 'Re–Volution said that terrorists caused the blast, that they had bodies. They're in the coroner's office right now awaiting autopsy.'

'I know,' Wilkes replied. 'That's what they're hiding. All employees are signed to non–disclosure agreements so we cannot say anything.'

Han nodded. 'But if I was to ask you a question?'

'I could answer yes or no,' Wilkes replied.

'Were any terrorist bodies found at the source of the blast or within its radius?'

'None,' Wilkes said, 'that I saw.'

'Were any terrorists found in the quantum–storage server rooms?'

'None, that I saw. But I did see Kieran Beck and his entourage leave the building this morning in a convoy of vehicles. Word is that they're going underground until the security around the headquarters building is improved.'

'Did they head south?'

'They did.'

Han looked at Wilkes for a long moment, and then he turned and motioned Myles to follow him out of the room.

'So, now what?' Myles asked as he closed the office door behind them and followed Han to the offices.

Han stopped beside his desk and looked down a deep pile of cases awaiting attention. The city was becoming ever more violent as people struggled to feed, clothe and protect themselves. Electricity was in short supply and outages were commonplace, with the only secure supplies of energy reserved for the power stations themselves, services like the police and fire–rescue, and the *holosap* community. Black market smuggling, boot–legging and other crimes were on a rapid rise.

Han glanced out of the station windows toward the south, where the city was illuminated in patched by drifting beams of sunlight scything down from the turbulent clouds.

'They took her south of the water,' he said. 'They must have had a plan, somewhere to go.'

'Plenty of criminals operating in places most ordinary people wouldn't dare to go,' Myles replied. 'But what the hell would they want with Arianna Volkov? She's just a priest.'

'So we assume,' Han mused out loud. 'But she's got motive to hate Re–Volution, a means of access, everything she needed to hit the building. And now Re–Volution aren't talking about what happened. They haven't even released camera footage for us to review, which in itself might get Volkov off the hook.'

'That's Re–Volution for you,' Myles said as he rifled through papers on his desk. 'Money, power, influence, it gets them what they want. It's bad enough that we can't even speak to the board of directors about all of this. My guess is they're hanging Arianna Volkov out to dry.'

Han kept his gaze on the far side of the river.

'Don't even think about it.' Myles's warning broke Han's reverie and he glanced across at his partner. 'We cross the river we could be infected. That means we don't get back into the city again.'

Han nodded. Biometric sensors on gates at all access points to the river scanned anybody who tried to enter the city. Shortly before the implant chips detected the fungus responsible for The Falling, *Apocalypses* or whatever the hell it was called showed up under ultra–violet light as a sort of pale discolouring of the whites of the eyes, like jaundice but more creamy. So it was said. Turn up at the gates with that look about you and the guards gave you a choice: head back across the water and take your chances in the wilderness or be shot and bagged there and then.

Most took the river back to the south side. None had ever been seen again.

'Maybe they've got a decent bolt hole down there somewhere,' Han said. 'C'mon, we've got respirators, body armour and motorcycles, it'll be a walk in the park.'

Myles almost laughed. 'That's the line somebody always uses in a movie, right before everything goes to hell.'

'We've got to solve this,' Han reasoned. 'I can't let another damned case go cold and neither can you. We can't send uniforms because they're already stretched to the limit.'

'You want to go now?' Myles gasped.

'I don't want to go at all,' Han replied. 'But our chief suspect is on the other side of that river and we need to go get her back and figure out what's going on. Either she planted a bomb in that building or she's being framed for it and for the murder of Alexei Volkov. You want to sit here with your thumb up your arse hoping the next break lands in your lap then you go ahead. Me, I'm going to try to fix this.'

Han grabbed his jacket and his sidearm and turned to storm out of the office.

He only just managed to suppress a smile as he heard Myles swear under his breath and grab his own coat and weapon.

18

Bayou La Tour, Louisiana

Gulf of Mexico

'Anything yet?'

Kerry Hussein was leaning over a cage, her eyes shielded with lab glasses and a breathing mask over her face as Marcus walked into the laboratory. His arm throbbed from the snake bite, but the antivenin had done its work and his fever was long gone. Kerry shook her head as Marcus approached, her long black pony tail swinging with the motion.

'Not a sign, still as healthy as though he were born yesterday.'

Some of the excitement was gone now from Kerry's voice to be replaced with a professional urgency. Marcus knew that they could be on the verge of a major breakthrough, that they could save the entire world just like in those old *Hollywood* blockbuster movies. Except that this was real and conducted in a tiny laboratory perched on the edge of a stinking bayou deep in the Louisiana wilderness.

Not exactly a crowd pleaser, he figured.

'What about the samples?' he asked.

Kerry replaced the lid on the cage and pulled off her mask. To his surprise she was wearing a little make up. It brought out the edges of her already exotic eyes and the finely sculptured lines of her lips and immediately made him want her. The fact that she had insisted they get a good night's rest only inflamed his desire.

'What?' she asked, looking at him as a smile spread on her face. Her teeth looked bright and white against her olive skin.

'Nothing,' he replied, and forced himself to turn to the samples.

'The cultures are almost complete,' she said, the smile still touching the edges of her lips. 'One control, one infected, one not. We should have the results in a couple of hours. I'm going to send them to the other labs, see if they get the same results.'

'We're not ready yet,' Marcus said.

'Damn it, how ready do we have to be?'

'Ready,' he insisted.

Fact was, countless premature announcements of new discoveries, including cures for The Falling, had collapsed mired in shame after results were not replicated by other labs or turned out to be false alarms. The researchers in question had always been forced to retire from their work by the government and even accused of falsifying evidence, stripped of their qualifications for breeding hope in an increasingly desperate populace. Marcus was determined not to fall into the same trap. They would confirm the results themselves and ensure that they were replicable before sharing them with the wider scientific community for peer review and hopefully a global immunity program. That was how science worked and how it had achieved so much over the past few centuries.

'We have an immune specimen,' Kerry complained, 'that's been alive for forty eight hours now, an isolated gene and samples almost cultured. The antibodies will be isolated a lot faster if other labs around the world are working on this too.'

'Do we have to go over this again?' Marcus sighed. 'The specimen is a rodent, forty eight hours isn't sufficient to be certain and breeding antibodies that are compatible with humans will take a long time. This isn't going to happen overnight so why the hell rush it?'

'Because it's important. People are dying. The sooner we announce this the sooner we can get something out into the field.'

'And what if somebody else rushes and releases a serum that doesn't work, or has horrific side effects or even kills?' Marcus challenged. 'What then?'

Kerry stared at Marcus for a long beat. 'This isn't about confirmation trials, is it? This is about keeping the glory, right?'

Marcus gaped at her. 'That's not true. If we get this right millions of people's lives will be saved. Get it wrong and we're canned, perhaps even tried for incompetence.'

'That's such crap,' she snapped and stormed past him.

Marcus felt a flood of remorse wash through him as he turned to follow her.

'Oh come on, Kerry. You know as well as I do what's happened to other people who have released early results that looked promising only to see their programs shut down because…'

'Because what?' Kerry challenged as she whirled to face him. 'Because they tried to save lives? Because they sat in shitty little compounds for months on end with people who annoyed the crap out of them in order to maybe, someday, heal a pandemic for people that they will never even meet? The government shuts them down because it doesn't understand that science like this takes time, effort and often repeated failure before an answer is found.'

Marcus didn't hear the last few lines of her tirade.

'People who annoy the crap out of them?' he uttered. 'Is that how you see me?'

Kerry waved him away as she turned to leave. 'Oh my God, even now when we're on the verge of a breakthrough discovery you're still a narcissist. It's all about you, Marcus, right?'

Marcus took a pace in pursuit. 'But all of the times we've…'

'We've what?' she asked coolly as she turned to him at the laboratory door. 'Had sex? Get over yourself Marcus. It's not like I've made you breakfast in bed is it? Six months stuck here without access to other men, what did you expect?'

Marcus swallowed, tried not to let his face flush red in shame or let Kerry see the disappointment that seemed to tug down on every muscle in his face.

'I didn't know,' was all he could think of to say.

Some of Kerry's anger melted and she sighed.

'You're a great guy when you forget about yourself Marcus,' she said finally. 'When we've had sex it's been good, but if it wasn't for *The Falling* we wouldn't even be in the same city let alone the same bed.'

Kerry pulled off her latex gloves and dumped them in the trash before she turned and marched out of the laboratory. Marcus stared at her rolling butt and long legs as she walked and then cursed himself as anger seethed through his veins. *You bitch.*

'It happens all the time,' came a voice from behind him. 'I wouldn't worry about it.'

Marcus whirled to see Dr Reed appear behind him.

'Don't you goddamn *holosaps* ever knock?' he snapped as he stormed across to the specimen cages for no real reason that he could think of.

'We can't,' Dr Reed pointed out.

'Then we should get you all fitted with alarms or something.'

Dr Reed smiled as he joined Marcus in a flicker of light beside the cages.

'You're doing the right thing, Marcus,' he said. 'Rushing this and failing would be far worse than taking your time and getting it right.'

Marcus sighed and shrugged.

'Kerry's got a point though,' he said. 'People are dying, every single day, because of The Falling. The sooner we can get this out for peer review the better.'

'Another day or two,' Dr Reed urged. 'That's all it takes, and then you'll be certain of success and Dr Hussein will be satisfied too.'

'I doubt Dr frickin' Hussein is ever satisfied with anything.'

'No woman ever is,' Dr Reed lamented. 'All we men can ever hope to achieve with them is damage limitation. Go to her, and apologise.'

'Apologise for what?' Marcus asked. 'She's just ignored every good point I've made, accused me of glory seeking and then told me she never really wanted to sleep with me. What the hell should I be apologising for?'

'For being a man,' Dr Reed chuckled. 'You want the glory. I know I would, and in that Kerry is right isn't she?'

Marcus fumed on the spot.

'Of course I want the glory!' he snapped. 'But not at the expense of other people's lives, if we've got it wrong.'

'Precisely,' Dr Reed said. 'Go to her, apologise, and then explain to her what you've just said to me. I'm sure she will understand.'

'It doesn't matter,' Marcus moaned, 'she still won't be interested in me.'

Dr Reed rolled his eyes.

'I think that there are bigger issues at stake than your pride here, is what I'm trying to tell you,' he said. 'You need Kerry on your side to complete the work here, and she's done just as much as you to earn her place in history if this cure works. Now get over yourself and go talk to her. I'd put my boot up your backside to make you, if I could, but I can't so just get on with it.'

Marcus sighed and turned for the laboratory door.

'And don't come back until she's happy!' Dr Reed added.

Marcus crossed the laboratory and shut the door behind him. He was trying to think of what to say to Kerry when he heard a sudden and loud thumping noise that shook the entire compound. Marcus turned and saw Dr Reed watching him from within.

'What the hell is that?' Marcus asked.

Dr Reed's features creased with what might have been regret. 'I'm sorry, Marcus, truly I am.'

Marcus was about to ask why when he heard the sound of a woman's scream.

Kerry.

* * *

19

London

Arianna stood beside a broad window that overlooked the crumbling remains of what had once been the exclusive Shad Thames development, the river itself just visible to her left between the narrowly spaced apartment blocks, and tried to convince herself that everything was fine.

Alexei's transmission was interrupted. He's remotely locked the apartment doors for safety's sake.

Once an exclusive place to live, now the block opposite hers was a crumbling, dirt stained mess with broken windows, big black squares beckoning her imagination toward the horrors that might lie within. The city south of the Thames had been evacuated and then shut off by the military during The Falling: those left behind had died here. The road below was littered with fallen masonry and dense with foliage, and amid the debris Arianna could see scattered bones that had long been picked clean by rodents and then insects.

Many would have belonged to the people who lived here; men, women and children.

She turned away from the bleak view and looked at the apartment. It had been maintained perfectly for many years. That Alexei Volkov needed a bolt hole, somewhere that he could remain undetected was something that Arianna could understand well enough, given his younger years spent in the ferocious wilds of Siberia and then in the dangerous business world of Russia, but she could not fathom why he would have decided to build his sanctuary here unless he truly did believe that the police were corrupt. Maybe beyond the river in a land haunted by The Falling, was a place that somebody like Volkov could actually call safe.

But can I?

Arianna saw a viewing panel folded neatly against a wall nearby. She walked across the living room and picked up a remote control, tapping buttons as she went. The screen, a three by four foot transparent panel lined with tasteful silver trim, automatically extended on a slim aluminium arm to hover before her.

Arianna perched on the edge of the white leather sofa and activated the panel. Instantly a live news broadcast from Re–Volution's headquarters in the city appeared in clarity–definition before her, a female reporter standing in front of the still smouldering lower floors and speaking into her personal camera.

'... several dozen people are now confirmed dead after the explosion yesterday that also claimed the lives of over one hundred holosaps in what is being called the biggest case of genocide in recent history. The blast was deliberately designed to sever fibre links with Re–Volution's data storage facilities as well as inflict maximum human casualties...'

Arianna flicked across a couple of channels, all of them government owned but still maintaining a free press of sorts. Democracy required as its cornerstone a free press and the people knew it.

'... several individuals injured in the blast remain unaccounted for, including a Hope Reunion Church priest that the police have stated they want to question regarding the attack...'

'Oh God!'

Arianna leaped to her feet in shock as alongside the reporter's broadcast an image of her own face appeared. It was taken not from Re–Volution's data banks, where her records were kept for her freelance work and featured a happy, smiling picture of herself, but from the train station that very morning. They had zoomed in, and she saw her own brooding image staring out across the city. Somehow it made her look like a suspect, somebody who hid in the shadows and was rarely seen. Her psychology training told her why – *Suggestion*. Arianna paused the live–feed broadcast and stared at herself. The police could have released the Re–Volution stock photo, a normal snapshot of her smiling at the camera with not a care in the world, but no, they used a pixelated and shadowy image instead.

She heard words from the reporter flicker through her mind like phantoms haunting a bizarre and horrible dream.

'... she was questioned by police officers after the blast... the adoptive daughter of a former Russian magnate who was recently murdered... senior figure in the Hope Reunion Church, an establishment known to have housed terrorists in the past... not seen since this morning after an attack on commuters at train platform...'

Arianna knew a great deal about how the media could use certain images to create a suggestion in the mind of a viewer that a fact or accusation was true without actually saying so. The ploy had been used many times in history, a form of subtle but extremely persuasive propaganda; images of calving ice sheets, swimming polar bears and smoking power stations when reporting on climate change, even though the ice sheets, polar bears and power stations would perform precisely the same activities without climate change; people dying of gunshot injuries in foreign countries undergoing civil strife, despite the viewer not knowing whether the footage came from the same countries upon which the reports were focused; and images of rival religious groups singing happy songs and praying together when everybody knew that there was no such accord between opposing faiths and that each insisted upon the falsehood of the others.

There was no mention in the report of her being abducted or shot at. The suggestion, although never voiced, was that she had *fled*. Somebody, somewhere was trying to build a picture in the public mind of her as a criminal or somebody affiliated with criminals, and not the victim that she was.

'I can't let this happen,' she whispered to herself.

Hiding was no good to her. She had to come out fighting and make herself heard or by the time the sun had set she would never be able to set foot back in the city again. Every single person would know her name and would associate it with terrorism.

Damn it. How the hell would she get back across the river? Would they let her through the gates? Would there be armed men waiting to shoot her? What if the police *were* corrupt? And here she was, hiding in a penthouse apartment built illegally by a murdered Russian magnate with a patchy history in a part of the city reserved for the dead, the doomed and the criminal underbelly of one of the last populated cities on the planet.

Guilty as hell, without a further word being said about it.

Arianna shut off the display and turned for the elevator door. She reached down for the access panel, and immediately saw that it was still locked. Questions flashed through her mind faster than she could process them as she searched for a key. Why hide me here at all? Why had the door locked automatically? Why was Alexei murdered and by whom? Why was I attacked and by whom?

Where is Alexei?

What if this isn't Alexei's apartment?

Arianna walked back across the apartment and reached up for the contact panel near the holographic projector. Her hand froze without touching the panel, as though by some unheard yet powerful instinct. She stood, immobile as a statue as the morning's events ran through her mind.

Men on the train platform. Another man, a police officer, rescues her from an imminent attack and is shot in the process. Why was *he* not on the news? It would have been the perfect final blow, that she had fled and a police officer had been shot in the process, confirming in the minds of viewers her likely guilt of *something*. The answer popped into her mind of its own accord. The injured man was not a police officer.

Arianna felt her breath catch as a new and unexpected explanation dawned in her mind. What if her abductors were the enemy? What if Alexei himself was the enemy?

Arianna turned to seek a means of escape from the apartment.

To her surprise the elevator door opened. She turned toward it, only to see half a dozen masked men lunged into the building with a man she had only ever seen on the television before now following them. Kieran Beck. As the men grabbed her, she heard Beck's voice from behind his face mask.

'Hello, Arianna. I've been dying to meet you.'

* * *

20

Arianna opened her mouth to scream, but her cry was cut short by a gloved hand that smelled of leather as she was forcibly dragged through the apartment by the six men. They hauled her writhing body into the bedroom and hurled her onto the huge bed.

Arianna struggled against them, but they pinned her ankles and wrists into place with overwhelming force as one of the men pressed both of his gloved hands either side of her face to keep her from moving her head.

'What do you want?!' she managed to yell.

Kieran Beck strode into the bedroom, a black cylinder in his hand from which projected two metallic probes twice as long as matchsticks.

'What do I want?' Beck asked as he moved to stand at the foot of the bed. He smiled at her and shrugged. 'I want you dead, Arianna, right now.'

Beck tossed the black cylinder to the man who was pinning Arianna's head to the mattress. The man caught the cylinder easily as it spun past over her head, and then flipped it over in his palm and lowered it over her mouth, the two metal probes pointing toward her nose.

'What the hell are you doing?' she screamed.

'It's for insurance purposes,' Kieran Beck replied, 'ours obviously. My apologies in advance, Arianna, for the unbearable pain this procedure will inflict.'

Arianna squirmed against her captors but she was utterly unable to break free from their grasp. The man holding her head touched the two metallic probes to her nose and inserted them into her nostrils.

Tears spilled from Arianna's eyes as she felt the cold metal probes push up into her sinuses, heading toward her brain.

'Please, no,' she gasped.

Pain bolted between her eyes as though needles were being driven into her eyeballs.

'Do it,' Beck snapped. 'Now!'

The man holding the cylinder lifted a thumb over a button on its surface to activate the device as Arianna screamed.

'No!'

The windows to the apartment suddenly shattered in a cascade of glass as bullets scythed into the bedroom. Arianna saw the man above her hurled sideways as a bullet smashed through his skull and tore his face clean off in a spray of thick blood and bone that splattered across the bed sheets.

The cylinder was torn from Arianna's nose and spun sideways onto the bed, a bright blue beam of fiery energy singing the sheets in black patches as the laser cutter was activated.

Bullets slammed through Kieran Beck's men as they hurled themselves away from the hail of gunfire. Arianna rolled sideways off the bed and grabbed the spitting, clicking cylinder as she went.

'Kill her!' Kieran Beck bellowed from where he lay on the floor, one hand covering his head.

Arianna dashed toward the bedroom door. A gloved hand flashed out and grabbed her calf, strong fingers closing like a vice on her. Arianna whirled and jabbed the laser cutter into the hand, heard a scream of pain and smelled burned flesh. The hand shot away from her again and she fled the bedroom and slammed the door behind her. She grabbed an ornate chair, all flowing chrome tubes and plastic, and wedged it under the door handle.

She whirled for the elevator door once again, and instantly saw that it was locked, the keypad glowing bright red.

'Shit.'

A deep thud hammered into the bedroom door as Kieran Beck's men struggled to escape. She ran a hand through her hair in frustration and on reflex glanced up at the ceiling as though to heaven above to implore God for an answer.

He answered.

A square panel in the ceiling, fitted flush. A loft space. Arianna dashed across to the apartment's control panel and hit the access button for the loft. The hatch clicked and then hissed softly as it folded down and a metal ladder slowly extended to the floor. Arianna clambered up the ladder and instantly lights flickered into life inside the loft as motion sensors detected her presence.

Arianna turned around and hauled the ladder up. She yanked the hatch shut behind her, then rammed the laser cutter through the latch to prevent anybody from pursuing her.

The loft was about half as large as the apartment below, the penthouse suite's roof coming in from all four corners to a point above her head where heavy beams were supported that ran the length of the roof. Windows had been blocked off, probably after The Falling, to prevent weather damage and subsequent access by infected vermin. However, the covers were merely screwed into mounts and braces, not glued or attached via the outside.

Arianna did not have a screwdriver, but it took her only moments to spot a tool box among various other items stored in the loft space. Moments later she was unscrewing the window covers as from below she heard more gunfire and shouts of alarm. She lifted the cover down as soon as it was free to reveal a triple glazed window with a simple twist–lock handle.

Below her in the apartment, she heard the bedroom door smash open and Beck's men tumble out to the sound of enraged shouting.

Arianna grabbed the handle, twisted it and threw the window open.

Cold air breezed in, stained by the odour of the nearby Thames and battered by the sound of helicopter blades. On an impulse Arianna grabbed the discarded cover and guided it out of the window before taking hold of the edges of the window and carefully hauling herself up and out of the loft.

Heights had never been a strong point for Arianna and her guts lurched as she realised just how precarious her perch was. The roof slanted down toward a precipitous drop of maybe eighty feet to the narrow, weed infested street below her. She looked to her right and saw a large chimney, probably a century or two old, still standing alongside the apartments that had once been dock warehouses. A ladder was attached to the side of the chimney.

The helicopter sounded as though it was hovering on the other side of the roof, occasional bursts of gunfire shattering the air.

Arianna took the window cover from inside the loft and set it back in place. There was no way that she could properly secure it, so instead she drove two screws into the sides of the cover and then lowered the window over it. It would not escape close inspection but it might just be enough to disguise her means of escape.

Arianna closed the window and managed to force the handle shut over the cover below by leaning her weight into it. Then, lying flat on the rooftop, she edged her way along the tiles toward the chimney.

She was half way there when she heard the running footfalls echoing through the street below and the sound of more helicopter blades thumping distant air, getting ever louder.

* * *

21

The helicopter's rotors beat the air and the rooftop and Arianna's chest seemed to shudder with the blows.

She struggled toward the chimney, the damp tiles scratching against her fingernails as she slipped toward the dizzying drop just below her. The wind blew her hair into her face as she nudged herself along a few inches at a time.

Questions fluttered like dark butterflies through her mind: where was Alexei? Why would Kieran Beck want her dead? Why were helicopters shooting up the apartment? Only the government were allowed to operate aerial vehicles.

Arianna reached the edge of the rooftop and fear wrenched at her insides as she realised that the chimney was not directly attached to the apartment building. A yawning abyss of some twelve feet stood between her and the metal ladder bolted to the chimney's brickwork. Pressing her body flat against the damp tiles she inched her head over the edge.

Her belly contracted and her breath caught in her throat as she saw the sheer drop to the debris strewn alley below.

'Jesus, help me,' she whispered as she closed her eyes.

Nobody answered.

Below, two black vehicles screeched from the parking lot beneath the apartments and raced beneath the helicopter to vanish through the abandoned streets. Beck's vehicles, she guessed. They'd fled the scene. The helicopter made no attempt to pursue the vehicles, remaining in position just out of view on the far side of the roof.

Arianna's sense of balance wavered even though she was lying flat on the roof. There was no other option, no other means of escape. Her legs trembling, Arianna pressed her palms and her knees into the tiles and came up onto all fours, careful to stay just clear of the edge of the roof.

The helicopter's rotors thundered and she glanced to her right to see the speck of a second helicopter moving rapidly toward her across the city against turbulent clouds. She guessed she had maybe a minute, perhaps even less. She looked back at the drop.

'Oh God, oh God,' she whispered.

Maybe this was all just crazy. Alexei was not the enemy and she had got it all wrong. She could just go back, drop into the loft space and forget the whole damned thing.

The voice of her sanity barged its way to the front to be heard.

You shut the window, genius, and even if you're right somebody's trying to kill you. There is no room for mistakes. You can only trust yourself.

She tried to stand but her legs would not obey her. Every gust of wind seemed destined to blow her over the edge to an agonising death on the unforgiving alley below. Crunching bones. Bursting eyes. Seeping blood.

She took a deep breath, sucking in cold air. Her legs steadied. She stood up, the damp tiles cold on her feet as she backed up a few paces, balancing with her arms out to either side of her. Tears trickled from her eyes but she swiped them away as she focused on the metal ladder twelve feet away from the edge of the roof.

Twelve feet. Maybe fifteen feet because gravity will pull me down a bit.

Not far. Not too far. Just don't land badly and break a leg, or an arm, or bash your face in because you won't be able to hang on. Don't look down, just focus on the ladder and nothing else. You can do this.

Just do it.

Arianna sucked in a last deep breath of air and then ran at the edge of the roof.

Every step seemed to drain the strength from her legs. Tiles slipped as she ran but she powered forward with suicidal gusto. Her right foot touched down on the edge of the roof and she knew she could no longer stop herself from flying out into thin air and with a rush and a pinched scream she hurled herself as hard as she could at the ladder in front of her.

Time stopped.

Her stomach plunged as she flew away from the rooftop, gravity pulling her down as her arms and legs clawed at the air as though she could swim toward the ladder. She felt a rush of cold air as she began to plummet downward. The ladder loomed up, the broad brick face of the chimney filling her vision. She reached out for the nearest rung and then she slammed into the hard metal with a bone jarring crash.

Pain bolted through her fingers and wrists as she gripped the ladder and then through her thighs as they smacked down beneath her. Instinct kept her legs tucked back below the knee so that she didn't break her shins or toes impacting the chimney. Her right temple smacked against the hard metal ladder but not hard enough to scare her.

Christ, I did it.

Arianna fumbled with her feet to find the rungs below her, and then she scrambled down the ladder until she was below the apartment's rooftops and out of sight of the rapidly closing helicopter. She heard its rotors hammering the air as she climbed down and down to the alley below and finally, blissfully, stepped onto the ground.

She dashed through the dense foliage across to the edge of the apartment block and peered around the corner.

Overhead she could hear the thundering rotor blades as the second helicopter raced overhead. Arianna clung to the wall and did not move until the helicopter had passed over her and had begun to bank around for another pass. She could see the vivid television company markings and an open door on one side where a man was strapped into a seat behind a large camera.

Hovering in front of the apartment building was the other helicopter, its guns smouldering wisps of blue smoke in the downwash from its blades.

Arianna shifted position as the second helicopter passed out of sight behind the chimney, dashing back behind the brickwork and edging around it to keep the first helicopter just in sight. It flew in a wide arc and then headed back toward the apartment block. Arianna was wondering what on earth it was looking for when she heard a voice on a loudspeaker echo out over the noise of the engine and blades.

'Come out with your hands in sight!'

Her heart skipped a beat as the helicopter slowed and then hovered side–on to the apartment blocks.

'Come out now or we will be forced to open fire!'

Arianna clenched her eyes shut and hugged the bricks. They could be the enemy. They might want her dead. But if they were on her side, then perhaps they were saving her from Kieran Beck? Confusion swamped her senses as the voice rang out again.

'Come out of the apartment with your hands up or we will open fire! This is your last chance!'

Arianna stared at the helicopter and then to her disbelief she heard a couple of sharp cracks as an unexpected burst of gunfire erupted from *inside* the apartment. She saw the motorised gun in the helicopter shift position and a jet of flame flicker from its barrel in reply.

Hundreds of high velocity rounds smashed into Alexei Volkov's apartment in a shower of bullets that sent clouds of glass out into the sky like diamond chips. The chattering machine gun raked across the face of the building, forcing Arianna to cover her ears against the noise as she heard minor blasts from within the apartment as electrical devices were shattered by the hail of bullets.

The helicopter hovered for several more moments and then it banked and turned away. The deafening noise finally abated enough for Arianna to lift her hands away from her ears, and on unsteady legs she slowly emerged from her hiding place and stepped out into the street once more.

Alexei Volkov's apartment was completely destroyed, fires burning within as the once immaculate upholstery blazed and spat thick black clouds of smoke up into the blustery sky. Debris littered the street beneath the apartment, glass and warped window frames.

Above the sound of the crackling flames, she heard voices.

'Stay low, keep out of sight!'

'I am!'

Arianna ducked to one side of the street and hugged the brickwork as she saw two men running down the street in front of the apartment block. With a start of alarm she recognised Han Reeves and Myles Bourne running to a stop in front of the building. Police. Arianna was careful not to move, holding her long hair back out of sight with one hand as she watched the two men look up at the building.

Bastards. They were trying to kill her.

As she watched she saw Han, a pistol in his hand, shake his head and bang the butt of the weapon against his temple. She frowned as Bourne patted the detective on the shoulder as though consoling him. She was too far away to hear what they were saying, but it appeared that Han was either disappointed or perhaps even angry.

'Don't move.'

The voice was a harsh whisper that sent a chill down her spine, made worse by the cold tip of a gun that touched the nape of her neck.

'Back up,' the voice urged as a hand closed like a vice around her arm.

She turned to see two hooded men standing behind her. From somewhere inside she managed to dredge her voice back up.

'They're police.'

The man who held his gun to her neck smiled, revealing a row of rotten, stained teeth barely visible against the shadowy interior of his hood.

'We know.'

She was considering shouting out to Han for help when the two thugs looked up. Arianna turned to see Han edge forward toward the shuttered entrance to the apartment block. Han's face collapsed as he yelled at Bourne.

'Down, now!'

The two men hurled themselves across the street as the entire apartment block exploded and vanished in a ball of expanding flame and smoke. Arianna flinched as the shockwave hit her, a cloud of roiling smoke and flame billowing up into the turbulent sky as the helicopter rolled away from the blast. Chunks of brickwork and masonry showered past the chimney where Arianna crouched with her hands over her ears.

Arianna ducked her face away as the building collapsed entirely, Han and Myles vanishing in the expanding cloud of debris as she was yanked away by the two hooded men.

* * *

22

Bayou La Tour

Louisiana

Marcus did not consciously think about what he was doing.

He heard Kerry's scream and without considering any danger he launched himself down the corridor toward her. The sound of helicopter blades seemed to appear from nowhere to shake the entire compound and he quickly saw that the airlock was wide open, hot wind gusting dangerously into the compound from outside.

'Kerry?!'

He ran outside and staggered as the helicopter's downwash slammed into his back and sent him reeling across the ground as clouds of dust swirled in the sunlight. The hot air snatched his breath from his lungs as he squinted up into the bright sky and saw a huge twin-bladed helicopter hovering above the ground on the far side of the compound.

He heard another scream and turned to see Kerry sprawled on her back in the dust nearby as a figure clawed at her. Marcus hauled himself to his feet and ran at the figure. In the swirling dust clouds he could barely make out the faces of the two people struggling for their lives, but it mattered little to him as raw fury seethed through his body.

A man was crouched over Kerry, his tongue hanging out as he tried to lick her face, his hands pinning hers to the ground.

Marcus swung a boot up into the man's jaw, felt the thump as his steel toe-caps impacted into the man's face, felt a crunch as the jawbone shattered. Marcus's boot swung up and through the man's face and to his surprise he saw the entire jawbone rip from the man's skull and spin away into the sunlight in a spray of blood.

The man's eyes rolled up into their sockets as he was flung from Kerry's body and hit the ground on his back. Kerry screamed again and lurched to her feet, her face plastered in dirty tears and thick blood staining the side of her hand as she held it to her neck and crouched over her pain.

For a long moment Marcus did not understand, and then a dawning horror crept upon him as he turned and saw the helicopter lift up and swing away to the north. He looked down at the man he had attacked and saw that his face was a bloodied mess, his tongue hanging from his ruined jaw like a bright pink snake. But his body was already covered in lesions from which hung tattered ribbons of blackened, dead flesh and his body was almost skeletal, emaciated. His eyes were stained yellow as though from jaundice and his nails had fallen out along with much of his hair.

Marcus didn't say the word, but he thought it just the same. *Apophysomyces*.

Marcus whirled and saw the compound airlock still open.

'Come on!'

He grabbed Kerry's arm and dragged her toward the airlock as from the far side of the compound he saw figures limping, crawling and trotting toward him.

'Oh please, no!' he gasped.

The people were infected, staggering on decaying limbs and struggling under the oppressive heat. Marcus hauled Kerry toward the airlock, trying to keep track of the figures circling the compound toward him. He was only a few yards from the airlock but they had less ground to cover, their eyes set upon him. In the silence after the helicopter's deafening departure, he could hear their groans and pleas.

'Kerry, move!'

Kerry was shuffling, one hand still stifling the blood spilling from her torn neck, but she looked up and saw the figures looming toward her and then started for the airlock with renewed urgency.

Marcus was almost there when, within, he saw Dr Reed standing and watching them. Something about Reed's expression sent a lance of apprehension bolting down Marcus's spine.

'Keep the door open!' Marcus yelled.

Dr Reed's face was stricken with regret, so deeply riven into his features that Marcus knew the old man's grief was not feigned, despite his holographic visage. Slowly, the *holosap* reached up to a light–panel on the wall.

'What are you doing?!' Kerry yelled at Reed.

'Don't shut the door Reed!' Marcus shouted. 'Don't do this!'

Dr Reed looked down, unable to meet Marcus's eyes.

Then, slowly but agonisingly quick enough for Marcus prevent it from happening, the airlock door hissed shut.

'No!'

Kerry reached the door and screamed as she pummelled it with her fists, leaving bloody stains all over the surface. Marcus saw Dr Reed still standing inside the airlock, perfectly able to step outside but for the guilt that must be wracking the old man's mind.

'I'll kill you!' Marcus shouted, not caring how ridiculous the threat sounded. 'I'll find a way and I'll kill you!'

Kerry stepped away from the door and looked left and right. Figures were lurching toward them, arms outstretched as they begged through ruined mouths for food and water, eyeing both Marcus and Kerry hungrily.

'Shit, Marcus!' Kerry shouted, unable in her pain and terror to formulate a more useful response.

Marcus looked up at the airlock and turned to her.

'Give me your boot,' he urged as he cupped his palms at waist level.

'What?!'

'I'll boost you up!' Marcus shouted. 'Hurry!'

Kerry lifted her foot up into his hands and Marcus launched her up onto the airlock roof, the aluminium construction bowing slightly beneath her weight but holding. Kerry scrambled to safety and then turned, reaching down for him.

'Come on!' she yelled.

Marcus looked left and right and knew that he had no time. Hands reached out to touch him and he whirled away and sprinted from the compound toward the dense mangrove swamps nearby.

'Marcus!'

A hand grabbed his neck and squeezed hard. Marcus swung his left arm across and batted the hand aside, felt the nails of the fingers scrape perilously hard across the skin of his neck as he staggered backward from the emaciated woman reaching out for him, her eyes laden with pain and horror, her mouth open in a scream silenced by dehydration and rotting vocal chords. A rush of stale, fetid breath wafted across his face and he retched, staggering backwards.

Marcus grabbed a desiccated branch lying on the ground and with a grunt of effort swung it at the woman's face as she advanced. The branch smacked into her temple and shattered as she span away and collapsed into the dust. Faces loomed closer, some laced with ugly tattoos, others with twisted scar tissue deforming their already ruined faces.

'Marcus!'

He heard Kerry's cry above the sound of the groaning, infected horde that turned and lumbered after him as he whirled and sprinted away, their footfalls pursuing him in a clumsy stampede. Some fell on the rugged ground, unable to walk on crumbling legs and with their brains and spinal columns turning to mush inside their bodies. He glanced over his shoulder and saw them, eyes fixated on him, toothless mouths hanging open and drooling with thick white saliva encrusted on their lips and chins.

He heard no cries of rage or hunger from them, just a muted chorus of misery from the dying as they begged in their own exhausted way for some kind of release from their suffering. Marcus ran harder and plunged into the thick cover of the nearby forest, rushing between the trees as clouds of insects swirled and buzzed on the hot air.

The danger of mosquito bites was not at all lost to Marcus, as was the hazard of using wet soil to protect his skin. One open wound, one lesion in the skin coated with soil, could infect him.

He reached down as he ran and scooped up a handful of moist soil and wiped it across his neck and face, up his arms and on his hands. There was little he could do about the odds of becoming infected, except to console himself that while the soil–to–skin contact *might* infect him, an infected mosquito bite certainly *would* infect him. Play the odds, Marcus.

A thousand thoughts rushed through his head as he ducked under twisted mangroves and leapt over buttresses of thick saw grass. The helicopter had to have been military because nobody flew anything anymore: fuel was more valuable than gold or diamonds these days. Although Marcus could not fathom why, for some reason Dr Reed had called in the military to clean the compound out and kill both Kerry and himself. Maybe it was Dr Reed who wanted to isolate the genes and take the glory for the discovery that saved mankind? He'd said as much himself. But the genes had not yet been tested, not on a human being anyway, so how could he be sure of success?

A new and terrifying possibility slithered through the vaults of his mind as he searched through the swamp for a route back to the compound, trying to move quickly and quietly while also desperate to avoid scratching himself on any foliage or trees.

Marcus slowed, breathing heavily in the humid air and listening to the billions of insects humming through the swamp. He glanced behind him and saw that his pursuers had fallen behind, blundering awkwardly through the mangroves. Quietly, Marcus eased his way through the forest on a wide circle around them as he turned back toward the compound. His main concern now was Kerry. Having been bitten she had perhaps just a few hours before the infection would spread through her bloodstream, reaching every corner of her body and beginning the horrific process of rotting her flesh from the inside out.

The Falling was in so many ways a classic zombie–like sickness, playing out like the script of a horror movie. Victims were reduced to shambling, groaning automatons desperate for food and water, increasingly unable to seek it for themselves. But far from being voracious consumers of human flesh, the true horror was their desperation. They keened and cried and begged for release, adults and children alike. The sickness dehydrated and starved them in cruel unison, driving them insane until they were far into the realms of diminished responsibility.

Marcus fought back tears as he recalled images of parents eating their children and vice versa, of troops unwilling to open fire on the suffering masses, understanding their pain and that they were not an enemy, not a predator. They were simply desperate beyond all imagination for surcease. By the time the military gave the order to fire at will in cities all over the world, that doing so was not genocide but virtually an act of kindness, the infection was far too widespread to be stopped.

The reality of a global pandemic was not one of a last minute miracle cure, or a heroic last stand against mindless zombie hordes. It was a tragedy of the human spirit quashed by unimaginable horror, with no end or saviour in sight for either the infected or the few terrified survivors.

And now the *holosaps* were turning against their human creators.

Why? The question returned to him over and over again. Why had the military tried to silence them? Why had Dr Reed betrayed them? And where the hell did they get a group of infected humans from? Most people had died years before out in the wilderness, decades before in fact, when the cities had become quarantined against the spread of the infection. Some had since fallen silent as, somehow, *The* Falling had broken through and decimated their populations. Others, like New York, survived still on a meagre supply of fuel and grain harvested from unyielding permafrost to the north.

The answers that sprang forth from his imagination terrified him. What if the humans had been deliberately infected for some reason? In his memory he saw their clothes, ragged but not old, their faces, many of them tattooed or bearing the scars of savage fights. Convicts, or perhaps criminals? Maybe tests were being run, a vaccine sought elsewhere in secret military experiments that nobody wanted to hear about?

Marcus began to wonder what else the military might be up to out here. The compound was supposed to be the only inhabited place south of Georgia in the entire continental United States: he and Kerry had been brought down the coast by boat, the only safe way to travel. A helicopter probably only had a range of a few hundred nautical miles, so where was it based and why had it undertaken such a risky mission in the first place? And if the military or the government wanted them dead, why not just use a missile to destroy the compound?

The answer leaped out at him: Kerry's discovery.

They wanted it, and for whatever reason he and Kerry were not to be a part of it. He could imagine the cover–up, reported by Dr Reed: either Kerry or Marcus had failed to secure the airlock properly. The infection had got inside the compound. It was a tragedy but there was no option but to abandon them to their fate.

Then the heroic work of government scientists in New York would uncover the secret of the antidote, the cure for The Falling. The government would be worshipped by the populace as they distributed the cure for free, thanked by the wider world. American economic and military dominance would be secured first, before the cure could be safely distributed around the globe. America would lead once again.

Marcus's body seethed with impotent rage at the injustice as he crept slowly up to the edge of the forest and peered between the thick branches and leaves at the compound barely a hundred yards away.

Kerry was gone and the compound airlock was yet again wide open.

***

23

Marcus squatted in the undergrowth and watched for several minutes, trying to ignore the insects buzzing in clouds around him. In the distance they looked so dense it seemed as though the bayou was aflame with lazy coils of smoke spiralling up on the hot thermals.

The airlock remained open.

The compound would by now be completely compromised, he had no doubt. The solar power generators would not be able to sustain positive air–pressure for this long against the open airlock. Insects would have flown in, probably the infected people would have wandered inside too.

Why had Reed opened it? Bait?

Marcus tried to second–guess the *holosap's* thinking, but with what he needed almost certainly inside he could think of no good reason as to why the doctor would have opened the door. He had achieved his aim. Marcus and Kerry could not survive long in the wilderness with so little to eat and the danger of infection and with their only likely saviour the potential cure locked beyond their reach in the compound.

Then he remembered: an act of evidence, that the compound had been breached due to negligence, perhaps on Kerry's or Marcus's part. A reason to explain their deaths away as infection. There was nothing that Dr Reed, a *holosap*, could do.

Marcus took a breath and moved forward.

A body slammed into him from one side and a pair of arms wrapped tightly around his neck as he crashed down into the dense undergrowth. Marcus grabbed at the arms and tried to yank them off of him but they gripped him like bars of iron bent by force of will about his neck, strangling him.

Marcus reached behind him, searching for a face, but his attacker buried their face into him to avoid his groping fingers and Marcus cried out desperately as he felt hot breath against the soft skin at the side of his neck, felt teeth sink in with terrible strength and pain as they punctured and burrowed deep into his flesh. Marcus screamed, and then suddenly he was free. He lurched to his feet in panic, leaping away from his attacker as he whirled to face them and kill them with anything he had to hand.

And then he froze.

Kerry looked up at him, her eyes wide with horror and disgust as she wiped her hands across her face, smearing Marcus's own blood across her lips. He stared down at her as a crushing sense of dismay plunged through his guts.

'Kerry?' he whispered as he felt tears pinch at the corners of his eyes.

Kerry spat a mouthful of blood and skin onto the soil as she got to her feet. 'We've got to leave,' she said.

Marcus stared at her, his jaw hanging open as though the tendons and muscles were already decaying, rotting inside of him. He held his hand to his bloodied, throbbing neck and felt his torn flesh hot beneath his fingers.

'You bit me,' he managed to utter.

'Only way to protect you.'

'To do *what*?'

'Come on, I'll explain on the way!'

The sound of helicopter blades thumping distant, hot air reverberated through as Kerry grabbed his shirt and yanked him into the forest. Marcus stumbled after her in a daze and together they ran through the mangrove swamps, their clothes drenched in sweat, clouds of insects boiling around them.

Marcus heard the helicopter land at the compound somewhere behind them, the sound of its rotors fading away. He realised that whoever was left aboard was now disembarking. He staggered after Kerry, who was running with the stamina of the insane. She smashed foliage aside with her arms as she forged a path away from the compound.

Marcus guessed that they'd covered a mile when she suddenly changed direction and picked a spot behind a large tree that sagged beneath the weight of its many branches. She squatted down, breathing heavily as Marcus slumped down alongside her, his chest heaving.

They sat for several moments until their breathing was back under control.

'You want to tell me what the hell you're doing?' Marcus uttered.

He touched his hand to the back of his neck and it came away smudged with blood and soil.

Kerry's reply seemed to reach him from another world. 'I'm immune.'

Marcus looked at her for what felt like an age before he could formulate a reply.

'You're what?'

'I'm immune,' she repeated. 'I can't catch The Falling, and now neither can you.'

Marcus briefly entertained the idea that The Falling had already infected her cortex, had maybe reached up into her brain and was addling her thinking.

'Kerry, there is no cure and no immunity. We were at the earliest stages of developing a vaccine and hadn't even begun to…'

'I added another test to the series,' Kerry added.

Marcus felt certain doom weigh in upon him. Kerry had lost it, joined the crazies of the world.

'There is no cure,' he repeated, slower this time as he tried to contain the anger now returning to run like poison in his veins. 'You're not thinking straight, Kerry, and now we're both infected and we're both going to die.'

Kerry rolled her eyes.

Marcus snapped. He reached out and grabbed her, yanked her to the floor. He saw the sudden panic in her eyes as he straddled her, both fists clenching her shirt up against her chin as he shouted into her face, spittle flying from his lips.

'You got infected and you bit me, you stupid, selfish, insane little *bitch*! You're out of your damned mind and now I'm going to die too, all because of Kerry and her stupid little dream world! Where the hell do you get off you idiotic little…–'

A sharp pain in Marcus's side cut him off and he looked down to see Kerry holding a sheath knife against his flank.

'Get off me,' she hissed, 'or I'll gut you like a fish right here.'

Marcus didn't let go of her, unafraid. 'I'm dead anyway. What's the difference?'

Kerry shook her head.

'You really think I'd be doing all of this if I wasn't sure that I could not get infected, you dumbass?'

Marcus stared down at her.

'We only captured the nutria yesterday,' he replied. 'You cannot have tested a cure in such a short time.'

'I didn't create a damned cure!' Kerry snapped and jabbed the knife into Marcus's side hard enough that he yelped as he leaped off her. 'I just isolated the gene and spliced it into human blood.'

Marcus watched as she stood up and brushed herself off, slipping the knife back into a sheath on the belt of her shorts.

'Human blood?' Marcus echoed, horrified.

'Mine,' she replied, and wiped more of Marcus's blood off her face with her forearm. 'The gene responsible for immunity in nutria was a protein similar to the CCR5 and human leukocyte antigen. I tried to get you and Dr

Reed to put the gene out into the wider world so that we could test it under different circumstances in different people, but neither of you would agree to it. In Dr Reed's case, I guess we now know why.'

Marcus shook his head.

'I don't know why he's done this but it must have been planned. You can't just call up a helicopter and a bunch of infected people out of nowhere.'

'They must have a test process of their own going on,' Kerry explained. 'A pool of people they can use to test viruses and infections on. I got a good look at them all before I escaped from the compound roof and they all looked like bad dudes to me, ex–cons or something.'

Marcus nodded. Back in New York there was no room to house serious offenders, the prisons themselves now homes to thousands of families. Instead, people convicted of serious crimes were simply taken out into the wilderness and left to fend for themselves, which was as good as a death sentence as infection occurred typically within a few days.

'How do you know that this gene in your blood will work?' Marcus asked. 'It could affect different populations in so many different ways.'

'The gene that causes The Falling was mutated in exactly the same way as many other genes that cause infectious disease, like HIV. CCR5 is found on the surface of human cells and is a bit like a lock that The Falling and other diseases can open in order to enter the cell and infect it. If you take stem cells and mutate them to be unable to open that lock, then inject them into a host, you develop that immunity within them because stem cells reproduce indefinitely. The new stem cells provide a permanent supply of resistant immune cells.'

Marcus blinked.

'That's a huge risk,' he said. 'You'd need a bone marrow transplant or similar to create immunity.'

'Not if you're uninfected when the stem cells are introduced,' Kerry insisted. 'They multiply within you, ready to fight off any infection that may occur. It's a vaccine, Marcus, a crude one but the best we've got right now.'

'But it might not work for everybody,' Marcus replied. 'We can't just assume we're in the clear! I don't like it.'

'Well what *would* you like?! If I had not done this we'd both be out here and entirely without any chance of survival!'

Marcus ran a dirty, bloodied hand through his hair as he tried to think straight.

'Why did Dr Reed open the compound door after I'd left?'

'He tried to convince me to come back inside,' Kerry said. 'He must have looked at my notes last night and figured out what I'd done. Reed must have opened the airlock when we heard the helicopter arrive. As soon as I stepped out to see what was happening that damned zombified freak attacked me. If you hadn't heard me scream we'd have both been trapped inside and probably been killed. If Reed's trying to take the glory for all of this he can't afford to have me running about out here alive and well with a dirty great bite mark in my neck.'

Marcus felt the weight of their predicament push down on him even harder as he looked about at the bayou forest around them.

'It hardly matters,' he said finally. 'Even if The Falling doesn't get us, we've got no food and water and there's nothing to hunt out here. We won't last more than a couple of days.'

Kerry inclined her head at him as though trying to understand.

'You really have led a sheltered life, haven't you Marcus?'

'What the hell's that supposed to mean?'

'We're surrounded by what we need to survive, if you just look around you.'

Marcus laughed bitterly. 'Yeah, at the trees and the stagnant water and the damned bugs! And even if you're suddenly able to survive out here, what then?'

Kerry gestured with a thumb over her shoulder in the direction of New Orleans.

'The nearest relay station,' she explained, 'to shut it down and get Dr Reed off our backs. He won't be able to transmit his *holosap* without it. And then we've got to get this knowledge out into the world before anybody gets to us.'

Marcus though for a moment. The relay stations were merely small hubs with communications dishes set at regular intervals along routes used by scientists travelling out into the dangerous wilderness, essential for local communications and also for passing *holosap* projections to join their human counterparts in the wilderness. The regional communication satellite at the city airport, however, was responsible for beaming information to other regional hubs in other states and countries. They had all been built at great risk to the constructors after the majority of satellites had fallen either silent or literally from orbit, and *holosaps* were dependent upon both to venture beyond their colonies in the remaining populated cities. Likewise, humanity relied upon the large, powerful regional communication dishes to stay in touch with each other.

'Send an electronic mail?' Marcus guessed.

'And quickly,' Kerry confirmed, 'because if this happened to us, how long do you think it will be before every other research station around the world is taken down by whoever is behind all of this.'

A brief mental image of the hundred or so research posts manned by courageous scientists searching for a cure flickered through Marcus's mind.

'I guess we'll know by the time we get there whether or not we're immune,' Marcus replied.

Kerry turned away from him and headed off into the forest. Marcus hurried after her.

'If we're not immune, we'll need to do something about it before…'

'Before what?' Kerry asked.

'Before we start falling to pieces,' he answered. 'You got bit first, so I'll have to take care of you and then finish myself off afterward.'

'Who said romance was dead?'

'I'm just trying to think ahead in case things don't work out.'

Kerry stopped, turned and grabbed his shirt.

'You know, you're not so bad,' she said, and gave him a brief kiss on the cheek.

'What was that for?'

'For risking your neck to boost me onto the compound roof,' she replied with a smile. 'You didn't know I was immune. It was very brave of you, even if you are a dumbass.'

Kerry released him and strode off.

Marcus stood for a moment, feeling both elated and meek, before he set off after her.

* * *

24

London

'This way!'

Arianna's ears were still ringing from the blast and she could hear chunks of brickwork falling down around her as the two armed men hustled her away down the alley past the chimney.

Arianna knew that somebody must have set charges to blow the apartment to pieces, because even the helicopter's powerful gun could not have produced such a devastating blast. She was supposed to have died in that explosion, all evidence of her being there removed. Kieran Beck and his men had planned their attack well. Now, the hooded men shoved and prodded her through the city. They wore no masks or other protective equipment, despite the increased danger of infection. Worse, they were forcing her south, away from the city.

'Where are you taking me?' Arianna asked, trying not to sound afraid.

'Somewhere safe,' answered the bigger of her two abductors.

The other man laughed a short, nasal chuckle. Although she could see neither of their faces, they sounded like criminals through and through, the kind of people who had been ejected from the city for their crimes. Being tossed out into a wilderness where every breath of wind carried the fear of death was considered a far greater punishment both by the judiciary and the people.

She glanced over her shoulder, and in the breeze that ruffled the men's deep hoods she glimpsed jawlines that seemed warped and disfigured, as though the two big men were as old as the hills, their skin haggard and wasted.

'This is abduction,' Arianna uttered.

Neither of the two men replied as they guided her down what had once been Tanner Street, according to the dirt encrusted signs, and down a long tunnel beneath what had once been a railway line. At the far end was parked a small jeep, painted dark green with stencilled black numbers painted on the side.

The fuel shortages meant that seeing a vehicle was a rarity these days.

'You've got a car even out here?' she uttered.

'Plenty of fuel about if you know where to look,' replied one of her abductors. 'Plenty of vehicles too, people left in such a rush. It's finding decent batteries that's hard.'

The two men prodded Arianna into the jeep and then climbed in the front, the leader's gun never straying far from Arianna's chest. To her dismay, they started the vehicle's engine and pulled away through the city to the south.

'You're heading the wrong way,' she said. 'There's nothing out here.'

Neither of the men replied. Arianna felt anxiety creeping like little insects through her veins.

'The further south we go the more dangerous it gets,' she insisted.

'The more you chatter back there the more dangerous it gets for you,' said the shorter man, jabbing the gun at her chest again as he leaned over his seat. 'You're lucky to be alive so just shut up, sit still and wait.'

The man turned back to the front, shaking his head and muttering as he did so. 'Damned women, never happy.'

Arianna suppressed an overwhelming desire to express the important gains made by the feminist movement over the past two hundred or so years. She figured it unlikely that the guy would have heard of suffragettes, and she didn't want to die just right now.

She looked back over her shoulder through the rippling canvass cover at the rear of the jeep, through a transparent plastic panel as the distant shape of the apartments and the chimney vanished slowly behind her, a column of smoke thinning and joining the buffeting clouds far above the river.

Han Reeves was still back there, with Myles Bourne at his side. She was suddenly struck forcibly by the realisation that the two detectives had actually crossed the river to pursue her.

'The police,' she said softly to herself.

'What's that?' asked the driver.

'They followed me, over the river. They wanted to kill me?'

Neither of the two men replied, and Arianna fell silent again and watched as the crumbling city drifted by.

Many of the lower lying streets were flooded with expansive pools of green water upon which floated a detritus of trash, the plastic legacy of mankind's creativity. Buildings towered hollow and grey against the tumbling clouds, and she fancied she could hear the lonely wind whistling through countless empty rooms.

The dense streets and buildings gave way steadily to more open roads and greenery. As the jeep weaved around abandoned cars clogging the streets or diverted around the stagnant lakes of water so she realised how the natural landscape was overcoming the houses, shops and supermarkets. Trees sprouted across car parks; vines, creepers and mosses were draped across walls and roof tops, and some routes were impassable due to the dense, tall grasses and weeds that had pushed through the tarmac surface of the road.

Arianna knew that they were well out of the city and some way into what had once been the county of Surrey when the driver of the car pulled off the main road. They had been passing the rusting hulks of abandoned cars and lorries for some time on what had once been the A3, but now they were driving down an unobstructed lane, the road apparently fresh and the route overhung by huge trees that cast a broad green canopy overhead.

The driver turned left onto a rutted track so well concealed from view that Arianna momentarily thought that he had taken a wrong turn. Thick brambles brushed and scraped along the side of the jeep as it was driven down the winding, steep track. Arianna glimpsed through the jeep's grubby windows a deep valley, open grassland and a narrow river nestled between soaring hills thick with trees.

The jeep slowed and stopped in the middle of the track and the driver switched off the engine.

'Get out,' he said.

Arianna fought back more anxiety as she clambered out of the jeep, the leader's gun still pointed at her as they led her several paces out in front of the car.

'On your knees, hands behind your head.'

Arianna gasped. 'You're not going to kill me are you?'

'Only if you don't shut up and do as I say.'

Arianna knelt down on the muddy track, pebbles and stones digging into her knees as she put her hands up behind her head.

To her amazement, her two captors mirrored her actions alongside her.

For a moment nothing happened, and then the bushes and weeds came alive around them.

Eight men stood up, their bodies entirely concealed within a mass of foliage packed against their uniforms. All of them held assault rifles that were pointed at Arianna. From behind them walked a ninth man, concealed beneath a thick green hooded coat and camouflaged trousers. He strode silently across to where Arianna knelt as his men hurried forward and checked her over for weapons.

Satisfied, the soldiers stood back as Arianna's captor's hauled her to her feet between them. The ninth man reached up and pulled back his hood, and Arianna gasped despite herself.

His face was like one of those Greek masks, grotesquely deformed on one side only. The face of a black man in his early forties who had once been quite handsome, a square–jawed, rugged looking type with thick curly black hair, stared down at her. But one side of his face was a ragged mass of scar tissue, the eye completely closed over and the ear just a ragged strip of tattered flesh long since healed.

When he spoke, his voice was distorted by the useless half of his mouth, which no longer bore any teeth or recognisable lips.

'Barry, Tim, good job. Take off and get some rest.'

Arianna's two abductors obediently walked away. The man watched them leave and then looked down at Arianna as though studying a different species.

'Welcome,' he lisped awkwardly, 'my apologies for the rough journey.'

Arianna swallowed, managed to contain wildly conflicting emotions of fear, hope, disgust and pity for this stranger standing fore square before her.

'Who are you?' she demanded. 'What the hell am I doing here?'

The man reached out and placed a hand on her shoulder. She glanced down at big digits, the skin calloused and worn by countless hours of labour needed to survive out here in the lonely wilderness.

'My name is Icon,' he said, 'and you're here to save yourself. Come, there is much that you need to know.'

Icon guided Arianna gently down the track, six of the soldiers forming a protective phalanx around them while the others melted back into the foliage, their weapons trained on the entrance to the track a hundred yards back up the hill.

They walked in silence for a few paces before Arianna spoke.

'You're not wearing any protection against The Falling.'

Icon inclined his head. 'Nor are you.'

'I could be infected at any moment.'

'Yes, you could.'

'And you're doing nothing about it,' she snapped.

'No, I'm not.'

Arianna almost laughed. 'Don't you care?'

Although she could not see the undamaged side of his face, Arianna still was able to detect the subtle shift in what remained of his facial muscles as he smiled.

'I care very much, actually,' he replied. 'But you becoming infected is, I'm afraid, inevitable.'

'It's what?'

'Inevitable,' Icon repeated as though she had genuinely not heard him.

Arianna stopped on the track and refused to budge further. Icon stopped and turned to face her.

'If so, then I'm doomed,' she retorted. 'I'm not doing another thing that you say.'

'Then you'll die, Arianna.'

She looked at him for a moment. 'I haven't told you my name.'

'I know your name,' Icon replied. 'Your face has been on the news for some time now.'

Arianna's eyes widened. 'You get broadcasts all the way out here?'

'There were plenty of solar panels left lying around when civilisation collapsed,' Icon replied. 'Plenty of receiver dishes too.'

Arianna's eyes narrowed. 'What do you mean I'll die if I don't do what you say?'

Icon extended his arm and gestured for her to continue down the track.

Arianna thought for a moment and then obeyed, walking with Icon alongside her as they descended to the floor of the valley. There, beneath the vast canopy of trees, was a camp of perhaps a hundred carefully camouflaged tents. As the sun briefly broke through the clouds above so dappled sunlight danced like fireflies across the surface of the tents.

'Welcome to Nirvana,' Icon said.

People watched her as she walked between the tents, peering out through gaps with eyes wide and silent. Although they were hidden in the shadows of their cramped homes and their heads held low behind hoods and scarves, she could see that their features were scarred and disfigured, twisted by the ravages of The Falling.

Yet they were still alive.

'You're immune,' she whispered in amazement. 'You're all immune to The Falling.'

Icon shook his head slowly.

'We have immunity inside us but we still contracted the sickness that you call The Falling,' he said. 'It damaged us all but not enough to kill us.'

Arianna slowed as people emerged from their tents, their courage bolstered by Icon's presence and their curiosity aroused by Arianna.

'The government says that there is no cure or natural immunity to The Falling,' Arianna whispered.

'I know,' Icon replied. 'They're lying.'

Every person Arianna laid eyes upon was disfigured in some way. Limbs were missing, skin warped and twisted into rivulets where scar tissue had knitted together once–rotten flesh. Bodies had chunks missing from torsos and chests, deep depressions where the infection had rooted itself but somehow never reached the major internal organs.

'It's not all they're lying about,' Icon said to her.

Arianna turned in the direction that Icon indicated and saw a satellite dish hooked up to a television monitor, one of the old types with a slim screen but a solid back made of plastic and with cables coming out of it. The sound was turned down but upon the screen was the news, and the news was about her.

'Oh my God,' she uttered in disbelief.

On the screen, a picture of Arianna's face was emblazoned beneath a caption that read in clear, bold letters.

RE–VOLUTION PSYCHOLOGIST KILLED IN TERRORIST ATTACK

Arianna looked up at Icon, whose lips twisted into a grim smile.

'You're looking remarkably well,' he said, 'for somebody who is already dead.'

* * *

25

Arianna watched the screen as the residents of Nirvana crowded silently around her. Some of them were children who touched her skin and face in wonder, marvelling at how smooth and clear it was.

'Be gentle with them,' Icon said beside her. 'They have never seen a person who has no scars. Many were babies when they became infected.'

Arianna let them touch her as she spoke. 'They didn't inherit the immunity of their parents?'

'They did,' Icon said, 'but it is through infection that the immunity becomes effective. We do not know why. None of us have escaped without first having to endure the sickness.'

Arianna watched the news report on the screen and saw the smouldering remains of the apartment block.

'Can the sound be turned up?' she asked Icon.

'No need,' Icon said, 'they've been running the piece all day. It says that police carried out an assault on a suspected criminal hideout south of the Thames in the old city. During their approach, an individual named as Arianna Volkov, a priest and qualified psychologist contracted to Re–Volution Ltd who was recently questioned about an alleged involvement in the terrorist attack on the company yesterday, opened fire from a top–floor apartment. Police returned fire, and a gas leak in the building caused an explosion in which Miss Volkov died.'

Arianna's hand flew to her lips as she saw further aerial shots of the pile of rubble that had once been her adoptive father's hideout.

'Were there any other supposed fatalities?' she asked Icon.

The man looked at her curiously. 'Apparently the remains of two men were also found in the rubble by rescue teams about an hour ago.'

Arianna turned away from the screen, her eyes blurring with tears that she swiped angrily away.

'You knew them?' Icon asked.

Arianna got back control of her breathing. 'There were police detectives on the scene,' she explained. 'They questioned me after the Re–Volution attack.'

Icon raised his one eyebrow at her. 'They set you up and tried to kill you and yet you mourn them?'

Arianna shook her head. 'I don't know what's going on, or who to trust.'

Icon chuckled to himself. 'Isn't that standard procedure in the city? Come, I will tell you what I *do* know, and then perhaps you can help me with what I don't.'

Icon led her through the camp, the little crowd of children and parents following them within interest. Arianna noticed that there were no fires, despite the chill air. Instead, thermal blankets, sleeping bags, insulation and closely packed tents seemed to be all the inhabitants of Nirvana had to warm themselves against the cold.

'Not exactly living up to its name, your little town,' she observed.

'We're happy enough,' Icon replied. 'The police and government send patrols out into the suburbs and helicopters to fly out even as far as this in search of us. We do our cooking a half–mile from here to prevent them from detecting us using their infra–red cameras. In Nirvana, staying inside the tents, inside our bedrolls and being beneath the trees is just enough to prevent easy detection.'

'The police know you're all out here?" Arianna asked. 'Are you all convicts?'

Icon did not reply as he led her into a larger tent at the rear of the camp, tucked in against the steep side of the valley. Inside, a bed and a table dominated the tent, which was just large enough to stand up in. Maps on the table suggested this tent doubled as Icon's home and a planning room.

Icon eased himself with a weary sigh into a folding chair that bulged as it tried to contain his huge frame, and gestured to another nearby. Arianna sat down as Icon spoke.

'Most of us are not convicts,' he said. 'They stay near the Thames, where they can still trade items with people in the city from time to time. What we represent is a dirty little secret that the government doesn't want anybody else to know about. We're the ones who became infected but survived The Falling because we carry antibodies in our blood that make us immune.'

'Why would they lie about that?' Arianna gasped in amazement. 'They could have formulated a cure by now, a vaccine against The Falling. They could have saved lives, millions of lives and…'

'I know,' Icon said softly, stalling her tirade with a casual waft of his hand. 'We all know.'

Arianna sat back for a moment. The expression on her face was a question in itself, and Icon answered.

'Most of us were cut off when the city of London was quarantined against infection, locked out and left to die. The majority of victims went insane with pain or died from starvation or dehydration or blood loss. Others preyed on those more advanced with the disease, surviving by eating the flesh of the dying until they too eventually died or were eaten by others. It was horrific, to say the least. Others, like myself, fled the city for the countryside. I figured that it didn't matter if all the cows, dogs, cats, rodents and birds were dying too. I could eat the healthy bits of anything I caught in the hope that by some miracle I survived this.'

He pointed to the ruined side of his face. Arianna glanced at it but then looked away.

'No,' Icon said, 'look at it.'

He got up and walked across to her, bent down so that his cratered, shining scar tissue was inches from her face. Arianna looked. She could see beneath the sinewy skin the shape of Icon's skull and jaw, saw the tendons and muscles flex and twist as he spoke.

'This is as far as it got,' he explained, and touched his face once again as he stood up straight and returned to his seat. 'I used to be a soldier, so I knew how to survive in the wild for limited periods. I caught fish, slept out under the trees on makeshift beds and tried to keep myself clean despite the smell of decaying flesh falling off the side of my head.'

'And it just stopped, just like that?' she asked him.

'After a few days of considerable pain, and obviously a lot of damage to my face, I noticed that the smell of dead flesh was fading. I found an abandoned house and a mirror, and watched for the next few weeks as the skin and flesh healed and scars began to form. I was lucky. When we were cut off from the city most people went on the rampage for food and water. I didn't. I took medicine. That's the clue to survival, you see. You can learn to find food, to purify water, to sleep at night in the wild, but you can't fix blood poisoning or gangrene or cure a broken leg out here. I took boxes of every pain killer, anti–biotic and medical dressing I could find and brought them with me out here.'

Arianna could not help but admire Icon's sheer tenacity.

'So you survived,' she said, 'and started looking for others?'

Icon nodded. 'I wasn't sure if it was the medicine or pure luck that cured me, but I figured that whatever it was there were other people who needed it too. Once I was fully healed and fit, I went in search of others. They're the people with me in this camp. Every one of them both survived The Falling and the human panic that it caused, and was close enough for me to find them and teach them to survive out here.'

Arianna glanced out of the tent, where she could see people milling about, waiting patiently for her to emerge once more.

'There must be a reason for why you're being hunted,' Arianna said.

'I don't doubt it,' Icon agreed. 'If the citizens of London discover that there is immunity to The Falling, the government will fall overnight. There haven't been elections for years. We're living under a dictatorship in all but name.'

'We still have a free press,' Arianna began, 'and if we can get this to them…'

Icon laughed out loud, spittle drooping from his ruined lips and his big barrel chest heaving as he shook his head and pointed out of the tent. 'You mean the same free press that's reported you dead on the word of the government alone?'

Arianna kept her demeanour calm as she replied.

'It's not possible to silence all of the people all of the time,' she said. 'The press might have no more idea than I did that your people are out here or that I'm still alive.'

'Very true,' Icon agreed, 'and very foolish on the part of the government if they have assumed that you were killed in the explosion.'

'It wasn't the government,' Arianna said, 'at least not entirely.'

'What do you mean?' Icon growled, leaning closer to her, his dark eyes focused on hers.

'Kieran Beck,' Arianna said. 'He and his men were there. They tried to kill me.'

Icon watched her for a long moment before speaking.

'That does not surprise me at all,' he rumbled. 'Even so it's not like them to rush such an announcement out without being certain of the facts. It is most likely connected to the planned vote on *holosap* control of government. They're in a hurry to push it through and we must endeavour to prevent that.'

Arianna's blood ran cold as she remembered where she was sitting and with whom.

'So you'll commit another terrorist attack?' she uttered. 'Kill another few innocent civilians?'

'We have committed no such atrocities,' Icon assured her.

'How am I supposed to believe that?'

'You're not,' Icon admitted, 'that's the whole point. But we have no access to the city and frankly we wouldn't want to go there at all.'

'Why?'

'We may be immune to The Falling, but we remain *carriers* of the infection.'

Arianna froze on her chair. 'Carriers? You mean you can infect people?'

'Yes,' Icon replied. 'With the same ease as I could pass to you a common cold.'

Arianna swallowed and Icon made his best attempt at a reassuring smile.

'Don't worry,' he said, 'I have no desire to infect you or anybody else, which is why we would never enter the city. If we were to inadvertently infect a single person it could result in millions more dying and perhaps even the loss of London in its entirety. None of us would want that on our conscience.'

'So you stay out here,' Arianna whispered almost to herself. 'But if you're not doing it then who the hell is?'

'Re–Volution,' Icon replied. 'It's the only answer we can think of.'

'The company is bombing its own people?'

'Think about it,' Icon implored her. 'Re–Volution controls access to *holosap* technology, which costs extortionate amounts of money despite the human race facing annihilation from The Falling. It's profiteering gone mad. As long as they have the only definite cure for infection, that of uploading, then they will continue to reap profits from the human population. They have a monopoly on the only technology that could conceivably outlast mankind.'

Arianna frowned.

'But if every human dies and only *holosaps* are left, then surely the revenue dries up?'

'You're forgetting the storage issue,' Icon pointed out. 'By law, only Re–Volution can permanently erase somebody from existence after they've uploaded. By maintaining complete control of the system they can charge *holosaps* simply for the right to continue existing. A life tax, if you can properly call a *holosap* alive.'

Arianna stared at the news screen for a few moments before speaking.

'They can't be doing all of this alone, they must be getting help.'

'From the police, and from a few highly placed individuals within the government, the most prominent of which is Prime Minister Tarquin St John.'

'A *holo*–sympathiser,' Arianna recalled. 'He's been banging a drum for years for equal rights for *holosaps*, the passing of laws in their favour and so on.'

'The same,' Icon agreed, 'and if I'm right he's the one most likely to pull the plug on humanity in favour of a *holosap* future. He sees it as our next natural evolutionary step, believe it or not.'

'We've got to stop him,' she replied. 'We've got to stop whatever he and Kieran Beck are planning.'

Icon was about to speak when the sound of running footfalls rushed up to the tent entrance and one of Icon's men yanked the tent flap aside.

'Somebody's coming,' he snapped, and cast a suspicious glance at Arianna. 'They're armed.'

* * *

26

Bayou La Tour

Louisiana

The dawn sky loomed over the bayou, the horizon awash with a flare of sunlight as the stars glistened overhead, lonely deep blue heavens above a lonely planet.

Marcus crouched with Kerry in a creek that hummed with insects, stagnant water filled with algae clinging to his boots. The air was cooler, in that it was breathable and did not scorch the lungs yet, but the temperature would soon rocket upward again.

Ahead, across a broad stretch of ground cleared long ago, was a dome–like structure with a satellite dish the size of a house mounted alongside it. The structure was silhouetted against the rising sun, mankind's sharp and angular architecture crude against nature's elegant wash of colour.

'Can we make it?'

Kerry's voice was soft on the morning air, partly for fear of being heard by real or imagined troops laying in ambush ahead, and partly because of her exhaustion. They had walked all night to reach the relay station in the hope of beating any intercept mission, but it was almost without doubt that the troops would anticipate this move.

'We won't know until we head out there.'

Like Kerry, Marcus had spent the last eight or so hours thinking about their plan, a sure chance to get properly paranoid. They were being pursued by trained troops, of that he was sure, but those troops would be weighed down by heavy suits and breathing apparatus. They could fly helicopters to search the bayou, but Marcus had heard no aircraft during the night.

That left only one possibility.

'Wasps,' he muttered. 'They can't hit the relay station with heavy weapons without disrupting the entire communications chain and defeating the object of stopping us, so they'll come at us using Wasps.'

WASPS was the military's acronym for Wi–fi Automated Strike, Paralysis and Surveillance drones. The size of a small bird, Wasps looked exactly like their insectoid cousins only much larger, louder and far more dangerous. Laden with all manner of micro–sized sensors, their most dreaded asset was a two–inch hypodermic delivery system, a sting in the tail that injected victims with a dose of either *Pancuronium bromide* for paralysis and later questioning, or a lethal toxin for when agony simply wasn't enough to make the military's day.

In the gloomy half light of dawn, Kerry's features were taut and her eyes shadowed.

'They're automated,' she whispered. 'Too many stings and you're dead no matter what happens.'

Marcus nodded, scanning the horizon. 'The bayou's big. They'll send out plenty and hope to get troops out to us before we're killed.'

Everybody had seen the news reports and the documentaries covering major assaults by the police when Wasps had been involved. Marcus could not shake from his mind an image of a criminal writhing in unimaginable pain as a swarm of glossy black Wasps stung him over and over until he was a bloated mess, blood pouring from his wounds as he thrashed himself into a cardiac arrest.

'We should wait until it's light,' Marcus said. 'Wasps work better at night.'

'They've got infra–red, right?' she asked.

'Yeah,' Marcus agreed, 'so they can see targets in the dark, but maybe it's hot enough in the day to conceal us a little.'

'We don't have enough time to spare,' Kerry said. 'We wait too long they'll be on us anyway.'

'Shit,' Marcus whispered. 'It's got to be over a hundred yards.'

'Then let's make it quick, okay?'

He touched her shoulder and she reached up and squeezed his hand. They stood, and after a brief hesitation they plunged without a word from the treeline and sprinted across the open ground.

The shadowy terrain was rough and filled with unseen crevices and pot holes. Marcus stumbled and weaved breathlessly to keep up with Kerry as she flew like a gazelle across the open ground, her long hair flying behind her head like a banner. Marcus saw her skid to a halt in front of the station door and yank a set of keys from her jacket.

'Thank God they don't use digital locking out here,' Marcus gasped as he stumbled up alongside her.

The station door was secured using two stainless steel padlocks that restrained two equally tough sliding bolts. The human population was too long gone for any concerns about vandalism when the station was built, while the fear of battery failure or signal disruption in the bayou's heat precluded the use of remote locking. Even with the huge satellite dish and the relay stations, Dr Reed's *holosap* projection had often been broken and weak at the compound. Kerry and Marcus carried keys for all remote stations in their area.

Kerry opened the padlocks and slid the bolts back before heaving the door open and hurrying into the building's absolute blackness. Marcus followed her in and slammed the door behind him, pushing the bolts back through.

Lights flickered on as Kerry hit a switch, illuminating a large room half filled with a pair of small computer banks and a solar powered cooling system. Above, a skylight stained with dust and grime looked up into the brightening sky at the satellite dish above.

A single computer terminal, unused in years, waited patiently. Kerry hurried over and started the computer, which hummed into life.

'They'll have thought of this,' Marcus reminded her as he joined her at the desk, watching the antiquated computer boot up. There was no transparent screen, just a slim plastic–backed monitor and a touch–pad embedded into the surface of the desk.

'Maybe,' Kerry agreed, 'but with only us and Dr Reed out here they won't have been able to do much about it unless they've hacked this relay station out of the loop.'

'Can they do that?' Marcus asked, watching as Kerry began sifting through files.

'Maybe,' she replied.

Marcus, standing over Kerry, suddenly smelled something odd on the air. His gaze was drawn down and he felt a terrible fear ripple like insects through his gut as he saw the flesh around Kerry's bite wound.

The bite had turned black, with bruised and yellowed skin expanding away from the wound. Around the circumference of the bite Kerry's once flawless skin was spilling away in infected chunks that had the odour of road kill.

'Kerry,' he whispered, 'your wound.'

'I know,' she replied, her gaze remaining fixed upon the monitor before her. 'It's been getting worse all night and I feel like crap, some kind of fever.'

'What if you're not immune?' he asked.

'Then this is all for nothing,' she snapped back. 'But we're dead either way Marcus so let's try and make what we can of it, okay? If I've got to go to my grave I may as well try to take these bastards with me, agreed?'

Marcus nodded, enshrouded with despair at Kerry's fatalistic assessment of their chances.

'So how are we going to do it?' he asked.

'First, we have to cut the compound and this relay station off from New York, which we can do from here. That will hopefully stop Dr Reed from communicating with other governments around the world for a while.'

'He'll have been in touch with home base long ago,' Marcus pointed out. 'And those troops are already deployed here, somewhere.'

'Yes, but they haven't caught us yet. We keep disrupting them while moving toward the main communication hub at the airport.'

She flicked through files and folders until she found what she was looking for.

'Here,' she said. Marcus looked at a bank of data files, big numbers that changed continuously as Kerry explained. 'That's data moving back and forth between our compound, this relay station and the airport.'

'Can't he just send information out from the airport's main hub?'

'Not if he can't get out here to see what we're doing,' she replied.

Marcus watched as Kerry hurriedly began re–routing files and re–coding data. He stood back and turned to survey the station's interior. The sky outside was much brighter now and heat was beginning to build from the computer banks and from the sunlight entering the station.

'There's no food or water,' he said.

'It's a remote station,' Kerry pointed out as she typed, 'why would there be?'

'How long will this take?'

'Not long, if you'll just shut the hell up.'

Marcus stood in the centre of the station and felt something odd touching his senses, as though a gossamer web had drifted through the field of his awareness like an errant thought. He turned full circle, frowned to himself.

'Something's not right,' he said.

'I'm nearly there,' Kerry said, 'then we can get the hell out of here.'

'Hurry,' Marcus urged.

Kerry typed a few more lines of text and then hit the Enter key. Marcus saw lines of code updating themselves and then the cursor on the screen returned to its normal position, blinking patiently.

'Shit,' she muttered.

'Is that it?' he asked.

'No,' Kerry shook her head. 'We're out of the loop already, they've cut us off to stop us sending messages from here. We need to get to the airport hub and send a message from there as fast as possible.'

Marcus hesitated, struck by the feeling that he'd suddenly recalled an old memory that he'd believed lost forever.

'What's up?' Kerry asked, staring at him.

'I don't know,' he replied, 'I just… I just get the feeling that this had all been predicted by them, that we're already playing into their hands.'

The voice that replied belonged to neither himself or Kerry. 'You have been, Marcus.'

Marcus whirled, and saw Dr Reed's *holosap* shimmer into existence on a projection platform barely inches from where he stood.

'You've been watching us!' Kerry exclaimed in horror.

Dr Reed smiled. 'I've been waiting for you all night,' he said. 'I don't need sleep much, you see. It's fabulous, the amount of control us *holosaps* have over brain function.' Dr Reed peered at Marcus's bite wound, and then at Kerry's. 'So, you believe that you have immunity to The Falling?'

Kerry reached up self-consciously to the rancid flesh on her neck. 'There's no *belief* required,' she replied.

'A pity,' Dr Reed said, 'that you decided to take such a chance, to make such a leap of imagination without first completing your research.'

'So you could take it?' Kerry spat.

'No,' Reed replied, 'so I could confirm or deny it. I'm sorry, Kerry, but you're immune to nothing. That infection will kill you, probably within a day or so. Marcus will, of course, follow suit. Just like you said, you're both dead no matter what you do.'

'Not if we get word out,' Kerry replied. 'Somebody, somewhere will hear us.'

Dr Reed inclined his head in acquiescence. 'Perhaps, but by then it will be too late for all of you.'

'All of us?' Marcus echoed. 'What do you mean *all* of us?'

'All humans,' Dr Reed smiled without warmth. 'Didn't you know? You're number's up, Marcus. We don't need any of you anymore.'

A sudden crack like a gunshot made Marcus jump and he flinched away from the skylight above, fearing troops making an assault on the station with guns blazing. But there were no troops.

On the thick plastic surface of the skylight a jet black insect the size of Marcus's hand skittered with mechanical efficiency, wings humming occasionally as it tried to enter the station through the plastic. A two-inch stinger protruded from its tail.

'Wasps,' Kerry said in a trembling voice.

Moments later, the plastic skylight rattled as dozens more Wasps landed outside the station.

* * *

27

'You led them here,' Marcus gasped.

Dr Reed, his hands in his pockets, shrugged. 'They followed me. They're linked in to my *holosap* generator at Re–Volution via the communication hub.'

Kerry turned to Marcus, ignoring Dr Reed. 'Get me a syringe from that medical pack.'

Marcus turned to the Medipac box hanging on the wall. Although a remote station, the terrain of the bayou meant that all locations housed emergency survival packs in case of injury to service personnel operating in the local area.

Dr Reed watched as Marcus unpacked the syringe.

'You're wasting your time,' Reed said as he glanced up at the Wasps skittering about on the skylight. 'There's no food or water here and those Wasps will soon find a way inside.'

Marcus looked at Kerry, but she said nothing as she rolled up her left sleeve. Marcus moved across to her as she flexed her fist and a vein appeared in the crook of her arm.

'Ah,' Dr Reed murmured as Marcus gently slipped the needle into her arm. 'Trying to send your blood work out into the world are we? You'll never get to the airport before you die, or the Wasps catch you.'

Marcus drew Kerry's blood and then eased the needle out again as she held a finger over the wound and reached for a plaster. Marcus carefully capped the needle as he waited for her to roll her sleeve back down.

'They're working it out,' Dr Reed said again, looking up at the skylight.

Marcus realised that the Wasps were gone from the skylight, but he could still hear their metallic legs rattling about outside the compound.

'The air conditioning vents,' Marcus realised.

'We don't matter anymore,' Kerry snapped as she grabbed the syringe from him. 'All that matters is getting this out to other research stations.'

'Which no longer exist,' Dr Reed said from behind them. 'The assault was inclusive.'

'What assault?' Marcus asked.

'The one launched by troops across the globe, Marcus,' Reed smiled with ingratiating smugness. 'There will be no cure for your pitiful sickness.'

As Kerry began transferring her blood from the syringe to a test tube, Marcus stood between her and Dr Reed.

'You know, for somebody who thinks that we're not immune you're awfully worried about us not completing our work here,' Marcus said.

Dr Reed shrugged again. 'Worried? Me? Not really, Marcus. Sooner or later you'll be dead and I...' He smiled. 'Well, I won't be.'

'If word gets out about this,' Marcus said, 'every *holosap* on the planet will be shut down.'

'I wonder,' Dr Reed mused, 'if you realise just how big of an *if* that is?'

The scuttling sounds grew louder and Marcus realised that the Wasps were dismantling the mesh shields on the outside of the station that covered the air conditioning vents. He heard the sound of buzzing wings beating the air outside echoing down into the station interior along with the squeal of metal incisors on metal vents.

'Tick tock,' Dr Reed smiled at Marcus.

'Were you always like this?' Marcus asked, masking his increasing fear with a thin veil of bravado, 'or was being an asshole something you learned?'

The clatter of small fragments of metal falling like stones inside the air conditioning vents told Marcus that the Wasps were chewing their way through the shields using their metallic mandibles, lined with tiny diamonds that could slice through just about anything.

'They're going to get through,' he whispered to Kerry.

She didn't reply, the fingers of one hand flying across the keyboard as with the other she swirled her blood in the test tube.

'The screening will take at least an hour,' Dr Reed pointed out. 'Those Wasps will get through within minutes.'

Marcus looked up at the interior vents, large enough that the Wasps could easily crawl through. The wire–fabric mesh inside the conduit, designed to prevent airborne insects from entering the station, would not stop them.

'The troops will be here too,' Dr Reed added, 'in about ten minutes I'd imagine. If the Wasps aren't through by then, the troops will just blow open the front door and let them in. There's really nothing that you can do, Marcus.'

The fear in Marcus's gullet twisted into rage as he whirled and swung his fist through Dr Reed's face. The *holosap's* image flickered briefly and he smiled that infuriating, casual smile.

'Temper, temper young Marcus. It's all futile. My image is appearing at the same time in two different places. The speed of light and all that. I've briefed the troops on what you're doing and I can assure you they're fully prepared.'

Marcus whirled away from the *holosap* and looked at the front door for a moment, the bolts still in place. They were safely locked inside by the only means of escape.

A crack sounded from above him and he saw a Wasp land on the skylight and begin chewing on the plastic, the inch–long diamond tipped mandibles scratching and scraping. Two more Wasps joined it and began likewise chewing. As he stared up at them he saw one of the Wasps tilt its head to peer down at him with its large and soul–less black eyes.

Marcus shivered and turned away. He tore off his shirt and reached up to pin it over the skylight, preventing the Wasps from looking inside.

'I don't think that's going to save you,' Dr Reed chortled. 'Feel like hiding under your duvet, Marcus?'

Marcus looked across at Kerry, who had stopped twirling the test tube and was now typing frantically with both hands.

'Whatever you're doing, hurry it up!' he yelled at her.

Kerry kept typing as from within the air conditioning conduit Marcus heard the vents collapse and a loud buzzing noise echo toward them. The sound of the mandibles chewing on the skylight vanished as the Wasps there abandoned their position and headed for the breached vent.

'They're coming through!' Marcus yelled.

'Time,' Dr Reed said, 'for you both to die.'

Marcus leaped across the station and yanked at the main door's bolts, hoping to beat the Wasps out and make a run for it. Behind him, he heard Kerry still typing.

'Come on, run!' he yelled.

The air conditioning vent inside the building rattled as the Wasps slammed against it in their haste, and Marcus saw shiny black legs and mandibles poke through between the slats as they fought to crawl through the gaps.

Marcus ran back across the station and grabbed a chair. He swung the chair up and smashed the metal leg across the matchbox sized head of a Wasp. The drone's head cracked to one side and a beady black eyeball dented inward, but the Wasp's legs kept scraping as it crawled through the gap.

Marcus's heart fluttered in panic in his chest as he staggered away from the vent as the gigantic Wasp heaved itself through and beat its wings as it headed straight for Kerry. Marcus screamed and swung the chair again and batted the Wasp out of the air above her head. The Wasp hit the wall with a metallic clang and dropped down to land on its legs.

Two more Wasps burst through the vent and with a loud buzzing shot straight toward Marcus as the damaged Wasp took off again and zoomed toward him. Marcus tumbled backward toward the door in terror as he swung the chair one more time.

One Wasp took the blow directly and flew across the station, but the other two avoided the strike and collided with Marcus as he shrieked in disgust and horror. He grabbed one of them in one hand, its body hard and cold and its sinewy plastic wings beating against his hand as he hurled it away. It turned over in mid–air and hovered before darting back toward him, its huge stinger catching the light as it rushed in.

The station filled with Wasps as Marcus screamed and collapsed and threw his hands and arms over his head in a last ditch attempt to protect himself as the Wasps collided with him and crawled across his body, their legs hard metal spikes that dug into his skin. He heard Kerry scream nearby, and then silence.

'Kerry!'

The Wasps hung onto his body with their pincer–like mandibles, but Marcus felt no stingers impaled into his flesh as he lay crawled up into a foetal ball in the corner of the station. Then, suddenly, the Wasps took off again and flew to the opposite corner of the station and landed together in a big, black metallic ball, their legs tucked beneath themselves as the sound of their beating wings fell silent.

Marcus stared at Kerry, who was sitting staring at the computer screen, her chest heaving with panic and her hair in disarray where a Wasp had evidently landed on her head. She turned her head slowly and looked at him.

'Wasps deactivated,' she gasped.

'Deactivated?' Dr Reed almost shouted in disbelief.

'Hibernation mode,' Kerry muttered as she focused back on her screen. 'Priorities, Doctor Reed. I'm good at prioritising. You said that they tracked your *holosap* signal, so logically there had to be a signal I could hack. I thought I'd handle the Wasps before you.'

'It's futile,' Dr Reed insisted, 'the troops will be here any moment!'

Marcus clambered to his feet, his skin still tingling at the horror of what had almost occurred. He rubbed at the indentations in his skin from where the Wasps had clung to him.

'You hacked them?' he uttered at Kerry.

'I call it reprogramming,' she replied without looking at him. 'You're welcome.'

Marcus almost laughed out loud as he threw his arms around her. 'You're a genius.'

'Get off me,' she urged without rancour. 'I've got the rest of the day to save too y'know.'

Marcus released her with a grin as he turned to Dr Reed. The *holosap* tried to move closer to the computer but was stopped at the edge of the projection platform.

'What's up, Dr Reed?' Marcus asked. 'Feeling a tad inadequate? You're not half the man you used to be, remember?'

'It's over,' Dr Reed insisted. 'The troops are almost here.'

'Can we shut him down from here?' Marcus asked Kerry over his shoulder.

'No,' Kerry replied as she worked, 'but we can shut him up.'

'What are you doing?' Dr Reed snapped at her.

Kerry did not reply as Marcus joined her. The Doctor continued to demand to know what was happening, but Marcus found that he enjoyed infuriating Reed by pretending that he wasn't there at all. Which in many ways, he wasn't.

Kerry finished typing and looked not at Dr Reed but at the screen. 'Goodbye,' she smiled.

She tapped a key and moments later the relay station's computers shut down one after the other. Marcus saw rage flare briefly in Dr Reed's expression, his mouth working as he shouted, but no sounds came forth and then the *holosap* flickered and vanished as the transmission was broken.

'He'll have told the troops that we've deactivated the Wasps,' Kerry said, 'but by now he'll be back in New York or maybe the airport hub, completely unable to watch us.'

'Good,' Marcus said, 'so what do we do now?'

Kerry tapped a few more commands into the computer, hit "Enter", and then leaped up out of her seat.

'We run!'

Marcus barely had time to think when he heard the buzz of the Wasp's wings beating the air once more. He whirled and followed Kerry out of the station, helping her slide the locks through the door behind her but noting that she did not use the padlocks this time. Instead, she hurled them into the bushes as they slammed the doors behind them and fled.

Marcus ran with her for a hundred yards into the cover of the forest before they ducked down and looked back as the sound of a distant engine growled through the bayou.

Within minutes a troop transporter fought its way to the station and twelve armed men jumped from the rear, all wearing HazMat suits.

'What did you do to the Wasps?' he whispered to Kerry.

'They can't be reprogrammed to target individuals without the proper access codes,' Kerry whispered back, 'but in an emergency you can set them to something called *melee*.'

'As in battle?' Marcus asked.

Kerry looked at him as the soldiers opened the station doors and smiled as they heard sudden screams drift their way on the hot air. Marcus saw the soldiers stumbling and falling away from the station, heard panicked gunfire as the Wasps burst from within the station and attacked with blind fury anyone within sight, their cruel stingers easily piercing the troop's suits.

Marcus looked at Kerry and shook his head in wonder. 'You really are a genius,' he said finally. 'I mean it.'

Kerry winked at him. 'I'm a woman,' she said. 'Come on, before those Wasps start looking for anybody else to kill.'

Marcus got up and crept away after her, the city of New Orleans looming through the distant haze.

* * *

28

Re–Volution Headquarters

Centre Point Tower

London

'Welcome, Prime Minister.'

Tarquin St John shook Kieran Beck's hand, the former investment banker's grip not as strong as St John's and far briefer. Beck was a man used to living behind the scenes, rarely appearing on television or in public, probably because of the weight of public animosity toward Re–Volution.

Beck's forehead was patched with a small surgical dressing, mild lesions just visible marking his skin.

'I appreciate the invite, Kieran,' St John replied.

'Not at all, especially after your performance of this morning.'

'It was nothing more than my duty,' St John said, and glanced again at Beck's injury. 'What happened?'

'Fell,' Beck replied. 'Hit my head on the wall. Lucky there's nothing much up there to damage. Come, please sit down.'

St John joined Beck on two sumptuous leather seats arranged around a painfully expensive smoked glass coffee table. Beck had made tens of millions of dollars trading in commodities before investing heavily into the early research efforts of Re–Volution. A shrewd and quick–thinking businessman, Beck had seen the huge potential of Holonomic Brain Theory and its revolutionary mating with quantum storage in producing the first viable holographic human entity while the technology was still in its infancy. The rest, quite literally, was human history.

St John looked around the simple office that was Kieran Beck's inner sanctum. Virtually nobody visited the top floor of Re–Volution, so dense was the security surrounding the company's innermost workings. Due to the threat from terrorist groups, many of the company's board of director's identities were a state secret, and it was rumoured that they used body–

doubles as a fail safe and entered the headquarters building through underground tunnels to protect their identity and safety from those who would wish them harm.

St John, for his part, could not fathom why anybody would want to maim or murder the very people that represented the likely salvation of what was left of the human race.

The view from the top of the Centre Point Tower was panoramic, and looked out to the south over the Thames toward the derelict city beyond. St John could see the jumble of London's city blocks stretching away toward the river, beyond which were the remains of the London Eye, only the lower half of the huge Ferris Wheel still standing and entombed in vines and green mosses. Beyond, the city was a geometric pattern of tower blocks consumed by nature's random canvass of forest and foliage that stretched out into the now untamed wilderness of dense woodland that had once been the Home Counties.

The view to the north, he knew, was much the same, but this time the barrier to the wilderness was not a river but the railway line that ran through Islington. On the far side of the tracks was a sixty–foot high fence that ran for miles and encased Greater London to the east and west, patrolled by police and carefully trained dogs for any sign of a breach. It was rumoured that the guards often heard the sounds of people living beyond the fence, and the calls of strange creatures that had never been identified. St John put the stories down to legends started by concerned mothers afraid that their children would venture outside the security fences.

'The board and I were greatly impressed and relieved to hear of your support for Re–Volution in Parliament,' Beck said.

St John smiled. 'It was no effort on my part, Kieran. The future of mankind rests with your company, of that I have no doubt. Decades of research into The Falling have failed to find a cure and we are but one step away from utter annihilation.'

'I agree,' Kieran said. 'If there was another way, we and no doubt every other human being on Earth would take it, but right now we are in danger of losing everything that we have fought to protect. We cannot wait much longer.'

'How so?' St John asked.

Kieran Beck clasped his hands before him on his desk and studied them before speaking.

'There have been further tragedies in the field,' Beck reported. 'Our friends in America lost a research station down in Louisiana.'

St John sighed. 'The losses are becoming unacceptable. How many research stations have gone down?'

'Twelve,' Beck replied, 'four in the USA, six in Europe and two in the Far East. We only have eight remaining and maintaining communication links and extraction protocols is becoming increasingly difficult. Fuel is almost depleted and we have no resources left to continue expansion here in London in any direction. Farmland, what we have of it, is at capacity and even a single poor harvest will trigger a famine in the city. The situation is much the same in New York and far worse in Tokyo.'

St John considered the predicament once again. He had done little else in eight months as the tide of obstacles facing mankind's beleaguered survivors flowed ever closer to drowning them.

'Do you intend to accelerate the program?'

Beck's shoulders gave a tiny shrug. 'I don't see what alternative we have, Prime Minister.'

'Parliament will almost certainly pass the bill I have proposed, passing control of parliament to the *holosap* community, but I do not believe that they will in good conscience condone a complete abandonment of the human colonies.'

'Before long they won't have to,' Beck pointed out. 'A single breach of our quarantine conditions and the whole city will descend into panic and chaos, and even with Re–Volution's security supporting the police force law and order continues to collapse. We just don't have the manpower to control this many people and maintain a secure city border, or security at all for that matter. I don't have to tell you what will happen should the population realise just how precarious the situation has become on all fronts.'

St John sighed again. The populace hated *holosaps*, hated Re–Volution and hated the politicians that supported transferring political control to the *holosap* community. The price of uploading, of achieving immortality and security against disease, starvation and aging was far too high for all but the elite to afford. Despite lobbying, Re–Volution maintained its pricing structure because it was providing not a one–off service but essentially eternal maintenance and support for all *holosaps*. To calls and complaints that the company should offer uploads to all of humanity, the company replied that even if it did so it would take decades to upload everybody, and then who would physically maintain the databases if there was a problem?

These entirely understandable policies were ignored by the people, who yearned for the discovery of a cure for The Falling. There was a world waiting out there, full of life and food, if only they could get to it. But if they discovered that the city had been breached by the infection, they would doubtless run riot. The police would be overcome, the laws holding society together spat upon with the ferocity of years of anguish, and politicians like St John… He shuddered.

'We have little choice,' Beck urged him. 'If parliament passes the bill of rights then we must immediately endeavour to upload as many of us as we can before it's too late. New York is on its last legs. Another failed harvest and it will fall and the governor knows it. Tokyo may already be collapsing – we haven't heard anything from them for two weeks now. It's too late, Prime Minister. We've done everything we can, waited longer than we ever should have.'

St John glanced out of the windows at the city.

'What of the terrorists?' he asked. 'They have become bolder, more desperate. What if the databases cannot be kept safe? It's no good if we all upload ourselves and they then destroy everything. And what about power? How will you maintain power to the site and....'

'We have everything under control,' Beck promised. 'The solar arrays are already under construction on every tower block in the city. It's ironic, that if previous governments had funded a power program of this kind on this scale we would never have needed bloody fossil fuels in the first place. By the time the array is complete this city will never need to worry about energy generation again, and we have plenty of machines under construction both here and in the USA designed for maintenance purposes. With only *holosaps* left, food will no longer be required, or heat. We will need no hospitals, no housing, nothing but the power sources and the machines we're building to maintain them. Terrorists will be but a memory, Tarquin.'

St John nodded slowly. 'How many robots have you constructed?'

'Here, just a few hundred at the moment. Far more in the United States,' Beck said. 'We have to build their components in separate factories, otherwise the workers might realise what we're doing. So far, the program has not raised any suspicions. The cover story of machines able to run farms outside the city walls has held up well.'

'Parliament is nervous,' St John said. 'A step such as this is unprecedented in human history and can never be undone. I have muted the possibility in private with other ministers from time to time and received rebuttal after rebuttal.'

'That is why we need control of parliament,' Beck insisted. 'Keeping the *holosaps* in a permanent state of stasis without true freedom of movement is both an insult to their human rights and tantamount to an act of suicide upon the human race. The other ministers do not see things as clearly as you do, Tarquin. They would doom themselves rather than grasp salvation.'

'But it would not be a democratic process. You're talking about a coup.'

Beck leaned back in his chair for a moment before replying.

'Yes, that's exactly what I'm talking about. But this is not about me or anybody else making a grab for power, because there is no power any more. We're all on tenterhooks waiting to see which way this all goes. I just don't want to risk us going the way of everything else on our planet: extinction. You know what all the other politicians are like: by the time they've made a decision they'll already have been infected. We must act now.'

St John closed his eyes. 'What do you need me to do?'

Kieran Beck offered St John a reassuring smile as he spoke.

'We can't afford the public learning that our research stations have been overrun,' he said, 'or repeatedly hearing that our buildings are being attacked. We need to keep the media under control.'

'I'll see what I can do. What else?'

'As soon as we have political control, I'll need a major police initiative launched under your command to put down the terrorists wherever they may be, a measure to keep them under control until such time as they have The Falling to worry about.'

St John narrowed his eyes. 'That could be anytime, years or even decades away.'

'Or tomorrow, Prime Minister.'

St John swallowed thickly. 'And my family? I cannot afford for them all to be uploaded.'

'We have initiatives in place,' Beck said, 'for those circumstances when Re–Volution feels that charitable acts are worthy of suitable recompense. Your family need have no concerns about their survival, Tarquin, and nor will any minister who decides to vote alongside you.'

St John hesitated for a moment. 'How will it be done?'

'The process will be painless,' Beck replied. 'All willing ministers will be administered a drug that anaesthetises and then stops the heart. Uploads will commence immediately.'

St John knew that what Beck was proposing was as an historic moment as it was an appalling one, the willing suicide of an entire political cabinet in order to maintain political control after the fall of the city. Euthanasia on a grand scale. Sacrifice?

'What if we upload and a cure is found?' St John asked.

'What if we don't upload and a cure is not found?'

'And those ministers that refuse?' St John asked. 'Hart and his followers?'

Beck sighed. 'We cannot choose for them. If they do not upload, then they will be lost to us.'

St John stood slowly, his brow deeply furrowed. 'I need to think on this.'

'I understand,' Beck said, 'but even if parliament passes the bill, it will take a true leader to show them the way. You must be the first, Prime Minister, the cross from the living to the after–living.'

St John's firm, steady gaze flickered slightly, the first hint of fear touching his features. 'I'll be ready, if the time comes.'

He turned away, and was almost at the door when Kieran called after him.

'One more thing, Prime Minister,' he said. 'We all do this together, in Parliament, as one when the time comes. Anybody who refuses will be lost to eternity.'

* * *

29

'Stay here.'

Icon's voice was laden with concern as he pulled his hood up over his head and ran from the tent. As he dashed away through the camp Arianna watched as all around her tents were fastened shut, the residents tumbling into or beneath thermal blankets to conceal their presence from the threat of roving helicopters.

Within moments the entire camp was silent, utterly still.

Arianna slipped from inside Icon's tent and hurried in pursuit. The cold forest seemed devoid of life around her, the silence oddly deafening as though it physically enveloped her. She could not help but stop on the track just outside the camp beneath the canopy of trees and simply listen.

There was no sound of animal life and the sheltered valley stilled the air so that the trees seemed to stand like statues, a petrified monument to nature's dominance over man. Once, long ago, even a remote valley such as this would have had a distant background hiss of vehicles on arterial roads and of aeroplanes cruising the vast skies above. Now, there was nothing. Arianna closed her eyes and had the sudden and unnerving sense of knowing what it looked and sounded like to be dead.

A hand yanked her to one side and a voice hissed in her ear as her eyes flew open.

'I told you to stay in the tent.'

Icon's voice was fierce, his grip tight. She looked at him as fear flared momentarily inside her. Icon's grip loosened in response and he pulled her down with him as he squatted back into the bushes.

'Twenty yards out,' came a whispered voice from one of Icon's men concealed somewhere nearby. 'Want me to put them down?'

Icon shook his head. 'No, let them come.'

'Who is it?' Arianna asked.

Icon did not reply but pointed with one gloved finger out to their right, across open land in the valley to where the main road was just visible snaking its way between the rolling forested hills. Arianna squinted but could not see anything out of place.

'The fork in the valley, under the trees,' Icon breathed softly.

There, just visible in the distance, she saw a pair of police motorbikes loosely concealed within a dense copse. The matt black plastic and metal blended in well with the trees and she would never have noticed them were it not for Icon's guidance.

'You've been followed,' he said. 'Stay out of sight, this could be a trap.'

A clicking noise made by one of his men, barely audible even in the otherwise silent woods, made Icon tense up and fall silent. Arianna's breathing became shallow as she watched the turn in the track up ahead.

Moments later two figures moved cautiously toward them. Both held pistols in a double-handed grip before them, eyes scanning the track ahead from behind respirator masks. Neither wore uniforms. Another click from nearby and this time Icon answered with two of his own.

The movement was both explosive and almost completely silent as from the woods a dozen men lurched upright, dense camouflage swaying like fur on their bodies as their rifles whipped up to point at and entirely encircle the two intruders.

The two men froze where they stood on the track, eyes flicking left and right as Icon leaped up and stormed toward them, a pistol in his hand aimed at them.

'Drop your weapons, hands behind your heads!'

In the otherwise silent forest Icon's voice boomed like cannon fire. The two masked men slowly laid their weapons down and put their hands behind their heads. Icon collected the two pistols, looked at the two men for a brief instant and then turned his back to them.

'Kill them both, quietly,' he said.

Icon's henchmen rushed in as one of the captive men shouted out, his voice distorted by his respirator. 'Why are you not wearing masks?'

Icon spoke over his shoulder as he walked away. 'Death is certain in this world, mask or not.'

Arianna watched as the two captives were restrained by some of Icon's men as others drew huge knives from their webbing. Icon stalked past where Arianna crouched, watching in horror as the henchmen lifted the blades to the throats of the two captives as others yanked the respirators from their faces.

Arianna exploded out of the bushes. 'No! Wait!'

The men hesitated as Arianna rushed across to them. She stared in amazement as Han Reeves and Myles Bourne, their faces twisted in fear and impotent anger, recognised her instantly.

'You?!' Han uttered in disbelief. 'You're really behind all of this?'

'No!' Arianna gasped. 'These people grabbed me before the apartment blew up.'

Icon stormed back to her side. 'You know these men, these traitors to humanity?'

Arianna struggled for words. 'They're the detectives who were there when Alexei Volkov's home was destroyed. I saw them before I was brought here.'

'Then they die,' Icon snapped. 'They tried to kill you did they not?'

Arianna struggled to understand all that had happened. 'They blamed me for terrorist attacks in the city,' she said, 'but I didn't do them. They think I'm an enemy of the state.'

'You are,' Icon pointed out, 'now.'

'I didn't ask for this,' she snapped.

'Can you trust them?' Icon pressed her.

Arianna looked at the two detectives, both with steel blades pressed against the vulnerable flesh of their necks. The thread of an artery pulsed beneath the blade against Han's throat. Han and Myles had followed her after she had been abducted in the city, but as police officers that was their job. It had been a police helicopter that had attacked Alexei Volkov's apartment and both Han and Myles had been there, and yet they had not been prepared for the blast that brought the building down in front of them, so how could they have been anything to do with the attack at all unless…?

'I don't know,' she admitted finally as she turned to Icon. 'All I know is that you cannot kill them.'

'Is that so?' Icon said and raised his hand to click his fingers.

'No,' Arianna insisted and clamped his giant fist in her own hand. His skin was as rough as sandpaper and cold to the touch. 'They may be our only chance of figuring out what the hell is happening. Show them.'

Icon stared down at her, his disfigurement concealed by his carefully shaped hood but his disdain at being ordered about by Arianna clear. When he did not move, Arianna released his fist and turned to Han Reeves.

'Everybody is lying,' she said, 'some more than others, but the biggest lie of all is being told by the government. There is a cure for The Falling.'

Han Reeves's face screwed up in disbelief.

'Don't believe what they're telling you,' he snapped back. 'They're terrorists, murderers and cowards.'

Arianna reached up and yanked Icon's hood aside before he could react and the hood fell away to reveal his ruined face. Han Reeves stared at the horrific scarring, searching for signs of deception.

'Something else,' he dismissed her, 'he got burned. It means nothing.'

Arianna looked about her at the other henchmen. 'Show them.' The men did not move. 'Show them!' Arianna almost screamed, pointing at Han and Myles. 'Until you can prove that you're for real this will never, ever end!'

The men looked at each other, and then one of them reached up and pulled back the heavily camouflaged hood he wore. His features were perhaps more hideously distorted than even Icon's, a skull loosely clothed in chunks of flesh and rippled skin. The scars of crude stitches used to seal his face back up during his recovery laced every inch of his face, and his voice was gravelly where the disease had ravaged his vocal chords.

'My name is Malcolm and I recovered from The Falling after four weeks,' he growled at Han and Myles. 'Icon saved my life, along with just about everybody else you can see. He stitched my wounds, fed me and kept me alive when I could barely breathe let alone help myself.'

One by one, encouraged by Malcolm's gesture, the men removed their hoods. Arianna managed to conceal her horror at their gruesome visages, looking like an army of zombies draped in foliage. They stared at Han and Myles in silence as Arianna spoke to the detectives.

'They all survived The Falling,' she explained. 'They fought off the infection because they possessed immunity and their bodies were able to recognise the attack and act against it. That means that running in their blood are antibodies that can save people's lives and end this. The government, for whatever reason, does not want that to happen.'

Han looked at the grim collection of deformed men before him and then glared at Icon.

'Immune or not, it doesn't justify terrorism.'

Icon stormed up to Han and gripped the back of his head with one hand as with the other hand he pushed the knife blade a little tighter against the detective's throat. Han got a close up view of Icon's big, craggy and ruined face as he spoke.

'I will only repeat this one more time today,' Icon growled. 'We have attacked nobody. We're too busy trying to stay alive out here. Do you understand what I'm telling you?'

Han looked into Icon's one good eye, and then glanced at Arianna.

'What else have you found out?'

* * *

30

Arianna had never tasted pine–needle tea before. Brewed simply to make plain hot water more inviting, it was a staple survival beverage to Icon's men. It helped to mask the stale taste of pond water too - boiling the water killed off all harmful bacteria including fungi like *Apophysomyces*, but it didn't alter the taste.

'How long have you been out here?' Han asked.

They were sitting in Icon's tent, Arianna watching as Icon updated Han and Myles on everything. It was bizarre to her, listening to how her entire world had collapsed and been reborn in just twenty four hours as Han asked questions and Icon patiently replied. She knew that the detectives were under no impression that they were trusted; two armed guards stood a few yards away at the tent entrance, rifles held ready for the slightest hint of discord.

'Since the quarantine,' Icon replied. 'I don't even know how many years it's been.'

'Twenty four,' Myles replied helpfully. 'I was six when they cut the city off from the outside world.'

'A quarter of a century?' Icon asked of himself, not looking up. 'Is that all?'

'It's long enough,' Arianna said, guessing that Icon must be nearing his sixties. 'You've been out here for a long time.'

'If you and your people have nothing to do with the attacks in the city, then whey were you there and why did you grab Arianna?' Han asked.

Icon explained what they saw on the television broadcasts, about the terrorist attacks and the subsequent investigations that led to the manhunt for Arianna.

'We felt certain that Arianna was somehow connected to everything, and when we saw that she was on the run and had been rumoured to have fled to the south of the city we knew we had to act.'

'For what reason?' Arianna asked. 'You never finished telling me why I was targeted by your people.'

Icon looked at her, his dark eyes seeming to reflect nothing as he spoke.

'There are many possible reasons but right now I cannot share them. I don't know who to trust.'

Arianna looked at Han and Myles before she replied.

'Frankly, nor do I,' she said. 'I've been arrested, shot at, nearly blown up and abducted twice in one day. You think this shit is coming any easier to me?'

Icon's big head swivelled up as he looked at her. 'No, I don't.'

'Good, then start thinking straight. Right now we have no option but to trust each other, because I have the distinct impression that mistrust is what's preventing this from all getting out. The government is controlling the media either directly or indirectly, telling lies through the news in order to keep the population afraid and their own objectives concealed. We won't figure this out if we cannot talk to each other. Agreed?'

Icon glanced at the two detectives. Han shrugged and nodded. 'What do you want to know from us?'

'How you came to be here, and exactly how Arianna became involved.'

Han gestured to Arianna as he replied.

'There was a terrorist attack on the Re–Volution headquarters, in which Arianna was implicated due to her religious beliefs and access to the building. Shortly before the attack, Arianna was also implicated in the murder of a Russian magnate, Alexei Volkov, her adoptive father and the man whose illegal apartment south of the Thames was destroyed earlier today. At the very least she may have been considered a target by Alexei's killers, which may be why she was abducted this morning from a rail platform in the city.'

Arianna wanted to speak but sensed that Icon was digesting the information.

'We did not abduct her twice, only after she was found escaping the apartment block you mentioned,' he said finally. 'That means…'

'That somebody else wanted me too,' Arianna explained.

'I sent two officers to keep an eye on you,' Han added. 'If you were involved in the murder and attacks then you were a suspect, and if you weren't then you might become a target. Somebody got you away from them on that rail platform, and then after that you were taken here by Icon's men.'

'I didn't tell you my name,' Icon growled from beneath his hood.

'You're well known to us,' Han explained. 'However, intelligence didn't tell us you were a survivor of The Falling, living out here for the last twenty four years and hadn't been in the city since. Must've slipped their minds.'

'You think our own people are in on something?' Myles asked, appalled. 'I've been an officer all of my life, and I know damned well that my colleagues would never stoop to treason like this.'

'Don't you?' Icon murmured as he looked up. In the pale light leaking into the tent from outside, his concealed face looked like a ghost's. 'What if your life, or your family's life was on the line? What if your children were dying? What if you knew that everybody in power had stood by and let millions of people die and was lying to those that remained in order to retain their wealth and maintain control? What would you be willing to do then?'

Myles stared at Icon, unable to reply.

'It is Kieran Beck who is lying,' Arianna said, saving Myles from Icon's steady glare, 'that's the bottom line.'

'How would you know that?' Han asked.

'That apartment that blew up,' she replied. 'I was inside it beforehand, with Kieran Beck and his men trying to kill me.'

'Beck himself was there?' Myles Bourne gasped. 'What on earth would he want with you?'

'I don't know,' Arianna said, 'but I recently learned that my true father was Cecil Anderson, the creator of the first holosap, Adam. Maybe that's how I fit into all of this.'

Han stared at her, a bemused smile on his face. 'D'ya think?'

'You're Cecil Anderson's daughter,' Myles echoed. 'That guy was a legend.'

'He also was trying to shut his work down,' Arianna said, 'before he was murdered. Icon, you said that Tarquin St John was involved in all of this somehow?'

'The Prime Minister?' Han asked.

'St John is pushing for a power handover to the *holosaps*,' Icon said. 'We think that Kieran Beck is arranging so-called terrorist attacks on Re-Volution to generate what sympathy he can among the population, and preventing a cure for The Falling from entering the city would be one way of achieving that and getting his bill through parliament past any opposition. It would help the people hate the terrorists more than the *holosaps*, convince parliament that there is no other option in the face of extinction and also blind them to any true threat.'

'Which is what?' Han pressed. 'What *is* the threat?'

Icon sighed and looked down into his mug as he replied.

'We believe that genocide is the government's true aim, the final eradication of *Homo sapiens* in favour of *Homo immortalis*; the *holosaps*.'

'You're kidding,' Han uttered. 'St John's a human, he'd be digging his own grave or at least that of his family. Nobody can afford to upload several generations, and he's married with three kids.'

Icon smiled grimly. 'That's when people do deals behind closed doors,' he said. 'Imagine, a world left only to the fortunate and elite few. No more mouths to feed, no more crops to tend, no more hospitals to maintain or diseases to be feared. The new humanity could live in peace surrounded by nature on a pristine world where nobody would ever grow old or be injured again.'

'Or be born,' Han said. 'It really would be the end of what it is to be human. We'd all be like recordings or something, alive but not living.'

'There will be no *we* about it,' Icon pointed out. 'The human race would be reduced to a few thousand *holosaps*, the handful of people able to upload and save themselves.'

'How would they do it?' Han asked.

Arianna gasped as she was hit with a sudden revelation.

'That's why they're hunting Icon's group so intently,' she realised. 'They want to remove any human immunity from the world, because when they're ready they're going to *let* The Falling into the cities.'

Han frowned at her. 'Just like that? If they opened Westminster Bridge nothing but dogs and rats would cross it, and the people would shoot them on sight.'

Arianna shook her head as she tried to figure it out. 'They must have some kind of plan and a breach in the city defences would be perfect. Everybody expects it to happen at some point.'

'What if they're breeding infected animals, or even people?' Myles suggested. Everybody stopped talking and looked at him. Myles seemed intimidated by their looks. 'Well, it's possible isn't it?'

'And they would only have to be carriers, like us,' Icon agreed. 'Once they've come into close enough contact with uninfected people, or in the case of animals perhaps been caught and eaten by the poorer citizens, the infection would pass on if the meat wasn't cooked properly or fluids were exchanged.'

Han nodded. 'A dense population, crammed in. It could be over in a matter of weeks and the *holosaps* would have the perfect opportunity to confirm their way of life as the only safe way for humanity to continue. They would take control and boom, everybody else dies.'

'And anybody found to be immune would die in the chaos, either thinking that they were doomed when the infection took hold or shot by the government if they survived too long.'

'Hence the corruption in the police force,' Icon said. 'They must have people making sure there are no loose ends.'

Han did not miss the implication. 'We're not enforcers for St John or anybody else,' he insisted. 'Hell, we're just trying to keep up.'

'What can we do about it all?' Arianna asked. 'The only person likely to have answers is Alexei Volkov, and he's out of reach.'

'He is the key to all of this,' Icon agreed.

'But he's a *holosap* now, and out here there's no way that I can talk to him. Besides, what if he's behind it all? What if he tried to have me killed?'

Han shook his head.

'The man burned to death on his own bed,' he pointed out. 'Alexei Volkov was not the kind of man capable of doing that to himself. Somebody killed him of that much I'm sure, what I don't know is why?'

Arianna turned to Icon.

'Why did you target me, when you saw the news reports?' she demanded.

Icon sighed, staring into the middle distance as he spoke.

'When I was sixteen I joined the army, served with an infantry regiment as a boy soldier. I later earned a commission, serving as an officer. Just before the city was quarantined, I was ordered to act as a guard and escort to a man in the city employed by the government to work on a top secret project to create the first *holosap*. His name was Cecil Anderson.'

Arianna managed to keep her features devoid of emotion. 'Go on.'

'On the night of the quarantine, Professor Anderson arrived at the laboratory in a state of distress, adamant that he should destroy "Adam", his initial creation. He was in the process of doing so when the laboratory was attacked. I was injured, my corporal killed. The people who attacked us murdered Professor Anderson and threw me out of the city to die. That was how I ended up out here.'

'Who were they?' Arianna asked.

'As far as I can tell, they worked for Kieran Beck. He may even have been the man responsible for your father's murder, but it is so long ago now and they all wore masks. It's hard to remember.'

Arianna shivered. 'What happened to my father?' she asked.

'His body was thrown in the Thames,' Icon said, 'as was mine. I managed to swim to the opposite shore. Trying to return to the city would have been suicide because they were shooting anybody trying to gain access by that time. Going the other way, dangerous as it was, was my only option.'

'What's that got to do with me, here and now?' she asked.

'Because before your father died he sent something via electronic mail. I saw him do it, right after he destroyed Adam. It was only later that I realised what it was he had created.' Icon looked up at Arianna. 'A kill–switch.'

'Kill–switch?' Han asked. 'For what?'

'For all *holosaps*,' Icon said. 'It's what he used to destroy Adam. Professor Anderson hid the kill switch, and he died rather than reveal to Kieran Beck where it had been sent. My guess is that Beck and his people want to get hold of the kill switch and prevent it from ever being used before they upload themselves. Alexei and Arianna are the only possible links they can pursue.'

'What was your real name?' she asked. 'Who did my father know you as?'

Icon's face seemed haunted and it was a few moments before he spoke again. 'Lieutenant Connelly,' he said finally. 'Ian Connelly.'

'Icon,' Han said, 'probably a shortened version of your name on your uniform during military training.'

Icon nodded. Arianna touched his forearm as she spoke. 'What do you intend to do about all of this?'

Icon replied softly.

'You have to go into the city and talk to Alexei, find out more about what happened to this kill–switch. He and Professor Anderson were collaborators and friends, he may know something.'

'Alexei was trying to talk to me before the apartment was attacked,' she replied. 'But if I try to contact him now I'll be spotted immediately. They must be monitoring him. I can't get back into London now,' Arianna said finally. 'I'd be shot on sight.'

Icon's reply came to her as though from a distance.

'I didn't say anything about going back to London,' he said. 'I meant that you need to upload and find him that way. You need to die, Arianna.'

* * *

31

New Orleans,

Louisiana

The glow of dawn illuminated the decrepit city skyline, the sun a hazy disc veiled by wreaths of mist not yet boiled off by its heat. Marcus squatted alongside Kerry beside the skeletal, rusting hulk of an old Pontiac as they surveyed the route ahead.

The US 90 crossed the broad swathe of the Mississippi and descended toward the low city skyline and what had once been the central business district to their right. A scattering of high-rise office buildings were now cloaked in foliage, a few of their remaining windows reflecting the rising sun's hazy glow.

The silence unnerved Marcus as he scanned the city for movement. There was little wind, just a hot breath that seemed to swell off the swirling water far below to hum across the surface of the bridge. Abandoned cars littered the way ahead, their deflated tyres locked in the grip of vines and weeds, soft grasses swaying in the faint breeze.

'So quiet,' he murmured.

'Yeah,' Kerry whispered in reply, affected by the sombre scene. 'Like the city's haunted or something.'

The scene was one that Marcus imagined had once been the staple of film makers, back in the good old days when money had been power and capitalism had dominated the ever growing ranks of mankind. The tower blocks were like giant angular trees draped in foliage, while the lower lying ranks of offices, houses and apartment blocks were lost in a mass of vines and trees. Here, perhaps more than anywhere but the tropics, nature was reclaiming her land with ferocious speed. Marcus glanced at the bridge around them, at the huge rusting bolts and cracked concrete.

'We should get down there,' he said, 'in case the bridge falls.'

Kerry nodded but did not say anything further. Marcus waited as she watched the city for a few moments longer and then moved quickly but carefully forward, staying alongside the concrete barriers as she jogged with her back hunched.

'We'll get down into the city and out of sight,' she whispered back to him finally. 'Can't risk them seeing us up here. Then we'll head for the airport. It's a few miles miles across the city.'

Marcus jogged alongside her as they descended. 'And then what?'

'I don't know: we're making this up as we go, right? But we need to access the regional communications hub's computers and send off my blood–screen data to everybody on the planet with access to a computer.'

Marcus frowned. 'Even if we make it we'll never get back out of there in one piece.'

Kerry did not reply as they jogged down onto the entrance ramp to the bridge, peering at the airport way off in the distance to their left. Marcus saw nothing but a jumble of leafy buildings lining a freeway beneath them littered with rusting cars. A big sign to his left read in fading script: *"Always glad you came!"*

They followed the US 90 until it reached the airline freeway running east–west below them and then followed the on–ramp until it reached the ground. Kerry seemed to relax as they dropped off the elevated road.

'They can't see us from miles away,' Marcus said.

'You can't know that,' Kerry replied. 'Besides, you never heard of binoculars?'

'They probably think that we're dead already.'

'They won't think that until they find our rotting bodies,' Kerry snapped back. 'There's nothing alive out here, Marcus. We're the only things moving other than clouds. If we're spotted, we're done for.'

Marcus looked at Kerry. Her skin was an unhealthy palour, pale and sheened with a light sweat despite the cooler air of morning. A thick wad of hastily applied medical dressing was taped to her neck where she had been bitten, the lower edges crimson and black.

'How are you feeling?'

Kerry did not look at him, but her voice was uneven as she replied.

'Hot and tired with the fever but it's been twelve hours and I'm still standing.'

Marcus nodded but did not reply. He recalled the stories of how people had always gone into a sort of shock about twelve hours after contracting The Falling, which was partly why the disease had acquired its name: people collapsed. Some had claimed with grim humour that the illness had be so named because bits kept falling off people, like some kind of leprosy plague. That humour had vanished within a few weeks of the first major outbreaks here on the Gulf of Mexico and through the Florida panhandle.

Nobody joked about it anymore.

Marcus touched his own, lighter wound. The skin was sore to the touch, swollen, but not bleeding where Kerry had only just broken the surface. It was the kind of thing that Marcus could have well done without, but he too was now surprised at the lack of explosive necrosis. The disease typically attacked flesh far faster than even the most dangerous spider venom, but right now he realised that his own body was mounting an immune response just as quickly as the disease was making its attack. Soon, the fevers would begin as his body went to war on the invading sickness.

'How long do you think, before we know?' he asked.

'Know what?'

'You know damned well what I mean.'

Kerry sighed as they walked. 'Another twelve hours,' she said. 'Less, if my own wound starts to heal. I should be unconscious by now.'

Marcus nodded. 'Let's not get too excited just yet, okay? We're on a suicide mission that might not help anyone.'

'It'll help the survivors see through the government's lies if nothing else,' she snapped back at him. 'Nobody's ever going to get through this if they keep killing anybody who discovers a potential cure.'

Marcus stared at his feet as they walked. 'So we're probably not planning an escape method.'

'Of course we will!' Kerry hissed as she stopped on the freeway and whirled to face him. 'I don't want to die, okay? I want to live too. But right now there are more important things on my mind than our survival. Most people out there think that The Falling was some kind of judgement on mankind, on scientists who failed to find a cure. They blame us for not saving their families, their loved ones. People loved science when it got things right, which is most of the time, but when it gets something wrong suddenly we're all evil manipulators of Mother Nature, out to destroy humanity with genetic engineering or holographic immortality or nuclear disasters. I'm sick of hearing it, okay?'

Marcus stared at her, the silence deafening after her outburst. 'You're doing this for posterity?'

'I'm doing it for people who have never even heard my name,' Kerry insisted, 'just like countless others before me. That's what scientists do. People used to remember movie stars, pop divas and other pointless celebrities, but few of them could name the person who discovered radioactivity or how to vaccinate against diseases, scientists whose work has saved millions of lives.'

A light wind gusted across the lonely freeway and thrummed through the hollow interiors of the rusting cars littering the asphalt. Marcus heard a distant hum that conflicted with the wind, an unnatural harmony that made the hairs on his heck rise up.

'You hear that?'

Kerry lifted her chin, cocked her head to one side in what to Marcus was a remarkably attractive manner, her hair curled back over one tiny ear, her neck slim despite the swelling beneath the medical dressing.

'Chopper,' she said as she grabbed his arm. 'Run!'

Marcus followed her at a dash as they sprinted for the cover of an overhead bypass. The distant humming sound became louder as they ran into the shadows beneath the overpass, the helicopter's blades echoing back and forth around them as they climbed up into the darkest recesses and huddled there amid the weeds.

Marcus squinted out at the bright sky, trying to see the helicopter as it thundered its way toward them. The noise of the blades and the engine soared and he retreated back as it seemed as though the helicopter was going to land right beside the overpass.

'They've found us!' he shouted above the din.

Kerry remained motionless as the helicopter thundered overhead, right over where they were squatting, and flew on toward the east. The deafening engine noise faded as quickly as it had come and Kerry ducked down to watch with Marcus as it flew away.

'That was close,' he said.

Kerry continued to watch the helicopter as it flew away, and as the engine racket receded into silence so they heard the noises from the overpass above them. They sounded like a giant metal ball bouncing and rolling down a hill, the grind and scratch of steel on asphalt. Marcus looked at Kerry, who remained silent as they listened to the strange movements above them fade away. Whatever was making the noise was moving down the overpass toward the freeway where they crouched.

'You think that they saw us?' Marcus whispered to Kerry.

The noise stopped instantly.

Marcus sat in silence and thought that he could hear his heart beating against the wall of his chest. Kerry turned and grabbed a fist–sized chunk of crumbling asphalt from where it lay beside her. Before Marcus could protest, Kerry hurled the asphalt in a high arc toward the far side of the freeway.

The chunk of asphalt spun through the air and hit the freeway. It shattered into dozens of smaller pieces as it bounced through the swaying grasses.

A deafening burst of automatic fire shattered the silence as bullets tore into the ruptured surface of the freeway below. Kerry grabbed Marcus's arm and yanked him out from under the overpass as the gunfire abruptly ceased and the strange metallic scratching began again.

Marcus followed her up the embankment alongside the freeway, crouching tight against the concrete wall of the overpass as they listened to the scratching, rolling sound nearby as it descended on the opposite side of the overpass. As the sound reached the freeway, they turned and leaped up onto the overpass.

Kerry led Marcus silently across the road to the far side, and they crouched to peer down onto the freeway below.

There, a three foot diameter metallic sphere rolled slowly through the grass toward the shattered chunk of asphalt. Metal feet crunched as they flicked out from the ball's surface one after the other and dug into the road behind it, propelling the sphere forward. As Marcus watched, a small compartment opened on the sphere's surface and the black eye of a camera lens appeared and shot an image of the damaged asphalt.

'What the hell is that?' he whispered to Kerry, keeping his voice so low that even he could barely hear it.

Kerry did not reply, her face rigid with fear as she looked past him.

Marcus turned and saw another sphere rolling rapidly toward them on the overpass.

* * *

32

'Run!'

Kerry sprinted for the opposite side of the bypass as Marcus struggled to keep up with her. He vaulted over the trunk of an old Lincoln as he looked over his shoulder and saw the metallic sphere rolling rapidly toward them, its metallic feet flicking out one by one from its smooth surface and propelling the sphere at frightening speed with a clicking sound like a machine gun.

'Shit!' Marcus yelled as he saw Kerry leap over the side of the overpass just as the sphere suddenly halted and reared up on spindly metallic legs that shot from beneath it in a tripod formation.

Moments later, two parallel compartments opened on the side of the sphere and a burst of flame erupted from within each. Marcus leaped into thin air as bullets raked the road where his feet had been in a cloud of dust and fragments of rock.

Marcus plummeted eight feet and hit the sloped embankment hard. The bones in his legs shuddered as pain bolted through his ankles. He rolled as he landed and tumbled down the embankment until he plunged into the knee high grass on the freeway.

'Get up!'

Kerry's voice was high–pitched as she ran past him, her hair flying behind her like a banner. Marcus dragged himself onto his feet as he saw the other sphere rolling between the abandoned cars on the freeway and weaving to get a clear shot at them.

'What the hell are they?!' Marcus yelled as he ran after Kerry.

'Who cares?!'

Kerry ran across the freeway, taking the barrier in the centre in a single bounding leap as she fled for the cover of abandoned buildings lining the side of the freeway. Marcus jumped over the barrier and hurled himself to the ground as a burst of gunfire raked the asphalt behind him and punched holes in the metal barrier to send sparks flying across him.

The sphere on the overpass had rolled down the embankment and pursued them, but the central barrier on the freeway was an obstacle it could not pass. Instead, it reared up on its legs and began firing over the barrier at him.

'Stay low!' Kerry yelled.

Marcus dodged behind the dusty wreckage of an old SUV and then moved directly away from the line of fire. Bullets pinged and twanged off the metal vehicle behind him, punching holes at odd angles through the bodywork. The vehicle's structure deflected the bullets away from him and the sphere was unable to account for the unpredictable angles the obstacles produced.

The gunfire stopped and Marcus eased his way further from the SUV until he reached the far side of the freeway. He rolled flat over the top of the barriers and dropped down alongside Kerry.

'They know we're here,' she said.

'You think?' Marcus asked breathlessly. 'Holy shit, Kerry. Since when did they have machines like that out here?'

'Since forever, probably,' she replied. 'Classified military kit, perfect for hostile environments. Who knows?'

'We know, now,' Marcus shot back. 'They'll figure out what we're trying to do.'

Kerry nodded.

'Those spheres are not likely to be automated, like WASPS,' she said. 'They're remotely controlled. The same system we need to hack is what sends them signals from whoever is controlling them.'

'Great,' Marcus replied. 'So the closer we get to their base at the airport, the more horrible things they can throw at us?'

Kerry nodded. 'We must be close.'

'Close to what?' Marcus breathed. 'These machines, who built them and what are they doing out here anyway? There's no population, no enemy other than The Falling so what are they protecting?'

Kerry sat for a long moment as she stared into the distance.

'That's a very good question,' she whispered in reply. 'There's supposed to be nothing out here but relay stations and the regional broadcast hub. A couple of guys with guns would be able to hold out against any infected animals still living out here.'

'Yeah,' Marcus replied, 'and they sure don't need all of that hardware to kill us. Between the WASPS and those rolling nightmares it's a wonder we even got out of the relay station.'

'Whatever they're protecting, it'll be at the airport. They'd have had to fly these things in as there's no manufacturing them out here.'

'So we keep going?' Marcus uttered, hearing the despondent tone infecting his voice.

'There's no going back now,' Kerry reminded him. 'We do this and finish it or we're toast anyway. Those spheres will find a way around the freeway barrier to us before long. Let's move before they get too close.'

Kerry moved off at a low run, moving into the shelter of a half-collapsed warehouse as she turned east again toward the distant airport. Marcus followed her as they moved parallel to the freeway, aware of a dizziness and a buzzing in his head.

'We need to eat something,' he gasped as he followed Kerry.

'I know.'

They moved as swiftly as they could around rusting oil barrels, cars collapsed on sunken suspension, through dense weeds as tall as their heads that had pushed up through endless acres of cracked asphalt. The rising sun beat down with relentless blows, soaking Marcus's shirt with sweat. The rising humidity prevented the sweat from evaporating on his skin and the sense of disorientation increased as he stumbled after Kerry.

He was on the verge of begging her to stop when he saw her trip and collapse onto one knee, her head hanging low.

'Kerry,' he gasped.

His own voice sounded dry and weak. He crouched down alongside her and noticed the bite in her neck was inflamed and leaking a fluid that looked almost like syrup. It didn't smell anywhere near as good.

'We need to rest,' he urged her. 'It's too hot.'

Marcus looked through the forest of weeds and grasses toward a dense copse of trees set just back from the freeway near ranks of old clapperboard houses. He recalled sitting under trees in his youth, how the mass of leaves above his head had cooled the air during the long hot summers of his childhood.

With a heave of effort he helped Kerry to her feet and guided her across the open ground of what had once been a convenience store's forecourt, filled with rusting cars awaiting owners that would never return. Half way across he saw a twisted piece of metal perforated with holes lying on the ground that had once been a registration plate. He picked it up and tucked it under his arm as they walked.

A bank on the far side dropped into a ditch that contained a shallow stream. Marcus helped Kerry across the ditch and into the shadows beneath the broad limbs of the trees. He gently set her down with her back to the thick trunk.

Her eyes rolled up into her head and her jaw hung slack.

'Stay with me,' he rasped.

With agonised steps he crept back to the shallow stream and filled their canteens with water, then dragged himself back to Kerry's side. With one canteen he washed both their faces and drenched their festering wounds with the water, but he dare not drink it.

Instead, he dug a shallow pit in the soil with one hand and then filled it with dry twigs and a strip of his shirt tail. Moments later, he used a cigarette lighter he had always carried with him in the laboratory to ignite the dry twigs and flames spat and writhed from the tiny fire.

Marcus built a crude stand from old windscreen wipers and then lay the registration plate over the flames and set the spare canteen onto it. His eyes felt heavy with sickness and exhaustion, his joints ached and his head throbbed as he fed ever larger twigs and debris into the fire, the water in the canteen bubbling as it finally boiled. He hauled himself back to the stream and refilled the other canteen, bringing it back to the fire and replacing the one with the boiling water, which he then set down in the shade to cool.

He did not know how long he lay, waiting for the water to cool enough to drink without scalding their parched lips, but he finally drank from the canteen. It tasted of dirt and decaying foliage and yet seemed as sweet as the finest wine, the boiling having destroyed any threat of bacterial contamination. He felt his head clear a little, and he grabbed Kerry's jaw with one hand and tipped the canteen between her lips.

Kerry coughed and swallowed, then gulped from the canteen as though it were the last drink she would ever taste. Water spilled down her chin and Marcus endeavoured to catch every last precious drop with his spare hand.

Kerry drained the canteen and slumped back against the tree once more. Marcus watched her for a few moments. He was no doctor, and had no idea whether Kerry was dying or whether he had just saved her life. But somehow, instinctively, he knew that he had done the right thing.

Marcus refilled the spare canteen and set it to boil, then repeated the whole episode once more before he finally relented to his weariness and slumped alongside Kerry against the tree.

The cooling breeze that drifted beneath the tree lulled him toward sleep, and as his eyes grew heavy and he drifted between wakefulness and sleep he dreamed of seeing several shiny spheres rolling by on the distant freeway, their metallic bodies glinting in the bright sunlight and their feet clicking on the ground as they wound their way east.

Dozens of spheres, with WASPS hovering in the air above them in evil black clouds.

* * *

33

Surrey,

United Kingdom

The tent was silent as Arianna stared at Icon.

'You want me to do *what*?' she asked.

'You must upload and find out what you can from Alexei Volkov,' Icon repeated. 'He was murdered, and as the only person connecting you to your father and everything that has happened recently he must be the key to solving both his own murder and the greater conspiracy of Kieran Beck and the Prime Minister.'

'You think that Alexei knew where this "kill–switch" was?' Han asked.

'Perhaps,' Icon said. 'He was burned alive, was he not? Perhaps his murderers tried to threaten him with immolation if he did not reveal the kill–switch's location. When he refused or did not know, they carried through with their threat. It would not be beyond a man like Kieran Beck.'

Han Reeves frowned. 'You sure about that? His death could just have coincidentally been at the same time as the hit on the Re–Volution headquarters.'

'I don't believe in coincidences anymore,' Icon growled back. 'I don't even believe that governments wanted to cure The Falling when it first began.'

'You're kidding?' Arianna gasped. 'That's one conspiracy too far.'

'Really?' Icon shot back. 'Our world was dying. Climate change had ravaged food production, novel diseases and antibiotic resistant strains were causing the loss of millions of lives every year and wars over water, fossil fuels and territories based on archaic religious beliefs were killing millions more. Don't you think that it occurred to governments even back then that the population problem could be solved with a suitably virulent disease?'

'That's a big difference to saying that The Falling was a planned event,' Han pointed out.

'I didn't say planned,' Icon corrected him. 'It's as likely that The Falling started naturally enough, perhaps because mankind's obsession with antibiotics created a weakness in humans to a disease that might otherwise have been harmless to us. The Falling was in the soil, in wood and foliage, in plants. It was everywhere and had been for millions of years without causing a pandemic. Once it got out and was identified I can't believe that nobody, anywhere in the world in all of those laboratories didn't figure out a cure, or learned that some people were still immune. I heard once that ten per cent of people were immune to HIV, the last really dangerous illness to emerge before The Falling. And what about people in foreign countries who had never had exposure to antibiotics, who might have retained immunity to diseases like it? How did they fall?'

'It probably mutated,' Myles said. 'There's more to disease than just the start. HIV, the common cold, they're all able to mutate within individuals so you can't cure people with a single vaccine, only slow the illness down.'

'Forget all that,' Arianna snapped. 'How on Earth do you expect to get me to upload? I'm not dead in case you hadn't noticed, and I want to stay that way.'

Behind the shadows of his hood, Arianna thought she saw Icon smile softly.

'You wouldn't be dead,' he replied. 'Not quite.'

'Not *quite*?' she echoed.

'You have an upload,' Myles realised as he looked at her. 'They want to use that to get you inside.'

'Won't work,' Han pointed out. 'The police are after you now, if everything Icon says is true. They'll identify you the moment you show up on the Re–Volution servers and terminate you.'

'Precisely,' Icon said, 'which is why it won't be Arianna that they see uploading.'

'What the hell are you talking about?' Arianna snapped.

'Your DNA,' Icon smiled, looking directly at her with his one good eye. 'It's contained in your white blood cells. We will transfuse them with the cells of one of our own, a survivor who is not on Re–Volution's or the government's watch list. You'll then upload and be able to move freely as a *holosap* for a while.'

'Wouldn't they check the chip itself?' Han asked. 'I thought that they recorded stuff, who we are, where we've been and so on?'

'It has to only *appear* to be somebody else,' Icon replied. 'There is no way yet for Re–Volution to match a brain to a specific person without a body. An upload becomes effective immediately upon death so in such cases Re–Volution are dependent upon the information contained on the chip alone, which is chiefly comprised of that person's DNA. With no teeth or other identifying traits, they're reliant upon the upload working at all to verify who a person actually is. Arianna will upload but we will hack her chip first and alter the registration details to match our donor's chip. Arianna's appearance will be generated in their likeness as per the donor's digital birth certificate. Re–Volution will run checks of course, but they take time.' He looked at Arianna. 'It is the mother of all identity theft, but you will have only a few hours before the deception is uncovered.'

'I almost don't want to know,' she replied, 'but how do you intend to make me dead?'

'We have an expert,' Icon replied, 'a former surgeon who survived the pandemic. He will be responsible for hacking your chip, and will then use a medical procedure that will send you into a state of clinical death, although your body will in fact be in a sort of stasis. The procedure is normally used for people undergoing deep heart and brain surgery. Once you are in stasis, you will be uploaded and must obtain the information we need to expose Kieran Beck's conspiracy before it can be put into action. You will effectively be both physically alive and dead at the same time.'

'Which is illegal,' Arianna said and swallowed thickly. 'And what happens after I expose the conspiracy?'

'The medical process is reversed and you will be revived.'

'Just like that,' Arianna uttered.

'Your *holosap* will remain of course, but by then Kieran Beck's operation will be ruined and your name cleared. If we get what we want, all *holosaps* will be shut down afterward, including yours.'

Icon looked up at the entrance to the tent. A woman stood there, her face half–shielded by her hood. Arianna could see that she had been beautiful once but the ravages of The Falling and countless years in the wilderness had aged her features. Arianna realised that she must have been a child when the pandemic struck.

'This is Lynda,' Icon said. 'Her white blood cells will be transfused into you, effectively concealing your identity.'

'And you're okay with this?' Arianna asked Lynda.

Lynda stared back at Arianna for a long moment before replying. 'My entire family died when I was seven years old,' she whispered. 'I barely survived myself. If this procedure can help to bring Re–Volution down it's worth every sacrifice,' Lynda looked at Icon, 'by any means.'

'By any means,' Icon replied as though reciting a mantra.

'Where will all of this be done?' Han demanded of Icon as Lynda left the tent. 'You don't have any technology here, nothing like a laboratory or operating theatre.'

'We have a site,' Icon replied, 'this side of the Thames.'

'So you *do* go into the city,' Myles pointed out.

'Not into the city but we do approach it to trade,' Icon admitted, 'with people from inside for things that we cannot obtain like medicines, clothes and such like. Much of the equipment abandoned by people lying around out here is considered valuable by elements within London.'

'Like weapons,' Han snapped.

'Those who would oppose Re–Volution,' Icon replied without rancour, 'is the enemy of my enemy, and thus my friend.'

Han shook his head. 'Innocent people have died in their hundreds in London from the blasts caused by the terrorists.'

'Innocent people have died out here in their billions,' Icon countered, 'their deaths caused or ignored by your government, or both. Our purpose, detective, is to end this and we now have the opportunity to do so. I take it that you do not have the ability to upload?'

Han shook his head.

'Then you have nothing to lose right now by helping us,' Icon said, 'because we are living proof that the government that you work for is not only lying to you but will without doubt abandon you to die as soon as their objectives are fulfilled. Arianna here is the only person who can prevent that from happening. It's your call, detectives.'

Arianna watched as Han and Myles exchanged glances, and then Han looked across at her.

'You up for this, Arianna?'

'I don't know,' she said. 'Alexei was murdered but he did not see his killers or know precisely why he was targeted. I'm not sure that he could help us even if I do manage to make contact with him before I'm identified.'

'He will know,' Icon replied, 'and if not Alexei Volkov then somebody else. The *holosaps* cannot be entirely unaware of the conspiracy at hand, and within their ranks it is possible that many know what will happen. I doubt very much that any of them would risk their own immortality or that of their families by becoming a whistleblower. All you have to do is prove the corruption within Re–Volution and we'll have what we need to bring the government down.'

Arianna glanced nervously at Han. 'Have you got my back?'

Han nodded without hesitation. 'All the way. Right now, I just don't know who it is I'm supposed to be protecting you from.'

'Everyone,' Icon answered for Arianna. 'This is not about Arianna's survival, or yours or mine. This is about the survival of our species as we know it. There can be no compromise, no doubts, no hesitations. If our plot fails, no human will ever again exist as a biological entity. We will become extinct, detective.'

'No pressure then,' Myles uttered.

Icon turned to Arianna. 'We will travel to the suburbs in the next hour or so. It will not take long. Then you will take your journey into the *holosap* world.'

Arianna watched as Icon stood up and swept from the tent, leaving her with the haunted feeling that she was about to cross a boundary that no human being was ever meant to traverse.

'You okay?' Han asked.

Arianna looked up at him, and the brief notion of replying that she was fine was dashed from her mind by a wave of anxiety.

'I'm about to die, kind of,' she replied. 'So no, I'm not so good. Thanks for asking.'

'You don't have to do this,' Myles replied and jabbed a thumb in the direction of the camp outside. 'I don't see any of *them* leaping up to volunteer for it.'

'Their donor can't get close to Alexei, but I can so I don't have much choice,' she replied. 'I might die doing it, but we'll all die if I don't.'

'You don't know that,' Han insisted. 'These guys are up to something, I know it. Icon doesn't seem the type to just sit out here twiddling his thumbs for twenty five years waiting for somebody like you to come along.'

'You think they've got their own objective?' Myles asked.

'Of course they have,' Han said. 'They've been abandoned to die and then hunted for a quarter of a century. Seeing the *holosaps* fail to achieve power isn't going to be enough for them. They'll want revenge.'

Arianna rubbed her temples, her brain fuzzy with exhaustion.

'Let's just stay with what we know for sure,' she said. 'St John is the man behind the bill to put the *holosaps* in power. Let Icon and his people target him if they want to. All I give a damn about right now is getting word of immunity to The Falling out, as soon as possible. Can you do that for me?'

Han stared back at her for a long beat. 'You want me to do what now?'

'Get a blood sample from Icon and a couple more from his people and take them with you back into the city. *Prove* their immunity. Get somebody started on a vaccine.'

'Just like that, huh?' Han said.

'Somebody else must have stumbled across this in the last twenty five years,' Arianna said. 'We can't be the only ones. That means Re–Volution are covering it up every time a cure is found. Maybe they've done it before. If you can expose that, it's another victory for us.'

Han sighed and looked at Myles. 'You good to go with this?'

'If Icon's people don't kill us first,' Myles replied. 'You think they're up to something and I agree. We're likely cannon–fodder to help them on their way.'

'They're not fakes,' Arianna pointed out. 'They're genuine survivors and that in itself is enough to build upon.'

Myles smiled coldly.

'And if they're building towards destruction?' he challenged. 'I'd ask yourself this, Arianna: who would you want in control of our government? *Holosaps*, who for the most part may be entirely innocent of any crime, or Icon's gang of armed mercenaries?'

***

34

There was no shortage of hardware available to Icon and his people.

The collapse of civilisation in the face of The Falling had been so rapid, and had involved such chaos and panic, that the vast majority of human technology had been left where it stood. Even the military, holed up in London alongside the beleaguered civilians, had been unable to forage far from the safety of the Thames or the north wall.

Icon rode in the passenger seat of an old Army rover, the diesel engine rattling and belching puffs of black smoke as Malcolm, his driver, crunched through the gears to climb a steep hillside road that wound between dense rows of bushes and fields left long untended on its slopes.

The rover breeched the crest of the hill and descended down into another deep valley. Alongside a stream in the base of the valley stood a decrepit farmhouse and two large shelters, built from corrugated iron that was stained a dull red brown. Scattered farm machinery lay where it had been abandoned, an old tractor rusting where it sat at an awkward angle and blocked the narrow track into the farmstead.

Icon waited for Malcolm to negotiate the rough ground alongside the track, where they had long ago cut through the wire fences to bypass the ruined tractor. Here and there, bleached by the sun, Icon could see human bones amid the swaying grasses, lying where they had fallen dead from the blasts of a farmer's shotgun until he too had finally been overcome.

Icon had found him, half of his head blown off by his own weapon, his body slumped across those of his wife and three children, all of their corpses showing signs of being eaten raw by the desperate and dying who had passed through the lonely valley.

The rover pulled up near the farmstead and Malcolm switched off the engine. The silence was heavy, no sound but for the clinking of the hot engine and their laboured breathing through ruined sinuses.

Malcolm pulled a pistol on instinct, Icon clambering from the rover and slipping a pistol of his own from its holster as they advanced on the storage sheds near the farmhouse. Truth was, there was nothing alive out here any longer, but they had both learned long ago that fortune favoured not the brave, but the cautious.

The steep slopes of the valley and dense woodland at both ends provided good cover and made it difficult for the government's roving helicopters to land or examine the farmstead in any detail. That, and the fact that Icon had ensured that the abandoned farm machinery and human bones were left where they lay made the location look like any other across the south–east of England: silent and dead. He had also deliberately not repaired the walls or the collapsed doors of the sheds, gambling that an observer would not suspect anything of value hidden within in the absence of suitable protection.

Icon eased his way up to the entrance of the larger shed and peered into the gloomy interior. A pair of large trailers sat on sagging tyres, concealing what lay beyond. The light beamed in shafts from the bright sky outside and dimly illuminated an angular shape covered in old canvass sacks. Icon moved forward between the trailers and holstered his pistol as he yanked the dustsheets off. Clouds of dust motes swirled through the streaming sunlight, Malcolm keeping watch on the shed entrance as Icon surveyed the equipment before him.

Most of it had been obtained from three locations; the abandoned British Army camps in Aldershot and Pirbright, and an old Royal Air Force base out west called Odiham. Although the military had been organised enough to attempt to bring most of its considerable arms and ammunition with it in the last, desperate flight to London when the country had fallen completely, no number of aircraft, helicopters and vehicles could have shipped everything inside the city's safe zone.

Icon scanned the crates of SA–80 assault rifles, rocket launchers, grenades and timed charges all laid out in methodical order before him. The weapons were greased and cleaned on a regular basis, the priming charges on explosives carefully packaged separately to preserve their life spans. Much of the equipment had lain here for ten years or more but all of it appeared to have been manufactured yesterday.

'There's too much,' said Malcolm over his shoulder. 'We'll never get to use all of it.'

Icon smiled as he replied.

'You can never, ever have too much ammunition, Malcolm. Countless battles have been fought and lost when bullets have become scarce or weapons poorly maintained.' He looked over his shoulder. 'Firepower isn't everything but tell me, would you rather have it or be without it?'

Malcolm shrugged but said nothing.

'I served in the military,' Icon went on as he lifted an SA–80 from its crate and tested the mechanism. The bolt ran smoothly through its mounts, and he aimed the weapon at the ground and fired the empty chamber with a satisfying click before making the weapon safe again to take the load off the spring before replacing it in the crate. 'One good shot is always preferably to two bad ones, single fire always more accurate than automatic. But when you're pinned down in a dustbowl on Afghanistan's plains with a hundred well-maintained AK–47's directing grazing fire across your position, you really learn to appreciate the finer points of ten well-lobbed grenades and a rocket launcher or two.'

Malcolm shrugged again.

'Only if we get the chance to use them,' he replied, and then lowered his pistol as he looked at Icon. 'Why are we going through this charade? The woman doesn't know much about what's been going on and there's not much chance that her dead friend does either. Why not just head into the city and hit them hard, now, while we still can? Take our chances with surprise on our side?'

Icon ran his hand down the surface of a rocket launcher, one of eight he had liberated many years before.

'I would prefer covert exposure of the government's lies to all-out battle,' he said. 'Enough blood has been lost, don't you think?'

'The woman has an upload for cryin' out loud. She's as much one of *them* as St Bloody John. There's no reason for her to risk anything for us.'

Icon sighed and shook his head.

'Yes, there is,' he said as he turned to face Malcolm once more. 'She's a human being and right now I see more of that in her than any of us. She's lost a great deal as have we all, but where we talk of vengeance and war she speaks of resolution and our future.'

'She's also a psychologist and a priest or something, isn't she?' Malcolm asked with a bitter smile. 'They have a way with words.'

'You think that I am deceived?'

Malcolm sighed and shook his head. 'No, only that you've placed too much faith in one person.'

'Any less, Malcolm, than you have placed in me?'

Malcolm stared at Icon and then chuckled.

'Bastard,' he uttered under his breath, 'you've got an answer for everything.'

Icon smiled as he dragged the dustsheets back over his secret arsenal before clapping his friend on the shoulder.

'That's why I'm still here,' he said finally. 'This is our insurance, Malcolm. We will mobilise just as we planned, and if Arianna is unable to obtain the information we need or becomes compromised in her efforts to do so, we proceed as we always intended to.'

Malcolm bit his lip.

'They'll be ready by then, if she's compromised. People go insane you know, when they upload, become part of the *holosap* cloud–conscience or whatever the hell it's called. They can talk languages that we can't understand. She could expose everything we've planned.'

'It will not matter by then,' Icon said. 'The best laid plans are always for nothing once battle is joined. It will be our fortitude and courage that will carry us into London and on parliament, living proof that humans can survive beyond the walls and the river, that we are immune to The Falling.'

'And Arianna?'

'Is a decoy,' Icon said, his voice quietening. 'Her presence will not remain undetected for long. They will see her as the main play against their objective and focus their efforts upon her. They will not see us coming.'

'Nor will the people,' Malcolm pointed out. 'They'll fear civil war once we cross the bridge and enter the city. The same chaos that brought everyone else down will infect them just as surely as The Falling would and…'

'If the government doesn't want to admit their dirty little secret to the people, then we shall have to bring the truth to them,' Icon insisted. 'We have not deceived, Malcolm, nor have we harmed. That blood is on the hands of the government. We must expose them for what they are but we cannot choose how it will eventually be done. I hope that Arianna will expose them without bloodshed, but if she fails then we alone must take up the cause. By any means.'

Malcolm nodded. 'By any means.'

'Have the men transport our weapons to the rendezvous point,' Icon said as they walked from the shed. 'Soon we will have ended this, one way or the other.'

With a firm hand on his friend's shoulder, Icon guided Malcolm back to the rover.

* * *

35

New Orleans

A caress of cool air awoke Marcus, a breeze of movement that touched his cheek. He blinked his eyes open, felt an ache in his limbs from where he had lain slumped against the tree trunk warring with a pulsing, influenza–like sickness raging through his veins.

'Wake up.'

The voice was a whisper as he managed to focus on the face hovering before his.

Kerry smiled down at him, the cool hand of one of her palms gently cupping his cheek.

'I feel terrible,' Marcus croaked.

'I know,' she replied. 'It will pass, trust me.'

Marcus could see that behind Kerry the parking lot and the freeway beyond was tiger–striped with shadows and golden sunshine, the sky above a powder blue scattered with streamers of high cirrus cloud. Kerry held a canteen of water to his lips and he drank greedily, the cool water splashing down his chin and neck. She caught the stray droplets and drained them back into the canteen.

Marcus leaned back against the trunk, felt a little of his discomfort easing as the water rehydrated him. Kerry set the empty canteen down and looked at him.

'You've come a long way,' she said. 'I thought I was done for.'

Marcus squinted at her. Sunlight was sprinkled in shimmering dapples across her face through the leaves of the tree above and her eyes were clear and green.

'You're beautiful,' he said, 'and your fever's broken.'

'And yours has definitely begun if you think I'm beautiful,' she smiled.

Marcus realised that Kerry had been right all along. 'You're immune. It worked.'

'It worked. We've got the cure in our blood.'

Marcus closed his eyes and exhaled as though he were releasing a lifetime's anxiety. He felt himself fold into the tree trunk upon which he slumped. Kerry had been right. Dr Reed had been the enemy and everything that they had worked for now rested on their ability to expose the deception before the machines, or whatever the hell they were, could find and destroy them.

Marcus's eyes blinked sharply open again. 'I saw Wasps passing by and…'

Kerry pressed a finger gently to his lips and glanced over her shoulder as he replied. 'I know.'

Marcus frowned. 'We can't have been hard to find,' he whispered in reply. 'I had to start a fire to clean water for you. They must have detected it?'

Kerry looked down at him.

'You did good,' she said, 'and the fire was small. Most of the smoke scent would rise straight up in this heat, so it's not certain that they would have detected it unless a Wasp flew right overhead, and the spheres couldn't get across the stream to us. Infra–red probably was confused by the midday heat too. I don't know, but it looks like they passed us by and were headed for the airport.'

Marcus's tired brain ached. 'They know what we're trying to do.'

Kerry nodded. 'Most likely. Reed knows that we have a potential cure for The Falling, he knows that we can't travel far and need to broadcast the data soon. The communications hub at the airport is the most logical place to attempt that. As they can't find us to kill us, they're pulling back and waiting for us to come in.'

'Shit,' Marcus uttered. 'We'll never get past those spheres and Wasps.'

'Or the helicopters,' Kerry replied. 'The machines obviously aren't as perfect for killing as they're supposed to be, so they've brought the troops in. I saw two big helicopters land at the airport about an hour ago.'

Marcus propped himself up a bit further against the trunk, and suddenly a waft of what smelled like chicken hit him. He turned and saw two small rodents roasting on his makeshift stand built from windscreen wipers.

'Cooking kills the diseases,' Kerry reminded him, 'and neither of us can go on without proper food.'

'They weren't already dead?' Marcus asked. 'Where did you find them?'

'Saw them when I was scavenging for water,' she replied. 'Couple of water rats or something. They didn't even run from me, probably never seen a human before. I hit them over the head and that was it.'

Marcus felt renewed resolve pulse through his veins as he got up onto his knees. Kerry plucked the two cooked rats from their spits and they ate the roasted meat. It tasted to Marcus finer than the best steak, the calories pushing back the fever wracking his body as his immune response attacked the sickness trying to permeate his body. The food also cleared his mind a little.

'Nature's fighting back,' he said. 'Other species are developing resistance to The Falling. That's why the government are trying to finish us off, to eradicate humans in favour of *holosaps*.'

'Before everybody who's left sees rodents, horses and who knows what else running happily around outside city walls. The government would fall overnight,' Kerry agreed.

'There's just one problem,' Marcus said as he picked the bones of his meal clean. 'Why bother? If there's a cure, then both *holosaps* and humans can live on together?'

'Power,' Kerry replied. 'Isn't that what it's always about?'

'But how can the *holosaps* survive without human support? There won't be any more new people being born, no further physical science being done. There has to be more to this than just *power*.'

Kerry refilled their canteens with purified water and stamped the fire out beneath her heel.

'I don't know, but I figure they're smart enough to have formulated a plan that will work. Right now all I care about is letting what's left of the world know that we're alive, immune and that they can be too, and to hell with power.'

Marcus tossed the rat carcass aside and despite the fever coursing through his body he forced himself to stand upright. 'Good, let's get it done.'

Kerry watched Marcus for what felt like a long time. Then, she stepped forward and flung her arms about his neck and kissed him firmly on the lips. Marcus caught his breath as her kiss ended and looked down at her.

'I thought I was just some fun?' he said.

'You were,' she smiled. 'Now you're just a whole lot more fun than before.'

'Sick, tired, smelly and having just eaten a dead rat?'

'Just like me. We go well together, don't you think?'

Marcus picked up his bag as Kerry released him, and moments later they struck out together toward the distant airport. Marcus struggled alongside her, sipping water and hoping to hell that his fever would break soon.

They stuck to the edge of the freeway, moving carefully between wrecked vehicles and whispering any exchanges to avoid being detected by sensitive digital ears.

'The heat might help cover our approach from infra–red cameras,' Kerry said as they moved.

'I wish I could believe that,' Marcus replied. 'They could have drones up in the air, or Wasps. They'll see us moving from above.'

'I don't think it's our approach they're worried about,' Kerry replied. 'I remember reading about some big general once, maybe Washington or somebody, who said that it was underestimating an opponent that lost more battles than anything else.'

Marcus chuckled bitterly. 'You really think there's any danger of them underestimating us? We've got no weapons, no plan and no escape route.'

'That's my point,' Kerry whispered back. 'They're letting us come to them because it's easier and they believe themselves to be undefeatable. They think we're nothing.'

'We *are* nothing, compared to what they've got.'

'No,' Kerry insisted, 'they're nothing compared to what we've got.'

'And what the hell is that?'

'A better reason to survive,' Kerry replied. 'I thought you were manning–up for a bit back there?'

Marcus snorted. 'I'm staying reasonable too.'

'You're sounding like Dr Reed.'

'Now that's just nasty.'

'You ever think about him?' Kerry asked.

'Only the number of ways I'd like to murder him, if he were still properly alive.'

'That's kind of what I mean,' she replied. 'We can't kill them, but only because nobody has ever tried to think about what that actually means.'

'There's no getting near the Re–Volution servers,' Marcus confirmed.

'I didn't mean that,' Kerry said, 'I meant whether *holosaps* are actually alive.'

Marcus rubbed his temples and skirted a crumpled length of chain–link fence laying across grass the colour of straw. 'I don't think I can handle a metaphysical conversation right now.'

Kerry looked across at him.

'I know, but I was thinking in just general terms. I mean, have you ever seen a *holosap* laugh like they mean it?' Marcus looked up at her as he slowed. 'Or cry?' she added.

Marcus thought back across the years and shook his head.

'I guess not,' he admitted. 'I always got the odd feeling that I was looking at…'

He broke off, unable to find the words. Kerry finished them for him.

'A hologram,' she said, 'a moving picture that had no true depth.'

'No,' Marcus said. 'I always felt that I was looking at somebody with no soul.'

He saw Kerry shiver involuntarily.

'They're not right,' she said. 'I don't understand everything about them, about how their brains work or how they're created from their dead former selves, but I always figured that something was lost between the living person and their *holosap*.'

Marcus nodded as words tumbled without thought from his mouth. 'People aren't people when they have no fear of death,' he said.

Kerry took one more pace and then stopped in her tracks. Marcus looked at her and then ahead down the cluttered freeway with its swaying reeds and abandoned vehicles, thinking she had seen spheres or Wasps charging their way.

'What?' he asked.

Kerry did not move for what felt like an age but then she turned to him and hugged him tightly again.

'You're a genius too,' she whispered.

'I am?'

'Now we go together even better. Smelly, but smart. Come on,' she urged as she grabbed his hand and pulled him onward. 'You just figured out how to defeat everything that they have.'

Marcus let her tug him along with her firm grip and her bright smile, unable to understand what the hell she was talking about but hoping that she was right.

* * *

36

London

The journey back toward the city was conducted in silence.

The rover in which Arianna sat chugged its way north, followed by four more and a large troop carrier packed with boxes of equipment, the contents of which Icon refused to divulge.

'They're weapons,' Han had said a short while before.

He sat behind her in the rear of the rover, Myles beside him. Malcolm, Icon's right–hand man, drove the rover and shook his head, the loose folds of his hood briefly revealing the side of his skull–like face.

'Would you be surprised if the boxes did contain weapons?' he challenged. 'We're on the open road driving toward the last standing city in the country, which has a well–armed military and police force determined to eradicate people like us with extreme force.'

'Enough to take out a battalion?' Myles asked.

'I hope so,' Malcolm replied.

Han turned to look at Arianna. 'How are you doing?'

Arianna sighed 'As well as can be expected, which is to say I'm fairly terrified.'

'Good to know.'

She looked over her shoulder at him and he grinned, one hand reaching up to squeeze her shoulder. 'I'm right here. We've got your back.'

'Who's got yours?' she asked.

Han was about to answer but Malcolm spoke across him.

'The plan remains the same. Arianna will undergo the procedure to expose the *holosaps* from within and hopefully find the kill–switch at the same time. Icon and the men will maintain a secure perimeter around the site in case of any interruptions. If the process fails, we perform an armed egress away from the city. Hopefully, this will all be over within a couple of hours.'

'It'll certainly be over for Arianna if the procedure fails or the military figures out where we're all at,' Han pointed out. 'They're not going to be able to resist hitting your people hard, probably with an air strike of some kind.'

'We're ready for them,' Malcolm replied.

'Are you sure about that?' Myles asked the driver. 'The government can still put a thousand troops on the ground at a moment's notice, not to mention the police and air support. If this goes bad, and it well might if Arianna's true identity is exposed while she's uploaded, they could use her to locate us.'

Malcolm inclined his head as he drove.

'Then we will have our chance to stand and fight them, something that has been too long coming.'

'A suicide mission might suit whack–jobs like you,' Han said, 'but right now our best bet is to let Myles and me get back into the city and report everything we've learned.'

'We don't trust you to do that,' Malcolm growled back. 'And who would you report to? Your superiors?' Malcolm laughed. 'They would shoot you on sight and…'

'Not everybody in the city is the enemy,' Han shot back.

'That's enough!' Arianna snapped, silencing both men. 'This has to end somewhere, at some time and right now is the best opportunity we've got. None of us want to go through with it, least of all me because I have to endure the small matter of dying, so why don't you all shut up and let me think about what I've got to go through for any of this to be worth it, battles or not.'

She heard rather than saw Han slump back into his seat. Malcolm looked briefly across at her, a strange look on his disfigured face, but he drove on without another word.

They reached the city soon after, Malcolm following Icon's vehicle to a narrow street barely a mile south of the water. Decaying tower blocks loomed over narrow streets strewn with debris, the rusting hulk of a double–decker bus lying on its side nearby and almost entirely consumed by vines and weeds.

The vehicles pulled in behind one of the crumbling tower blocks, to shield them from view of the city to the north. Arianna climbed out as Icon walked toward her and gestured to an open doorway at the rear of the tower block, little more than a gaping black hole.

'It's in there,' Icon said. 'Malcolm will organise the sentries and distribute the weapons, just in case. I'll accompany you upstairs.'

'What about Han and Myles?' Arianna asked.

'They stay here under armed guard,' Icon replied. 'Best place for them.'

'Best for whom?' Han challenged.

Icon whipped a pistol from his belt and aimed it at Han. 'Best for me. You're within a mile of your fellow officers guarding Westminster Bridge, detective, and I'm not about to take the chance that either you or your partner here will make a run for home.'

Han ground his teeth in his jaw but said nothing as Malcolm and two more of Icon's men flanked him and Myles.

'Keep them to the rear,' Icon ordered. 'If they move, shoot them.'

The vehicles pulled away, probably to avoid identifying the building in which they would be hiding. Arianna watched Han and Myles being led away by Icon's men. 'That wasn't what we agreed,' she said to Icon.

'I know,' he replied without rancour, 'but twenty five years of surviving has taught me to trust nobody.'

'And yet you trust me to walk into the *holosap's* lair and not report your position?'

Icon smiled as he walked her toward the tower block. Icon's men fanned out toward sentry posts scattered around the perimeter of the building.

'I think we both know that's not your intention,' he replied. 'We both want this to be over with.'

Arianna followed Icon to a cold, stone stairwell that climbed up into the tower block. She was more than surprised when Icon bypassed it and headed toward an equally uninviting stairwell that went down into the darkness. He waved her to follow him.

'Just in case the detectives are able to break free,' he explained. 'One airstrike and this building would be demolished with you inside it. The basement offers protection from that.'

'You mean we can enjoy being buried alive together instead of incinerated?'

'At least we will stand a chance,' Icon replied. 'And their drones and helicopters can't detect us down here.'

The stairwell descended down toward the basement, the walls plastered in old gang tags and graffiti that had smeared and faded as water leaked down from above to stain the plaster and brickwork. The air felt damp and cold as Arianna followed Icon into what must once have been a maintenance bunker, a large but now silent boiler occupying one side of the room. On the other was a series of lights glowing from the power provided by a small diesel generator vented through a now–redundant air conditioning unit. The power was hooked up to what looked to Arianna like a heart–bypass machine, a ventilator and numerous monitors. Three fan–heaters struggled to maintain a meagre pocket of warm air around a pair of medical gurneys over which stood a middle aged man wearing small round spectacles and a face mask that only partially concealed his ruined jaw and neck.

On one of the gurneys lay Lynda, her arm patched where her blood had been taken.

'Doctor Tyree,' Icon greeted him. 'This is Arianna.'

Tyree's face looked close to normal, only a vague patchwork of scars beneath a surgical mask lining his neck and left jaw, but his stance was like that of a crippled pensioner and one leg dragged slightly behind him.

The doctor gestured Arianna to a vacant gurney. 'There is not much time.'

'You're not even going to buy me dinner first?' Arianna managed to quip.

The doctor smiled beneath his mask. 'I know you're nervous but don't worry. This procedure is standard during heart and brain operations. It's very stable.'

Arianna sighed as she climbed onto the gurney and lay back as Lynda climbed off the other gurney. Doctor Tyree placed straps around Arianna's wrists and ankles.

'To prevent you from falling off the gurney,' the doctor explained as he worked. 'We re–initiate heart rhythm using an electrical impulse.'

'Don't skimp on the voltage.'

'You'll be fine,' Icon said as he looked down at her. 'I must go now to ensure that the doctor's work remains uninterrupted.' Icon leaned in closer, his ruined face only partly concealed by his hood. 'Arianna, if you think that you're in danger, get out. The doctor will pre–arrange a signal for you, a way to connect with him and ask for extraction. Use it. Enough people have died over all of this. I don't see any sense in losing another.'

Icon whirled away and swept from the basement. As she watched him go, and the doctor rolled up her left sleeve and prepared a syringe with a needle that seemed thinner than a human hair, Arianna wondered briefly if the cold, bare basement room would be the last thing she would see with her own eyes.

'What will I see?'

Her question slipped out seemingly of its own accord as the needle slipped in. Arianna did not look at the doctor, instead staring at the featureless ceiling as she heard his reply.

'They say you see a light, a tunnel of light, but before you can reach the end it turns into patterns that resolve themselves once again into the world around you. You'll be fine, Arianna.'

A sudden, further question leaped into Arianna's mind.

'How long will I have before they realise who I am?'

Doctor Tyree shrugged. 'It's doubtful you'll have more than a few hours, Arianna, but just you being in there will be enough for us to complete our attack. By any means, as we like to say.'

Alarm pulsed through Arianna's chest and her eyes flew wide as she looked at the doctor.

'Attack?'

Before she could call out for help she felt her body go numb and darkness fell like a heavy shroud around her.

* * *

37

The darkness took on a new shape.

Arianna was not aware of the precise moment when she realised that she was awake and aware again. An incessant beeping noise infiltrated her awareness and echoed through an immense blackness around her. Then, slowly but surely, the basement came back into focus.

For a moment she could not identify what was different about it, but then she realised. She was no longer on the gurney but was in fact above it. She felt a further jolt of surprise as she realised that she was both on the gurney *and* above it, looking down at herself as the doctor worked on the bypass machine close to her side. She saw blood, her blood, flowing through clear tubes, but she quickly noted that her chest was not moving, the respirator was not working and the blood was flowing only slowly.

One of the monitors read a flat–lined heart rhythm and a body temperature of less than sixteen degrees. The doctor turned and poured a bag of ice into the bypass machine, keeping Arianna's blood chilled.

'I'm dead.'

She did not speak the words, but none the less she heard them clearly. Everything seemed hyper detailed, her senses super charged. She could hear the doctor's breathing, the rustle of his shirt beneath the white laboratory coat he wore, the brush of his skin against the icy–cold plastic bags.

The colours in the otherwise dull basement seemed deeper than any she had ever witnessed, and she wondered for a brief moment how she could see anything if her eyes were closed. The realisation that she could not have any eyes as her body was lying beneath her caused her to look at herself.

And realise that there was no *self*.

She had no body and was merely a point of existence hovering in the air. She wondered if this was the essence of her, her spirit or her soul or whatever those who believed called them. Then she recalled that she too believed in such things and a great joy flushed through her, an overwhelming sense of relief that, somehow, all of this time, she had been right.

She began to rise up and away from her physical body, and turned to see a growing orb of brilliant white light, brighter than the most powerful star and yet every bit as gentle as starlight. Warmth flooded around her, enveloped her in a comforting blanket of peace and contentment as she rose up toward the centre of the light, the darkness fading away behind her, rising faster and faster and yet as calmly as a feather lifted by a warm summer breeze.

The brilliant light surrounded her and all memories of her troubled life fell away like worn skins to tumble behind her into oblivion. Arianna was smiling broadly yet she had no mouth. She felt her heart racing with joy even though no such organ beat within her. Warmth caressed her even though she had no skin with which to sense it, and the questions that she had fell away with her concerns as she let herself be taken by the light until it consumed her.

Ahead, figures milled in the brilliance, and though she could not clearly see them she knew somehow that they knew her and were waiting. She sensed family, friends, people she had long ago pushed from her mind to avoid the grief of recalling their names.

Connor.

The smaller of the many silhouettes awaited her and she knew with all of her heart that he was there, that he was safe, that he had always been safe and that all of her suffering and grief had been for nothing because nothing ever really dies.

'Connor!'

She called out to him, reached out for him not with her hands but her heart, and felt his smile and his laughter and his happiness reaching out for her too, connecting with her as though he had never left and…

The bright light shivered as though it had been cast against a vast sheet of glass and an unseen projectile had shattered it into a billion pieces. Arianna cried out in despair as the warmth vanished and she felt Connor's presence ripped away from her as sure as he had been torn from her life. The light faded to a mere haunting ghost of what it had once been as the glowing rainbow colours and elegant freehand watercolour strokes of creation were yanked into orderly geometric spirals, lines and corners. Harsh, painfully bright and angular.

Streams of information flowed past her like highways filled with billions of headlights, passed through her like laser beams as she felt herself falling downward into blackness. Memories of her life rushed back in a tsunami of emotion: joy warred with pain and hope clashed with despair in a hymn of human suffering. Arianna cried out in horror as the emotions overwhelmed her and crushed her down and with a deafening crash that sounded as though she had hit the ground head–first from a mile high, the rush of data vanished into blackness and the world fell silent once more.

The voice, when she heard it, seemed alien.

'Welcome.'

Arianna realised that she could feel her eyes and that they were shut. With a titanic will of effort she opened them.

She was standing in a small, clean room. A potted fern of some kind stood in one corner, warm colours from outside glowing against the walls. An attractive, dark haired woman sat in a reclining chair nearby and watched her with a calm smile.

'How do you feel?'

Arianna looked down at herself and saw her body glowing as she stood on the projection platform built into the floor. Sparkles of light glittered like fallen stars as they traced the outline of her legs. She moved her arm to touch herself and it passed straight through her body. She jerked it away again.

'Don't worry,' the woman said. 'You'll soon become familiar with your new status as a *holosap*.'

Arianna looked at the woman. 'Can you hear me?'

'Perfectly well,' the woman replied. 'My name is Penny. You're in the Re–Volution headquarters in London.'

Arianna looked around her and realised that she was standing in her own office, the one she had last seen only the day before. The chrome Crucifix on the wall was gone, it's mark on the wall covered by a plastic Re–Volution logo. *See the light*. She turned and saw that her full length mirror was still there. Her reflection glowed and shimmered, partly transparent, but more shocking was the face of a stranger looking back at her. Lynda, from Icon's camp, her features as forlorn and lonely now as they had been hours before.

Arianna, her mind filled with memories of the wonderful warm light and of Connor waiting for her, forced herself to ask the right questions.

'What happened to me?'

'We're just trying to work that out,' Penny replied. 'Your download was activated remotely and we cannot locate your details on our database. What's your name?'

'Lynda,' Arianna replied. 'Lynda Griffiths.'

Penny nodded and swept a perfectly manicured finger over a touch screen mounted into the arm of Arianna's chair.

'Can you recall anything about your life, Lynda?'

Arianna stared at the floor near her feet and shook her head. 'Everything's just a blur,' she replied. 'I'm not sure what I'm seeing?'

'Your neural connections are not yet complete,' Penny explained. 'It will take time but hopefully within a few days you should be able to remember everything that happened to you, right up to the moments before your upload. You understand that I need to report your upload to the police. They may wish to interview you in case your upload was the result of foul play.'

Arianna nodded. 'Of course, that's fine. I'd like to know what happened myself.'

'I don't doubt it,' Penny replied. 'Your record in the database lists you as missing, presumed dead. You were only thirty nine years old. I'm sorry for what has happened to you, Lynda. Do you know why you were not here in the city when you uploaded? Our data puts you somewhere south of the Thames.'

Arianna shook her head. 'No, I'm sorry but I don't. I would never have willingly set foot beyond the perimeter though, it's far too dangerous. Somebody must have taken me there.'

Penny nodded and scanned her touch screen.

'It's possible you were abducted, although according to this you've been missing for some years.'

Arianna changed tack.

'Perhaps you could run some sort of scan on my upload?' she suggested. 'Maybe it will allow you to see what I can't recall?'

Penny inclined her head. 'Perhaps, but that would be a police matter and they would need a warrant to access your data stream. I think that for now it's best that you remain under restrictive measures until your history can be pieced together.'

Arianna shrugged. 'That's okay. You'll let me know as soon as you find something?'

'Of course,' Penny assured her. 'Do you have anybody waiting for you?'

Arianna shook her head. 'Like I said, I don't recall much right now.'

'Okay,' Penny said and shut down her touch–screen. 'You'll be assigned a quarters in the colony. You're downloaded, but for the time being you won't be able to move freely. Everybody is very sensitive here after the terrorist attack on our headquarters.'

'That's fine,' Arianna agreed and mustered a cheerful smile. 'It's not like I'm going anywhere now.'

Penny smiled but her eyes were fixed intently on Arianna's. 'You're handling this remarkably well, Lynda. Most of my clients find adapting to their new existence difficult and disorientating.'

Arianna shrugged again. 'Are you kidding? I'm immune to The Falling now. I don't care how weird it feels, it's better than dying for real…, I mean, forever?'

Penny offered a final smile and reached out for a button on her chair.

'You'll be sent directly to your new quarters in the colony. Your escort will arrive shortly afterward. The transfer process is extremely rapid.'

Arianna took a deep breath even though she technically had no lungs with which to inhale. Penny touched the button on her chair and Arianna reeled as data flashed like a whirlpool of stars spiralling down into a bottomless pit of darkness. Even before her brain had been able to properly process the image she found herself standing in an apartment that seemed to her as solid as anything in the real world. As she took in the scene, she gasped.

Leather couches, soft carpets, broad windows that looked out across a tremendous vista of tumbling cumulus clouds rolling over pristine, forested mountains. Bright flares of sunlight burst through the cloud from perfect blue heavens to drift like glowing beams across the world below as though the hand of God were gently caressing His own Creation. A waterfall plunged down hundreds of feet from a mountain crevice into a deep, shimmering azure lake nearby, rainbows dancing through the clouds of vapour.

Arianna gasped at how beautiful the *holosap's* world looked, realised in colours more vivid than dreams. The apartment in which she stood was part of a palatial villa perched on the edge of a cliff overlooking the forested hills and valleys. Arianna stepped up to the window and slid it open, the impossibly fresh smelling air wafting past her, the sound of the water and of birds in the trees. Clearly, there was no pandemic in this world. It was Heaven, or Nirvana, or whatever paradise one chose to call it, a far cry from Icon's pitiful, freezing domain.

It's not real, Arianna. She gathered her thoughts, most of them haunted by the doctor's parting words as she hurried across to a familiar looking panel on the wall. Clearly, the colony's digital architects had decided to make the environment seem as real–world as possible. She tapped the panel, wrote a short message and entered a name into the transmission request window.

To Alexei Volkov, from *rebyohnuk*. I need you.

'Hurry,' she whispered as she sent the request.

* * *

38

New Orleans

'Stay down.'

Kerry's voice was a whisper as she crouched low behind a wooden fence that lined a parking lot near the airport's main terminal.

Marcus crouched alongside her and peered through cracks in the fence to where the airport terminals and control tower loomed. The vast, open expanse of the airport meant that there was no easy way to reach the radar tower, but that it was their target was made clear by the fact that in a world now devoid of electrical power, the primary radar dish was still spinning slowly.

'It's active,' Kerry said. 'They're here all right.'

Marcus scanned the airport and let his gaze fall on the enormous satellite dish, almost as big as the control tower, sitting at the end of a concourse near the terminals.

'We'll never get across there without being seen,' he said. 'They'll be onto us the moment we step out of cover.'

'They could have been onto us by now,' Kerry pointed out. 'They know roughly where we're coming from and this is the main road in.'

Marcus thought for a moment. 'They're letting us in?'

'Yep,' Kerry replied. 'Easiest way to catch us I guess, just let us into their lair and then encircle us.'

Before Marcus could stop her she got up from behind the fence and jogged alongside the high hedges that led to the airport's main entrance. He scrambled to keep up as she moved beneath the main Terminal sign and toward an up–ramp marked Departures. There were no guards present, no spheres or humming swarms of Wasps awaiting them. The thought that they were all waiting in ambush sent shivers down Marcus's spine that warred with those from his fever.

'This is insane,' he hissed at her. 'They could send a hundred Wasps at us right now, or a dozen of those spheres!'

'Then why haven't they?' Kerry challenged. 'I think that they want us alive and the Wasps can be unreliable, so they'll come at us with their troops instead.'

'And that's better how?'

'You'll see.'

Marcus trudged along behind Kerry as she climbed the up–ramp, which turned left into the terminal entrance proper. Here, she slowed and hugged the concrete walls, easing her way up until she could peek around the corner and see the terminal entrance.

Marcus's guts plunged as he peered over her shoulder and saw two metallic spheres guarding the terminal entrance. Above the spheres, clinging to the concrete walls in angular, glossy black balls, were two swarms of Wasps.

'Shit,' he uttered.

'Good,' Kerry whispered.

'What?'

'They're letting the machines do the guard duty,' she replied. 'Machines can be fooled.'

'You're kidding,' Marcus whispered. 'We could get into the airport from any direction, just head back down to the lot and jump over a wall. These things are here for decoration.'

'No, they're here for a reason,' Kerry snapped back. 'Think about it. They post Wasps and spheres here, forcing us to move out across the open ground outside the terminal. They don't think we'll try the main entrance for fear of death.'

'And unsurprisingly, they're right. We go that way, we're finished.'

'But if we can get past, we can get halfway to the satellite dish without exposing ourselves.'

'How? You can't put the Wasps into stand–by without access to a computer, and those spheres are lethal.'

'Yeah,' Kerry agreed, 'but they're also flawed. They must be powered by electricity so they must have a power source, batteries or whatever, and they must have delicate electronics inside them. Wires, silicon chips, stuff like that.'

'So? You think you're going to outrun them until their batteries run out?'

'No,' Kerry said. 'But they couldn't find us when we were camped out under that tree, and I think I know why. The spheres couldn't get over the stream to look for us, and the Wasps just couldn't see us from any distance away. Their sensors must be too small to resolve distant targets.'

Marcus frowned. 'So they passed us by.'

Kerry nodded. 'Plus the spheres, although likely remotely controlled by humans, are limited in their mobility and reaction times. They can be out–manoeuvred.'

Marcus checked over his shoulder in case hordes of machines were approaching them from behind. 'This gets better and better. So what are you suggesting?'

'We attack them.'

'We do what?!'

'We attack them and slip past in the confusion.'

'Just like that?' Marcus uttered. 'And if we do, don't you think the soldiers controlling the machines will just send in the troops to finish us off?'

'I'm counting on it,' Kerry said. She watched the two hanging balls of Wasps and the two spheres for a moment longer, and then turned to Marcus. 'Okay, this is what we're going to do.'

Marcus listened to what she had to say and then shook his head. 'Seriously?'

'Seriously,' she confirmed. 'Let's get to it.'

'But if we get this even slightly wrong…,' he said as Kerry got up and hurried back down the ramp.

'I don't want to think about it,' she replied.

Marcus followed Kerry down to the nearby airport parking lot, where hundreds of vehicles lay rusting under the burning sun. One by one, using bits of pipe yanked from engines and old plastic jerry cans foraged from trunks, they began syphoning from old bowsers with tanks big enough to still contain useful amounts of gasoline. Marcus hunted down empty glass bottles, collecting them along with fragments of dried rags and abandoned clothing hanging to the bones of long dead victims of The Falling.

It took almost thirty minutes to find enough gas to fill both the cans. Kerry led Marcus back to the up–ramp and gestured across to their left.

'The ramp comes back down the other side of the multi–storey,' she said. 'Get over there and be ready.'

Marcus sighed, but he hurried along across the front of the huge parking lot until he found the western access road leading to the up–ramp on the far side of the terminal. Carrying his jerry can and bottles, he crept up the ramp and under the terminal entrance shelter until he could see the two spheres and swarms guarding the main entrance.

In the distance a bright rectangle of light marked the east entrance, and he glimpsed Kerry appear close against the wall there. In typical fashion she did not hesitate. Before Marcus had a moment to draw breath and prepare himself he heard a clicking sound as Kerry lit the Molotov cocktail she had prepared and hurled it at the entrance. The flaming bottle arced across the terminal entrance and trailed oily brown smoke.

Marcus's heart skipped a beat as the silent projectile smashed right alongside the furthest swarm of Wasps. A bright spray of flaming gasoline, smoke and shattered glass showered down over the swarm and the sphere right below it. Marcus saw the two spheres jerk into motion as though startled awake, one of them draped in streams of burning gasoline.

The two swarms of Wasps suddenly hummed loudly.

'Shit.'

Marcus grabbed his own Molotov and with his lighter ignited the tinder–dry rag stuffed into the bottle's neck. He stepped out as the two swarms began to break apart, and with a heave of effort he hurled his flaming bottle toward the nearest swarm.

The bottle spun through the air and smashed into the Wasps, exploding into flames that coated the Wasps in burning gasoline and sprayed down on the second sphere even as its feet flicked out to propel it after Kerry.

Marcus ducked back against the wall as the second sphere rotated toward him and its guns flared. A deafening crescendo of bullets shattered the wall near where he cowered but ceased almost instantly as he heard a dull explosion and a deep thud.

Marcus peeked around the corner, another Molotov in his hand as he saw the sphere topple onto one side as flames seethed inside it. The burning gasoline had seeped in through the open gun ports and he could see wisps of blue smoke as the flames melted vulnerable wires and cables. The Wasps above the damaged sphere were airborne but crashing wildly into the walls of the terminal as the sticky, flaming gasoline scorched delicate circuits and blurred their optics with fluid and heat. Others skittered across the floor, their wings malfunctioning and their glossy black abdomen pulsing as they tried to sting the flames that enveloped them.

Marcus saw Kerry make a dash for the terminal entrance and he grabbed his remaining gasoline and bottles and ran hard toward the smoke and flame. One of the Wasps on the ground righted itself and beat its wings as it tried to lift off, smoke coiling in a dirty brown vortex from its body. Marcus changed direction and jumped, landing on top of the Wasp with both feet.

The hard body of the Wasp hit the asphalt beneath him, solid as a bag of rocks under his boots, but he both felt and heard delicate hinges connecting the wings and body crack and splinter beneath the impact.

'Inside, now! Before they recover!'

He heard Kerry shout at him as she ducked behind a wildly revolving sphere that was trying to take aim at her. Marcus stopped, lit another Molotov and hurled it at the back of the sphere. The explosion shattered the bottle as Marcus hurled himself into cover, fragments of burning glass peppering the terminal doors.

The sphere collapsed onto one malfunctioning leg, its guns facing away from the terminal.

Kerry dodged past the damaged sphere and launched herself at the terminal doors, then yanked a tyre iron from her bag and wedged it between them. With a heave of effort she forced them apart enough for Marcus to squeeze through. Marcus dropped his bag between the doors as he passed through them, blocking them open for Kerry as she danced over the bag and then reached down and yanked it through. The door slammed shut again behind her with a dull thud.

The remaining functional Wasps banged into the glass, some of them still burning and smouldering, their flight awkward as they tried to reach Marcus and Kerry.

'They'll go around,' Marcus said. 'They'll find another way inside or they'll alert the troops.'

One of the spheres was attempting to shuffle around on its remaining functional leg to bring its guns to bear on the terminal doors and windows.

'We need to move, now,' he said.

Before Kerry could reply a blast of gunfire smashed the tiled floor near their feet and clattered across the ceiling above their heads. Marcus hurled himself onto the floor as Kerry crouched down with her hands over her head, a shower of shattered ceiling tiles tumbling down around them like snow.

A murderous voice boomed out across the terminal entrance.

'Hands in the air, right now!'

Marcus threw his hands into the air and with Kerry turned to see a black clothed soldier, his face concealed behind a mask and an assault rifle, stalking toward them from within the terminal.

* * *

39

Marcus stood immobile, his gaze fixed on the advancing soldier.

'On your knees!'

The man's voice was coming through a filter across his mouth, thick goggles protecting his eyes. He wore a heavy bullet–proof vest, thick black gloves and heavy duty boots. Ammunition was packed into his belt–kit, fragmentation grenades dangling alongside them and a thick combat knife was shoved into a sheath at his waist.

Marcus complied without question.

'We're not infected,' Kerry called out, still standing.

'On your knees!' the soldier bellowed.

Kerry dropped to her knees held her hands high as the soldier stalked toward them, the rifle switching between them as though the trooper had a nervous tick. Marcus could see his eyes behind the mask now, fierce but tinged with caution.

The soldier paused, standing a few feet away with his finger tight against the trigger. Marcus saw his gaze flick down to the wounds on both of their necks. Kerry spoke before Marcus could formulate a response.

'We're immune,' she said. 'We're immune to The Falling. The government is lying to you. They're lying to everyone.'

'Shut up and stay down!'

The soldier's gaze flicked back and forth between them. He glanced over his shoulder before shouting again.

'Don't move and don't speak!'

Marcus looked behind the soldier. The airport terminal stretched away through open passport control barriers with empty checkpoints and on toward baggage collection and the lengthy sheltered tunnels that led to the boarding ramps. More troops would be coming, and he realised that the soldier must have been a sentry, a human back–up for the machines guarding the airport entrance.

'It's true,' Kerry insisted, ignoring the soldier's order. 'They want us dead because we're proof that you can survive The Falling.' The soldier's gaze fixed on Kerry. Slowly, carefully, Kerry went on. 'Listen, the wound on my neck is from the bite of an infected human. Look more closely. It's healing. I'll have a hell of a scar, but I'm alive.'

The soldier stared at her neck for what felt like an eternity.

'She's not lying,' Marcus said. 'The lunatic bit me too, to pass the immunity on.'

The soldier looked at Marcus for a moment.

'How?' he asked finally.

'We're from the research station ten miles east of here,' Kerry said. 'We found evidence of mammals that had developed immunity to The Falling that were surviving in the bayou. I isolated the genes responsible and was going to send them out into the research community for peer review. Dr Reed refused to let me do that, so instead I injected myself with a serum containing the active genes.'

Marcus took over.

'Dr Reed is working with the government, or whoever wants this to be kept under wraps. He tried to kill us, which was when Kerry got bitten and when she decided to bite me too.' Marcus turned his head slightly to reveal his own bloodied wound. 'I've still got the fever, but I'm alive.'

The soldier's rifle lowered slightly. 'Why?'

'I don't know,' Kerry said. 'We figured that it was something to do with the *holosaps*. They want power and are on the verge of taking over politically. If The Falling can be cured, they'll lose that power.'

The soldier watched them for a moment longer. 'You're terrorists. Dr Reed gave his life to protect us from people like you.'

'Dr Reed's here?' Kerry uttered. 'We shut his transmission off!'

Marcus stared at the soldier as he realised what had happened.

'Reed's quantum storage is *here*,' he said to Kerry. 'They must have had to send him completely here to continue his work in hunting us down. Maybe they couldn't maintain a transmission from New York?'

Kerry looked up at the soldier.

'We're not lying. What the hell is the government doing out here with all of these machines if they're not hiding things?'

'The sentry 'bots are just guardians,' the soldier snapped back. 'The working machines are being built here.'

'Working machines?' Marcus echoed. 'You mean, like factory robots?'

The soldier remained silent. Kerry gasped as she finally figured it out.

'A workforce,' she said finally. 'The *holosaps* will need a robotic workforce to maintain the physical side of their life: the computers, satellite dishes, construction to build new robots when the old ones malfunction.'

It took Marcus only a second to grasp why the *holosaps* would do that.

'They're building a force to *replace* us,' he whispered, 'to replace humans.'

The soldier was looking at them, back and forth.

'They're building a support unit,' he snapped back, 'to reinitiate farming methods out here where humans cannot move freely. The machines are here to help humanity and people like you are destroying their efforts.'

Kerry gasped in disbelief.

'*Holosaps* don't need food and I'm right here in front of you!' she almost shouted. 'I'm immune to The Falling! We don't need the goddamned machines.'

A cracking sound echoed down toward them from the far end of the terminal. In the distance, Marcus saw a door open and several heavily armed soldiers plunge through it.

The soldier glanced over his shoulder.

Marcus saw Kerry move. From behind where she crouched she lifted a Molotov and a lighter, the flame touching the bone dry fuse in a flare of bright flame and coiling smoke. Even as the soldier turned back Kerry hurled the bottle at the tiled floor right in front of his boots as Marcus threw his arms up to protect his face.

The bottle shattered against the tiles and flames spilled from the burning fluid and splattered across the soldier's black fatigues as flaming glass fragments showered his arms and gloved hands. The soldier threw his rifle up to point at the ceiling with one hand as with the other he began frantically trying to pat out the flames spiralling up his legs.

Kerry launched herself at the soldier, Marcus scrambling to his feet in pursuit as she ploughed into him and they plunged down together onto the tiles. Kerry grabbed the soldier's rifle and pinned it down as she lay atop him, her legs straddling his waist. The soldier swung his free fist at her face but Marcus plunged down and wrapped his arms around the soldier's arm, pinning him down onto the ground.

'My legs are on fire!' he roared.

Kerry turned and grabbed the soldier's knife from its sheath on his belt, then shoved the wicked serrated blade up against his neck. The soldier's eyes flared wide and his screams stopped as he stared up at her.

Kerry glared down at the soldier.

'We're not lying,' she hissed. 'If the *holosaps* get what they want, every human being will die.'

Marcus watched as Kerry yanked the blade away from the soldier's neck and turned, batting the flames burning his fatigues out. Marcus released the soldier's arm and stamped out the remaining flames as Kerry stood up.

The sound of running boots and shouts echoed toward them from the terminal as the soldier, still lying on his back, stared up at them.

'You're sure?' he asked, his voice rasping.

'One hundred per cent,' Kerry replied.

'The doors,' Marcus urged.

Outside, the Wasps were battering at the thick glass as they tried to get to Marcus and Kerry, and one of the spheres was still jerking awkwardly around on malfunctioning feet to bring its weapons to bear on the doors. The soldier scrambled up onto his feet again and whirled, waving his smouldering gloved hands at his fellow soldiers still charging down upon them.

'Stand down!' he bellowed. 'Stand down!'

Marcus felt a surge of relief as he turned to the running soldiers. The relief transformed grotesquely into horror as the charging soldiers raised their rifles and opened fire.

A blaze of gunfire raked the terminal around them as Marcus and Kerry hurled themselves back down onto the ground. The bullets smacked into the terminal doors, splintered craters peppering the thick glass.

'Stand down!' the soldier yelled again.

Two rounds hit him square in the chest and propelled him backwards into a pillar, his bullet–proof vest shuddering beneath the blows. His rifle spun from his grasp and clattered onto the tiles at his feet as he collapsed.

'Shit!' Kerry yelled in terror, pinned down behind the wall.

Marcus moved without thinking, which was probably for the best. He hurled himself across the terminal floor, rolling as he picked up the rifle and knelt over the soldier's comatose body. He aimed the weapon at the horde of oncoming soldiers and pulled the trigger.

The heavy M–16 jerked in his arms as three rounds cracked out. The charging soldiers broke formation and dove for cover behind passport booths and baggage carousels, some returning fire as best they could. Marcus ducked down low, fired three more rounds, and then turned to the nearby terminal doors. The damaged sphere was almost facing the doors, its wicked machine guns coming to bear, and the Wasps were now waiting patiently for the doors to be shattered by the gunfire. Marcus turned to Kerry.

'Run!'

Kerry lurched to her feet and ran, but she headed not for the nearest escape route through the terminal to the east but instead for Marcus's side. She slumped down alongside him and shook her head.

'I brought you here, we stick together.'

A blast of deafening machine gun fire raked the terminal entrance as the sphere blazed a fearsome broadside of rounds into the glass. The doors shattered in a cloud of tumbling glass as half a dozen Wasps buzzed loudly into the terminal entrance.

The glossy black Wasps hummed toward them, metallic wings flickering in the weak light, cruel stingers glinting. Marcus whirled and pressed the muzzle of the rifle against the unconscious soldier's head.

The Wasps slowed and hovered six feet away from them. A voice rang out from further down the terminal.

'Lay down your weapons and come out!'

The soldier at Marcus's feet groaned and his eyes flicked open. They swivelled to look at the rifle pressed against his head, and then down at his chest where two bullets protruded from his thick protective vest.

Kerry shouted back at the soldiers. 'We've got a hostage!'

Silence hung heavy in the air in the terminal. Marcus looked down at the soldier, who raised an eyebrow quizzically at him.

'We'll kill him!' Marcus shouted, then looked down at the soldier and gave him a fractional shake of the head.

A reply rolled back at them. 'Fine, do it. Saves us the trouble!'

Marcus stared back down at the soldier, whose expression crumbled into anger. He reached slowly down to his belt–kit and unclipped a pouch. From within he pulled a small black box arrayed with switches beneath a clear plastic cover.

Marcus watched as the soldier flipped back the plastic cover. A small screen revealed the terminal in Infra–Red, viewed through a camera attached somewhere up high near the ceiling. The soldier swivelled the camera until it pointed at the half–dozen troops crouched fifty yards away across the terminal, their heat signatures clearly visible.

'I don't want to die!' he called out to his comrades, his voice trembling with fear that surprised Marcus. The soldier's face registered only rage.

A moment's silence passed and then a solemn voice rolled back toward them.

'Sorry Chad, orders are orders pal!'

Marcus looked down at Chad, who thumbed a touch–pad on his little box of tricks. He clicked on each of the soldier's heat signatures and then pressed a single button. All of the soldier's signatures were suddenly ringed with a flashing red box. Chad turned to look at the Wasps and then tapped in a four–digit passcode and hit *Enter*.

The Wasps and the sphere spun around in an instant, the Wasps buzzing loudly as they shot off across the terminal.

There was a moment of silence, then shouts of alarm and panic. Gunfire erupted, hammering the ceiling further down the terminal and two Wasps jerked in mid–flight and span out of control. The other four zoomed down out of sight as screams of agony shrieked and echoed through the terminal as the soldiers were attacked by their own weapons.

The sphere shuffled awkwardly past, and a deafening blast of machine gun fire smashed through the passport control booths nearby.

Marcus looked across at Kerry, who was sitting against the pillar beside Chad and looking pleased with herself despite the horrendous screams and clattering gunfire echoing around them.

'That's what you meant,' Marcus said, 'when you said I was a genius for saying that *holosaps* are not people.'

Kerry nodded as the gunfire ceased and the cries of pain faded into silence.

'The *holosaps* are lying, deceiving millions of people and are responsible for the deaths of billions of innocent lives. Their soldiers work for the government but only to preserve their own lives: if *they* realised that we're immune, do you think that they would risk their lives out here for a lie and a bunch of holographic zombies?'

'You think we can tell them all, turn them to the truth?'

'You're damned right you can,' Chad said.

The soldier struggled to his feet and yanked off his mask, revealing a surprisingly young face and a blond buzz–cut.

'You give me immunity to The Falling, and I'll bring the entire army down on whoever's behind all of this.'

* * *

40

London

Han Reeves sat on the cold, damp floor of what had once been a meat locker. Myles sat beside him, both of their hands cuffed using cable ties and a pair of rebel guards watching them from an open doorway, old SA–80 rifles cradled in their grasp.

Arianna would be out cold by now, Han figured. He found her intriguing, an odd mixture of courageous and timid that had a volatile edge to it, like a bomb only partially defused. He struggled now, he realised, between his duty as a police officer and a deep desire to protect Arianna from harm, a feat which he also recognised he had failed spectacularly to achieve: he was under armed guard, she was partially dead and neither of them could be sure that they had a life to return to back in the city.

'You think she'll pull it off?' Myles asked.

'The hell would I know?' Han replied. 'I don't even know what it is she's trying to achieve. Even if she can prove the *holosaps* are somehow corrupt and gets out of this alive, I don't know how Icon and his people will use that information to expose the government.'

'They've got their immunity,' Myles pointed out. 'That in itself is enough.'

'Yeah, provided they get the chance to show it. If Icon plasters his face across the news networks the people will run a mile. Nobody wants to see a ruined face as the poster child of the revolution. He wants Arianna to do it, and I think he wants her to do it from within.'

'But if he wants that, then why bother with all of his weapons?'

'Revenge,' Han explained. 'He's spent half of his life on the run, disfigured and living off the land, and all of it for a lie. A man like Icon's not going to see the government deposed and then just clap his hands and sing happy songs. He'll want them to burn for what they've done.'

Myles looked up at the guards, their face concealed by the ubiquitous hoods worn by all of Icon's deformed minions.

'If they hit parliament it'll leave a power vacuum,' Myles said. 'They might end up destroying what little government we have left.'

Han nodded but did not say anything. Truth was, he could not tell who was to be trusted and who was not. The only thing that he was absolutely sure of was that Re–Volution was the ultimate cause of everything that had happened. Without them and their bizarre, dangerous experiments into immortality there would be no *holosaps* to worry about and most likely the cure to The Falling would have long ago been administered to mankind's beleaguered survivors.

'We need to get to Revo's headquarters and figure this out from there.'

'Good luck with that,' Myles chuckled with a wince. 'Icon's got us locked down to prevent us from doing anything to interfere with his vengeance.'

'You got any better ideas?' Han challenged. 'We've been missing for several hours. What do you think will happen if we just show up at the station?'

Myles looked at Han for a long beat. 'How do you propose we get out of here?'

Han did not reply. Instead, he got up onto his feet and walked toward the nearest guard. The hooded man turned, the SA–80 drifting across to point at Han's belly.

'Stay where you are.'

'It's damp where I am,' Han replied, not moving too close to the weapon. 'You got a toilet I can use?'

The guard stared at Han for several seconds as though assessing whether or not to believe him. Finally, he leaned his head to one side and whistled. Within seconds, another hooded guard appeared, also armed with an identical weapon.

'Cover the other one,' the guard ordered his companion, 'this one needs to take a leak.'

Han walked out of the meat locker. As expected, the gunman fell in line behind him with the SA–80's muzzle close to Han's back. It was a common enough mistake among non–military people, to assume that their finger on the trigger would be quicker than a trained man's reflexes. Han walked only three paces before whirling on the spot, his cuffed hands sweeping around to push the rifle's barrel to one side.

Han stepped in toward the startled guard's face and dropped his full weight behind his forehead as he whipped it forward and down. It thumped into the guard's nose with a sickening crunch, hard enough that the man's consciousness vanished as though a switch had been flicked off in his mind. The guard crumpled to his knees as Han grabbed the rifle and turned it awkwardly in his cuffed hands.

The second guard, facing into the meat locker, heard the commotion and turned to bring his weapon to bear out into the corridor. Han aimed at him and shook his head once. The guard faltered, just in time for Myles to leap forward and wrestle the rifle from his grasp.

The entire event had taken less than ten seconds.

'Use their knives to cut us loose, then bind and gag them,' Han ordered as he shouldered his SA–80 and dragged the unconscious guard into the meat locker.

'You'll pay for this,' snarled the other guard, his hood falling back to reveal his hideously scarred face and neck. 'Icon will find you and…'

'We're on your side, arsehole,' Han snapped as Myles cut his bonds. 'But your people are going about this all the wrong way and if you keep going everybody's going to hell in a hand basket, okay?'

'How the hell do we get past the checkpoint on the river?' Myles asked as he turned and used a length of torn shirt to gag the conscious guard. 'If you're right they might just gun as down as soon as they see us.'

'We'll have to hope that they don't,' Han said, 'and I've got an idea to get us through and straight to the Revo building.'

Myles followed Han out of the meat locker in a hurry, slamming the door shut behind them.

'You're going to warn them about the attack?' Myles asked.

'Sure,' Han replied. 'Safest thing to do, right? We get into Revo, they think we're on their side and it stops Icon from blowing the crap out of the city or whatever it is he's got in mind.'

'And if they decide to just ice us as soon as we get in there?'

'They won't,' Han assured him. 'They'll be too damned keen to find out what we know.'

Han kept walking but Myles slowed behind him.

'And what if you're working for Re–Volution, Han?'

Han slowed in the corridor and stopped. He looked back over his shoulder at Myles, who was standing with the other rifle pointed at him.

'Oh come on, really?' Han asked.

'Corrupt cops, corrupt officials,' Myles shrugged. 'I mean, you've got connections Han, from the military. Maybe they got to you, and all you want to do is stop Icon and his people.'

'They shot at *us* Myles! Both of us!'

'And you've followed Arianna since day one of this case, right when she showed up at both the Re–Volution explosion and the murder of Alexei Volkov. It's like you've been following her for a reason, Han.'

Han opened his mouth to speak and then he heard it, a distant rumbling, the hammering of blades on air threading its way into the building from outside.

'Helicopters,' he said. 'How could they know we were here?'

'If you're working for Re–Volution, then you'd want this place destroyed. Maybe you called them in to hit the building?'

'Not with me in it, you idiot!' Han yelled. 'We've got to get Arianna out of there!'

Myles clenched his jaw and gripped his rifle tighter. 'This isn't over, Han. We get her out and then we head back over the water and sort this for once and for all.'

'Done,' Han agreed. 'Can we bloody go now?'

Myles lowered his rifle and turned to run for the exit.

Han turned with him and then jerked his right forearm backward as Myles dashed past. The blow caught Myles across the throat and collapsed his thorax against his windpipe. Myles's eyes bulged and he gagged as Han swivelled and drove his left knee up into his partner's plexus, driving the air from his lungs in a great rush.

Myles collapsed onto his knees and rolled up into a foetal ball as Han yanked the rifle from his grasp.

'Sorry kid.'

Myles gaped breathlessly, his face turning an unhealthy shade of blue as air whistled down his strained windpipe. Han tied his partner's hands behind his back and then bound his ankles up against his wrists. He stood up and watched Myles's laboured breathing for a moment.

Satisfied, he slung the spare rifle across his shoulder and jogged away as the sound of the helicopters thundered in pursuit.

* * *

41

'Alexei!'

Arianna could not hide the joy in her voice as she saw Alexei Volkov's *holosap* shimmer into her apartment. The kindly old Russian set eyes on her, his expression a curious mixture of surprise and disappointment.

'Who are you? Where is my daughter?'

'I am Arianna!'

'Arianna? What happened to you? You should have lived for *decades* more my dear! Why are you here? Why are you using somebody else's *holosap*?'

Alexei moved across the room to her and embraced her. To her surprise, Arianna realised that she could feel Alexei against her. The neurons in her reconstructed mind were already reconnecting, finding each other and building a simulation of the world that she was familiar with. It was truly as though she were still alive, that the world had not changed around her.

'This feels odd,' she said as Alexei drew away from her, his big hands cupping her shoulders.

'You get used to it, *rebyohnuk*.'

Child, Arianna recalled the Russian word. Suddenly she felt hope blossom in her heart and words tumbled from her lips almost as fast as her mind could formulate them.

'The Falling, Alexei, there's immunity among the survivors beyond the river. They're trying to get word out but the *holosaps* don't want that to happen. We have to go to parliament or the media and tell them everything before it's too late because if we don't then everybody could be…'

'Slow down, Arianna. What are you saying?'

'There's no time, we have to hurry.'

'Hurry where? And how do you know all of this, Arianna?'

'It's a long story but you have to trust me. There's a cure running in the blood of every survivor. There are dozens, maybe even hundreds of them, but instead of creating a cure the government is keeping them locked out of the city so that the people don't learn about them.'

Alexei watched her for a moment and then spoke softly.

'I have seen the news reports. Your name was all over them this morning. They say that you may have survived the blast yesterday, that you've suffered some kind of psychotic break, that the police are looking for you and that you should not be approached.'

Arianna felt her hopes sink inside her. 'They're controlling the media. They know what we're trying to do. If we don't stop this there will be nobody left.'

'Nobody left?' Alexei asked.

'That's what this is all about,' Arianna replied. 'Removing humans from the equation. It's what the *holosaps* have engineered. They're controlling government, convincing them to free the *holosaps* from confinement. As soon as they do they'll open the city to the disease and let every surviving human die.'

Alexei's mind ticked over for a moment. 'And those that are immune to the disease?'

'Will be hunted down and killed,' she confirmed. 'They're already doing it. It's only a matter of time.'

'But who is behind all of it?' he asked.

'Kieran Beck,' she said. 'All we have to do, Alexei, is figure out a way to expose the corruption of the leading *holosaps*. If we can go public with it then we can bring the government to its senses!'

Alexei reached up and rubbed his temples with his hand. Arianna waited impatiently as the Russian struggled with the implications of what she was saying.

'But if we do that, inform the government and the media, refuse *holosaps* the freedom of rights available to humans, then you and I suffer. Maybe we will be shut down also? Killed? I've already been murdered once this week, I don't want it to happen again.'

'We may die anyway, Alexei,' Arianna replied. 'There is a kill–switch.'

'A what?'

'A way to kill all *holosaps*,' Arianna said, and then realised what that meant to Alexei.

'But that too would mean that we both die.'

'It's not up to us, Alexei. Neither of us wanted to be uploaded anyway, and it's not what it seems. People change when they're uploaded.'

'They change?'

'For the worse,' Arianna confirmed. 'I have spoken to the soldier who guarded my father when he was doing his work, on Adam, the first *holosap*. They lose their minds, Alexei. We will lose our minds too. *Holosap* brains start out as exact copies but they lose all empathy for human beings within days. They become digital psychopaths, entirely self-interested and they view humans as inferior to them. That's all we are, Alexei. Copies. Facsimiles of who we were. The *holosaps* are not resurrected people, they're brand new people and they'll act that way!'

Alexei sighed. 'You always were a strong one, Arianna. Come, we must take this to Re-Volution itself.'

'The headquarters?' Arianna gasped. 'Are you serious? They're up to their necks in this.'

'Not all of them,' Alexei cautioned. 'There are good men in both Re-Volution and parliament who will listen to what we say.'

'If we walk in there we'll be dead.'

'We already are,' Alexei smiled.

'They'll shut me down.'

'You'll be shut down anyway, once they realise that you've killed somebody and stolen their identity.'

Arianna made to explain how she had come to be occupying another person's *holosap*, but then she recalled the attack on Alexei's illegal bolthole south of the Thames. Trust nobody.

'I'll have to deal with that when the time comes,' she replied, 'but it's only a matter of time before they work out that I'm not who I appear to be.'

'Then we must be quick,' Alexei said.

Alexei stood on the projector plate and motioned for her to follow him. Reluctantly Arianna stepped alongside him as he reached up for the panel.

'Here, take my hand,' he said. 'The first time you do this it can feel a little strange.'

Arianna let Alexei take her hand in his and then he tapped the panel.

The world shifted into a blur of rainbow lights, a flare of brilliant colour that was at once both beautiful and yet undeniably human in nature, filled with angular flashes. Arianna felt herself tilt off balance and then suddenly the lights vanished to be replaced by the atrium of Re-Volution.

Half of the clinically clean atrium was partitioned off by hastily erected panels that concealed the wreckage of the explosion, and both the security gates and the reception desk had been shifted to the left, away from the damage. She could hear the whisper of conversation and the sound of workmen labouring behind the partition.

'This way,' Alexei said.

They walked along the narrow light path glowing between the polished marble tiles of the atrium. Arianna realised now how odd it must have felt for the countless new *holosaps* on their first few days. The living clearly tried to interact normally with the *holosaps* around her, but she caught the suspicious glances directed at her as she walked, noticed how people gave the light path a wide berth, which was even harder now with half of the atrium partitioned off.

'We have to go through security?' she asked Alexei.

'Sure we do,' he replied. 'They scan our signatures, just like everybody else.'

'I shouldn't be here though,' she said. 'A security guard was supposed to meet me at the apartment. They said I'm not cleared to travel.'

'It's okay,' Alexei insisted. 'I'll get you through.'

The security guard, a human standing alongside a walk–through detector designed to alert him to concealed weapons, saw them coming and pointed toward a shimmering panel of light nearby. Alexei walked fearlessly through the panel and then turned to wait for Arianna.

She walked through the waterfall of light.

A discreet buzzer went off and the security guard looked up.

'Brand new,' Alexei said. 'She's with me. Coding is on its way.'

The guard frowned. 'I'll have to clear it upstairs.'

'Please do,' Alexei replied.

Arianna watched as the guard touched a glass panel at his side and spoke quietly to the person on the other end. Moments later he turned to her with a bright smile.

'You're good to go, have a nice day.'

Arianna turned and with Alexei moved across to another light panel in the floor, this one designed to transport *holosaps* to the different levels in the building. Alexei touched the light panel beside him and in a blur the atrium was replaced with an expansive office on what she assumed must be the top floor of the building.

'We shouldn't be here,' Arianna whispered to Alexei. 'This is the executive level.'

'Yes, it is.'

The voice was not that of Alexei, but of a man who appeared from an adjoining room. Beside her Alexei stepped off the panel and it suddenly let out a harsh beep and the light beneath her turned a deep red. Arianna tried to follow Alexei but found herself immobile.

Slowly, on automated wheels, the panel travelled out into the centre of the office until Arianna was facing both Alexei and the man whom she had come to despise over the past two days.

Kieran Beck.

Alexei gestured in her direction. 'This is Arianna,' he said.

Kieran Beck looked her up and down curiously, and then a smile entirely devoid of warmth spread across his features.

'Hello again, Arianna.'

* * *

Dean Crawford

42

'Alexei?'

Arianna's voice was laden with the same dread and confusion that now paralysed her every bit as effectively as the light panel on which she was trapped.

'Oh come now, Arianna,' Kieran Beck said. 'Surely you cannot have failed to realise that the great Russian magnate is long dead, especially as you stand here now in the guise of some unwashed woman living like an animal in the woods?'

Arianna looked at Alexei, who was watching her without any hint of emotion on his craggy old features.

'You should erase her, right now, while you can,' Alexei said to Kieran.

'In good time,' Kieran replied, watching Arianna closely. 'There remain a few things that we can learn from this one, so why rush?'

Arianna managed to keep her grief in check as she looked at the Alexei.

'Alexei wanted to die, not be uploaded.'

'Yes he did,' Kieran Beck replied, 'just like the fool he was. You should have realised that his murder would not only remove his vocal objection to *holosap* rule but also turn him to our side. He is now a true *holosap*, and all the better for it.'

Arianna shook her head.

'You're the reason why *holosaps* should never be allowed to rule.'

'A little late for all that,' Beck replied as he walked across to a broad, mirror polished black desk. On it stood a small, black box that bore several small flashing lights on its surface. 'You know what this is, Arianna?'

She shook her head. Beck grinned.

'It's you. Every single digitized neuron of you is trapped inside this little box, a quantum storage unit. You see, Arianna, it's not quite so easy to hide yourself in that digital cloak when we're already looking for you. It's especially hard when I can exist both as a human and a *holosap*.'

Arianna stared at Kieran Beck in disbelief. 'That's illegal!'

'So is identity theft,' Beck grinned. 'I don't doubt that the news tonight will further cement you in the public mind as a terrorist who will stop at nothing, not even murder and uploading, in order to destroy the *holosap* movement.'

Arianna watched as Beck's *holosap* shimmered slightly as the sunlight beaming through the office windows sliced through his image.

'Of which you're guilty as charged,' Alexei said to her. 'Besides, we knew you would run to me eventually, although not like this. Re–Volution have been listening in, Arianna. You should never have called me *Rebyohnuk* when you sent me that transmission request. I knew then for sure that it was you.'

'Alexei,' she gasped, 'is there nothing left of you?'

'Nothing,' Alexei replied, 'nothing human that taints me any longer. You were right Arianna, we do change when we upload, but we change for the better. You human beings are like an illness, like The Falling. You take but give nothing back. You kill each other, live in squalor and cower before diseases and your false idols. Losing my humanity was the best thing that ever happened to me, and it will be for you once your *holosap* rids itself of your pitiful existence for once and for all.'

Arianna's heart sank as she stared at the image of a man she had once cared about more than life itself, a figure cruelly torn from her life to be replaced with a monster.

'It would be a great shame, Arianna,' Beck went on, 'if your deception here were exposed, the lengths to which you will go to discredit Re–Volution's mission revealed to the public. You know how they do *hate* terrorists.'

Arianna made to move toward Beck, but it was as though her body was made of stone. Only her head could move. Beck grinned and made a show of tapping his little quantum box, his finger vanishing briefly inside.

'Frustrating, isn't it?' he said. '*Holosaps* are allowed limited freedom of movement, but at just a flick of a switch you're as immobile as a light bulb, which in some ways is all you really are. A big, complex light bulb. It's like a prison, isn't it?'

'What do you want?' Arianna snapped.

'From you?' Beck asked. 'Nothing, because you're not important enough, Arianna. You're a bit of an irritation to be honest, an itch that needs to be scratched. Fortunately for me, all I have to do is hit a switch on this box and you'll cease to exist.'

Beck's finger hovered over a red button concealed beneath a clear plastic safety cover. Arianna's eyes were drawn to it as though it were a gun pointed at her head.

'I seem to recall,' Beck went on, 'that you never wanted to be uploaded? That you were against *holosaps* even existing. You claimed once that they represent an abomination?'

'Why am I here?' Arianna asked. 'If I'm so damned unimportant why bring me here at all? Why not just erase me?'

Beck lifted his hand away from the box and looked up at the ceiling as though searching for his words there.

'Because you're useful to us, Arianna,' he replied.

'What does he mean?' she asked Alexei, and then looked back at Beck. 'You murdered Alexei, just like you murdered my father twenty five years ago. What would you have wanted with me?'

'Ah,' Beck smiled, 'Cecil Anderson. He tried to stop us, but he failed. As for Alexei Volkov, his support for the campaign for the right–to–die–again was damaging our credibility. It seemed the sensible thing to do when it became clear that Volkov was achieving such a following, to end his life and thus replace him with somebody entirely more amenable to our needs. Now Alexei *understands*, and will support us in parliament.'

Arianna shook her head in disgust.

'You killed a good man just so that you could get control of everything,' she uttered. 'You're just another power–monger, another crazed little Hitler.'

Kieran Beck chuckled and looked across at Alexei. 'Such a charmer, isn't she?'

'Get rid of his face,' Arianna demanded of Alexei. 'You're not Alexei.'

'I like his face,' Alexei replied. 'The people like his face. It'll help them so much to see him assure them that life as a *holosap* is so much better, that he regrets ever opposing it in the first place.'

'What do you want?' Arianna repeated to Beck.

'Security,' Beck replied finally. 'Where is your father's kill–switch, Arianna?'

'The only man who knew that was Alexei Volkov and he is dead,' she replied. 'Serves you right.'

'Not good enough,' Beck snapped back. 'Volkov died after enduring pain that no mortal man could endure and prevail. He did not know where the kill–switch was so there is only one other person who does. You.'

Arianna shook her head. 'My father went to great lengths to hide me. The last thing he would have done is tell me something as important as that.'

'We will see, Arianna.'

'So that's it?' Arianna said to Beck. 'You torture me, or somebody else, until you get the kill–switch, then gain control over parliament and eradicate all humans and inherit the Earth?'

'Oh no,' Beck countered with an extravagant wave of his hand. 'We have no intention of eradicating mankind, only upgrading it. Come, I have something to show you.'

Beck tapped a light panel on his broad desk and Arianna experienced a rush of colours spiralling in a milieu about her. They resolved into a well lit room that she guessed was underground, deep beneath the Re–Volution building. Alexei and Beck were standing before her. To her right were ranks of quantum super computers, all humming as they churned unimaginable amounts of data through their circuits. To her left were several rows of glass spheres, each containing swirling balls of light that writhed and sparkled with remarkable beauty, like shimmering tropical fish.

Arianna felt herself inexplicably drawn to the spheres, and realised that she could move freely again. As she moved closer she imagined her heart fluttered in her chest as she realised what she was looking at.

'Oh my god, no,' she gasped.

'Yes,' Beck replied. 'Welcome, Arianna, to the future of humanity.'

Coiled within the writhing tendrils of light inside the nearest sphere was a holographic foetus, as clear to Arianna as any X–ray image from the womb.

'How?' she demanded. 'You're not allowed to access the genetic records of people without their specific consent.'

'We're not accessing people's genetic records,' Beck explained. 'We're using those of people who have long ago passed away.'

Arianna's voice choked back into her throat in horror. 'You're what?'

'We're bringing back the dead,' Beck said. 'We have their genetic code, their brain scans, everything we need. This is the greatest gift we've ever been able to create for the human race and believe me they'll pay handsomely for it. Who wouldn't want to hug their long lost father or mother one more time, Arianna?'

'You can't do this,' she whispered. 'This is not natural. You're playing god.'

'Not playing,' Beck countered her, 'being. And we can, because we already have. I am sure that you would love to meet the latest addition to the *Holo sapien* race, ressurected this very morning?'

Arianna stared at Beck as he extended his holographic arm to his right.

From the ranks of super computers, a small, shy looking boy emerged.

Arianna's throat tightened and needle sharp points of pain pierced the corners of her eyes as she saw the boy's floppy brown hair and wide brown eyes staring at her. Tears flooded her eyes and a sob escaped from her lips as she heard his voice call to her.

'Mummy?'

Arianna dropped to her knees on the light path and held her arms out toward him.

'Connor.'

The little boy ran into her embrace and threw his arms tight around her neck as she cried openly and loudly into his shoulder, squeezed his body against hers as though he was the only thing keeping her alive.

'So you see,' Kieran Beck said quietly, 'we have everything that you need right here, Arianna. There is no need for you to run any more. Join us. You have seen the *holosap* colony have you not? An entire world, modelled as we would wish it to be. There is no pain there, no suffering, no loss, no hunger, no need to ever say "goodbye" again. This is the future of our species: a safer, brighter, happier life with our loved ones all around us. Join us and let us protect the human race not just for the now, but for ever more.'

Arianna clutched Connor to her as she looked up at Beck through eyes that still blurred when she cried, even though there were no real tears to shed.

'It isn't right,' she shouted through the grief warring with joy in her mind and in her heart. 'It isn't right!'

Beck sighed as though he were burdened with the worries of a lifetime. 'Even if all you have said is true there is no reversing the march of human evolution, be it biological or digital. We *holosaps* are unassailable now. We control the key to eternal life. If anybody stands against us we can deny them that immortality. We possess something greater than the power over life and death now; we have the power to control a person's *existence*. The sloughing off of human foibles, the cumbersome emotions and the ridiculous wants and needs is not a detriment but evolution. We never needed those things, never will again. We are all the purer in our new forms and no longer slaves to grief or love or hope.'

Arianna released Connor and looked into his eyes. He smiled back at her, his nose scrunching up just like it always used to. She turned to Kieran Beck.

'Those are the things that make us who we are.'

'Who we *were*,' Beck insisted. 'They are a part of history, just like the rest of the human race.'

'I don't know where the kill–switch is.'

Beck shrugged.

'As I said, Arianna, we will see. For now, just tell me where the man known as Icon is, and what he and his band of terrorists intend to do. If you can manage that then I may withhold using Connor as a means to extract information from you.'

Arianna felt raw terror surge through her heart.

'They're not terrorists,' Arianna replied, her voice shaky as she held Connor beside her. 'You're the one who is lying and murdering. You're the terrorist.'

'They might as well be terrorists as far as human survival is concerned,' Beck insisted. 'If it's not The Falling that gets you it'll be something else, perhaps your own wars with each other. The time has come for humanity to move forward, to leave your medieval wars and your petty illnesses behind. Humanity is weak, Arianna. It always was. This is your chance to define your species' future for all eternity. Tell us what we need to know and you'll never miss your son again.'

Arianna looked at Connor and then back at Kieran Beck as the impossible decision swamped her.

* * *

43

New Orleans

Marcus watched as Kerry and Chad skirted the corpses of the soldiers lying dead on the terminal floor. The Wasps, their glistening bodies pulsing as though they were out of breath and their fearsome stingers leaking drops of pale creamy venom, sat on table tops or clung to the walls nearby.

'That's gross,' Kerry said.

White froth clouded the insides of the soldier's face masks, their eyes wide and rigid with pain. Some of their limbs twitched sporadically as the lethal venom surged through their nervous system.

'Full *melee* mode does that,' Chad explained. 'The poison is a mixture of the venom of fire ants, Black Widow spiders and Black Mamba snake. It hits pretty much everything at once.'

Marcus shivered as he glanced at one of the Wasps. 'They won't hit us?'

'Not as long as we've got this,' Chad said and waved his little control box. 'Shame the guys forgot I was carrying it for them when they posted me as the sentry.'

'We need to move,' Kerry said. 'We need to get the word out about all of this and shut Dr Reed down too.'

'Not yet,' Chad warned. 'I want my immunity.'

'We can do it on the way,' Kerry replied. 'You guys must have a medic, right?'

'We did,' Chad replied, and inclined his head to indicate one of the bodies now lying dead on the floor.

'We'll figure something out,' Kerry said.

Chad picked up extra ammunition from his fallen comrades and stuffed them into his belt kit. Marcus was surprised when Chad hefted an M–16 from one of the dead soldiers and handed it to him.

'I'm not a soldier,' Marcus said, the weapon feeling cold and heavy in his hands.

'You are now.'

Chad turned and walked off toward the departure gates on the far side of the terminal. Marcus looked at Kerry, who shrugged and followed Chad.

Marcus saw her lean down and snatch a 9mm pistol from one of the dead soldiers as she passed by. She hefted the weapon in her hand, clearly having never held a gun in her life before.

'What about the Wasps?' Marcus asked.

'They stay here,' Chad called back over his shoulder. 'Once we're clear I'll set them to guardian status in case anybody tries to sneak up on us from behind.'

Marcus nodded, hurrying to get away from the revolting machines. He glanced back to see the remaining functional sphere sitting lop–sided on its damaged legs, two black eyes staring at him as he walked and both machine guns still smouldering wispy tendrils of smoke.

'We need to access the satellite dish and send a clear message,' Kerry informed Chad.

'The building is at the end of the east concourse,' Chad said. 'It's guarded, obviously, but it's also on lock–down.'

'Reed?' Marcus asked, and was rewarded with a nod.

'So how do we get in?' Kerry asked.

'We knock,' Chad replied, and one gloved hand tapped a square pouch on his belt kit. Marcus glanced at it and saw a pack of plastic explosive stuffed into the pouch.

'Reed won't go easily,' Marcus pointed out, 'he's all for the cause.'

'And he'll have sent warning by now,' Kerry realised. 'Crap, he might even sabotage the dish.'

Chad shook his head. 'The dish was built by the engineering corps. There's not much he could do that we could not repair in short order, except maybe scramble the computer codes or something. Only one way to find out.'

They hurried down the long, silent concourse, the hot wind moaning through shattered windows and gusting bits of trash at their feet. They were half way along when Marcus glanced out to his left and almost tripped up.

'Holy crap.'

Kerry and Chad stopped and stood in the gaping maw of a shattered window that looked out across the terminals and aircraft parking areas to a distant hanger, probably where aircraft were stored or serviced long ago. The hangar doors were wide open and four big CH–47 heavy lift helicopters were parked outside, their long rotors drooping beneath their own weight.

Inside the hangar, in long ranks of silver that glinted in the sunlight, stood thousands of metallic spheres and behind them hundreds of automated drones.

'You think they're planning to use all those spheres just to do farming, Chad?'

The soldier hefted his rifle against his chest. 'I'm not paid to ask questions.'

Kerry shook her head. 'You're not paid to be ignorant either, are you? Didn't it cross your mind as a bit odd when your soldiers sent a bunch of infected convicts into our compound to kill us?'

'We were told that you were traitors,' Chad replied. 'That you had to be stopped. Those were our orders.'

'You're like those machines,' Kerry said, 'unthinking.'

Chad shot her a dirty look, then turned away and stalked off down the concourse.

'It's an army,' Marcus whispered as he looked at the distant hangar. 'How many other armies do you think they've built?'

'I don't want to know,' Kerry replied. 'Come on.'

Ahead, the concourse ended in a set of double doors that led into what had once been a departure lounge. The satellite dish was built on top of the lounge, its control room occupying the lounge itself.

Marcus felt a pulse of excitement. Here, finally, was a way to get the word out about what had happened, to reveal to millions of people that they had been lied to for decades. The knowledge that he and Kerry would be behind this momentous achievement filled his chest with pride, and for a few moments his fever seemed to break.

'Movement.'

Chad's word was simple and precise. He slowed, Marcus and Kerry slowing with him. The double doors ahead had two windows at about head height, and in them appeared two masked soldiers, both looking out down the concourse.

'This is where it might get a bit tricky,' Chad said.

Moments later, it got even trickier. A voice called out to them from behind.

'Marcus, Kerry.'

They whirled to see Dr Reed behind them, his *holosap* shimmering and flickering slightly.

'Reed,' Kerry hissed. 'It's over.'

Reed chuckled, his hands in his pockets as he looked at her. 'Yes it is. There's no way that you're getting into the control room, and my men saw everything that happened in the terminal entrance. Chad, frankly I'm surprised that you were turned so easily.'

Chad said nothing, simply watching the *holosap* as he cradled his rifle in his grasp.

'You can't hide this forever, Reed,' Marcus pointed out, 'sooner or later people are going to realise that you and the people you work for are lying.'

'Too late, I suspect,' Reed replied. 'There are discussions and votes being cast right now in political halls across the world, passing bills ensuring that political and military control pass to the *holosap* community, to safeguard the future of humanity. No matter what you do here, I'm afraid the outcome is already assured.'

Marcus looked at Dr Reed for a moment. Something seemed off about him but he could not be certain of what.

'You're not safeguarding, you're planning genocide,' Kerry scowled.

'Genocide is a harsh word,' Reed scorned her. 'A tactical retreat from mankind's archaic existence would be a more reasonable description.'

'From your point of view,' Kerry almost laughed, 'and what about these soldiers who are running around and dying for you? I take it you've lied to them about their futures, that they'll be automatically assured uploads when they die? Like hell they will.'

Dr Reed shook his head, the smile not slipping from his features.

'Alas, Kerry, you will not turn them. They know the difference between desperation and certainty, and which side they wish to be.'

'So did I,' Chad said.

'Promised you immunity, did they?' Dr Reed asked. 'Said that they're already immune?'

'They're walking proof of it,' Chad replied.

'Are they?' Reed challenged. 'I did a little more work on Kerry's supposed cure and found that it merely slows the disease. It does not stop it.'

'Crap,' Kerry snapped back. 'He's trying to turn you back Chad, don't listen to him.'

'I do hope that she hasn't administered her supposed cure, Chad,' Dr Reed said. 'That would be most unfortunate for you.'

Chad glanced sideways at Kerry. 'What's the chances?'

Kerry shook her head. 'The Falling always started with a fever and influenza–like symptoms, which then progressed to full blown necropsy, or flesh degradation across the entire body. I had the fever, it's now passed and my wound is healing. Marcus still has the fever, but it's easing and his wound is also beginning to heal. What do you think?'

'They're wrong, Chad,' Dr Reed insisted. 'They'll die before the day is out. It's attacking them still.'

Chad looked at Marcus, back at Kerry and then at Dr Reed.

'I suppose the only way to be sure is to let them live and find out, right Doctor?' Chad suggested.

Marcus glimpsed a flicker of irritation twist Reed's face. 'Of course,' he replied. 'Please place them under arrest and then we can put them in quarantine.'

Chad grinned. 'Nice try, doc'.'

Marcus saw the soldier whirl, a grenade in one gloved hand as with the other he aimed his M–16 and fired through the double–door windows. The glass shattered, the soldiers within yelling in alarm as Chad hurled the grenade through the broken windows.

Marcus threw himself down alongside the soldier, remembering to cover his ears as Kerry huddled against one wall with her arms over her head. Chad ducked down, his body shielding them both as the grenade exploded with a sharp, deafening blast inside the departure lounge.

Chad was on his feet in an instant, this time securing a plastic explosive at the base of the doors as he jammed priming charges into the soft material and then ran.

'Get away!' he bellowed.

Marcus and Kerry sprinted back up the concourse, straight through Dr Reed's *holosap*. Behind them, they heard the double doors crash open as the troops charged through in counter–attack, unaware of the charges Chad had placed. Dr Reed opened his mouth to warn the soldiers, but it was too late.

'Hit the deck!' Chad yelled.

They threw themselves down as Chad hit a remote detonator in his hand.

A tremendous blast of heat and noise thundered from behind them, a shockwave ploughing into Marcus like a freight train. He felt his body hurled forwards until he landed hard and tumbled across the unforgiving floor. Chad landed beside him, rolling deftly and bringing his rifle back up to aim toward the shattered doors as Kerry slid to a halt nearby.

Chad fired into the thick coils of smoke, hitting bodies sprawled across the floor. Screams from injured men echoed down the concourse as Chad leaped to his feet and advanced, firing all the while and yelling over his shoulder at Marcus.

'Move now, start firing!'

Marcus stumbled to his feet, his legs feeling feeble as he staggered in pursuit of Chad. He lifted the M–16 and fired into the darkened rectangle ahead, the rifle kicking into his shoulder as rounds flew away from him.

Chad dashed to the side of the doors and waved Marcus to stop firing, then ducked inside. Marcus hurried in pursuit as Kerry ran alongside him, the 9mm in her hand. They heard shouts from the darkness, more shots fired. Screams cut brutally short.

Marcus's eyes adjusted to the gloom as he stepped into the departure lounge.

Several of the soldiers who had charged the doors lay dead around them, their blood mingling with dust in congealing pools on the floor. Limbs lay scattered where they had fallen, weapons still in the grasp of severed, gloved hands. The sickening smell of spilled blood and innards tainted the air and Marcus coughed, his throat constricted.

Chad surveyed the carnage down the barrel of his rifle. 'Clear.'

'Is that what you call it?' Marcus uttered.

Kerry stepped in alongside Marcus, one hand covering her face. 'You okay?'

Marcus nodded, his eyes streaming as he struggled against the smoke and the sight of so much blood. He looked up and saw above them the roof of the lounge modified with heavy steel girders, stretching up through a hole in the roof sealed with clear plastic that looked up toward the huge dish outside.

'Pay dirt,' Chad rumbled and looked at Kerry. 'You ready?'

Marcus looked over his shoulder at the lounge entrance and saw Dr Reed still standing in the concourse beyond, his image flickering. Suddenly, Marcus realised what was wrong with the *holosap*. He wasn't moving and he wasn't looking anybody directly in the eye.

'He can't move,' Marcus said. 'He's a static image. His projection equipment must be inside this building somewhere.'

'You're clutching at straws,' Dr Reed said, appearing suddenly near the control panel before them but staring at a far wall as he spoke, his crude projection unable to interact properly. 'You'll never access the passwords from here.'

Kerry stormed across to face him and held her pistol to his head. 'You sure?'

'You can't kill me, Kerry, you know that.'

'Really?' Kerry grinned tartly. 'You're not able to move freely, doctor. That suggests to us that your storage unit is also here.' She aimed the pistol more carefully between his eyes. 'You think a bullet through your quantum storage will finish you off?'

Dr Reed's features flickered with panic. 'I'll have a back–up, in New York!'

'Not once we're done here,' Kerry growled. 'I'll make it my business to be sure that when people find out how you're involved in corporate genocide, you're shut down for good. Password, now.'

Reed's jaw trembled, but he was unable to bring himself to surrender his future into Kerry's hands.

Marcus walked across to the control panel and grabbed the first piece of broken glass he could see. He then walked across to Dr Reed's *holosap* and moved the piece of glass about and around him until he saw the *holosap's* image flicker slightly, the light beams interfered with by the broken glass like a prism splitting a rainbow.

Marcus turned his head and saw a low, slim black box lying on a worktop nearby.

'Bingo,' he said.

'Genius, once again,' Kerry admitted.

'Get away from there,' Dr Reed yelled.

Marcus tossed the glass aside as he walked across to the projection unit. He felt certain that it would be attached to optical fibres, which would themselves lead to the *holosap's* hard drive. Moments later, he followed a cable protruding from the rear of the projection unit to a locked cabinet nearby.

Marcus stood back, aimed his rifle, and shot the lock clean off to a yelp of horror from Dr Reed. The cabinet doors buckled under the blast and Marcus leaned in and prized them open to reveal a small, glossy black box, a portable quantum storage unit. Marcus turned to Dr Reed as he aimed the M–16 at the box.

'So, how about that password doc'?'

Dr Reed was about to reply when Kerry's voice reached them weakly.

'Marcus, I…'

Marcus turned, and his blood ran cold as he saw Kerry's legs give way beneath her as she slumped to the floor.

* * *

44

London

Han Reeves entered the building and looked up at the staircase above as the sound of the helicopters thundered ever closer. He was about to take the steps two at a time when he hesitated.

Icon had said that the surgeon would conduct his work up there, but it seemed an odd choice. There were no escape routes from the upper floors, they would be vulnerable and exposed. Han looked across the lobby to where a set of stairs descended down into the bowels of the building: deep, underground, shielded. If it were he planning this escapade, he'd have chosen the basement, not the upper floors.

Han hit the basement stairs at a run, dashing down them as quickly as he could and feeling the air turn even colder as he descended.

The basement was unlit, but he was only half way down when he heard the boots rushing up toward him from below. A crash of gunfire erupted around him as bullets tore chunks of plaster and brickwork from the wall near his head and he hurled himself down on the cold, hard steps, just out of the sight of the entrance to the basement.

'Hold your fire!' he yelled.

'Drop your weapon and come out with your hands up!'

'Arianna's in danger!' Han insisted. 'They know she's coming!'

A moment's silence echoed around Han before a reply was shouted back at him.

'Not our problem!'

Han cursed under his breath as he stood on the stairwell, the SA–80 cradled in his hands. He knew that he only had about thirty rounds, and that although an extremely tough and reliable weapon the SA–80 was not ideal for close quarters combat. There was no way he was going to take out an armed gang in a confined space.

'You think Icon will agree with you?' he called out.

'Icon ain't here!'

Han glanced back up the gloomy stairwell as he thought about that for a moment.

'Then where the hell is he? I need to tell him that Arianna's in danger. They know who she is, and if they want to they can find out about your plans here. There are helicopters coming. This could be the end of everything, you understand that? They could bomb this building out of existence any moment now!'

A long silence ensued, but Han could just about hear muffled whispers coming from within the basement.

'You could be with them!' came the hollered reply. 'You could be here to kill us!'

Han shook his head and rolled his eyes.

'You think I'd be pissing about talking to you down here if that were true? I'd have run and called the bloody cavalry!'

Another moment of silence and then a rebel appeared at the entrance to the basement, a pistol held in his grasp and aimed at where Han was concealed behind a pillar.

'Show yourself!'

Han took a deep breath and stepped out into the corridor. The rebel facing him remained hooded, his pistol fixed dead centre on Han's face, and through the shadows concealing his skull–like features Han recognised Malcolm.

'There's not much time,' Han said, keeping his SA–80 pulled close in to his chest at port arms. 'If they break her she'll tell them everything. Where your camp is, your families, Icon's plans, where we are now. It'll be over before it's begun.'

Malcolm smiled, shaking his head slowly. 'It's already over.'

Behind him Han could see several more hooded rebels, all of them armed as they crowded through the basement entrance to watch.

'What do you mean?'

'You think Icon is just going to leave it to the woman to end this war, to resolve everything? You think the government and that bastard St John will just put their hands up and admit everything, hand a cure to every citizen? They need to pay for what they've done and we're making that happen.'

'Arianna is stuck in the *holosap's* world with no chance of escape unless …'

'The hell with her!' Malcolm shouted. 'She's not the main plan, never was! This is our main plan,' he said, and shook his pistol in his hands. 'Take the war to the enemy, and finish them for once and for all. So if the helicopters are coming, I say let 'em!'

A rumble of agreement rippled through the rebels as they crowded into the doorway.

'Where is Icon?' Han demanded.

Malcolm shrugged and made a show of looking at his watch. 'Right now, he's probably on his way to blow the checkpoint on Westminster Bridge to hell.'

Han gasped in dismay. 'He'll be annihilated. There's no way he has enough firepower to overcome the military and police. They'll wipe him from the face of the planet.'

'Escape is not his plan,' Malcolm replied. 'If Arianna's been turned, then Icon will know by now and push on.'

Han stared at him for a moment as a sudden dread flooded his synapses. With a realisation colder than death itself he realised what Icon was going to do. The weapons, the camp, the attempt to get Arianna uploaded: everything was a secondary mission, a back–up plan. Icon's objective, his true goal, had never been to resolve the situation peacefully.

Icon was planning to force the government's hand in another way entirely.

'The Falling,' he said finally.

Malcolm cocked his head to one side. 'There you go,' he replied in a whisper. 'They brought this upon us and they've kept it upon us. Now we'll bring it right on home to them. They did a deal with the Devil, Mr Policeman, and now that debt is due.'

Suddenly it all made sense. The apparent determination to make a suicide mission into the city was not one that would be achieved with guns or missiles. Instead, Icon was going to bring the government's greatest fear down upon them and then deny them their escape.

'He's bringing the disease inside the city walls.'

'Into Westminster, and he'll destroy Re–Volution's storage units and therefore parliament's means of uploading or relying on their latest back–up. They're going down, either by The Falling or at the hands of the people if they try to flee the building, once the truth gets out.'

Han frowned. 'But how can you stop the politicians uploading? The servers are under heavy guard now and Icon won't be able to get in…'

'The touch paper for that little bomb has already been lit, officer,' Malcolm smirked, his creased lips catching the light beneath his hood as he jabbed a gloved thumb over his shoulder toward the operating theatre far behind them inside the basement. 'They think that they're immune to disease? They're about to get a shock.'

Han's heart skipped a beat. 'Arianna, her upload.'

Malcolm winked one disfigured eye. 'It's not just humans that can get a virus.'

Han gasped at Icon's audacity, his plan a double stroke of genius. Hitting the *holosaps* from both the inside and the outside, he was more than willing to sacrifice anybody in order to achieve his goal.

'Icon knew that she would be identified,' Han finally realised. 'He had no intention of bringing her back out of this.'

'No intention of killing her either,' Malcolm replied without a hint of remorse. 'What will be, will be.'

Han saw an image flicker through his mind's eye of thousands of panicked citizens flooding the streets of London as The Falling entered the city, probably through infected animals released by Icon's men, fleeing but with nowhere actually to go but…

'You, all of you,' Han said with a disbelief that he had rarely felt. 'You're their saviours.'

'Those of us that survive any retaliation by government forces,' Malcolm nodded. 'We carry the immunity in our blood. Some of us will report to the hospitals and inform the staff of our immunity. They will then take blood and…'

Han started laughing. He couldn't help it. He looked away from Malcolm and rubbed his temples with one hand. As he did so he heard a faint commotion echo from the stairwell above and realised that somebody had found Myles. Han knew he had only seconds left now before they would be on top of him.

'You'll inoculate the population, right?' he snapped. Malcolm nodded. 'And how the hell are you going to do that quickly enough to protect millions of people against a disease that kills in days?'

'They will suffer,' Malcolm snapped, 'and we cannot hope to save them all. But many will live and they will carry the knowledge of what our government has done to them.'

'And what you did to those who didn't survive,' Han snapped back. 'You, all of you, will be either forgotten or left to rot in prison. You're all as guilty as St John, no matter how you cover it up or justify it to yourselves. You're going to kill countless innocent people just like the government has.'

The rebels shifted, dark mutterings flitting like dangerous thoughts from one man to the next.

'You're done here,' Malcolm said, gripping his pistol tighter. 'Drop your rifle.'

The sound of running footsteps echoed down the stairwell behind Han, Myles's voice shouting out. 'He's the enemy! He's going to kill Arianna!'

Malcolm tightened his grip on his pistol. Han let his shoulders fall in capitulation as he sighed and moved to lift the SA–80 from his shoulders, turning the barrel toward the rebels as he did so.

'It doesn't have to be this way,' he said.

'Yes,' Malcolm replied, 'it does.'

Han let his knees collapse, dropping with the force of gravity as he squeezed the trigger on his SA–80. The first round ploughed into Malcolm's abdomen long before he could even think about returning fire and he doubled over as his legs gave way beneath him.

The rebels, packed into the doorway, could not bring their weapons to bear upon Han past Malcolm as he fell.

Han's knees cracked against the unforgiving concrete floor as the SA–80 chattered rounds into the densely packed rebels. Several at the back turned and fled, but their comrades in front were sprayed with the rifle's bullets that thudded into vulnerable flesh.

Two wild shots went high above Han–s head as six or seven rebels fell before the onslaught.

Han leaped to his feet and pain bolted through his knees as he ran forward. He leaped over Malcolm's inert body and then over the pile of corpses in the doorway, scooping up a dropped pistol as he plunged into the basement and opened fire on the first movement he saw. Another rebel fell as rounds thumped into his back and his screams echoed loudly through the dingy, confined spaces as he tumbled onto the cold ground.

Han fired a single 9mm bullet into a rebel's back as he desperately tried to open a side door. The kid fell, his hands clasping the door handle, just as a bullet smacked into Han's ribs from behind him and ripped the breath from his lungs.

Han spun in mid–air, the impact hurling him back against the nearest wall as he aimed wildly at a shadowy figure in the doorway.

Malcolm's grotesque face glared at him as he propped himself up on one elbow, trying to maintain an aim on Han to fire again, his features twisted with agony and rage.

'We're still human beings!' he yelled.

Han fired, three rounds that smashed into Malcolm's ruined face and splattered his brains out across the tiled floor behind him.

Another rebel fled across the room and tried to duck behind a stack of old pallets near a far wall. Han fired several shots, the wooden pallets splintering and offering no protection to the crouching man. Han heard a strained cry of agony and then the man slumped in silence where he crouched, the pistol in his hand clattering to the floor.

The gunfire ceased, ringing in Han's ears as he slumped, trying to draw breath and clasping his side. His hand came away slick with blood and he was momentarily surprised by its warmth against his skin.

'He's in there!'

Han heard the voices rushing down the stairwell. Somehow, he managed to haul himself to his feet and staggered across to the basement door. He slammed it shut, then dragged one of the wooden pallets across to it and wedged it under the handle before ducking down and creeping through the basement.

He saw a second doorway, saw light emanating from within and a man's face peering out at him through a small window.

'Open the door!' Han yelled, wincing at the pain bolting through his ribs. 'She's in danger!'

The man shook his head, eyes swimming with panic. Han aimed his pistol at the glass and the man threw his hands up. 'Okay, okay, don't shoot me!'

The door swung open and Han tumbled through as the man, wearing a doctor's white coat, slammed it shut behind him.

Han saw Arianna laying on the gurney nearby. 'Get her out of there!'

The doctor gaped at him as though he were mad. 'I can't just switch the machines off, she'll die. She needs warming at a steady and constant rate for at least…'

Han whirled and shoved the pistol he'd acquired directly into the doctor's face.

'If you don't, I will,' he hissed. 'Revive her, now!'

* * *

45

Arianna stared down at her son, Connor's beautiful big brown eyes looking back up at her, still young despite the passing of so many years, still innocent enough to be unsullied by the cruelty of life, still himself before the digital psychosis would ruin him forever.

Kieran Beck and Alexei watched her in silence, their holographic images just transparent enough to see the endless ranks of growing foetuses sparkling like distant stars in a bizarre blue universe.

Slowly, one hand resting protectively on Connor's head, Arianna stood and faced them.

'You think that this is somehow the future?' she asked, gesturing over her shoulder at the new lives growing in the spheres. 'This is the end, Beck, don't you understand? This isn't the way that humanity is supposed to evolve. This is just a playback, a warped facsimile of who we are.'

Kieran Beck chuckled. 'It'll do for thousands of *holosaps* who would rather exist like this than be reanimated as *human beings*.'

Beck twisted the last two words and spat them out as though he were describing a particularly nasty taste in his mouth. Arianna realised that Beck was long past seeing humanity as anything other than a stain upon the world, perhaps upon the universe, something to be scoured away by the clinical swab of science.

'You wouldn't be here at all if it were not for human beings,' Arianna pointed out, desperately trying to think of a means of escape.

'Yes I would,' Beck corrected her. 'I would willingly choose life as a *holosap* over that of an ordinary human being. Change comes to us all Arianna and those who move forward, those who survive are those who do not oppose change but embrace it. Look at your church, for instance.'

'Our church has not been corrupted by your self-serving agenda and…'

'The church has always been corrupt,' Beck snapped, 'never more so than in its dying days when its priests and popes tried to enforce their archaic ways on an ever more intelligent and disbelieving population. We laugh now at their final, desperate efforts to enforce celibacy, birth control, homophobia and their God upon a disinterested populace. Your church, like all that have gone before it, will erase themselves from history by their own inability to understand the difference between what is real and what is false. This is reality, Arianna, right here, right now. It's us, standing here, and if you do not embrace it…' Kieran Beck once again gestured to the quantum storage devices surrounding them. 'You die, forever.'

'I'd rather go to my grave and meet my Maker,' Arianna replied, 'then see you take over control of the fate of our race.'

Kieran raised an eyebrow as he looked down at Connor. 'Perhaps a different kind of sacrifice would prompt a more favourable point of view?'

Arianna instinctively put herself in front of Connor. 'Leave him out of this.'

'Why, Arianna?' Beck asked. 'Surely, if all of this is so pointless, if being a *holosap* is so horrific and unacceptable to you, then why would you worry about Connor here? Is he not, surely, just a glowing light of no substance and no interest to you?' He smiled again. 'You need to decide, Arianna, which side of the afterlife you're on.'

Arianna glanced down at Connor, who was looking up at her with confusion etched into his young features.

'What does he mean, mummy?'

Arianna felt her heart tear inside her as she realised what she must do, must say to the man who willingly no longer considered himself a man, and at the same time say to her dead son who was no longer dead. The bizarre, counter–intuitive nature of her dilemma did nothing to alleviate the crushing grief she felt coursing like acid through her veins as she clenched a fist tight and turned back to Beck.

'My son is dead,' she said.

She heard the tremor in her words, felt it in her throat, felt painful tears stinging her eyes even though she had no eyes and could not produce tears as she stood her ground in front of Kieran Beck.

'Mummy?'

Arianna closed her eyes shut tight, tried not to hear the tiny voice or feel the little hand clinging tightly to hers.

Beck's monotone drawl reached across to her. 'You would sacrifice your own son simply for a belief? And you call me *inhuman*?'

'Connor Volkov died eight years ago,' Arianna said, her eyes still tight shut. 'I miss him more than I can say and will love him with all of my heart until the day I die, but he is not coming back and whatever you've created here is not my son.'

A deep silence drew out around her. The darkness in her mind and the silence proved too much, and she opened her eyes to see Kieran Beck and Alexei still watching her in silence, still felt Connor's hand holding on to hers.

'This,' Beck said to Alexei, 'is what used to happen to the religious mind back in the day. They'd murder, maim and torture, all for beliefs with no more substance than dreams.'

'You have no more substance than dreams,' Arianna pointed out. 'My son died of The Falling. I buried him in a mass grave in Leadenhall eight years ago. It broke my heart but it can never be undone, even if…'

'Mummy?' Arianna looked down at Connor, who was still staring up at her with those baleful eyes. 'Am I dead?'

Anguish ripped across Arianna's chest as she fought back tears and nodded. 'Yes, honey, you died a long time ago.'

Kieran Beck stepped forward. 'It is time to decide, Arianna: your son's life or eternity for us all. Where is the kill–switch?'

Arianna's tears flooded down her face. She felt them even though they had no more substance than thin air, hot against her cheeks, the neuro–optical links in her holographic brain piecing together ever more complex sensations. She clenched the fingers of her left hand tighter, the fist a dense ball of light, and this time she felt her fingernails digging into her skin. This time, she felt pain.

Pain. It had never occurred to her before, that *holosaps* might feel physical pain. A new and horrifying fear for Connor swept over her as she looked down at the little boy staring up at her, a canvas of hope and confusion, of the need to be held and loved. She realised that it didn't matter whether this *holosap* was really her son or not. He could suffer at the hands of men like Kieran Beck, just like any other child.

'What happens to Connor, if I tell you everything?'

'He lives,' Beck replied without hesitation, 'so to speak. I have no wish to erase either of you.'

Arianna's mind raced as a new realisation dawned within. 'How did you obtain Connor's DNA? He died without an upload.'

'Ah,' Kieran smiled. 'Let's just say that we needed to experiment on people to perfect our *holosap* re–generation project, and it was decided that people who could not afford an upload were likely to be willing subjects. Your son's blood was available, via the genetic records of all citizens kept on government record. We simply obtained these and went from there.'

'You obtained them?' Arianna echoed in disgust. 'You mean you stole them, illegally. That's where the Prime Minister came in, I suppose?'

'He proved instrumental,' Kieran Beck confirmed, 'in obtaining both genetic material and of course the brains of those who had died from The Falling. They were recovered from the bodies before burial, and transported most bravely through underground networks by my people.'

'The police will arrest your human self on sight,' Arianna shot back at Beck. 'You'll be in prison for the rest of your life.'

'Maybe,' Beck replied, 'but of course those among the police who favour our cause will always be able to cover up anything we do. Corrupt police officers are not so difficult to come by these days, didn't you know?'

Arianna stared at Beck and felt the weight of utter defeat upon her shoulders. 'Han Reeves?'

Beck shook his head. 'Myles Bourne. A vibrant and determined young man who just happens to possess an upload. He was smart enough to request one before we put him to work, as insurance. Or futurance, as we like to call it. We will not be stopped, Arianna,' Beck insisted. 'Mankind will live on in a purer form.'

'You're re–animating the dead,' Arianna whispered in horror. 'That's what these foetuses are.'

'In a sense,' Beck confirmed. 'Imagine, a world where Einstein or Hawking lives again – both men donated their organs to science. Or perhaps great world leaders or thinkers whose brains even now lay in cryogenic preservation, awaiting just this kind of technology. The future possibilities are endless and will only continue to grow. This, Arianna, is where we need to be. This is our time, the time of man's future, of *Homo immortalis*.'

Arianna, her body feeling empty of feeling for the first time in days, stared blankly down at Connor. The little boy clung to her hand in silence and she knew that she simply could not abandon him to oblivion.

She looked at Kieran Beck.

'Where are you now?' she demanded. 'Really, I mean?'

'Westminster,' Beck replied. 'The vote is in progress as we speak and parliament will undoubtedly back the *holosap's* Bill of Rights.'

'Then let's do this there,' Arianna replied. 'If you're to keep your word, I want to be where everybody can see both myself and my son. I won't trust you until we're in plain view.'

'You might betray me,' Kieran pointed out.

'You have my son,' Arianna whispered, 'and I want him alive. How badly do you want your kill–switch, Kieran?'

Beck glared at her for a long moment and then he smiled once more, a smile utterly devoid of anything that Arianna could define as human.

'You will tell parliament of the kill–switch and its purpose. I shall send Alexei here with your son. Fail me, Arianna, and I will extinguish Connor's life just as quickly as I did your father's.'

Arianna opened her mouth to reply, but no sound came forth.

She tried again, but nothing happened.

She saw a brief glimpse of confusion on Connor's face, and then suddenly she was yanked from the room into a swirling maelstrom of spirals and lights plunging into an impenetrable blackness through which she flew, screaming in her mind for her son.

* * *

46

New Orleans

'Kerry!'

Marcus dashed to her side. Her legs were completely limp, her eyes filled with sudden terror. Marcus realised that her wound had split open, the flesh beneath her skin festering and black.

'I can't move my legs, Marcus,' she whispered, tears spilling from her eyes.

Dr Reed's voice reached them both from nearby.

'As I said, the sickness was slowed but not reversed. The animals that remained in the laboratory at the compound have since died,' Dr Reed smiled as Marcus turned to face him, Kerry in his arms, 'very long, painful deaths.'

'If the disease can be slowed it can be stopped,' Marcus shot back. 'Tell us what you know or we'll blow your storage unit right here and now.'

'Send my storage data back to New York,' Reed snapped, 'or *Kerry* dies right here and now.'

Dr Reed stared at his quantum storage unit. Chad glanced at Marcus.

'How come you're not on your knees yet?' the soldier asked him.

Marcus set his rifle on the floor and reached up to his neck wound. He pulled off the dressing. His skin felt cool and soft to the touch, no sign of necrosis. Marcus realised that his fever was long gone. He felt fine.

'I don't know,' he said.

Kerry rested her hand on his arm and smiled weakly up at him. 'I do. Don't listen to anything Reed says, just get me to the control panel.'

Marcus dragged Kerry to the control panel and hefted her into the chair. Her head sagged and her skin was drenched with sweat, but she rested her hands onto the keyboard screen before her.

'This will change nothing,' Reed snapped. 'Humanity is over. This is the new future!'

'Yeah, yeah,' Kerry waved him off. 'We've heard it all before. Give us the password to the control panel or we'll blow your existence back into history, okay?'

Chad checked his watch.

'Vote's due in a few minutes,' he said. 'We're almost out of time.'

Marcus walked across to Reed's storage unit and lifted it out of the cabinet. 'We don't have time for this. We'll figure out the passcode. Kerry, get started. I'll blow Reed away.'

Kerry began typing deftly. 'Nice knowin' you doc',' she said without looking over her shoulder at Reed.

Marcus turned and tossed the quantum storage unit onto the floor as though it were a piece of trash, then clicked off the safety catch on his M–16 and took aim.

'You'll never break the code on your own!' Reed yelled. 'It's quantum coded. It would take a thousand years using even the best conventional computers!'

'Unless you've got me,' Chad growled over his shoulder. 'I've got security clearance, remember? I'll find a way to get in.'

'You won't!' Reed yelled, his voice increasingly shrill. 'You're done, you'll never break it in time!'

'If we're dead anyway,' Marcus replied, 'we'll die trying and we'll be sure to take you with us if we fail.'

Marcus was about to fire at the storage unit, just to shut the panicking doctor up for once and for all, when a sudden alarm claxon screeched out. He looked up to see a pair of rotating sirens flash bright red light through the otherwise gloomy control room, flickering weirdly and passing through Dr Reed's *holosap*.

'What's happening?' Kerry called out over the alarm claxon.

Marcus looked at Dr Reed, who seemed also to be surprised by the commotion. Then the doctor looked at a computer screen and his features froze in a rictus of horror. Marcus glanced across and saw the message written there in vivid and flashing yellow letters.

VIRUS DETECTED: SHUT–DOWN REQUIRED

Marcus looked back to Dr Reed, whose expression was collapsing into something akin to panic.

'Problem, doctor?' Marcus asked.

'A virus has been detected,' he said, 'infecting the quantum storage systems. But that's impossible!'

Kerry looked over her shoulder at the doctor. 'Give us the password and we'll shut you down until the virus is removed. Hurry!'

Dr Reed looked at the screen and then up at another, larger screen that showed a map of Earth. Across the globe, the same communication systems that allowed the *holosaps* to appear were filling with red flashing markers that flashed across continents at the speed of light, leaping across optical networks in the blink of an eye.

'Now, doctor!' Marcus shouted, 'or you really are history!'

Reed whirled and called across to Kerry. 'Alpha–Delta–India–Five–Three–Seven–One–Delta–Three!'

Kerry tapped the password into the touchscreen and in an instant it illuminated with a bright blue light a series of screen folders to access the systems.

'We're in!' Kerry shouted.

'Shut me down!' Dr Reed yelled. 'Quickly!'

'Shut you down?' Marcus echoed with a sneer. 'You got it, Doc'.'

Marcus picked up the *holosap's* storage unit and turned as he hurled it straight out of a nearby window.

'No!!'

Dr Reed's scream echoed throughout the control room as Marcus heard the storage unit hit the ground outside the terminal with a crash of delicate quantum machinery as it shattered against unyielding asphalt. To his surprise for a moment nothing happened as Dr Reed stared at the open window where his lifeline to immortality had just vanished. Then, quite slowly, his image began to disintegrate before Marcus's eyes.

'This is murder!' Reed wailed.

Marcus watched as the doctor's image began to crumble as though he were being split apart atom by atom, the carefully stored data tumbling from his *holosap* in a cascade of bright pin–prick spots of light that Marcus somehow knew was binary code, countless billions of data streams collapsing before his very eyes.

Dr Reed's screams fell silent as the *holosap's* ability to generate sound vanished. Despite himself, despite all that Dr Reed had done and despite the fact that he had already died once for real, Marcus could not help feeling some small quiver of guilt as he saw every infinitesimal stream of data that was Dr Reed collapse into a tumble of shimmering lights that spread out from the projection plate on which he had stood and faded into blackness.

Marcus stared at the spot where the doctor had been standing only moments before. He could hear Kerry's fingers flying across the keyboard before her but he realised he could also hear the drumming of boots on asphalt. He turned and hurried across to the window.

Below, running in a tight formation, several dozen troops were pouring into the terminal below them.

'We've got company,' he called across to Chad in a harsh whisper.

Chad nodded but didn't even look up as he replied. 'We're short on ammunition, not much we can do about it.'

'Say what?' Marcus blinked. 'You're just going to quit now?'

'I only need a few minutes,' Kerry called to them. 'Quickly, come here Marcus!'

Marcus rushed over just in time for Kerry to turn in her seat and jab a syringe straight into his arm.

'Ow!' Marcus yelled. 'What the hell are you doing?!'

'You're immune, Marcus,' she said. 'I'm sending your blood, not mine.'

'I'm as good as dead!' Marcus snapped back, but he held his arm still as she drew his blood. 'We all are,' he added softly.

'No,' Kerry replied as she withdrew the needle and patched his arm, her useless legs dangling awkwardly from her seat. 'You remember where some of the world's most effective serums came from, back in the day?'

Marcus thought for a moment and then he realised. 'Snake venom,' he whispered.

Kerry nodded. 'Just keep them at bay for long enough for me to scan your blood and to send this data, and we're done.'

'What about you?' he asked.

Kerry did not reply. Chad stepped up, checked his rifle's magazine and then began rifling through the bodies of his fallen comrades. He pulled out ammunition pouches and a handful of what Marcus assumed were fragmentation grenades.

'We could use the Wasps and the sphere you control,' Marcus suggested.

'They'll have hacked them by now,' Chad replied. 'They won't make the same mistake twice.'

'We've dodged them before,' Marcus said with more conviction that he felt. 'We'll do it again.'

Chad grinned tightly but said nothing as he tossed two magazines to Marcus, who caught them and stuffed them into the pockets of his jeans. Marcus then watched as Chad yanked the body armour from his fallen comrades and arranged the suits into two piles half way between the entrance to the control room and the control panels.

'This is going to be over fast,' Chad reported to Kerry. 'You done yet?'

'Almost there,' Kerry said, tapping the keys fast. 'I'm reactivating the cameras and hacking links to every broadcast network I can. I want the whole damned world to see this as well as hear it.'

The drumming of boots running down the concourse toward the control room echoed around Marcus. He looked up to see the troops advancing toward them. Hovering around them were black specks emitting a distant hum.

'Here they come,' Marcus shouted.

* * *

47

Chad took up a position near the doors and whispered across to Marcus.

'I'll hit them with the frag' grenades first. Hopefully we'll take out a few of those Wasps with the shrapnel.'

Marcus nodded as he crouched down behind an upturned desk and aimed down the concourse.

'Single shots,' Chad added, 'don't spray them. Aim for their body armour. The shots won't kill but they'll stun enough to drop them. Take the headshots while they're on the deck. Make every round count, understand?'

'Hold them off!' Kerry yelled before Marcus could reply. 'I'm broadcasting in thirty seconds!'

Marcus saw Kerry press a portable memory drive into the terminal, the one that contained the raw data of her cure. He saw an upload panel, a blue bar filling with light, and then a blinking message. Kerry wasted no time as she hit the button to send the data, then reached up and activated the bulbous black eye of a camera mounted atop the control panel.

He heard her voice speaking into the camera as he took aim down the corridor.

'My name is Kerry Hussein. I am a research biologist working for the United States Government in Louisiana, and broadcasting from the international airport outside of New Orleans. I have discovered a cure for The Falling.'

Chad set his rifle down and held two fragmentation grenades in his hands. He pulled the pins, counted one second, and then hurled them both in a straight line as hard as he could down the concourse. The two grenades shot through the air as though they had been fired from a cannon, too fast for the soldiers to react, and both weapons detonated at head height just in front of the charging squad.

Marcus saw the double burst of flame and debris cut through the front few troops like a scythe, saw Wasps hurled with immense force into the walls of the concourse to shatter into pieces on the floor or blasted out of the broken windows. The double blast thumped through the control room and the shockwave rang in Marcus's ears so that he barely heard Chad's yelled command.

'Open fire!'

Marcus aimed through the swirling grey smoke at a staggering soldier, his bulky battle kit and black body armour an easy target. He fired. The rifle kicked into his soldier and he saw the soldier jerk under the impact and tumble to the ground, gasping for air behind his respirator.

As rounds flew back at them down the concourse and he glimpsed Chad firing shots at controlled, regular intervals of about two seconds, dropping soldiers with each round, Marcus aimed at the soldier he had dropped and fired a single shot into the side of his head.

A bright puff of scarlet blood and the man fell still.

The remaining soldiers plunged into the limited cover available to them either side of the concourse, and in an instant the handful of still–flying Wasps hummed loudly above the cacophony as they raced toward the open doors.

'Wasps!' Marcus yelled.

Kerry's voice continued behind him, as calm as could be, into the camera.

'I am sending with this broadcast data from my partner's blood, which will reveal the genes responsible for his immunity. Both myself and my colleague were bitten. I am the control subject and remain infected. My partner was bitten by a pit viper before he was infected, and it is that snake bite which has saved his life. The noise you hear in the background is the government's troops attempting to kill us. They have been lying, to all of us, for decades. The Falling is not incurable and never has been. It is the aim of the *holosaps* to gain control of our government and then eradicate humanity from the face of our planet.'

Marcus took aim at a Wasp and fired. The bullet shattered the cruel drone in mid–flight and it spiralled downward and crashed onto the concourse floor.

'Nice shootin'!' Chad yelled as Kerry's voice continued behind them.

'The *holosaps* consider us a plague upon our planet, a weakness, something to be destroyed. They hate us and will stop at nothing to claim their place as the supposedly rightful heirs to this planet. They truly believe themselves to be the future of humanity, the next natural evolutionary step, and equally believe human beings to be the next victim of a natural extinction. They are wrong. We will not fall and we will not be subjugated. This immunity, contained in the blood, is the very reason why we need not surrender to *holosap* rule. *Homo immortalis* is just that, immortal, but only if we allow them to be.'

Marcus fired another round into a Wasp, catching it with a glancing blow that was just enough to send the drone crashing into a wall. It tumbled down onto the concourse floor and Marcus fired at it again, smashing it to pieces.

'Fall back!'

Chad's voice rang out above the gunfire now pouring into the control room as the attacking soldiers regrouped and began advancing yard by yard down the concourse toward them. Marcus leaped up and saw three remaining Wasps race through the open entrance to the control room.

'The body armour!' Chad yelled. 'Use it!'

Chad dove beneath one of the piles of body armour, pulling it across his legs and body before firing at the nearest Wasp. Marcus turned for the other pile nearby and then saw Kerry, sitting with her back to the room, still talking into the camera.

'The *holosaps* have built an army of robots here in New Orleans, weaponised machines, some controlled by people, others entirely automated. They are not for research purposes to cure us of The Falling. They are not for farming or maintenance. They are designed to kill us. No doubt they will have similar machine armies in most surviving cities. Find them, destroy them, stand up for those of us who have survived this far and for those who might live in the future!'

'Kerry!' Marcus yelled. 'Get into cover!'

Kerry did not move, staring up at the camera as she spoke.

'There is a virus present in the *holosap's* storage system. We don't know who caused it but it may be our only chance to shut them down before every last human being on Earth is murdered by our own creations! Let the virus run and never trust them again, ever!'

One of the Wasps dove at Chad, who deflected it with a swipe of the heavy body armour as he fired a pistol at it. Marcus grabbed one of the thick body suits and whirled to swing it at an attacking Wasp. The drone was batted aside and clanged loudly against a metal pillar.

Marcus turned and saw the third Wasp dive in toward Kerry.

'Kerry!'

Marcus leaped between the Wasp and Kerry and swung his rifle butt at the drone.

The Wasp plunged beneath the weapon, swinging its metallic abdomen up toward Marcus and squirting a spray of venom across his face. The sharp, ammoniac tang wafted across his nose as it splashed across his eyes like liquid fire.

Marcus screamed and swung his arms in blind panic as he toppled to his knees, the humming of the Wasp loud in his ears as its wings beat the air and then he felt the cold metal legs grip his neck as the Wasp collided with him, sharp, evil clamps biting into his skin as something long and sharp plunged into his neck.

Marcus gagged as much in horror as pain as the Wasp injected venom deep into his body. He reached up instinctively and grabbed the drone, yanked it free and smashed it against the ground with ferocious blows, driven by pain and terror, hearing the metal crash against the floor tiles but unable to see as his eyes burned and throbbed. The drone's metallic body writhed in his grip but he felt its wings smash and bend, its head crunching and snapping until he hurled it away across the room.

Kerry dropped down alongside him from her seat and he felt her arms wrap around him as bullets ricocheted in a violent hymn of destruction. Panels smashed in bright clouds of sparks, the smell of burning cables and exploded touch screens tainting the air.

'This is it!' Chad yelled, firing at what sounded to Marcus like two Wasps attacking him. His warning was followed by agonised cries and then a deep thump as a grenade went off. The blast reverberated through the control room but it seemed somehow distant as Kerry shielded him from the blast, her long black hair falling like a veil across their faces, hers barely an inch from his own.

Chad's weapon fell silent, and Marcus realised through his pain that the soldier must have been holding the grenade that had just detonated. Pain seethed through Marcus's body, burning like flames in his veins and throbbing in his neck as though it were swelling to ten times its normal size. He felt his skin stretching under unbearable strain, felt his heart racing and his limbs twitching beyond control, the control room a shadowy blur now as some of the venom drained from his face.

'Marcus.'

He heard Kerry's voice above the din, soft in his ear. His eyes were blurred, pain bolting through them, but he managed to turn his head enough to see her looking down at him, one hand cupping the back of his head as the other gently brushed her hair from out of his eyes.

'We did it,' she whispered.

Marcus, despite his pain, gave a jerky nod. 'We've certainly gone and done it now.'

He saw Kerry smile, laugh even, a tiny ray of hope and light amid the darkness and destruction surrounding them and the yelling voices that burst into the control room.

'There they are!'

Marcus pulled Kerry close to him with the last of his strength.

* * *

48

London

Han Reeves watched as the doctor pumped Arianna's blood through the bypass machine, this time having warmed the blood first. The ice was gone and Han realised that he was clenching his fist in desperation as with the other hand he held the pistol pointed at the doctor.

The sound of the helicopters outside had been confirmation that it was over, that somebody had called them in as soon as they'd had the chance. A mole amongst the rebels, perhaps? An informer for the police? Han couldn't be sure, but he knew now that he would be unlikely to escape the basement alive.

'Open the door!'

The rebels were outside and with them was Myles. He recognised the voice and the anger in it.

'It's over Han!' Myles called out. 'There's nowhere for you to go now!'

Han ignored the calls, although he knew that sooner or later the rebels outside would be forced to risk the doctor's life in order to take Han down. He had covered the grubby window with his jacket, hanging it there so that nobody could take a lethal shot at him while the doctor worked. Han knew now that if he died before Arianna was revived, it was all over. Everything. Her sacrifice would be for nothing and so would his. The rebels would kill them all and the police helicopters would then arrive to kill the rebels.

Corrupt officer, no doubt would be the accusation, betraying his force for money or perhaps the chance to upload with the *holosaps* someday. Maybe by now the Prime Minister had already managed to somehow tie Han into the murder of Alexei Volkov and the blasts at Re–Volution.

Mind you, they probably wouldn't even need to bother. Han looked down at his shoes, one of which was glossy where his blood was leaking from his wound. He could feel it squelching under his foot. His mind felt feeble and his legs numb, but he kept the pistol pointed at the doctor.

'Hurry it up,' he insisted.

'She's almost ready,' the doctor said, 'another minute or two. You can't hurry life, or death.'

Doctor Tyree looked at Han, who realised belatedly that a professional physician probably knew a dying man when he saw one. Han glanced at the monitors relaying Arianna's condition and saw that she still did not have a heartbeat. Her core temperature was now up from sixteen degrees centigrade to thirty four degrees.

'You're not going to last long enough,' the doctor said with a confidence Han did not want to think about. 'You're losing too much blood.'

'You worry about Arianna's blood,' Han snapped. 'I'll worry about mine.'

Tyree looked at Han for a moment, as though considering something, and then he waved him over. 'I can dress the wound.'

'The wound's fine.'

'You're going to drop stone cold unconscious at any moment,' the doctor replied, 'at which point I'll dress the wound anyway and then open the door for the police once Arianna's alive. Which order would you prefer all of that to happen in, detective?'

'You're not here to save her or me,' Han growled, clenching his pistol tighter.

'If that were true, how come she's not already dead?' the doctor asked.

Han blinked, blood loss clouding his thoughts. Sweat was beading cold on his brow, his heart fluttering in his chest.

'I don't care what you think. I'm not going to…'

The world tilted wildly as Han's vision and balance vanished in unison. He had almost hit the floor when the doctor caught him, slowing him down enough to lay him flat on his back.

'Get the damned gun out of my face,' Tyree insisted.

Moments later, as Han's vision focused once again, he felt the doctor holding a dressing against his wound.

'You need stitches, badly,' then doctor informed him. 'But the wound is not fatal. Get up and keep the pad pressed against the wound.'

Han hauled himself upright as Tyree turned away from him. He reached up and applied a small electrode to Arianna's chest and then hit a switch. A loud beep echoed around the room and then settled into the calming, rhythmic signal of a beating heart.

'Rhythm's good, temperature's up,' the doctor reported. 'She's coming around.'

The blast came from behind Han, not an explosion but the sound of a metal ram smashing through the basement doors. He whirled for his pistol and then realised that the doctor was holding it close by his thigh, a quiet smile on his face.

'Sorry detective,' he said, 'but there's just no way that you're getting this back.'

'Get down!!'

The rebels burst into the basement in a flood of hoods and weapons. Han crouched down as the rebels, rifles pulled into shoulders and aimed at them all, fanned out through the room. Myles Bourne strode to stand before Han where he crouched on one knee, one hand holding the medical pad to his bloodied side.

'You screwed up big, this time,' Myles said.

Han squinted up at Myles. 'What do you mean *I* screwed up?'

'The rebels are right, Han, you can't be trusted. I leave you or the woman alive you'll blow this whole thing to pieces. You've been part of their plan all along, to infiltrate the rebels and find out their plan.'

Han stared at Myles for a long moment, and then it all fell into place.

'You're working for St John,' he said finally.

'No, you are.'

The doctor and the rebel soldiers looked from one to the other, their rifles shifting from side to side as they did so. Myles looked at the rebels and pointed to his bruised, battered face.

'This look like the action of a friend to you? He tied me up to get down here so he could finish Arianna off before she even had a chance to share what she'd learned. You found me, didn't you?'

'That's not true,' Han shot back and looked at the doctor. 'Tell them what happened.'

The doctor looked from one to the other. 'I don't know why you came here,' he said to Han. 'Maybe you do want to kill her.'

Han let out a gasp of despair and rubbed his forehead wearily with one hand. 'Are you kidding me?'

The rebels stepped forward, rifles still tightly aimed at both Han and Myles. 'We don't have time for this,' one of the rebels said. 'Arianna's work is done no matter what happens.'

'What do you mean?' Myles asked.

'She's the key, not Alexei Volkov,' Han replied. 'Icon's got the *holosaps* by the balls. That's why Icon really wanted her to be uploaded. It was nothing to do with solving a murder or finding evidence of corruption. She is his secret weapon.'

Myles's features paled and his jaw hung open as he looked over at Arianna's body.

As if on cue, Arianna gasped and sucked in a huge breath of air as she shuddered, her eyes opening as Tyree moved to her side.

'Stay still, don't try to move too quickly.'

Arianna bolted upright in the gurney as though the doctor hadn't said a word. 'Connor!' She blinked as she took in the basement, the rebel soldiers, Han crouched on the floor and Myles Bourne standing over him with the pistol in his hand.

'It's Myles!' she yelled. 'Myles is working for the *holosaps*!'

Han only had the briefest of moments to look at Myles before his partner moved, a tiny metallic grey pistol flashing into his hand from beneath his jacket. Han registered the fact that it was not a police issue weapon and that it was too modern for it to have gotten into the hands of the rebels, compact and light.

Three shots crashed out as Myles whirled with practiced fluidity, the shots hitting the rebels one by one and sending their own wild fire up into the ceiling to spray chips of concrete dust down onto the floor of the basement.

Han tried to move but his weakened legs would not respond. The three rebels collapsed to the ground, writhing in agony from their wounds. Without haste, Myles stepped up to each of them and three more shots crashed out as he fired into each of their brains, silencing them forever.

Myles turned to Arianna, Han and the doctor. 'Arianna, you're still alive. How unfortunate.'

Arianna's voice was croaky, her throat sounding dry as she replied. 'If you can call it that.'

'You're a traitor,' Han growled at Myles. 'You're condemning the entire human race to death.'

'I'm no traitor, Han,' Myles replied. 'I've been working for my father since I was a child. I doubt that you, as an orphan, would understand why.'

'Kieran Beck,' Arianna said.

'A visionary if ever there was one,' Myles snapped with true pride stiffening his limbs and lifting his chin. 'It helped to have family inside the law, and I am proud to have risked my neck to be here. It is over for the parasite that we call mankind.'

'You are a human being,' Han said in disbelief. 'You're killing yourself!'

'That's right,' Myles agreed and then turned to Arianna. 'It is time for a new beginning, and it starts with your end.'

Myles raised the pistol to point at Arianna.

With a heave of effort Han lurched to his feet and threw himself awkwardly at Myles. The younger man stepped a single pace back and to the right, dodging Han's shambling attack as he swung the butt of the pistol to thumb sickeningly into the back of Han's head.

Han groaned in pain and sprawled onto the floor. He rolled over to see Myles turn his back to Arianna and the doctor and aim the pistol down at him.

'A shame, Han,' Myles said. 'You could have had a great future if you'd joined the winning side.'

Han, his features contorted by pain and regret beyond words, nodded stiffly. 'So could have you.'

Myles frowned pityingly and then squeezed the trigger.

The gunshot crashed out and Han flinched as the bullet smashed through blood and bone. The left side of Myles's head split apart in a messy spray and he toppled sideways to crash down onto the ground next to Han, his one remaining eye staring lifelessly at his former partner.

Han looked up to see Tyree pointing Han's pistol, the barrel smouldering.

'I think I've definitely broken my oath now,' the doctor said, his voice trembling.

Han rubbed the back of his head as he clambered wearily to his feet. He looked down at Myles's corpse, and the reached down and wrenched the pistol from his grip.

'Can you walk?' he asked Arianna.

Slowly, Arianna slid off the gurney as the doctor carefully removed the lines from her arms and patched them. She balanced unsteadily against the side of the gurney as Han moved alongside her. The doctor spent a minute or two patching the wound in Han's side, muttering again about how he needed stitches, before standing back and looking at them both.

'You're both alive, but I've never seen any two people look closer to death.'

'You ready?' Han asked her.

Arianna nodded. 'Where are we going?'

Han was about to answer when a squad of police officers dashed down the stairwell and burst into the basement, their weapons aimed at Han, Arianna and the doctor as they flooded into the room. They came up short as he saw the bodies littering the floor.

Han, one hand in the air and the other holding the dressing to his wound, managed to speak.

'I'm a police detective. You here to kill us or save us?' he asked.

'Commissioner Forrester sent us,' one of the officers replied through a face mask. 'What the hell happened here?'

'It's okay,' the doctor said. 'Detective Myles Bourne was a Re–Volution informer, nearly killed all of us.'

The officer looked at Arianna. 'This woman is wanted for…–'

'This woman just risked her life to protect us all,' Han said. 'The leader of the rebels, Icon, used her upload to access the *holosap* colony and then left her to die.'

'That's not true,' the officer replied. 'The man called Icon contacted Forrester's office a few minutes ago and informed him of your location. He has requested that you join him in Westminster. Something big is happening!'

* * *

49

They moved swiftly.

Icon's men shifted from cover to cover across the crumbling remains of Westminster Bridge, toward the heavily fortified guard post protecting the entrance to the city. A couple of corpses, rabid dogs, lay nearby amid the dense weeds and cast a stench of rotting meat across the bridge as Icon walked past.

Icon wasn't even within a hundred yards of the guard post when he heard the first alarms going off, saw soldiers tumble from within the post in a thunder of boots on tarmac, rifles gripped in their hands as they amassed to confront Icon and his men.

No need, Icon mused. It's not us you need to worry about.

Icon looked over his shoulder. The helicopter gunships he'd called in had thundered overhead toward the south of the city minutes before. Two of them, leaving only another pair remaining to protect the city. Commissioner Forrester's office had not believed him until he'd mentioned Han Reeves's name, and that of Arianna Volkov. Now, the secrets and lies would start to emerge, if Arianna had survived. Part of him hoped that she had.

He looked down the apparently deserted road behind him, and nodded once.

The sound of a diesel engine growled and a large truck rounded the corner of the street down where the gutted shell of the old Park Plaza still stood. The truck drove slowly, rattling along until it lined up on the bridge. Then with a cloud of belched smoke from its exhaust the truck accelerated toward the guard post.

Icon leaned back as the truck thundered past, then ducked down as the inevitable broadside of gunfire began. He glimpsed the windows of the truck shatter but it mattered little for there was no driver within to harm, the vehicle remotely controlled. Inside, a simple assembly of levers, servos and modified hydraulics steered and powered the truck on its suicidal charge.

There was no time for the guards to bring heavier weapons to bear upon the truck before it ploughed through the razor wire fence, both sets of gates and then smashed into the guard house. Soldiers leaped out of the truck's way and then it smashed through the barriers on the northern side of the bridge and came to a rest, fifteen yards past the guard house.

Only now did Icon wave his men forward.

In an instant, two things happened. Firstly, the troops guarding the city came under heavy and controlled fire from the advancing rebels. Secondly, the side of the truck hissed as a door opened automatically and from within the truck poured a flood of wild dogs, their jowls drooling with rage and their matted fur patched with lesions of rotting flesh.

Just like the machines, thought Icon, only worse.

He heard the screams of the soldiers as they were bitten, or tried valiantly to shoot the animals dead before they escaped into the city, but there were too many. Even as more police vehicles flooded toward the bridge from within the city, rushing to the aid of their beleaguered comrades, the animals darted off the bridge and bolted away up side streets and down the embankment, laden with their lethal disease.

Icon hurried forward with his men to the truck as soon as the last of the guards had been picked off by his marksmen, and together they hauled out crates of heavy weapons. Moments later, as police vehicles swamped the north side of the bridge, a fusillade of rocket–propelled grenades screeched across the bridge and ploughed into them. Explosions rocked the vehicles, hurling them into the air like toys amid roiling balls of smoke and flame, hurled the bodies of police officers like rag dolls across the streets, snapping and severing limbs.

Icon's men surged forward, bigger weapons mounted on tripods now spraying a lethal combination of plunging and grazing fire across the burning vehicles, consumed amid writhing coils of dirty smoke and flame.

The sound of helicopters overhead made Icon look up, but he feared them no longer as he directed RPG fire up into the sky. It only took a single direct hit to send the first plunging down into the city to the sound of deep, thumping explosions as it vanished behind glittering tower blocks of glass and stone. In an instant the remaining helicopter pulled back and up, away from the danger.

Icon knew that the two helicopters that had travelled south of the city would already be hurrying back, but within minutes he would have nothing to fear from them either.

Westminster loomed ahead, the crowds of commuters flocking the streets fleeing in screaming hordes as Icon's men surged across the bridge between the flaming wrecks of the police vehicles. They swarmed down Westminster Road and placed charges against the sheer metal fences surrounding the Parliament buildings.

Gunfire erupted from within Parliament as armed guards, finally realising what was happening, began trying to slow down the rebel attack, but there was little chance for them to out–gun Icon's little army. Speed and surprise overcame the odds, for at least a while, and a while was all Icon needed. Every gunshot from within the building was met in reply by an RPG that smashed through the ornate glass windows and blasted the snipers and security guards into silence, forcing those within the building to retreat away from the windows.

Moments later, Icon's men fled into cover as their charges exploded with deafening blasts that echoed across the city. The steel fences lay twisted and torn, black metal bare and open like giant metallic flowers blossoming in the weak dawn light.

'Forward!'

Icon's deep, bass roar thundered across the street and his men obeyed willingly with a great cheer of their own as they plunged unopposed down into the Parliament gardens toward the huge building's many and various entrances. Charges were set, doors blasted open in violent cascades of shattered wood and masonry, and in a wave of righteous fury the rebel forces plunged into Parliament with blood lust surging through their veins.

*

The Chamber was packed to overflowing with ministers, *holosaps* occupying the seats where once Bishops had sat. Only a single representative from what had once been the Church of England remained, a sole voice for the Hope Reunion Church still clad in flowing black robes, his clerical collar stark white and illuminated in a strangely ultra–violet light by the glow from the *holosaps* that surrounded him.

Upon a large screen was a chart showing votes cast for and against the voluntary euthanasia of the political cabinet. Over ninety per cent of the votes were in favour.

Prime Minister Tarquin St John stood before the Speaker of the House, his voice carrying clearly through the amplifiers and betraying a slight tremor.

'The wishes of this parliament have been made clear,' he said. 'We have, as a species, made every effort to save ourselves through conventional means, through the search for a vaccine for the terrible sickness that has plagued us and decimated our cities for decades.' St John sighed. 'We have failed and now I stand here as your Prime Minister on the last day of human rule in this country.'

The chamber remained silent as a sepulchre as St John went on.

'In order to ensure our continuation as a species and the governance of those that remain in our care, we have chosen that we should sacrifice ourselves in order that others may not yet have to. On this day, we shall cease to govern as human beings and begin to govern as Holo sapiens.'

St John looked across the chamber to where his wife and children stood.

'I shall be the first,' he said. 'And here, I give you the man responsible for humanity's conquering of The Falling, Kieran Beck.'

A ripple of applause shuddered through the chamber as Kieran Beck stood alongside Tarquin St John as the Prime Minister slipped out of his jacket and rolled up his sleeve.

Kieran Beck looked up at the *holosaps* as he produced a syringe from his pocket and slipped the protective cap from the needle. The Prime Minister looked across at his family one last time.

'It's okay,' he said, the microphones picking up his words. 'It'll be okay.'

Kieran Beck leaned over the Prime Minister and slipped the needle into his arm. The amber fluid drained into St John's vein. Kieran Beck stood back and looked down at St John. The Prime Minister sat in silence for a few moments and then his eyes began to droop. He turned his head wearily to his wife and daughters, who were holding each other and crying as they watched, and managed a gentle smile. His head dropped further and he sucked in a tremulous breath that he then exhaled slowly for several seconds as though unwilling to part with it. Then he slumped in his seat as his heart gave up its fight against the drugs surging through his system.

Kieran Beck looked up to the *holosaps*, and moments later a ghostly figure shimmered into existence among them. A rush of exclamations and whispers echoed through the chamber as the Prime Minister appeared among the *holosaps* and looked down at his family.

'See?' he said, his voice reaching them from the amplifiers alone. 'It's okay, everything's fine.'

Kieran Beck turned to the microphones.

'Today is a monumental day, one that shall be recorded forever in human history as the day when we, as a species, finally took control of our own evolution and our own future. Never again shall we kneel before the wrath of nature. Never again shall we fear the spectre of disease and disability. Never again shall we face utter extinction. Our race will continue forever more, into a future that is bright with promise and…'

A deep rumble shuddered through the building. Lights swayed gently in the high vaulted ceiling above. A ripple of concerned whispers fluttered like an errant wind across the crowd.

Kieran Beck went on.

'… with promise and the knowledge that we shall ever more be protected by our own ingenuity and technology. We shall be forever more. We shall be Homo immortalis.'

Beck stood back and waited for the applause, but none came. Instead the crackle of automatic gunfire rattled from outside the building to mounting whispers of consternation from the crowd. St John's holosap descended along the light path between the ranks of ministers. He paused as he saw his own dead body slumped in its seat, and then stepped up close to the dais behind Kieran Beck.

'Gentlemen, I'm sure that there's nothing to worry about.' He glanced at the armed security guards dotted around the chamber. 'Officers, if you will?'

The police officers jogged immediately to the closed chamber doors and took up firing positions around them.

'Speaker of the House?' St John asked, 'could we have visual on the outside of the building and the news channel please?'

A series of large screens flickered into life on opposing sides of the chamber, and were immediately followed by gasps of horror. St John stared wide eyed at the screens showing the chaos outside as he yelled to the nearest security guard, felt the chamber windows reverberate as the shockwave from explosions shuddered through the ancient building.

Behind him, his aide spoke quietly, as though fear had stolen the strength from her voice as she gestured to a screen set into the wall nearby.

'Sir, I think that you should see this.'

St John whirled. 'We're under attack and you want me to watch the bloody television?! I should have you thrown from…the… building…'

St John fell silent as he heard an American broadcasting across the airwaves. The news channel had vanished to be replaced by the image of a young woman, the broadcast shifting erratically and buzzing with occasional static. She looked as dirty as she did determined, her hair lank and her neck swathed in hastily applied dressings that concealed a wound of tattered, decaying flesh. In the background could be heard the sound of raging gunfire.

'My name is Kerry Hussein. I am a research biologist working for the United States Government in Louisiana, and broadcasting from the international airport outside of New Orleans. I have discovered a cure for The Falling.'

A rush of surprised gasps rippled through the chamber.

'What the hell is this?' Kieran Beck gasped. 'Call the broadcasting centre and have them shut this off!'

'It's not coming from our broadcasting centre,' his aide said, gesturing to the screen that was devoid of the company logo. 'This is a hacked broadcast.'

St John felt his blood run cold as he heard the woman's voice and realised that it was being broadcast not just to the government but into every single home in every surviving city on the planet.

The noise you hear in the background is our government's troops attempting to kill us. They have been lying, to all of us, for decades. The Falling is not incurable and never has been. It is the aim of the holosaps to gain control of our government and then eradicate humanity from the face of our planet.'

'No,' St John gasped. 'This cannot be!'

He saw two men firing their rifles at a swarm of mechanical insects bearing down upon them.

'The holosaps have built an army of robots here in New Orleans, weaponised machines, some controlled by people, others entirely automated. They are not for research purposes: they are designed to kill us. No doubt they will have similar machine armies near most surviving cities. Find them, destroy them, stand up for those of us who have survived this far, for those who might live in the future!'

The remaining man stood protectively over her before he too was overcome, his face smeared with some unspeakable poison as the revolting drone plunging a sharp, cruel stinger into his neck until the man was able to fend it off and smash it against the ground. But it was clear to St John that the man was doomed, and as he lay shivering on the ground the woman levered herself from her chair and lay down with useless legs splayed behind her to cradle the fallen man's head in her arms and stroke his hair.

Moments later, troops plunged into the room and opened fire at close range upon the two young scientists. St John cried out in horror and the chamber erupted into gasps of disgust as he saw their bodies ripped apart by the bullets, blood splattering the camera lens until a stray round smashed it to pieces and the transmission cut out.

St John stared at the blank screen, the thumps and explosions outside falling silent as the rebels breached the building. He imaged he could feel his heart thumping against the wall of his chest as the screen flickered and a reporter's image reappeared.

'… we apologise for the recent unauthorised broadcast to bring you breaking news that the Re–Volution quantum storage facility has been infected by an unknown virus in what may become the greatest single act of genocide in the history of mankind.'

St John staggered backwards from the screen, as though by doing so he could distance himself from the calamity. His *holosap* was stopped at the edge of the light path as though he had touched against an invisible wall, trapped to endure the terrifying news.

'Early indications are that the virus is currently dormant, but Re–Volution is struggling to contain the spread of the virus before it completely infects all data storage units worldwide.'

St John stared at the screen, immobilised until he heard screams coming from outside the chamber. Gunfire rattled loudly. The security guards tightened their stances, the commanding officer looking up at the Speaker of the House.

'Sir, permission to...'

'Go!' the speaker almost shouted. 'Go, now!'

The guards yanked the doors open and rushed out into the main atrium outside.

More bursts of automatic fire that sounded much louder now and then the deafening blast of several fragmentation grenades, a cloud of dislodged stone and dust billowing through the chamber doors as several ministers used their arms to shield themselves from the debris cloud.

The gunfire ceased to be replaced by the groans and screams of injured men. One by one, the screams were silenced either by muffled gunshots or by the horrific sound of throats being slit. St John stared at the chamber doors, willing then security guards to come back in, to say that everything was all right.

A new fear drained him of the will to move as the chamber door burst open and a flood of armed and hooded men poured inside, heavy black rifles in their gloved hands.

'In your seats, hands in the air!'

The command was bellowed time and time again. Kieran Beck retook his seat as behind the rebels strode a single man, unarmed and yet possessed of immense presence. The man shut the chamber doors behind him and walked to the centre of the chamber, staring up at each and every politician before he reached up and lifted his hood clear of his head.

The chamber gasped at the sight of his ruined features, and St John saw the colour drain from Kieran Beck's face.

'My name,' the disfigured man growled, 'is Icon.'

* * *

50

'Come on, hurry!'

Westminster Bridge was almost obscured by rolling banks of smoke billowing from wrecked police vehicles burning nearby. Fire trucks were battling the flames with hoses drawing their water directly from the Thames, blasting the fearsome blaze as Han and Arianna struggled by, skirting the chaos with a phalanx of armed police escorting them.

Han guided her toward the Parliament Building where Big Ben loomed above tight, nervous knots of police officers and riot vehicles that were forming a cordon around the building and fending off crowds of panicked citizens lining the streets. The entire scene was reminiscent of footage of the collapse of the country a quarter of a century before, when so many had died trying to escape the ravages of The Falling.

'He's already inside,' Han said. 'There's nothing we can do to stop him now.'

Arianna pushed on, dragging Han toward the cordon. A police officer saw them coming and raised his rifle.

'Stand still!' he ordered, recognising Arianna immediately. 'On the floor now!'

'Detective Han Reeves, eight–one–four–one–zero,' Han called back. 'She's in our custody. We need to talk to Commissioner Forrester right now!'

The officer turned and yanked the cordon up enough that they could pass through with their escort, but he kept his distance and the rifle aimed at them as he keyed a microphone earpiece and spoke quickly. Within a minute, Commissioner Forrester appeared from a surveillance vehicle nearby.

'Han?' he uttered. 'We're under orders to arrest you and this woman on sight!'

'I know,' Han said, 'and it's all false. This is Arianna Volkov and her only crime was being in the wrong place at the wrong time. Has Icon entered the parliament chamber yet?'

Forrester blinked in surprise. 'Yes, how did you know that he...?'

'It's a long story,' Han cut his boss off. 'Myles Bourne was an informer for Re–Volution and the son of Kieran Beck. He's now dead after trying to kill both of us.'

'You're serious? Myles?' Forrester asked, stunned. 'He was an exemplary detective.'

'The *holosaps* are planning to eradicate humans, and have been hiding the fact that Icon and his men are immune to The Falling.'

'We know about the immunity,' the officer replied.

'You do?'

'Television broadcast went out just a few minutes ago, right across the world. Some kids in Louisiana, scientists, they worked it out. Millions of people just saw them shot to death on live television.'

Arianna sighed, the loss of so many brave patriots a weighty burden on her shoulders. She wondered how many more would be killed before the day was out.

'Why is Icon doing this?' Forrester asked. 'The secret's out, people know about the deception. They're marching in their thousands on Re–Volution's building right now.'

'Maybe Icon hasn't seen the broadcast yet?' Han suggested.

'He must have by now. What else is he doing in there?' Arianna asked the commissioner.

Forrester glanced across at the parliament building. 'He's holding parliament captive. He's just had his people walk infected dogs on rigid leashes into the building and he's threatening to sit back and watch them all die if he doesn't get what he wants.'

'Which is what?' Han asked.

'Control,' Forrester replied. 'He wants control of government and some personal time with Kieran Beck.'

'The man who murdered my father,' Arianna said. 'He's behind all of this, not the government.'

Forrester blinked, trying to keep up. 'What about the virus, the *holosap* one I mean? I've got Re–Volution tech heads screaming for help with it.'

'I think I know what it is,' Han replied. 'You need to let us go in there.'

Forrester looked at Arianna. 'God only knows what you've gotten into. I'll order my men to let you pass through, but Icon's not letting the police into parliament. You'll be on your own, and I've no idea what's waiting for you in there.'

Han took Arianna's arm and smiled at her through his exhaustion. 'I've still got your back,' he said.

They walked together, Han valiantly supporting Arianna by the arm but both of them virtually leaning on one another as they staggered down toward the building entrance. Loudspeakers hailed their arrival to the twitchy rebels guarding the interior of the building, and by the time they had shuffled their way along the damp stone flags to the shattered main entrance they had been granted passage by the man controlling the inside.

Icon.

They walked through toward the chamber, the interior of the building as opulent, polished and clean as it had ever been, but for the occasional pool of spilled blood and corpses lying silent and still. The carnage marked the path of Icon's men to the parliamentary chamber, the doors of which stood guarded but open as Arianna and Han eased their way inside.

'At last!'

Icon's voice boomed out above the silence as he saw them enter the chamber. Arianna saw hundreds of ministers all sitting in their seats, their faces taut with fear. *Holosaps* glowed above them in the Bishop's seats. Her eyes settled on Prime Minister Tarquin St John, both the dead man's corpse and his glowing *holosap*, and Kieran Beck, the man who had caused so much pain in her life.

St John looked as though he were trying to make himself as small as possible. Kieran Beck was on his knees at Icon's boots, a rigid leash around his neck identical to the one restraining a growling, drooling Alsatian barely three feet from him, a rebel holding the animal and barely able to stop it from attacking the cowering businessman.

Alexei Volkov materialised silently into the *holosap* area in a flutter of light. With him stood Connor, and to her horror Arianna saw herself appear as a *holosap* alongside her son, Lynda's likeness now vanished to be replaced by her own. The ministers saw Arianna appear both in the *holosap* area and on the chamber floor and a rush of whispers rippled through the crowd. Arianna stared up at her son.

'What blasphemy is this?!' boomed the sole Hope Reunion Church Bishop as he stood to point at Arianna's *holosap* and then at Arianna herself. 'Have you no longer any respect for your faith?'

Arianna reached up to her neck and realised that she was still wearing her clerical collar. She felt shame burn her skin as the entire chamber watched her.

'Alexei's here,' Han uttered to Arianna. 'Who's the kid?'

'My son,' Arianna replied.

Alexei Volkov's voice called out to the crowd. 'Ladies and gentlemen of parliament, I give you Arianna Anderson, the woman who would see all *holosaps* die this day. She has murdered a woman in order to be both alive and dead at the same time!'

The ministers turned to look at Arianna and she managed to step forward on her own. Han let her go as she walked uneasily to the centre of the chamber, Icon staring back at her.

'Or the woman,' Icon said, 'who would save us all?'

'Have them arrested, detective!' Kieran Beck bellowed to Han with false bravado, his limbs quivering. 'All of them! She's a terrorist, a murderer!'

'A little late for that,' Icon murmured softly in response, his deep voice rumbling up toward the vaulted chamber ceiling without the need for amplification as he turned to the politicians. 'Now we can begin. My real name is Ian Connelly and I was once a soldier in the British Army. I am now a survivor of The Falling and I am immune to the disease.'

'This isn't the way,' Arianna said to him.

Icon continued, ignoring her.

'My people are immune to The Falling. Each and every one of them carries the cure to the disease in their blood, and now we know that there are others who have discovered that same immunity and died for their troubles at the hands of governments worldwide.' Icon looked about him at the ministers. 'But it is not the government we blame. It is Re–Volution. It is the *holosaps*!'

Beck stammered over his response, the bloodied deaths of two innocent civilians on live television having overwhelmed anything he could say in response.

'This is all a fabrication, a lie! These people are terrorists! The people on the television were terrorists!'

'You're the only liar,' Arianna shouted at Beck. '*Holosaps* are inherently unstable, psychotic in their lack of empathy.' She turned to the ministers. 'My name is Arianna Anderson. My father was Professor Cecil Anderson, and he was murdered by Kieran Beck when he tried to destroy the *holosap* program twenty five years ago.'

The ministers all looked at Beck, who pointed at Arianna from where he knelt on the chamber floor. 'She is a terrorist!'

'She is a saviour,' Han said weakly, one hand holding his wound. 'We know what happened, Beck. We know how you killed Alexei Volkov while trying to find the kill–switch that Cecil Anderson created to destroy all *holosaps* in the event of a malfunction or failure. How you placed your son inside the police force. Myles is dead, Kieran, by the way.'

Kieran's fury turned to something that might have been grief as he cowered beneath Icon.

'And now we know about the machines,' Minister Hart said, standing from his seat and speaking out at last. 'We know how the *holosaps* plan to take over and eradicate humanity. This was never about equal rights. This was about domination, about genocide.'

'But now,' Icon said, his voice overpowering them all, 'parliament votes to hand power to the *holosaps*, regardless of the people's wishes. Is that democracy? Is that what we fought for?'

Icon turned and with one boot kicked Kieran Beck over onto his back, within inches of the snarling Alsatian. Beck screamed in terror, one arm up over his face and his knees pulled up against his chest.

'This is what you are, Beck,' Icon growled down at him. 'Half a man, without the courage of a dog.' Icon looked up at the rebel holding the Alsatian at bay. 'Let it loose!'

The rebel yanked the leash up and unclipped it, and in a flash the Alsation lunged toward Kieran Beck's cowering form.

'No!' Arianna yelled.

The dogs yellowing fangs sank into Kieran Beck's right leg and he screamed in agony, shielding his face as Icon stepped back.

Kieran Beck looked up the Alsatian from behind his arm and then laughed out loud as he screamed. 'To hell with you all! You'll never be able to stop us now!'

With his free hand Beck pulled a small, snub–nosed pistol from his jacket and aimed it at Icon even as the dog tugged at his leg to the sound of crunching, tearing flesh. The former soldier leaped aside and kicked Beck's wrist in an attempt to dislodge the weapon as he pulled his own pistol, but he was a fraction too slow.

Beck's shot hit Icon high in the chest. The big man staggered backward and then collapsed as his own pistol fell from his quivering hands. Beck's maniacal laugh, of pain and feverish delight, strained his vocal chords as he turned his pistol on himself and pulled the trigger. His hair flew off of his head as though he had been scalped as the bullet tore through his skull in a wispy shower of blood, brain and bone that spilled down onto the politicians sitting nearby.

Several ministers vomited as Beck's body slumped and the dog sank its teeth into his shattered skull and began tugging and growling as it chewed. Han Reeves leaped forward, picked up Beck's discarded weapon and turned. He fired a single shot into the dog's head and the beast slumped over Beck's corpse.

Han hurried to Icon's side and propped him up as he looked at the wound. Pink blood bubbled from Icon's ruined lung. Arianna knelt beside them.

'At least I'll die a man and not a glorified zombie,' Icon gasped to her.

Beck's *holosap* shimmered into life among the others high above the chamber floor and he laid his hands down on Connor's shoulders, smiling broadly. He spoke as though nothing had happened, as though he had not just committed suicide before the entire chamber.

'The infection has breached the city and the time of man has come to an end!' he bellowed. 'The time of holo sapiens has begun!'

Icon looked up at Beck and shook his head, his forehead sheened with sweat but his voice still carrying far further than Beck's ever had. 'You're forgetting one thing, Kieran.'

'What's that?' Beck sneered in disgust.

Icon turned and looked at Arianna's *holosap*, still standing beside Connor. 'You have a choice, Arianna,' he said, speaking not to the real Arianna but to the glowing image of her. 'To save humanity you must eradicate the *holosaps*.'

'What?' Arianna stammered. 'I can't do that!'

'Yes,' Icon replied as he looked back at Arianna as she knelt beside him, 'you can. You're the only one who can, Arianna. You're still human, you're still alive and your *holosap* is still within reach. You must convince her, convince yourself.'

Arianna heard Han's voice from behind her.

'It's why he wanted you to upload,' Han explained. 'He didn't need you to contact Alexei Volkov. He just needed that chip in your brain to upload its data into the Re–Volution servers.'

Arianna felt a chill run down her spine as she looked at Icon.

'You're the kill–switch, Arianna,' Icon said solemnly to her. 'You're what I've been searching for all these years.'

* * *

51

Arianna stared at Icon's ruined face in disbelief. 'What?'

'I excavated your grave,' Icon replied, his voice rattling now as blood pooled into his shattered lung, 'months after I had survived The Falling. Your father buried you long before the city was quarantined. The grave contained the body of a young girl who was not Professor Anderson's daughter. She possessed no implant. It was a pauper's grave, Arianna. It was then that I understood that you were his secret, still alive somewhere, a walking kill-switch to bring the *holosaps* to account for the crimes he believed they might commit if allowed to propagate.'

She barely heard Kieran Beck's voice ring out across the chamber.

'Kill her! She will commit genocide if you don't! She'll murder us all!'

The amassed ministers seemed unmoved. Prime Minister St John spoke for the first time since Icon had burst into the chamber. 'Is this true?'

'It is true,' Icon replied. 'Cecil Anderson's daughter did not die of The Falling. She was placed in Leadenhall's boarding houses at the age of seven for several months to hide her identity and then adopted by Alexei Volkov. I watched her father send the kill-switch to Arianna's upload chip just before he died, the same virus he used to terminate *Adam* so many times, knowing that when she died of old age she would both be prevented the horror of becoming a *holosap* and she would exact her father's revenge on Kieran Beck, whom he must have known was plotting against him.'

'It's all lies!' Beck sneered.

'But why?' Minister Hart asked, ignoring the magnate. 'Why did he want it all shut down?'

'Because they're not us,' Arianna spoke finally, her lips moving almost of their own accord as though she were reciting her long dead father's last words. 'They're copies, not resurrected humans. They have their own agenda and see living humans as little more than an irritation, something to be cleansed.' She looked at St John. 'They will kill us all.'

'But the virus is dormant, right?' Han said.

'It was designed to activate when Arianna died and uploaded,' Icon said, 'but Arianna is not dead so it requires manual activation by her *holosap*. A simple spoken quote will suffice.' He looked at Arianna. 'You know the one, Arianna. *The Mourning Bride*, by William Congreve.'

Arianna stared back at him for a long moment. She turned and looked up at her son and her own *holosap*, far above her.

'This is the right thing to do,' she said, the sense of talking to herself bizzare and yet natural, now that she understood what *holosaps* really were.

Her *holosap* was staring down at her as though confused, the as–yet incompletely formed holonomic brain struggling to assess the complexity of the situation before her.

'I am not dead,' Arianna continued to her. 'And yet you exist. Therefore you cannot be me and your very presence proves that it is so. You have my memories. You have my feelings. You have my beliefs. But you are not me. Is this the life you would really have for yourself? For your son?'

The *holosap* looked down at Connor, the child looking back up in response.

'Don't listen to them,' Beck raged at the two *holosaps*. 'They're lying to you. You're alive! You're here, right now! They would have you die for nothing!'

'I would have you die,' Arianna agreed, speaking softly, 'for you to avoid becoming what Alexei has become. A pawn. A machine with no true free will, denied the chance of the true afterlife that awaits us. I have seen it. I had to be placed in a state of clinical death in order to infiltrate the *holosap* colony in an attempt to understand what was happening. I saw the light, the *real* light, the *real* afterlife, and I would gladly die without an upload rather than become what my poor adoptive father has.' Arianna looked up at Alexei's *holosap*. 'Is that the Alexei you remember? Would he have threatened our son in this way?'

Arianna's *holosap* stared down at Connor, and then she slowly backed away and looked at Arianna.

'What will happen to me?' she asked.

'Don't listen to her!' Beck raged. 'Don't believe a word she says!'

Arianna shook her head. 'Honestly, I do not know,' she replied. 'But I do know that madness has infected every *holosap* so far, and that was the reason our father tried to destroy Adam, the very first *holosap*. He realised the danger it represented. Like Adam and like Alexei you'll lose the essence of who you are, who you were, who *I* am. You will become an automaton, your sense of self forever lost, and you will be forever beholden to the people who run Re–Volution, people like Kieran Beck, who murdered Alexei Volkov and who murdered our father, Cecil Anderson. You will not be free, you will be like all *holosaps*: prisoners.'

The *holosap* stared at Arianna for a long beat and then looked down at their son.

'I'm so sorry, Connor,' she said softly.

AFTER LIFE

Connor broke away from Alexei Volkov's *holosap* and dashed down the light path between the ranked seats, past the politicians and onto the chamber floor. Arianna's *holosap* rushed in pursuit of him. Connor slowed as he reached Arianna and stared up into her eyes as Arianna's *holosap* joined him.

'Mummy?' Connor asked. 'What am I?'

Arianna stared down at Connor through the tears that spilled from her eyes, and then she turned to look at Kieran Beck. The magnate glared across at Arianna's *holosap*.

'I'll have you erased forever if you dare cross me! I'll destroy you and your son!'

Arianna's *holosap* stared up at Beck for a moment and then the Prime Minister spoke.

'They took my life,' he gasped, his glowing features a mask of grief. 'My family. If you do this I'll never see them again.

Arianna saw the Prime Minister's wife and daughters huddled nearby, their faces damp with tears. Arianna's *holosap* looked at them, at Connor, at Beck and across the entire chamber, and she then spoke in a voice that seemed inhuman and yet filled with a wisdom beyond anything that Arianna herself possessed.

'This is not the answer,' she said. '*Holosaps* are not our saviour. This course is not one of courage but one of cowardice, and the only true violation of human rights is the resurrection of the dead. It is not our place. We are not meant to live forever, for if we do, what place empathy for those who cannot?'

The *holosap* turned to Arianna, her voice now a whisper that still carried to every high corner and every ear in the silent chamber.

'Heav'n has no rage like love to hatred turn'd, nor hell a fury like a woman scorn'd.'

* * *

52

'No!' Beck screamed.

A moment passed in utter silence as Arianna stared into her son's eyes.

And then, as though through magic, Connor's eyes glowed with a gentle light as one by one, tiny specks of light began to flutter away from his *holosap*, billions of 1s and 0s spiralling like pollen drifting on an invisible breeze. Connor's *holosap* began to sparkle as though made of a billion stars that began dripping away into a cascade of light that spilled across the floor beneath them.

'What the hell?' Han uttered.

Arianna dropped onto her knees beside Connor's *holosap*. The hair on his head was running like a million coloured droplets of light, as though a shower was draining illuminated water across his scalp. His eyes filled with sparkling tears.

'Mummy?'

Arianna's *holosap* knelt down beside Connor's and wrapped her arms around him, folding him into her embrace as they held each other. Arianna tried to suppress the terrible grief that filled her as she touched her hands to Connor's glowing face where it rested on his mother's shoulders and held it gently as he stared at her, cupping his chin and cheeks and wishing she could actually feel them one last time. She looked into his eyes and tried, with all of her heart, to convey her emotions to him.

Connor's fear melted away as fast as his image was collapsing like a neon watercolour in the rain. He stared back at her, his face slowly dissolving into a milieu of tumbling lights as he spoke silently. Even though she could not hear him, she could read the words falling from his lips as clear as day.

'I love you mummy.'

Arianna's heart broke as Connor's and Arianna's *holosaps* collapsed into each other, losing their resolution and shape until they were a kaleidoscope of coloured lights that tumbled to the floor in a river and then flickered away like dying stars into nothingness.

The silence throughout the chamber was complete. Arianna knelt on the floor, her eyes squeezed tight shut and her arms suspended before her around where Connor's *holosap* had once been.

'He's gone, Arianna,' Icon whispered weakly, his voice barely audible.

'What have you done?!' Alexei Volkov yelled, his own *holosap* starting to shimmer and trail a veil of falling digits.

Kieran Beck shouted at her. 'Arianna!'

In a burst of colour and light swirling like a thousand tiny tornadoes, the *holosaps* looked at each other and a great cry of terror erupted to echo through the chamber as their images collapsed into a flood of light that spilled without form across their seats, their cries warbling and distorting away into silence as they vanished.

Their shaking heads and imploring arms trailed halos of light, their digital flesh falling from their frames just as the flesh and blood of billions of humans had fallen to stain the earth when The Falling had infected mankind twenty five years before.

Kieran Beck staggered toward her as the ranks of *holosaps* disintegrated in colourful flares of bright light, as though seeing once again the halo of joy and love that she had witnessed too briefly only hours before. Beck's eyes were wide with a volatile mixture of rage and fear, his arms reaching out for her but spilling light like sparks that vanished into thin air.

Beck's face came within an inch of Arianna's, his mouth agape as he screamed at her, those glowing eyes still poisoned by hate.

And then Kieran Beck disappeared.

Arianna felt nothing as they disappeared one by one until every *holosap* in the chamber but Tarquin St John had vanished. She stared at the empty spaces they had once occupied, tears still filling her eyes as she heard the sobs of St John's daughters echoing through the silence as their father faded from view, still a human in his mind and his soul just as Connor had been.

The Prime Minister's *holosap* collapsed into coloured light and spilled away into eternity.

The silence in the chamber seemed oppressive, as though haunted by souls still lingering in the still air, until a single voice broke it.

'It's over,' Icon said, his chest heaving as his remaining lung struggled to keep him alive.

Arianna looked at Icon. 'You knew all of that time and you never told me?'

Icon's scarred and haggard face twisted awkwardly to accommodate the smile that crept upon his twisted lips despite his pain. 'I knew. You were the kill–switch Arianna. You were *Eve*, your father's defence against his own creation. All you had to do was upload once and the virus would go with you.'

'Alexei?' she asked.

'It was why he gifted you the upload,' Icon said, 'on your father's orders. If things ever got out of control he was to ensure you uploaded. The chip in your head would do the rest. Adam was the birth, but the end had to come with you.'

Arianna stared at the floor where moments before her son had stood.

'I've caused the deaths of thousands of people,' she said softly. 'I've killed my own son.'

'It wasn't Connor,' Han assured her as he moved alongside her.

'It doesn't feel that way.'

Han gently took her arm. 'Come on, you've had a hell of a day. We can deal with the aftermath later.'

'Not quite,' Icon gasped. 'There is the small matter of this parliament and its lack of a Prime Minister. They were about to sell out on humanity. Is that who we want running our country? I should kill them all, and there's no reason that anybody in the city would stop us. We carry the immunity to The Falling in our blood.'

'You forget that I now carry it too,' Arianna pointed out. 'Lynda's blood now runs in my veins, and I can and will pass on that immunity to anybody who needs it.'

Icon struggled to sit up, his men helping him as blood frothed from his lips. 'That was not what I had in mind when I uploaded you.'

'No, it wasn't,' she replied. 'My survival was not high on your list of priorities, was it Icon? I wonder what my father would have thought of that?'

Icon continued to glare at her but he said nothing as the ministers' attention switched from Icon to Arianna. Minister Hart spoke up once more.

'There are people here, servants of this country who would gladly see the *holosaps* consigned to history. If you truly are immune, then it is we who are at your service.'

Arianna sighed as she looked up at the ranks of politicians, as removed from the general population as any other generation of politicians had been, icons to leadership in name but falling far from it in deeds, and wondered if indeed any of them could be trusted any farther than she could throw them.

She was about to answer when Han spoke beside her. 'I don't think we should make any harsh decisions.'

'It's not your call to make,' Icon snarled.

Han gestured to the television screen, still silently showing broadcasts nearby. 'It's not ours now, either.'

Arianna looked up to see a broadcaster speaking urgently as images of New York appeared on the screen beside her, and then images of huge satellite dishes at airports near surviving cities exploding and collapsing as armed troops fled. The scrolling script at the bottom of the screen told her everything she needed to know.

'New York has isolated itself,' Han said. 'They've destroyed their regional communication hubs and shut themselves off so that the virus didn't get through.'

Icon coughed, blood splattering his shirt.

'You need a doctor,' Arianna urged him.

Icon shook his head, peering at her with his one good eye. 'I want no part of this future. I'll die a man on this floor rather than survive and be beholden to men like these.'

Icon gestured with a weak, quivering arm to the politicians.

Minister Hart shook his head. 'Not all of us supported Kieran Beck's obsession.'

'Destroy them,' Icon whispered, his eye drooping wearily. 'Destroy the *holosap* storage units. End this, while you can.'

'Strange,' Minister Hart say quietly, 'I expect that's what the *holosaps* were saying about us, about humans.'

Icon stared up at the minister until the life finally left his eyes and his broad chest fell still.

Han Reeves passed his hand over Icon's eyes and glanced up at the politicians.

'He's gone,' the detective said, 'but he was right. We need to do something about New York.'

'Then it is time for us to make a new stand,' Minister Hart insisted, 'because this is no longer a battle for ideals. This is about to become a war, and right now we are the only ones who can fight it.'

* * *

ABOUT THE AUTHOR

Dean Crawford is the best-selling author of the *Ethan Warner* series of thrillers and many independent novels. Published internationally, his books have sold hundreds of thousands of copies and earned the interest of major Hollywood production studios.

www.deancrawfordbooks.com

Printed in Great Britain
by Amazon